Little Nicole Stood Motionless, Petrified With Terror . . .

"Hide, Nicole," Claire whispered fiercely. The late afternoon was alive with noise, the hiss and pop of the fire in the fireplace, the steady, nerve-wracking beat of the rain against the shuttered windows, the rattling noise of the wind at the door.

But it wasn't the wind. Someone was jiggling the back door, someone was trying to force his way in. "Go away," Claire shouted in a panic that almost equaled Nicole's.

To her astonishment, a voice answered in heavy, guttural French.

"He says he's a stranger. His car went off the road and he wants to call a garage," Nicole translated, her voice shaking, her eyes blank.

Again the voice came, as the back door rattled noisily. "He says he's wet and cold and wants to come in," Nicole whispered.

The rattling turned to a loud thudding, and the two of them watched in mute horror as the back door began to give beneath the barrage. Then the door splintered open . . .

SEEN AND NOT HEARD

Anne Stuart

SEVERN
SH
HOUSE

This title first published in Great Britain 1989 by
SEVERN HOUSE PUBLISHERS LTD of
40–42 William IV Street, London WC2N 4DF.
First published in the U.S.A. 1988 by Pocket Books,
a division of Simon & Schuster, Inc.

British Library Cataloguing in Publication Data
Stuart, Anne
Seen and not heard.
I. Title
823′.54 [F]
ISBN 0–7278–1752–3

Printed and bound in Great Britain

SEEN AND NOT HEARD

❧ CHAPTER 1

Felice Champêtre moved slowly through her stuffy apartment on the rue Broca, her faded silk skirt rustling softly as it bumped against whatnot tables, an overstuffed armchair, a precarious pile of fashion magazines. She was brooding on the inequality of fate. Her ankles had swollen dreadfully in this damp, rainy weather, and the arthritis in her hands made it almost impossible to make a decent cup of tea. It was miserable to get old, miserable and unfair.

She'd been a great beauty, sixty years ago. Paris had been between wars then, money had been plentiful, and life was very gay. Now she was old and alone in a tacky apartment that held all the things she couldn't bear to part with, the contents of a huge house squeezed into her present small flat. No one came to see her, and when they did, all she did was complain about how wretched life was. And then, of course, they didn't come back.

She edged her way into the tiny kitchen, peering out of the grimy window into the rain as it washed over the city she once loved and now hated with a grim, unrelenting passion. The kettle was too heavy for her—she'd have to make do with the iron-tasting tap water.

She sighed, leaning against the old sink, as the cold loneliness settled around her. There were times when she thought she'd welcome death, a release from all this misery. She was getting so tired of the struggle.

Of course, there were moments of pleasure still. That young man in the park yesterday had been very sweet, very gallant. It was odd to see him there—that park was usually the province of old people like herself. She didn't even know why she went there. She didn't like old people any more than all those young, arrogant Parisians did.

But the young man hadn't been arrogant. He'd been courteous, gentle, even mildly flirtatious. People no longer knew how to flirt. It had been wonderful for a few brief moments to forget she was an eighty-year-old woman, to become young and desirable again.

He said he might come to tea. She knew he wouldn't—he was only being polite. But she could hope.

Still, today might be the day. She could feel it in her ancient, arthritic bones. She would put the kettle on anyway, just in case he happened to climb the three flights of stairs to her apartment.

The kettle trembled in her hands, and she set it in the sink and turned the tap. The rusty water gushed out noisily, covering any sound in the apartment. Felice couldn't hear the tiny scratchings at the front door lock, couldn't hear the flimsy door opening and closing, couldn't hear the stealthy, silent footsteps through the living area.

But her apartment was a dangerous maze of jumbled furniture. She heard the crash as one precariously balanced table of china toppled over, and she turned to blink nearsightedly through the shadowy room.

"Who's there?" Her voice was sharp, honed from years of nagging her late husband. Her fierce expression softened. "Oh, it's you!" she said. "I was hoping you might come today. I was just about to put the kettle on for tea."

"There's no need," he said gently, moving into the kitchen, his feet making no sound at all.

"How did you get in? I always lock the door," Felice chattered, suddenly, unaccountably nervous. She turned back to the sink. The kettle was now full—it would be much too heavy to lift.

"Don't be frightened of me, Felice," he said behind her, his voice soft and soothing, like a lover's. She hadn't heard a lover's voice in thirty years, and for a moment she shut her eyes as a wave of bittersweet memories swept over her.

She opened them again, for a brief, startled moment, when she felt the hard thrust of the knife up, up into her heart. And then she closed them once more, dying with a soft, graceful shudder.

He'd done well. There was never much blood if he did it right. He'd botched it once, and had to take a shower before he left. But this time it was very neat, very fast. An artistic job.

The water was still running into the sink, overflowing the old kettle, the sound mixing with the steady drone of the heavy rain. He reached past her crumpled body to turn the tap off, then stopped. He would leave it.

He pulled the knife free and hoisted the old woman's body into his arms, carrying her back through the cluttered living room over to the narrow bed. He set her down, arranging her carefully, her hands together in a prayerful attitude covering the neat wound. She lay there like a repentant effigy from a fifteenth-century tomb, her faded, too observant eyes shut forever. He took off her shoes and stockings, placing them neatly beside the bed, and stared down at her for a long, thoughtful moment.

He bent down and kissed her on her mouth. It opened slackly beneath his, and he took his time. When he pulled back, he closed her lips, slid the knife into the special pouch inside his loose trousers, and walked out the door, turning up his collar against the heavy rain that would greet him when he walked out into the street. There was a gentle, dreamy smile on his handsome face. He had done well.

Claire MacIntyre wrapped her hands around her mug of coffee and stared out into the rainy afternoon. The heavy ceramic was warm and hard beneath her hands, and she looked down to see that she was clenching it, her knuckles white with strain.

She removed her hands carefully, dropping them into her

3

lap, keeping them loose, keeping herself from clutching them together. Rain made her tense. The thought of Marc driving back to Paris with Nicole in tow made her want to scream with anxiety. Instead she sat in the old kitchen of Marc's mammoth apartment and drank too much coffee.

Was it only six months ago that it had happened? The pouring rain that turned to ice on the narrow streets of Brockton, Massachusetts, the car wheels that lost all traction, the sharp, desperate turn? She could still feel twinges from the whiplash that had twisted her neck muscles. Could the child feel anything at all?

As usual she'd been fighting with Brian. She'd known better than to fall in love with a married man, but that knowledge hadn't helped her. For eighteen months they'd fought, culminating in that last fight as Brian drove too fast through the icy streets of Brockton.

Claire shuddered, taking a sip of the steaming coffee. She shouldn't be taking in any more caffeine, she knew that. But somehow the only thing she could do was sit there and drink coffee and wait till Marc came back safely.

Marc, she thought with that odd clutching of nervousness and desire that had become habit with her. What would she have done without him? He had saved her, become her shelter in a storm, her Prince Charming, her protector, her lover, and, for the last few months, her life.

Brian hadn't stopped for more than a moment. They'd both seen the child's body lying there in the icy rain, and then he'd reversed the car and driven on as fast as he could, ignoring her screams of protest.

It had all happened so quickly. Hit-and-run, the newspapers called it. Probably some drunk driver. There were no witnesses, no one had come forward. In all likelihood the case would never be solved.

Not if Brian could help it. And Claire had kept silent, knowing that she was an accessory, knowing that implicating Brian wouldn't help the nine-year-old girl fighting for her life at Mass General.

So she'd said nothing. She'd broken off with Brian, holed

up in her apartment, and turned off her telephone, waiting for the child to die, knowing that if that happened she would have to go to the police.

But when the newspapers reported that the child's six-week coma ended, not in death, but in a murmured word of recognition, Claire had given in to her friend Joyce's suspicious demands, given up her guilt-plagued vigil, and gone with her to a party in Boston.

She'd had every intention of leaving early. Now that she knew the girl would live, might even live a normal, healthy life, a huge weight had left her. All she felt was a great, empty exhaustion. But she drank the imported champagne, smiled a huge, insincere smile, and wondered how quickly she could leave.

Joyce worked for the Boston Symphony Orchestra in a managerial capacity that Claire never quite understood. This particular party was to honor Le Théâtre du Mime at the conclusion of their first American tour. Joyce had charge of the arrangements, and Claire followed in her efficient friend's wake, smiling blindly at the French artists. Until she met Marc Bonnard. And then her smile was no longer blind.

He was very handsome, but then, the room was full of handsome men. He hadn't been an inch taller than her own five feet eight inches, and his lean, graceful body probably didn't weigh much more than hers. He looked very French, with a sensual mouth, a strong nose, sleepy, laughing eyes, and a thick wave of black hair that tumbled enchantingly down his high forehead. He had taken one look at her and made up his mind, he told her later. Learning that she couldn't, and would never, speak French didn't deter him in the slightest. It added to the mystery, he said. He had enough English for both of them. Besides, he was a mime. What did they need with words?

She fascinated him, he said. With her huge, sorrowful eyes, her narrow, elegant face and hands, her untamed mane of red gold hair. What secrets lay behind those sad, haunted eyes?

She didn't tell him. She went back to his hotel room with him, back to his bed with him, where she found she didn't have to think, didn't have to remember. One week later she flew over to Paris to live with him in the huge old apartment he'd inherited on the left bank of the Seine. One month later she met his daughter Nicole.

Claire took another sip of coffee. It was cooling now, no longer the hot comfort it had first been. Maybe she should brew another pot, just to warm her up. The chill, heavy rain could reach inside your bones. It must be hell to be old in such a climate.

She'd known about Nicole, of course. If she'd stopped to consider, if she hadn't been so mesmerized by Marc and his seemingly inexhaustible passion, she would have known the lure of a motherless nine-year-old was part of her abrupt decision to leave. She had kept silent when her lover had almost killed one young girl. Perhaps she could redeem herself with another.

Nicole wouldn't have any part of it. She'd taken one look at the interloper, the American who thought she'd take her mother's place, and her response had been politely contemptuous. And for once Claire was glad that she couldn't speak French.

That hadn't helped an already tense situation. A bilingual nine-year-old couldn't comprehend that an intelligent thirty-year-old could have learning disabilities that kept her from understanding even the rudiments of a language Nicole considered far superior to English. The first two months of Claire's stay in Paris were a kaleidoscope of frustration, irritation, guilt, and an almost mindless pleasure. And the omnipresent second thoughts.

Things had settled down, of course. Nicole began to accept her, grudgingly. With her beloved *grand-mère* on an extended visit to her elderly sister in Los Angeles, Nicole had no one else to turn to.

Because her hostility extended to Marc. She eyed her father out of solemn, bespectacled eyes, her sallow face blank when he exerted all his charm to tease her out of her sulks. She was polite, too polite, to him, to Claire. It was only when she finally screamed at Claire, her stolid self-control vanishing, that Claire felt she was getting somewhere.

And then Marc had sent her away to school, removing her from the day school she'd been attending. Claire had fought him on it, but she had no leverage. Even Nicole seemed resigned to it, packing her clothes with her usual sober demeanor, giving Claire a chaste kiss on the cheek before following her handsome father out the door.

Marc and Claire had been left alone in the huge old apartment, lovers on holiday in Paris. The Théâtre du Mime was on sabbatical. All Marc had to do was make love to Claire, and he applied himself to the task quite diligently.

He wanted to marry her. Claire looked down at the dark, oily dregs of her coffee and felt her stomach knot. She could think of no reason not to. She loved him, she loved him to distraction. When he was around she couldn't think of anything but him, of the hours they spent together, of the fiendishly clever ways he had of arousing and teasing and ultimately satisfying her. Her sex life with Brian had been mundane, almost boring, a small part of her life. With Marc, it became the focus of everything, so much so that it sometimes frightened her.

And when Marc was gone, the doubts began to build, as they were building right now, doubts that she tried to push away. He was handsome, he was gentle, he was marvelous in bed, and he loved her. He was even wealthy—his wife had left him a great deal of money when her car had plunged over an embankment on the way to one of his performances in Nice. What more could she ask from life?

She stood, and the scraping of the chair on the parquet floor scraped along her nerves. It was early April, and it was raining. It seemed as if it had been raining for months, that the fabled Paris spring was a figment of some travel agent's imagination. Who could help but be depressed? The sordid, distressing news made things worse. The situation in Lebanon, in Central America, the politics of her homeland seemed as out of control as ever. And another old woman was found murdered. That brought the number to thirty-eight. Thirty-eight women over the age of seventy-five found murdered in their apartments. The Grandmother Murders, they called them. Claire found herself grateful that she couldn't understand French, couldn't find out the gory details. She'd seen the blurred news photo and known more than she wanted to.

Maybe that was her problem. When she'd flown over to join Marc she'd blithely assumed that most people spoke English. Marc, in his eagerness to have her come, had encouraged that arrogant assumption.

But the street signs and magazines and newspapers and television shows were in French, and they might just as well have been in Swahili. Claire was like a deaf-mute, unable to hear, to communicate with most of the people around her. That sense of isolation was probably to blame for her depression, her anxiety, her sudden, unreasoning longing for the narrow streets of Brockton. Streets where she'd seen a child struck down, seen and said nothing, she reminded herself with a stray shiver, rinsing her coffee cup out in the sink.

She looked around the kitchen. It was spotless, of course. It hadn't taken her long to realize that Marc was scrupulously neat, and that the only way she could be happy was to alter her cheerfully sloppy ways and be as compulsive as he was. She set the mug on the draining board, resisting the impulse to dry it and put it away. Marc wouldn't be back till late. He was a careful driver—he wouldn't take risks in this sort of weather. She'd have time to clean everything.

She leaned against the iron sink, staring out into the silver gray rain. She was going to have to give Marc an answer before long. And she knew, without his saying so, that there was only one answer that was acceptable. And her fingers clutched the edge of the sink, her knuckles white with strain.

Chief Inspector Louis Malgreave of Homicide swore fluently under his breath. God damn the murdering bastards! Another one, another helpless old lady found stabbed to death in her pitiful little apartment.

This time it was Felice Champêtre, an eighty-year-old widow. Three weeks ago it had been Marthe Bernard, a week before that Hélène Mersot. And thirty-five other women in the last two and a half years.

Two hundred extra policemen had been assigned to areas frequented by the elderly. A small fortune had been budgeted in the quest for the killers. They had come close, so very close. And still the death toll rises, he thought wearily.

There had to be more than one murderer. While he had no proof, he was certain that rotten little punk Rocco Guillère had been responsible for Marguerite Debenet and the nun in Notre Dame. Not to mention the ninety-year-old twins in La Défense.

But he couldn't have killed the Comtesse de Tourney—his alibi was airtight. And three more women were killed while Malgreave tried to keep him in custody. It was a lost cause. No sooner had Rocco's defense lawyer gotten wind of the latest murders than Rocco was a free man. And Malgreave was faced with more questions than answers.

The official theory, one that Malgreave grudgingly accepted, was that it was a copycat killer. The United States had dealt with the same sort of sickness. One person poisoned a box of medicine and suddenly dozens of people were poisoning medicine. One man with a hatred of old women started killing, and everyone who was ever spanked by a grandmother began to get murderous ideas.

He stared out into the pouring rain, reaching for his cigarettes. He was trying to give them up, but so far he hadn't had any luck. The city was gray and cold, and he shivered in his fourth-floor office. He hated the rain. It had been almost eighteen months, almost twenty victims before they noticed that the women always died on a rainy day. Malgreave found himself praying for a drought.

He'd have to go and view the body, of course. He knew what he'd find. The crowded, pitiful apartment of an old woman trying to keep her dignity in a world changing beyond her recognition. The shrunken, withered body,

9

stretched out like a penitent, the arthritic hands folded across a sunken chest. Sometimes there was blood, sometimes not. There had even been a fingerprint that had matched at two of the scenes. They hadn't been Rocco's.

God, he hated this business. It was no wonder Marie was unhappy. He wouldn't blame her if she started looking at other men. She was too young, too lively to be tied to a husband whose job was death.

He stood up, reaching for his battered raincoat. It was already after six. He'd be late again, and Marie would have already eaten. She wouldn't say a word, but he would read the hurt and anger and disappointment in her fine brown eyes, and his guilt would eat into his soul.

But he had to stop by the rue Broca and Felice Champêtre's apartment. Marie's life didn't depend on his getting home on time. Some other woman's might.

Claire put the mug back in the cupboard, in a straight line with the other ceramic mugs. Marc didn't like them, preferring the paper-thin Limoges tea cups he'd inherited. But she'd broken one, and the look he'd given her had been chilling.

Later she decided she'd imagined it. But she went out and bought herself a set of heavy, earthenware mugs, and never touched the Limoges again if she could help it.

Her thick, red gold hair was still damp from the shower. She should have finished drying it, but she was too restless to spend the time. She tugged at the fine wool of her dress, wiggled her toes in the silk stockings, and fiddled with a pearl earring. She would have liked to have greeted Marc in an old pair of jeans and a thick sweater on a cold, miserable night like this. Or maybe wearing a soft flannel nightgown, and she could have made hot chocolate for the three of them in front of the fire, and they could have been a real family.

But Marc had standards, and Claire had learned it was easier to conform to them. Particularly when he explained that he wanted her to dress well because she valued herself, not him. It made sense, and she did as he expected. But right now she would have loved something more comfortable.

The chicken was simmering, the air was redolent of tarragon and wine. At least she could cook. She hadn't had to change that part of her nature, she thought with that uncomfortable trace of defiance. Indeed, she'd had so little to do during the last few months that she'd developed her modest talent into something approaching art. She would have liked to study further. Paris was the perfect place for learning haute cuisine. But the cooking schools weren't bilingual, and French was the language, not only of love and ballet, but the language of food.

Through the endless corridors and rooms of the old apartment she heard the soft closing of the front door. Her ears had become very finely tuned. Living with a mime did wonders for your senses, she thought with a trace of humor. Marc used to be able to sneak up on her when she was completely unaware. She hadn't liked it, hadn't wanted to say anything and hurt his feelings. So she'd worked on listening. Marc hadn't surprised her in months. No, that wasn't true. He was always surprising her. But he hadn't managed to sneak up on her in a long, long time.

She took off her apron, folded it neatly, and set it on the spotless kitchen table. Her narrow, delicate hands were trembling slightly, and she frowned at them. It must be the excitement. She'd been left alone for two nights, and ever since the accident she hadn't liked to be alone. Now that Marc was back, and Nicole, things would be better. Things would be as they should be.

Smoothing her challis dress, she headed for the living room, setting a welcoming smile on her face. Only for a brief moment did she consider that she shouldn't have to call forth a smile to greet her returning lover. It should have come on its own.

Once more she cursed her depression, her indecisiveness. She was going to throw away the best thing that ever happened to her if she didn't shake herself out of it. Marc was home, and she loved him. Maybe it was time she made

11

it clear just how much she did love him. Maybe it was time to get married. And maybe it was time for her to tell him so.

But then, she didn't want to spoil Nicole's homecoming, did she? It could wait. Wait until Marc asked her again. This time, she would say yes. And to hell with second thoughts.

❧ CHAPTER 2

Rocco Guillère propped his feet on the battered table and eyed his pointy-toed black leather boots blearily. He would need a shine tomorrow. He liked having classy boots, with a real shine, not that plastic coating they had nowadays, and he spent a lot of money on them. He knew the places where you could still get a decent shine, and he tipped well.

He liked people's reactions. He'd stride up to the stand in the lobby of the best hotels, all black leather and menace, and take his place with the gray-suited businessmen, propping his huge black boots beside their hand-sewn Italian leathers. The others would pull away, as if he gave off a bad smell.

Rocco grinned, lighting a stubby Gitane and drawing the acrid smoke into his lungs. Maybe he did give off a bad smell. He wasn't one of the bourgeoisie, into hot baths and clean clothes. He lived in the roughest, nastiest part of Paris, and his life was rough and nasty. He had no time, no patience for the finer things in life.

It was just after midnight, the heart of the evening, and his work hadn't even begun. He had to waste another hour until he was needed.

It was a simple job tonight, if he chose to make it so. He'd been hired as protection during a drug deal. He would simply stand in the background, glowering, his huge American Magnum prominently displayed, while Achilles and the little Spaniard traded lots of money for a decent amount of cocaine. He'd been told to stand guard while the Spaniard counted his money and left, and Achilles would pay him with part of the drugs.

It would be good pay for an easy night's work. And if he could keep the stuff away from that greedy little tramp Giselle he could make a nice profit.

But there was another alternative, one he'd used occasionally. He could waste both Achilles and the Spaniard, take all the drugs and the money, and no one would be the wiser.

He didn't do that sort of thing very often. Word would get around, and his reputation would suffer. He'd had to be very careful since that fool Malgreave had arrested him. It had been a close call. Two months in that stinking prison, two months while Malgreave went his slow, deliberate way, trying to pin those murders on him.

In the end he'd failed, of course. Thirty-five old women had died at that point. And Rocco had only killed seventeen of them.

He stubbed the cigarette out, shifting in the chair and tilting it back further. It was a good thing he'd been so far ahead of the others. They'd had time to catch up during his enforced retirement. Four more women had died since he'd been arrested, and he hadn't touched one of them. By now Malgreave had to have given up on him.

He scratched his groin absently. It should be safe by now. Or safe enough. And he was badly short of cash. He'd take care of Achilles and the Spaniard, and then, when a little time had passed, he'd find an old lady. A sweet old grandmother, living alone. And the very next rainstorm he'd start taking care of his quota. After all, he couldn't let a bunch of amateurs get ahead of him.

He smiled, his shark's smile. It would be a pleasure to set Malgreave to wondering.

It was happening again. The cold, black, rain-slick night. Brian driving his BMW far too fast, his handsome mouth set, his beautiful hands clenching the leather-covered steering wheel as if he wished it were her neck. He wasn't yelling, he was saying quiet, bitter, cruel things. She was the one who was yelling.

He'd promised, how many times had he promised? He would talk to his wife, the separation and divorce would be amicable, and they could finally get married. It had been eighteen months of promises, and Claire had had enough. So, apparently, had Brian.

There would be no separation, he had finally admitted. Not right now. His wife was pregnant again, and it probably was his.

That was when she'd starting yelling. And that was when he'd taken his eyes off the road, his hand off the wheel and lashed out at her, his formidable temper breaking its tenuous control.

She could still hear the sickening thump of a body smacking against the car. She could still see the child's limp, rain-soaked form lying beside the road. She could still see Brian's panic as he drove away, ignoring her screams, ignoring her futile attempts to grab the wheel. He'd finally hit her, hard enough to stun her, so that she sank back, huddled in a corner of the leather seat, watching with numb, disbelieving eyes as he sped through the night, away from the child.

Claire lay in the wide bed, covered in a cold, clammy sweat. She hated waking up in the middle of the night, hated lying there, remembering, with Marc asleep beside her, his sensual face childlike in repose. She reached out to wake him up, to touch his firm, muscled shoulder, then drew her hand back. Marc would have one response to her wakefulness, to her fears. And for once in her life Claire didn't feel like being made love to.

An odd way to put it, she thought to herself, inching her body over a bit, away from Marc. He was always so warm, his firm, lithe body radiating heat like a furnace. Even in the coldest weather they didn't need more than a thin blanket, and in the heat of the summer it would be almost unbearable. Right now Claire would have given anything for a cooling breeze. The rain had stopped, but the sounds of Paris at night reached the second-floor windows, muffled noises, reminding her that people had lives beyond the walls of this apartment that were rapidly resembling a prison.

She looked over at Marc. There hadn't been much time for talk. First there had been Nicole, horribly sick with some stomach virus. Claire had spent two hours holding her head over the toilet and mopping her brow. In her misery Nicole couldn't summon even the rudiments of English, and Claire had cursed her lack of French for the hundredth time. By the time the retching had ceased and Nicole had fallen into an exhausted sleep, all Claire wanted to do was the same.

"*Chérie*, you look dreadful," Marc murmured, his voice low and soothing as he led her toward the bathroom. "You take your shower first and I'll join you in bed. What a hell of a homecoming, eh?"

For once in her life Claire wanted to protest. She didn't want to take the shower Marc always insisted upon, she didn't want to wait for him in bed, and she didn't want to make love. But she said nothing. The few occasions she'd told Marc no, he'd refused to listen. And within minutes he'd had her begging him, helpless in the response he could always bring forth. He was a very adept man, almost frighteningly so.

She looked over at him. How could she be frightened of him? He was the kindest, sexiest man. And how patient he was with Nicole, and what little he got in return. He'd gone to get her simply because her grandmother had finally returned from Los Angeles, the grandmother Nicole adored above all people. Nicole could stay here for the next few weeks, while Marc went on tour with the Théâtre du Mime, and his three ladies, as he termed them, could keep each other company.

She was looking forward to meeting Mme. Langlois. She was both anticipating and dreading the next month. She looked on it as some sort of test. If she could survive, even thrive, in Marc's house, Marc's life, without Marc there to cloud her thinking, then there might be a future for them. She would have time to think things through, to make up her mind. And when he finally returned she could greet him with all her doubts resolved. Or she could be gone.

That alternative was looking oddly attractive. But she couldn't leave Nicole. Not until she was sure that Mme. Langlois would be enough buffer against Marc's exacting nature. He was a good father, a loving father. He was just a tiny bit . . . cold, at times. And Claire couldn't rid herself of the feeling that Nicole knew it.

She slid down further on the soft bed, sighing. She'd forgotten to pick up the sheets at the laundry yesterday. No, she hadn't forgotten—she hadn't wanted to. For one thing, the rain had been so depressing she hadn't wanted to go out in it. For another, no one at the laundry spoke English, and each visit was a nightmare of humiliation.

But Marc expected fresh sheets daily, and she had made up the bed this morning with the last set. Rain or no rain, she would have to go out tomorrow. Humiliation or no, she would have to face M. Gorgogne. Perhaps Nicole could come with her and translate.

She shifted uneasily. The bed was too soft and too small, and the heavy damask hangings made her feel claustrophobic. While he was gone she could see about bringing in a queen-size bed, one with a good hard mattress, plenty of pillows, and plenty of room. If she was going to make the decision to stay, she would have to do so on at least some of her own terms. If Marc couldn't accept that, then there was no future for them, and she could go back to Massachusetts and face what she'd been running from so desperately.

"*Chérie*," Marc murmured, reaching out for her, his strong, delicate-looking hand clasping her wrist. Like a handcuff, she thought for a brief, disloyal moment. His skin was hot, almost feverish against her cold, clammy flesh, and his eyes glittered in the darkness. "Claire," he murmured, his mouth moving over her collarbone, his voice soft and loving, as other, incomprehensible words tumbled from his mouth against her sensitive skin. And she put out her other

17

wrist, accepting his imprisoning hand, accepting his imprisoning body, shutting out the night and the memories, leaving only pleasure in the stuffy bedroom.

Thomas Jefferson Parkhurst was in the midst of a creative frenzy. His long, deft fingers were flying over the ancient manual typewriter, he no longer shuddered every time he drained his wine glass, and the late-night traffic from the rain-wet Paris streets made an agreeable rumble. It would have been especially nice, he thought, leaning back and running a hand through his shaggy brown hair, if he could have worked by candlelight. But he had trouble seeing the ink-blotched print as it was, and candlelight would make it impossible.

And it would have been nice if some ripe young mademoiselle were lying in bed waiting for him to finish his night's work. Someone who would pout prettily, come up behind him and press her bare breasts against his back, someone who would lead him back to bed when his chapter was done.

But the bed was empty, and had been since Susan had left him and gone back to her yuppie life in Marin County. Somehow he hadn't been in the mood for transients. He'd thrown all his energy into the book, working on it endlessly, until his neck was cramped and his long, lean body grew stiff and weary.

He was a tall man, and for a while he'd tried Thomas Wolfe's trick of standing up and writing on the top of the refrigerator. But he always kept crackers and dishes up there, and he hated having to clear them off, and it was hard to see the paper when he perched the typewriter up there. Wolfe had written longhand, but Parkhurst knew that no one, himself included, could read his handwriting. Besides, the man at the pawnshop assured him this typewriter had once belonged to Hemingway himself. Maybe some of that creative aura still lingered.

God knows, he needed all the help he could get. He was running out of time. Two more months, and then he'd have to go back. He'd made a promise to himself, and he couldn't break it. He had two years to find himself, find his art. After twenty-two months he still hadn't gotten it right.

He pushed back from the rickety table, stretching his long arms out over his head, and surveyed his apartment with regret and nostalgia. It was the perfect artist's garret, from the crescent windows overlooking the city, the six flights of stairs that left even a marathon runner winded, the nooks and crannies and clear, bright daylight from the skylights. During his painting phase its ambiance had almost fooled him into thinking he had talent. During his play-writing stage it had helped him write bohemian tragedies. It had provided him with enough space to practice when he thought he might be a dancer, it had provided him unnervingly good acoustics during his very brief stint with the clarinet. Now, during the great new expatriate novel stage, it made him feel like a wonderful cross between Hemingway and Gene Kelly.

He pulled the finished page out of the typewriter and lay it face down on the table. He never read what he wrote, never revised. First things first, he told himself. He'd write the damned thing straight through, then sit down and read it. And if it had no value at all he'd burn it, book the next flight for New York, and go back and face life.

Susan would have him back. As long as he'd gotten over this artistic nonsense and went back to work she'd be more than willing to share his life. But somehow Thomas Jefferson Parkhurst wasn't sure it was going to be the same life. Even if the novel didn't work out, even if he did have to go back to the brokerage house, the last twenty-two months had changed him. Thank God.

He drained the last of the wine, then grimaced at the label. Park-Millet Vineyards. His first venture into modified creativity, buying an ancient vineyard in a barren, sparsely populated area in the northeast of France, had been a resounding failure. The wine was undrinkable, the vineyard unsalable. At least he could use the tax write-off.

His bed was an ancient iron affair, halfway between a twin and a double, with a sagging mattress, aging springs, and not enough pillows. It protested audibly as Parkhurst

19

threw himself down on it. For a moment he remembered the noise it made when Susan had shared it, remembered with a brief, salacious grin. And then he dismissed the thought, rolling over on his back and turning off the low-wattage bedside light.

It was raining again, raining hard on the metal roof just over his head. He used to like the steady drone of rain. Now it just made him depressed and restless.

He'd chosen Paris for his sabbatical because he'd always loved it. The clear, beautiful light that was now, too often, obscured by smog, the magnificence of the architecture, the self-possessed friendliness of the people. He always thought the French were like cats—charming on their own terms but not on anyone else's.

But the French had begun to lose their charm. For some reason the Grandmother Murders particularly depressed him. He'd imagined copycat killers were the province of places like L.A. and New York, not his beloved City of Lights.

Another old lady killed today, not three blocks away. He might have seen her in that park where the old ones hang out, he might even have seen her killer. Punching the inadequate pillow, he rolled over, searching for the one comfortable spot in the concave mattress. They were always killed on rainy days, and Paris was breaking records for rainfall this year. He didn't want to watch the death count rise. Maybe he'd stop buying the papers.

A cold, wet breeze blew in his open window, and he shivered lightly. Maybe it was time to go back.

Chief Inspector Malgreave leaned his weary face out into the rain, letting the cool mist cover him. He couldn't sleep—he never could on rainy nights. Not since they'd realized that the old women were always murdered in the rain. He would lie there, careful not to wake Marie, and picture Rocco Guillère skulking through the city.

He had to get over that fixation. Rocco was only part of the answer. There had to be at least three different people murdering the old women—Rocco was only one of them.

Homicide had borrowed some of the best minds in law enforcement in the world, and the physical evidence they were amassing was prodigious. But given the angles of the wounds, the saliva on the women's mouths, the traces of hair and fiber, it was certain they were dealing with perhaps a whole band of lunatics.

He shivered. His mother's mother had been a warm, comfortable farm wife in Provence, with a ready cuff to the ear and an inexhaustible supply of cakes for a greedy grandson. His father's mother had been more austere—a retired schoolteacher who stood no nonsense. He'd loved them both, grieved when they died, and then continued on with his life. Who could hate old ladies so much that they would deprive them of their last few years on this earth?

Of course, the lives that were snuffed out weren't always the most pleasant. The women lived alone, in tiny, crowded apartments, living out their days in discreet, genteel penury. He'd toyed with the idea that the murderers were fanatics, convinced they were doing the old women a mercy by ending their lonely existence.

But he didn't think so. It didn't ring true, any more than the notion of copycat killers felt right to a man of his remarkable instincts. But he had to be wrong about the latter. There was no logical reason for three or four people to be murdering old women.

He looked back over his shoulder at his wife's sleeping figure. She'd creamed her makeup off, and her mouth was open slackly as soft, polite snores issued forth. She would hate it if she knew he was watching her. At times like these she looked a bit as she would when she was very old. Like the old women who were murdered. And he loved her still. Would she still be with him when she grew old? Or would she leave him?

There was no sleep for him tonight. If he wasn't tormenting himself about the murders he was tormenting himself about Marie. Maybe if he rewrote his notes something new would catch his eye. Besides, he needed a cigarette, and Marie hated it when he smoked in the bedroom.

Carefully he closed the window, shutting out the steady,

merciless beat of the rain. His feet were silent on the carpeted floor as he left the bedroom, closing the door behind him. By the time he started making notes, Marie was forgotten. She lay alone in the tiny bedroom, her troubled brown eyes staring blankly at the rain-splattered window and the night outside.

Claire measured the coffee carefully, then returned the jar to the freezing compartment of Marc's state-of-the-art refrigerator. It was just after six, and the rain had finally let up. Maybe they would have a few days of sun.

Nicole was still sleeping when Claire had checked on her, her pale, plain face streaked with the telltale stain of tears. She must have woken some time during the night, Claire thought with a surge of guilt. Marc's bedroom was at the opposite end of the huge apartment, and Nicole never, ever entered that room. Claire hadn't figured out whether it was by inclination or Marc's command, but even when Marc was out of town Nicole avoided it.

Clear liquids for Nicole, fresh croissants for Marc. She'd found a baker who spoke English. She had to walk twice as far to get to it, but it was worth it. And she enjoyed the empty streets of the Left Bank, the sense of solitude. Early morning was like a piece of time stolen from a jealous god—it didn't even exist for those who slept through it. It was a secret, precious gift and Claire wouldn't have given it up for anything, not even the dubious comfort of her bed. The time was hers alone, away from suggestions, opinions, and spying eyes.

God, she was getting paranoid! She hadn't dealt with the accident properly, that was her problem. She'd been so caught up in guilt and misery and running away that she hadn't had a chance to come to terms with it. It was no wonder that it was affecting the rest of her life, making her unable to open up, to trust.

Maybe she could find a therapist who spoke English. She'd suggested it once to Marc, and he'd promised to look into it, but the subject had been dropped. She knew he didn't really approve, considered it a weakness. But damn, right now she felt weak.

The American embassy might be able to help. That was it. Once Marc left next week she'd go over there and talk to someone. They could recommend an American or British therapist living in Paris. They could probably even help her find a laundry where the people spoke English. She'd been passive too long. It was time to face things.

She'd left the address of the embassy sitting on the counter while she went out to the bakery. When she got back Marc was up, sitting there sipping coffee, smiling at her with lazy charm, extending his hand for the newspaper she never forgot to buy.

"*Merci*, darling," he said, opening the paper to the grisly picture of a dead old lady. Claire had deliberately folded it inward, hoping not to look, but Marc spread it out on the narrow table and she had no choice. Another murder, she realized with a shudder.

The scrap of paper with the embassy's address on it was exactly where she had left it. She went over and poured herself a cup of coffee, keeping her eyes averted from the table, when Marc's low, soothing voice reached her. "I did want to mention something, *chérie*," he said. "Did you know the American police are looking for you?"

⚜ CHAPTER 3

Gilles Sahut shoved his burly arms into the bucket of water and sluiced the blood from his skin. The water was already a murky shade, and the fresh red diluted swiftly, turning it even darker. Gilles pulled his arms back out, but they were still coated with a faint maroon cast. He shrugged his massive shoulders and wiped the rest off on a filthy towel that had once been white.

He glanced around, not even noticing the carcasses hanging from the rafters. He was glad it wasn't yet summer. It wasn't that he minded the smell of blood as it pooled on the cement floor at his feet, but the flies were a nuisance.

He'd been working since five that morning, hacking, slicing, carving. He was proud of his profession. He was a butcher, owner of his own boucherie in a tidy little back street in the Belleville section of Paris. He'd worked hard for it, with no one to help him. His foster parents hadn't given a damn for the brutish boy who'd been foisted upon them, and he'd cleared out as soon as he could, apprenticing himself to old Maître Clerc. He'd been diligent, patient, and not the slightest bit squeamish, not about butchering cattle, not about putting dye in diseased meat and selling it to nursing mothers, not about putting up with Maître Clerc's drunken affection. He'd put up with worse in his life.

And he'd waited. Waited until the boucherie had started to show a fair profit, waited until Maître Clerc's brother died, waited until he'd become indispensable to the old man. And then he'd given him a little push down the stairs and taken over the business he'd worked so hard for.

He no longer sold diseased meats. He had his own reputation to consider, not Clerc's. It was his name over the shop now, and every morning he looked on it with pride.

And he no longer had to put up with the drunken fondlings of a raddled old fag. Instead he could afford a clean, decent-looking whore who wouldn't complain if he liked it a little rough. He paid well, and he never marked them.

No, he thought, splashing some of the bloody water over his sweating moon face, life was good. He had his work, he had sex when he needed it, he had friends to drink wine with and play cards. And every few weeks, during the heavy rains, he had the old women.

Why had she lied to him, Claire demanded of herself. Surely she could have told him the truth after so long? Marc wasn't likely to pass judgment—he had a laissez-faire attitude about morals that sometimes shocked her.

After all, she was planning to marry the man. Was she fool enough to think a marriage would survive with secrets between them? Oh, by the way, Marc, I happened to have been involved in a hit-and-run accident just before I met you. One of the reasons I came to Paris with you was because I wanted to get away from the police in case they found out what happened. And you thought I came just to be with you?

He wouldn't like it. He wouldn't like it one bit. But she had lied to him, quickly, instinctively. "The police? Why in the world would they want to see me?"

Marc had smiled, his charming, beautiful smile. "I don't know, darling. I must confess, I lied."

Relief and confusion washed through her. "You lied?"

He nodded, glancing down at the grainy photo of the

murdered woman with only cursory interest. "I told the man from the embassy that you left me to tour southern France. I had no idea where you were, or if you were even still in the country."

Claire held herself very still. "Why did you do that?"

He shrugged, an elegant, classic gesture. "I have an instinctive distrust of the police. And I knew they could have no good reason for wanting to bother you. What was it—overdue parking tickets?"

Brazen it out, she ordered herself. Or confess. Don't just stand there doing nothing. "Something like that, I would imagine," she said finally. "I really don't know. It was thoughtful of you to help, but I'd better go talk with the embassy and see what it is they want."

"As you wish," he dismissed it lightly, turning back to his paper. And ever since she'd been cursing herself for a fool and a coward. The more she lied, the deeper the hole she dug herself.

It was a pretty afternoon—one of the best she'd seen in a long time. The sun had come out, bright and strong, and burnt away the soaking rain. Even the bare trees were delicate against the bright blue of the sky, and Paris was at her finest. The air was cool and fresh, hinting of a heat-drenched summer to come, but right now there was only light and warmth on an afternoon of simple pleasures.

Claire found herself walking aimlessly through a residential section. She could only be thankful she had an instinctive sense of direction. Street signs meant absolutely nothing to her, refusing to imprint on her stubborn brain no matter how hard she tried. She could find her way back by recognizing landmarks and houses, not street names, and with that she had to be content.

Marc had taken the pale and still unwell Nicole to see her grandmother, leaving Claire to her own devices. The old woman didn't approve of him, Marc had said humorously. It would be better to warn her of Claire's existence, rather than spring Claire on her unannounced. After all, her daughter had been dead less than two years, and *grand-mère* was still having trouble accepting it. She wouldn't like meeting her replacement.

So Claire had hours of free time and nowhere to go. The embassy was now out of the question. Since Marc had so innocently covered for her, she could simply stay in Paris, waiting. Waiting until things died down, waiting until she got up enough nerve to go to the authorities herself. Waiting for something.

She could always telephone back to the States. Telephone Brian, whom she'd sworn she'd never speak to again. The telephones in France were direct dial, thank God, and many of the public phones even had English instructions on them. It was her one defense against incomprehension, and she didn't want to use it lightly. Once she called, there might be no turning back. She would wait just a little bit longer.

She was heading in the direction of the tiny park. It wasn't far from Marc's apartment—less than a ten-minute walk, and she'd discovered it one winter afternoon when she'd been searching for an English-speaking druggist.

It was a small and pretty patch of green in the midst of the huge city, and the benches and pathways were always pleasantly filled with people. Old people, feeding the pigeons, reading the paper, playing checkers, gossiping with each other. On a day such as this the park would be packed with people wanting to take advantage of the good weather while it lasted. Claire didn't mind. As long as no one asked her anything in rapid, incomprehensible French, she was glad to be surrounded by people. She spent too much time alone in Marc's apartment.

Someone was even selling ice cream at the edge of the park. The sun was surprisingly hot, beating down on Claire's head. She'd let her red hair flow loose around her shoulders. Marc preferred a more formal style, but Marc wasn't there to see it. She opened the buttons of her stylish wool coat and stared longingly at the ice cream cart. Why couldn't she even remember the French word for ice cream? Why couldn't they have it written on the white steel sides of the cart as they would in the States? At that moment she would have given years off her life for a scoop of coffee ice cream.

Resolutely she moved onward, heading down the winding path toward the shallow, man-made pond. It couldn't hurt her to lose a few pounds around her hips, she told herself. There wasn't a woman alive who couldn't afford to lose a few pounds around her hips.

A woman was walking up the path from the pond, slowly, sedately, with the kind of inborn grace one only saw in royalty and the most expensive prostitutes. She was somewhere past seventy-five, with snowy white hair, dark, lively brown eyes, and softly creased skin. She was well-dressed, in a pale blue wool suit, and her hands were encased in white kid gloves. The gloves were stretched taut over knuckles swollen with arthritis, but the woman's face reflected none of the pain and discomfort that had to be her daily lot. She caught Claire's curious expression and smiled, a warm, friendly smile that was reflected in her youthful eyes.

Claire smiled back, breathing a small, sad sigh of relief as the woman passed her without speaking. She was always reluctant to respond to the friendliness of strangers when she couldn't even summon a word of French. There was no way she could explain to the chauvinistic French that her lack of the language wasn't arrogance or laziness. It was at times a torment for her, to be locked away in silence.

So intent was she on her brief moment of self-pity that she didn't notice the rough figure coming up the path behind the elegant old lady. That he saw her made no difference, he wasn't about to move from the center of the path as he continued on his way. He crashed into her, knocking her to one side, and moved onward without even a backward glance.

Claire had a jumble of impressions. The dark, twisted cruelty of the man's face, the iron hardness of the body that had plowed into hers, his huge leather boots with their incongruous shine. She'd fallen against another man, and his indignant protests washed over her as she stared after the dark man's disappearing figure. A slight shiver passed over her, as if a goose had danced on her grave, her grandmother used to say. And summoning her best smile, she turned back to offer an apologetic shrug to the voluble and much-offended Frenchman she'd landed on.

The apologetic shrug was not quite enough. The innocent smile, the damnable English words, "I'm terribly sorry, but I don't speak French" only seemed to make matters worse. There were times when Claire considered pretending she was Lithuanian. or Bulgarian, anything but English-speaking. Her obvious nationality never failed to elicit a negative response.

The gentleman was waving his arms and shouting now. He'd been eating an ice cream cone, and her ill-timed descent had managed to squash it all over his elegant black suit. It looked like coffee ice cream too, Claire noticed mournfully. She tried again.

"I'm really very sorry," she began, when a voice interrupted her, smooth and fluent, and a strong arm snaked around her shoulders, squeezing her very lightly, a reassuring squeeze, telling her he would handle things. She subsided, looking up at her rescuer as he reasoned with the angry man.

He was American, there was no doubt about that. He was also quite tall, well over six feet, with the bony sort of awkwardness that she'd always found oddly attractive. He had thick brown hair that was used to having hasty fingers dragged through it, bright blue eyes, and a big, friendly mouth. His hands and his feet were in keeping with the size of him—huge and well-shaped, and his rumpled blue jeans and jacket fit with what looked suspiciously like the faintest tracing of early spring freckling across his impressive nose.

He turned back to her, his long arm still firmly planted around her shoulders, and grinned. "The gentleman forgives you," he said.

Sure enough, the elderly Frenchman was no longer gesturing and shouting. He was smiling, a warm, paternalistic smile, and there was even a hint of worry in his eyes, as if he was afraid he might have upset her. He took her hand between his and spoke long and movingly. Her companion answered, the old man laughed, and then she found herself being walked back up the pathway, that strong, comforting arm still around her shoulders.

"What did you say to him?" she said finally, knowing she should shake his arm free, for the moment not bothering. After all, they were in a public park. The man didn't look like a lunatic, and even if he were, he couldn't hurt her, not with so many witnesses. And while she couldn't speak French, she could certainly scream at the top of her lungs, and that was a fairly universal sound.

He smiled down at her. It was a warm, enchanting smile, full of friendliness and nothing else. "I told him you were my pregnant wife and you had occasional dizzy spells."

She considered several outraged responses. Instead she found herself laughing. "Thank you. I'm afraid my lack of French didn't help matters."

"I don't imagine it did. By the way, my name's Tom Parkhurst. You ought to know who you're married to. That is . . . you're not really married, are you?"

Not yet, she should have said. "No, I'm not married." Tell him about Marc, she ordered herself sternly. Say thank you very much and get rid of him.

It had been so long since she'd spoken to anyone but Marc. So long since she'd heard the blessedly flat vowels of an American accent. Surely she could indulge herself for just a short while?

"My name's Claire," she said, deliberately omitting her last name. She wasn't sure why she did—it was just an instinctive gesture of self-protection. She stopped, and he took his arm away from her slender shoulders and shook her proffered hand. There was just the right feel to it, not too soft, not too rough, not too squeezing, not too limp. He was harmless, she told herself. A fellow American, and someone to talk to.

"I don't suppose," she said, "that you know the French words for coffee ice cream?"

* * *

Malgreave slammed the book shut with a nasty curse. His English wasn't bad, better in conversation than in literature, but this book, for all the effort he was putting into it, wasn't proving any help at all. He glared down at it. He'd gone to a great deal of trouble to get it. It was the latest American best-seller, chronicling the history of several of the copycat killers in the last decade. And there was absolutely nothing of value for his current case.

He leaned back on the uncomfortable, overstuffed sofa that Marie had banished to the back bedroom, the room they now called his office. It had been Margritte's room, until she got married, and for almost a year Marie had refused to change anything. But now Margritte was about to give birth to their first grandchild, an event Marie clearly anticipated and dreaded. On the one hand Marie loved babies, she loved Margritte, and she looked forward to having a new little one to dress up and play with.

On the other hand, being a grandmother meant getting old. And he knew very well that Marie had no wish to get old.

She'd lost weight recently. She'd been going to a health center and exercising, and her waist had come back. She no longer bought sweets, and she scarcely touched her morning roll. She was wearing more makeup now, and her hair had lost the becoming silver. No, she didn't want to get old. But was her sudden youthfulness for her own sake, or his? Or someone else's?

Margritte wouldn't be coming home now, and the spare bedroom was simply going to waste. And if Louis was going to bring his work home with him and smoke those nasty cigarettes, then he needed a place to work, she said. She wasn't going to give up her television programs because he wanted to concentrate. God knows, she said, she had little enough to entertain her these days.

She was going to leave him, he knew she was. And while the thought ate away at his soul like acid, there was nothing he could do. If he said anything, there would be no turning back. So he just plodded onward, his head in the sand, hoping she would change her mind.

And in the meantime, the weather forecast was for three days of rain.

Rocco Guillère strolled down the narrow street, away from the park, his cruel dark eyes following the old lady's elegant pace. He hated women like that. They looked like they had a broomstick up their ass and they'd rather die than admit it. Tall, straight, born rich and she'd die rich.

Sooner than she'd like. He looked up into the clear blue sky, peering into the fleecy white clouds scudding along. When he'd been a boy and lived outside of Paris he could tell what the weather would be from the clouds. He'd forgotten all that—now he only knew the weather from what landed on his skin. He'd wait, he had to wait. He'd promised, and promises like that couldn't be broken.

In the meantime, he knew where she lived. It wouldn't take long. Early spring was one of the rainiest times of the year. All he had to do was be patient and hope that fool Malgreave didn't realize he had anything to do with the two bodies found floating in the Seine last night.

He didn't have anything to worry about. The police didn't fuss too much about dead drug dealers, as long as they weren't part of a gang war. This way he had the money, the drugs, and Giselle had been able to enjoy herself, the greedy bitch. And in a few days, as soon as the rains came again, he'd get his reward.

Marc came up behind her, snaking his arms around her waist and pulling her pliant body back against his. His warm, damp mouth nibbled her neck, and his narrow hips pressed against her buttocks. He was aroused, and she waited for an answering surge of heat in her own body. It came, obediently enough, but it took a moment.

"Did you miss me while we were at *grand-mère's?*" he murmured in her ear.

She didn't move. There was absolutely nothing to feel

guilty about, she told herself for the twentieth time. All she did was share a park bench and an hour's conversation with a fellow American. And a coffee ice cream cone that was sinfully delicious.

It had been nothing. Just a sharing of idiotic things. Where they went to college. Where they'd worked. What pets they'd had when they were young. The miserable weather, and yes, the tragic deaths of the old ladies. The kind of conversation strangers had. And that's all she and Tom Parkhurst were. Strangers who would be unlikely to meet again.

So there was no need to tell Marc, was there? He was flatteringly jealous, but it wasn't a game Claire cared to play. There was no comparison between the two men. Marc was heat and passion and dark, mysterious depths. Tom was about as mysterious as a teddy bear.

No, there was no need to tell him. "Of course I missed you," Claire murmured, turning in his arms and pressing her hips against his. "Do I get to go next time?"

He smiled at her, his dark, dreamy eyes level with hers. "Not next time, darling," he murmured, his hands deft with her zipper. "There wasn't time to bring up the subject. But soon, I promise."

She felt the coolness of the air against her skin as the zipper parted company, and she squashed down the sudden surge of disappointment. She'd been looking forward to meeting Nicole's beloved *grand-mère*. Anything to break out of her seclusion. Marc would have no reason for keeping them apart, unless . . . "She does speak English, doesn't she?"

Marc's expressive face was answer enough, it didn't need his words. "I'd been hoping you wouldn't ask. Not really, darling. But I'm sure Nicole will translate for you."

"But she just spent almost a year in Los Angeles . . ."

He shrugged. "You will find that Harriette Langlois does not do anything she doesn't care to do. And she doesn't care to learn a language she considers an abomination." The dress slid to the floor, a pool of silk at her slender ankles.

"Don't worry about her, darling. As long as we have each other we don't need a disapproving old bitch like her. Let Nicole have her."

"But . . ." Her mouth was silenced, swiftly and effectively, by his. And Claire, thinking of Tom Parkhurst and guilt, kissed him back.

Harriette Langlois was washing her own dishes. She hadn't yet arranged for her cleaning lady to come back, and in truth, she didn't mind doing the dishes for a change. It helped her think.

But even giving her Limoges the care it deserved didn't take enough time. She scrubbed the wooden counters, threw out the leftover bread, and turned off the light, moving back into the airy, delicate living room that she'd missed so desperately when she'd been on her self-imposed exile.

The room was almost English, she had to admit it, much as she hated the English. The comfortable chairs and sofa were covered in a pink chintz, the watercolors were of the Lake District, the curtains were Irish lace. Well, even the worst abomination of a country could have its merits.

She moved slowly, carefully across the room to the little table that held her precious store of cognac. She poured herself a small glass and took a deep, warming sip. By this time of night she began to get a little weary, she had to admit it. But there was always one thing that could manage to give her energy.

The photos were arranged on the baby grand piano, each in its silver frame. Nicole, solemn, dignified as only a too-serious five-year-old could be, even in happier times. Isabelle, her mother, Harriette's only daughter, with her too-large nose and her laughing eyes that were now forever closed. Jacques, Harriette's husband, a man with too little imagination and too much morality, but a good man, nonetheless.

And Marc Bonnard. Handsome, charming Marc Bonnard, in a matching silver frame. He'd been startled when he'd seen it, and professed himself flattered. Harriette had only smiled sourly.

She moved to the piano and stared down into Marc's wonderful eyes. "You bastard," she said, the words a ritual, "you murdered my daughter. And I will make you pay for it." Holding her glass of cognac in a silent toast of vengeance, she drained it.

And ten blocks away, Claire shivered in Marc's arms.

❧ CHAPTER 4

There was rain that night. Claire lay on the too-soft bed, clutching the freshly laundered sheet in desperate fingers, digging her feet into the mattress. Marc's slender, delicate hands held her hips, allowing her no movement, as he used his mouth on her.

He was very good with his mouth, but tonight he was inspired. No matter how she writhed and struggled he wouldn't let her go, and she knew she'd have bruises on her hips tomorrow. She was sweating, aching, desperate, as he slowly, carefully brought her just to the point of orgasm. And then he backed off, just long enough for her to regain a small portion of her self-control, only to begin the slow, maddening process all over again.

He was relentless, indefatigable, and Claire was weeping, helpless, her heels drumming against the bed as she sought a release he refused to grant her. She bit her lip, hard, to keep her pleas from bubbling forth. It would do no good, it would only incite Marc further, and besides, she didn't want to risk Nicole hearing. She suffered in silence, her body convulsed in tiny spasms of useless reaction as he took his time in a ritual he had long ago perfected, but this night brought to astonishing heights. That it was closer to torture than to love occurred to her when her mind was too clouded and aching to block out the disloyal thought.

"Marc," she moaned, unable to help herself, "please . . ."

But it was endless long minutes before he finally took pity on her and ended her torment. As he gathered her trembling, weakened body into his arms she had the brief, unpleasant thought that tonight his lovemaking had been rather like a cat playing with a succulent mouse. And the tiny death it had ended with was unpleasantly like a real death.

Her shaky muscles tightened as she rejected the thought. Marc's body was dry and hot, wrapped around her, and belatedly she realized she hadn't been allowed to touch him at all.

"Marc," she whispered, her voice raw, "don't you want me to . . . ?"

"No need, darling," he murmured, biting her ear. He always bit just a little bit too hard, and once more her muscles screamed in tension. "You were so exciting that things just took care of themselves. Do you know how exquisite you look when you struggle against me?"

There it was again, the unpleasant image of an animal caught in a trap. She turned to look at him, and his eyes glittered in the darkness, his mobile, handsome face wreathed in tenderness. He could convey emotions so well with just the slightest twist of that face.

Claire was still shaking inside. She didn't want to kiss him, didn't want to taste her desperation on his smiling mouth. So she merely smiled. "I love you, Marc," she murmured, trying to believe it.

"I know you do, *chérie.*" He lay back, keeping possessive arms around her. His body was a furnace, hot and dry and perfectly relaxed. "I have a wonderful idea," he said, his hand trailing through Claire's flowing hair. "Tomorrow let's take the day for ourselves. We'll send Nicole to see her grandmother and you and I will just spend the time together. I have to leave Monday, and I'm going to miss you terribly. I want to go with the memory of a perfect day between us."

Slowly the trembling had stopped, slowly the sweat had begun to dry on her body as she relaxed beneath his

37

soothing hand. She was still too hot, but these moments, the gentle, comforting, loving minutes after they made love, were the most important to her. It made the darkness and the pleasure that was uncomfortably akin to pain worth it. "That would be wonderful, Marc," she said, pressing her face against his smooth chest, rubbing like a cat.

"I'll take Nicole to Harriette's," he murmured, "and then I'll come back and join you in bed. Then we'll find a wonderful café for lunch, and go for a long walk in the afternoon. I know how you love long walks."

"That would be heavenly." She was very drowsy, and her doubts and distaste had vanished into a haze of satisfaction.

"I'll take you someplace you've never been before." His voice was a soporific litany, lulling her to sleep. "A wonderful park where the old people go, and they sell the best coffee ice cream in Paris."

It took every ounce of strength and determination she possessed to keep from panicking. The sick feeling in the pit of her stomach stayed there, and the sweat on her body turned chilly. "That would be heavenly, darling," she whispered in the darkness, keeping her muscles relaxed, feigning a sleepiness that had now vanished.

And Marc Bonnard, his hand still possessively smoothing Claire's red gold hair, smiled into the dark, rainy night.

Yvon Alpert lay awake, listening to the rain. He'd been awake since three, since the rain started. Jeanne had left sometime after five, oblivious to his dark mood. She'd chattered on and on about how nice things would be next month, when they were married and she didn't have to rush home to change her clothes before work. He'd suggested more than once that she could bring things over, but Jeanne was a good Catholic, with a strict sense of propriety. Each time she spent the night she had to allow herself to be persuaded, had to convince herself that she was swept away by passion and emotion and it wasn't her fault. If she'd done anything as calculated as bring a toothbrush she could no longer believe in her own essential purity.

Yvon had been patient, understanding, but just before

dawn on a rainy night it took all his willpower to keep from screaming at her. She left, with a saucy bounce of her narrow hips and a cheerful wave, unaware of the torments her fiancé was suffering.

He didn't get out of bed to watch her walk down the street, as he did on other nights. He should get up, make some coffee, ignore the rain, and act like it was any other day. He stayed where he was.

The sheets smelled like sex. They smelled of Jeanne's middle-class perfume, and sweat, and that faint, ammonia-like odor of semen. He should get up, wash, and face the day. He didn't move.

He had no reason to be tormented. His job at the ministry was a good one, with ample money to support him. Jeanne was a good woman, affectionate, sexually inventive, and if she was a bit too Catholic he could overlook it, as long as she didn't try to drag him to mass. He hadn't been to church since he was nine years old and the orphanage had burnt down, and he knew he could never go again.

There were times he missed it. Times when he longed for confession and absolution, longed for a penance to wipe some of the evil from his tainted soul.

But then the sun would shine, and he would put such dark memories behind him and think ahead to the good life that awaited him. He would marry Jeanne next month, and they'd have children, lots of children. He was in line for a promotion—with luck they might be able to afford a small house in the suburbs, one with room for the children to play.

But there'd be no garden.

He still couldn't walk into a formal garden without feeling nauseated. It was the smell of roses that got him, he realized. The sickly sweet scent of pink roses in summer that reminded him of pain and fear and death. And the stench of flesh burning his nostrils.

The roses had burned along with the orphanage. Everything had been destroyed by the fire—he could remember the blackened timbers of the old wooden building that had been his home for three years, the skeletal branches of the rosebushes, pointing at him, the ashes of the gardener's shed in one corner of the decimated garden. With the remains of the gardener lying there in the embers.

Grand-mère Estelle had been found in the basement of the main building. The authorities had decided she'd fallen through when all the debris from the upper floors had collapsed. There was no need for Madame Marti to be in the cellar of the building. It hadn't been difficult to identify her—who else would be found dead in the orphanage she'd run for more than forty years? What remained incomprehensible, and was finally dismissed with a Gallic shrug, was the peculiar condition of her body. It had taken a strong-stomached employee of the district three days to find all the pieces of Mme. Marti. They never did find her feet.

Yvon sat up, nausea churning in his own stomach. He hated remembering, hated the sick, dark clouds that beat around his head. If only Jeanne had stayed, her incessant chatter could have drowned out the steady beat of the rain against the windows. Could have drowned out the things he didn't want to remember, drowned out what he had to do.

He moved over to the window, looking down into the wet, dirty streets. Maybe if he quit his job, moved to the country, maybe somewhere in the south. His employers thought highly of him—they'd write him a good letter of recommendation and he'd be able to find something suitable. In the south, in a climate where it seldom rained.

But he knew he couldn't do that. It would follow him, the memories, the nightmares, the pledge he'd made so many years ago. The longer he delayed the worse it got. There was no sleep for him on rainy nights.

And every now and then, when he least expected it, he'd catch the faint, inexplicable scent of pink roses.

The rain turned to spring snow flurries that scattered in front of the fierce wind. The sun was bright yellow in a clear blue sky, and the puffy white clouds scudded along, carrying the smog with them. It was a glorious day, Claire thought as she heated the milk for Marc's coffee. Surely nothing terrible could happen on such a beautiful day.

Nicole sat in silence, sipping at her hot chocolate, her small, spotless hands careful around the Limoges cup. Claire had wanted to get her something less fragile, but Marc had refused. "She must learn to eat and drink like civilized people, darling. It will do her no good to coddle her."

Claire nodded, disagreeing. As far as she was concerned, Nicole could have benefited from some coddling. Not that the child would let anyone close enough to do so. Maybe her *grand-mère* would be allowed to dispense affection. Someone to fill the terrible gap left by the loss of her mother.

Nicole fixed her flat dark gaze on Claire's face. "How did you cut your lip, Claire?" she asked, and Claire felt the color flood her face as the memory of the night before swept back through her.

Unfortunately Marc was there, listening. He dropped the paper and spoke to her in a cold, emotionless voice, and Claire flinched in silent sympathy. The relationship between father and daughter had gone from bad to worse. Marc no longer attempted to charm Nicole out of her bad moods. He was cold, clipped, distant with her, reserving his warmth and affection for Claire and Claire alone.

Whatever he'd said to Nicole had been effective. The girl's sallow face had turned pale and her opaque eyes grew even more blank. He might just as well have slapped her across the face, Claire thought dismally.

Once more she felt that clinging sense of desperation. She knew how much Marc loved his unpromising little daughter, and yet he seemed unable to show it. He seemed removed and judgmental, yet Claire knew it was all the act of a loving man who simply didn't know how to treat children.

During the last few months she'd tried to help, but had quickly learned not to interfere. The best the two Bonnards could do was muddle along, misunderstanding each other, wrapped in coldness, until something broke through. And that something wasn't going to be Claire MacIntyre, no matter how much she wanted to help them bridge the gap. They simply wouldn't let her.

41

Nicole muttered a graceless apology, and Marc once more disappeared behind the newspaper. Claire tried to give Nicole an encouraging smile, but Nicole swiftly turned her head away. In another, less stalwart child Claire would have thought she was blinking back tears. But as far as she knew Nicole never cried when she was awake. It was only during sleep that her formidable defenses gave way.

Claire glanced toward Marc, then looked swiftly away. The headlines of the paper were dark, bold, screaming of something ghastly. The photograph needed no translation. Another old woman had died.

It was a cold, blustery day. Not a day for a casual stroll in the park, but Marc, blessedly high-spirited, wouldn't take no for an answer. He'd bundled Nicole off to her grandmother's shortly after breakfast, then took Claire back to bed for another hour. It almost wiped out the memory of the night before. With the bright, chilly sunlight streaming in the windows Claire could almost forget the refined torture of the rain-swept night before.

The streets were empty. The day was more like January than early April, with a sharp wind whistling down the streets and around the buildings, sending a chill straight into Claire's heart. Her silk dress provided little protection against the cold, and the high, high heels on her leather shoes were making her ankles ache as Marc drew her along at a pace just a shade too brisk for a Sunday afternoon stroll.

"Where are we going, Marc?" she demanded, pulling back. "I'm not dressed for this weather."

He stopped, his hand still possessive on her arm, and looked at her with affectionate criticism. "Darling, my grandmother dressed in clothes that were no warmer than what you're wearing every day of her life, and she never complained about the cold. It's all that ridiculous central heating in America. Your blood's gotten too thin."

"My legs are freezing," she protested. "At least you should have let me wear jeans."

"You know I can't abide trousers on women," Marc said, his bright smile taking the sting out of the words. "Don't complain, sweetheart. It's just another block or two, we'll

42

take a quick turn around the park, and then I'll take you home and warm you up properly. I don't know what's gotten into me—I'm quite insatiable."

Claire ignored the little pinch of dismay, smiling into those dreamy eyes that were on a level with hers. "It's probably because you're going away," she said. "You know you're not going to be having any for a while."

"What makes you think I'm celibate when I'm away from you, Claire?" he countered gently. "Perhaps I have a new woman every night."

She wasn't even ruffled. "Then maybe I'd better find someone to fill in while you're gone."

They started back down the sidewalk, her arm tucked companionably into his. "You know I would kill you if you did." His voice was teasing. "Don't forget, I'm French. We're a very jealous, passionate race."

"So I've noticed." She was relaxing, despite the cold. Marc seldom teased—life was much too serious a business for him. She loved him best when he was tender, lightly mocking. "At least, the passionate part. I've never given you cause for jealousy so I'm not sure how you'd be."

"I would be dangerous." He steered her into the park. "Very dangerous, *chérie.*"

She could have wished he'd chosen another place. Not that she was feeling guilty about the American she'd met yesterday. There was nothing to feel guilty about. It was just an innocent encounter between expatriates, an hour and a coffee ice cream cone. But Marc wouldn't understand, wouldn't believe she'd already forgotten the man's name, the flattering warmth of his blue eyes.

"What do you suppose is going on?" Marc murmured in her ear, drawing her closer.

She would have thought the park would be deserted on such a blustery day. In part she was correct. There were no old people sitting on the benches, huddled against the sudden cold, no ice cream vendor plying his trade. In their place were close to a dozen uniformed police, with several plainclothes men just as clearly connected to the authorities.

"Let's leave," she said, pulling against his arm. There were other people there, a scattered crowd of curious bystanders, watching with great interest as the police milled about.

"Stay right here. I'm going to find out what's going on." He released her arm and headed toward the most official-looking of the men. She didn't even consider moving, much as she longed to escape. She didn't want to know what was going on. She wanted to keep walking on this cold, bright day and not think about the police.

She wrapped her arms around her shivering body. Marc was deep in animated discussion with the man, and she watched both, unconsciously comparing them. Marc never ceased to surprise her with his beauty. Every bone, every muscle in his body was perfectly formed, exquisitely trained. Even the unruly curl of dark hair obeyed him, landing at just the right spot in his well-shaped forehead. He caught her watching him, turned and smiled, that charming, possessive smile that never failed to warm her.

In contrast the man beside him was almost ugly. He must have been in his late fifties, with a lined, weary face and ancient eyes that had seen too much. He was tall, taller than Marc's average height, and his shoulders were slightly stooped, as if under a great weight that he just managed to support. His clothes were rumpled, as if he slept in them, and his thinning hair needed cutting. And yet there was something about him, a hint of compassion around a grim mouth, a suggestion of morbid humor in the dark eyes, that Claire liked.

A moment later Marc rejoined Claire. The tips of his ears were red from the cold, and he rubbed his hands together briskly before once more taking hold of her. "As I suspected," he said, looking mournful. "It's this nasty business of the old ladies. I didn't want to disturb you, darling, but another one was killed last night. She lived near the park, and the police suspect she might have been seen here yesterday."

"The poor woman." Even pulling the coat tightly around her, she couldn't seem to get warm.

"These people are animals," Marc said somberly. "They're going to post a warning at the entrance to the park. The inspector told me they simply couldn't guarantee the safety of the old people in Paris. They haven't got the manpower."

"How ghastly."

"Be glad you're thirty and not eighty." He smiled, dismissing the morbid subject. "As long as you behave yourself you're safe. Let's go, *chérie*. There's no ice cream on such a cold day, and I don't like the way all these men are looking at you." He pulled her up tight against him, pressing a soft, damp, open-mouthed kiss against her chilled lips.

It was too cold to respond, though she did her best. When he released her they started back toward the street. She looked about her curiously, wondering which of the busy policemen had offended Marc with his importunate eyes. They all seemed intent, unaware of the well-dressed couple heading out of the park. Marc's paranoia, she thought, dismissing it. She should never have responded to his teasing.

Still, she could feel the eyes on her. She turned to say something to Marc, casting a furtive glance over her shoulder.

The American was there, surrounded by a handful of shorter Parisians. He was looking straight at her, and his blue eyes were mournful.

Tom, his name was. Thomas Jefferson Parkhurst, she thought. And Marc had noticed him. Damn, and double damn.

"Let's take a taxi," she said, huddling closer to him.

Marc's eyes clouded in surprise. "Why, darling? We've only a short walk."

"Because I can't wait to get home with you," she said in a low voice.

He kissed her again, and she put all her enthusiasm into it, throwing her arms around his neck and pressing her hips against his. When they drew apart she was breathless, and if Marc had had suspicions she'd managed to banish them. "I doubt we'll find a taxi," he said, "but we can always run."

She laughed, suddenly happy. "Or at least walk very fast," she said.

"You always do." They hurried from the park, in perfect amity.

Louis Malgreave watched them leave. A good-looking couple, he thought. Not the sort who usually frequented this park, not the sort he ran into in the course of his days. Their kind didn't murder, their kind didn't rape or deal drugs. The man looked vaguely familiar, and it only took him a minute to place him. He was a mime. Marie had grown more interested in the theater, and he'd taken her to a performance of Le Théâtre du Mime last fall. He recognized the man even without the whiteface and baggy costume, recognized the bone structure and the graceful carriage. Malgreave prided himself on never forgetting anyone. In his job he couldn't afford to.

The woman had been a question mark. English, perhaps, or American, though she didn't have the brassy, self-assured look he associated with American women who slept with French men. Not married, he guessed. His assessing gray eyes slid over to the tall, unhappy-looking man down by the little pond. And perhaps not faithful.

That was the least of his worries. They had nothing to do with Marcelle Boisrond's death. For the moment that was all he could allow himself to think about, not Marie at home alone on a Sunday when he'd promised to take her to see Margritte. Not curious couples walking the icy streets of Paris. Only murder.

✦ CHAPTER 5

Thomas Jefferson Parkhurst didn't go straight home from the old people's park. He stopped first at a bistro and drank too much wine, comfortably anesthetizing himself before he made his way back up to his artist's garret. The wine was smooth and dry and a hundred times better than the vinegary substance produced by his own bankrupt vineyard, but for the first time in twenty-two months he longed for something harder. The smooth bourbon of his younger years, of his native Kentucky, would have blurred the edges much more effectively. Wine soured his stomach and gave him diarrhea.

He ducked in out of the wind and started the lengthy climb to his sixth-floor apartment, stumbling just slightly. The question was, why did he need his edges blurred today? Granted, he was cold as hell, and his apartment wasn't going to be much of an improvement from the icy streets below. But the sun was shining, the sky was dazzlingly blue, and Paris was magnificent as always.

He hated the fact that another old woman had died. He hadn't wanted to learn the details, but he'd already bought the paper to accompany his croissant and coffee, and his alternatives were to stare at his fellow diners in the small café or stare at his large hands. He'd read the paper.

She'd been in the park yesterday afternoon. He might even have seen her when he'd been talking to . . . He might even have seen her, he amended to himself as he gained the fourth-floor landing, panting slightly. He might have seen her killer.

The next flight of stairs almost proved his undoing. He'd drunk more wine than he'd realized, the unaccustomed quality of the stuff blinding him to the quantity. He slipped, banging his shins against the iron railing, and sprawled full-length on the stairs.

He considered staying where he was. No one else lived on the top floor—unless he had unexpected visitors he wouldn't be in anybody's way. And if someone did have the temerity to visit him unannounced they could damn well help him up to his apartment.

Except that the stairs were a lot less comfortable than his bed with the sagging mattress. And even lying stretched out on the stairs he couldn't avoid what was bothering him. Not the thought of another old lady being brutally murdered, depressing though that was. It was the memory of Claire.

He'd been cursing himself all night long that he hadn't found out more about her. He knew all sorts of things— where she grew up, what she ate for breakfast, what writers she read, and what she used to do for a living. He knew she couldn't understand a word of French and was miserable and embarrassed about her inability to do so. He knew she had a soft, vulnerable mouth, humorous eyes, and the most glorious red gold hair.

But he didn't know her last name, or where she lived. Or whom she lived with, he added bitterly, pulling himself to his knees.

He'd stayed up late last night. The novel needed something new, a sympathetic female character. He'd worked feverishly, and if the woman with the red gold hair had sounded vaguely familiar, it only added to his inspiration.

He'd called her Elizabeth, a name that suited her. The Elizabeth in his novel had been perfect; warm, glowing, sexually insatiable, and exquisitely beautiful. She'd haunted the book, haunted his dreams, so that he raced over to the park as soon as he'd finished his coffee and the gruesome details of the latest murder, and stayed there, shivering in the cruel wind, waiting for her to show up.

He never doubted that she would. That pull he'd felt had been too strong to be one-way. She'd come back, looking for him, and he'd be there, waiting.

When he first spotted her, standing alone, too lightly dressed for such a cold day, his first reaction was disappointment. She wasn't the vision he'd remembered. Her face was narrow, pinched with cold, her mouth thin and unhappy, her slender body graceless as she wrapped her arms around herself. The hair was still glorious, but the fantasy had faded.

He hadn't moved for a long moment, watching her, trying to reconcile reality with the dream goddess of the night before, when he saw the man. Very handsome, very French, very much her lover, he came up to the woman and put his hands on her.

Tom had waited to see her face light up. It hadn't happened. She'd smiled at the man, but it wasn't the same, open smile she'd given Tom just the day before. She kissed the man, her arms around him, seemingly lost in the public embrace. But Tom didn't believe it.

She saw him just before they left. She looked directly at him, her face blank. In less than twenty-four hours she'd forgotten him. And Tom headed out to get drunk.

He staggered the rest of the way to the top floor, slammed it shut behind him, and headed for the typewriter. Much as it went against the grain to revise before he was finished, this time it was too important. The saintly Elizabeth had to go.

Malgreave was walking, shoulders hunched forward, hat pulled down low on his head, hands shoved in his pockets. He ignored the cold, as he ignored everything when he was thinking. Possibilities and suspicions danced around in his head, and he had every intention of walking in the bitter cold until it all began to make some sense.

Josef was beside him, trotting at his heels like an over-eager terrier tracking a bitch in heat. Malgreave didn't mind—it gave him someone to talk to, to try his theories on.

When they'd finished up in the park he'd headed home, taking his assistant with him in a misguided hope that Josef's presence might deflect Marie's wrath at being abandoned one more Sunday. The effort had been wasted. The small, neat house in the suburbs was deserted, and there were frozen dinners awaiting him.

"Sorry, Josef. It looks as if Marie has gone to visit my daughter after all. We'll have to make do with these things." He gestured contemptuously at the brightly colored boxes lining the freezing compartment.

"I would consider it an honor, Chief Inspector," Josef murmured.

"The tragedy of that, Josef, is that you mean it," Malgreave said with a sigh. "No, I won't subject you to that. We'll find a café with something decent. God knows their food is probably from the freezer also. I don't know what France has come to. It's never failed to both enrage and amuse me, Josef, that the Americans have taken haute cuisine and in return given the poor French people frozen dinners with the taste and texture of cardboard."

Josef nodded solemnly, drinking in Malgreave's words, and once more the chief inspector sighed. Josef was a bright man, second only to himself in the department, and he combined a slavish adoration with a desperate ambition. The poor man was constantly being torn by those two conflicting emotions, hoping Malgreave would meet with disaster and be forced to resign, giving up his place to Josef, and hoping that Malgreave would once more triumph, bringing credit to the entire department. Malgreave had little doubt it was Josef's harridan of a wife who was responsible for the ambition. Were it left up to Josef, he'd be perfectly content following in Malgreave's footsteps, just as he was now.

Malgreave shook his head. "You'd best watch out if that pretty wife of yours starts buying these things, Josef. It's been Marie's only act of revenge for the long hours this job demands. You can tell her state of mind from the food she offers. If she's feeling generous and forgiving she'll leave tiny quiches, pastries, even a ragout to heat up. When we were young and just married she'd even wait up for me herself. Nowadays she's more than likely to reveal her displeasure in frozen fried chicken and peas the size and taste of goat pellets. It's a sad life, Josef."

"I'm certain Madame Malgreave loves you very much."

"Did I say she didn't?" Louis snapped. "No, you're right, Josef. But I'll give you another piece of good advice. There are times when love isn't enough." He slammed the freezer door shut. "Back into the cold, my friend. I need to walk."

And walk they did. Through the empty, windswept streets, they walked and walked until the nagging questions he had began to make sense.

"It was Rocco Guillère," Malgreave announced abruptly when they'd covered five blocks.

Josef was startled, his ferretlike eyes darting in his egg-shaped head. "What makes you say that? Not that I wish to disagree, Chief Inspector, but there is no proof, no clues, nothing to tie the man to this murder. I agree with you, he must have been responsible for a number of the old ladies, but I can't see why you suspect him of this one. This was scarcely his area of town."

"I know." Malgreave was weary. "I can only go by my instincts, and they seldom fail me. It was Guillère, all right. That elegant old lady in her beautiful apartment had been stabbed by a filthy hoodlum, then laid out on her silk-covered bed like a medieval effigy. God, it makes me sick to look at them. I'd rather there were more blood, signs of a struggle, not that damned formal lying in state, be they a comtesse, a nun, or a cleaning woman."

Josef shook his head, unconvinced. "It couldn't have been, sir. We've checked with everyone in the building. A man like Rocco would have stuck out like a sore thumb. We showed his photograph to everyone we could find, and not a soul had seen him."

Malgreave shrugged. "You know what your great strength is, Josef? Your stubbornness and adherence to facts. You know what your great weakness is? The very same traits. We know there are several people in Paris going around murdering old women, and Rocco Guillère is only one of them. Logic tells us that he isn't the one responsible for last night's killing. It wasn't his area of town, and people like him respect territory. A woman like Marcelle Boisrond would never have let a creature like Guillère near her. It stands to reason one of the other killers is responsible."

"Exactly," said Josef, not daring to feel smug.

"So when I insist that it was Rocco, despite everything, what will you think?"

Josef didn't even hesitate. He huddled deeper into the fancy British coat his wife had made him buy. "I'll know that Rocco did it," he said flatly.

Malgreave nodded. "Good man. I tell you, Josef, this was one murder too many. We're going to get him for it, and nothing is going to get in our way."

And Josef, torn between conflicting emotions, hunched his shoulders against the encroaching wind and followed Malgreave to the corner bistro.

The wind had finally stopped. There was a quarter moon, hung lopsided in a blue black sky, and the bare branches of the trees stretched upward, looking, Claire thought, like desperate arms reaching for rescue.

Morbid fancies, she thought, not turning away from the ghostly landscape. Marc was asleep in the bed behind her, his suitcase was already packed, and in another few hours he'd be gone. She should be back in bed, curled around his warm body, not standing barefoot on icy floors, staring out into the night.

Claire stared down at her clenched fists, deliberately relaxing them, stretching the fingers out. No rings. She'd told Marc tonight that she'd wear one; she'd marry him when he came back from the tour. It was a decision that had needed to be made, and she'd made it. She only wished she'd made the choice somewhere else, over coffee, in a bistro, even walking in that depressing park. It was a choice she would have made sanely, rationally. Why did she feel he'd wrung it out of her in bed that night?

She shivered. Was she simply afraid of commitment? Had she gone directly from a married man to a widower, subconsciously hoping both men would be too involved with their wives, both living and dead, to demand too much from her?

The next month would give her time to sort through her feelings, to decide where neuroses began and ended. And when Marc came back, she would tell him about Brian and the accident.

The Paris moon was a mournful one, she thought, looking upward. For all the talk about lovers and Paris, it wasn't a romantic sight. It was cold and lonely, shining down over the sleeping city, shining down on the corpses of old ladies, murdered before their time.

Claire shivered again, turning back to the bed. If she were very careful, Marc might sleep through the night. And tomorrow her last few weeks of freedom would begin.

"Tell me about this woman Marc lives with," Harriette ordered, leaning her frail body back against the chintz sofa and surveying her favorite grandchild with well-disguised fondness. "She's an American, I gather. Is she loud and vulgar?"

Nicole fiddled with her scratchy wool skirt. "Not really, grand-mère. She's very quiet and pretty."

Harriette snorted her disbelief. "Doesn't sound like she's Marc's type. He always went in for flashy blondes while your mother was still alive."

Nicole didn't flinch. She had no illusions about Marc—his fights with her mother had been too loud. Harriette had done nothing to foster the relationship, but most responsible for Nicole's dislike was Marc himself. Nicole had met him when she was four years old and her mother had gaily introduced him as her new father. She'd looked up into those dark, empty eyes of his and for the first time in her young life she'd felt fear. It hadn't been the last.

"Claire has sort of red blond hair," Nicole said. "She's very smart, very nice, really. She tries too hard, but then, what would you expect of an *Americaine?*"

"Apparently she doesn't try hard enough. Didn't you tell me she has no French? Barbaric!" *Grand-mère* sniffed.

For some reason Nicole found herself defending the woman. "Marc says it's not her fault. It's something to do with her brain."

"Heavens, don't tell me the woman is a mental deficient!"

"No, no. She tried to explain it to me once, but I wasn't paying attention," Nicole said patiently. "She said it was like being partially deaf. She could hear the noises but she couldn't make out the words."

"She's deaf?" Harriette demanded, incensed.

"No, *Grand-mère*. It's like she's deaf, but only when someone speaks in French."

"How very convenient," the old woman said icily. "Are you certain you don't wish to stay here with me while your stepfather is away? You can hardly be comfortable living with an afflicted stranger."

"I'm more comfortable with Claire than I am with Marc."

"That isn't saying much." *Grand-mère* picked an imaginary speck of dust from her silk crepe dress. "As long as you're happy and able to visit me every day I expect we can continue. The moment the woman becomes difficult you let me know, and I will have my lawyers deal with her. I don't trust Americans."

"If you met her yourself . . ."

"I have no need to. You forget, I just spent the last year in California." The old woman shuddered. "I know just what Mlle. Claire MacIntyre is like without seeing her. I know your stepfather's taste far too well, and it would take an idiot not to see through him. Therefore, she must be an idiot. Besides, she doesn't speak French—the interview would be a waste."

"But you speak English perfectly."

Madame nodded graciously. "True enough, *chérie*. But I have no intention of doing so. You'll simply have to be the go-between. I imagine we'll do just fine until your father comes back." She looked at her granddaughter piercingly, and once more Nicole felt that odd frisson of fear that was becoming far too frequent a companion. "You love your great-aunt Jacqueline, do you not?"

"Of course," Nicole replied, mystified.

"And California really isn't that bad. It's very sunny, and everyone has five color televisions and swimming pools and cars without roofs. You would enjoy yourself."

"Maybe Marc would let me visit," Nicole said. "Maybe you could take me."

Grand-mère smiled, a cool, distant smile that frightened her granddaughter very much. "We'll see, *chérie.* We'll see."

Gilles Sahut sat alone in his room over the butcher shop, staring out into the bright sunlight as he devoured his noonday meal. He hadn't taken the trouble to wash the blood from his hands, and the bread and cheese tasted of freshly slaughtered lamb.

He felt restless, angry, ready to jump, and the smell of blood and death from the animals below only increased his edginess. He shoved the heel of bread into his mouth and stomped over to the window, glaring into the bright spring day. He would have to buy a newspaper. Usually he didn't bother—he could scarcely read and seldom found it worth the trouble.

When the old women started dying he used to buy the paper, spending painstaking hours deciphering the details just to be certain. When he'd taken up his part he continued to read, curious whether anyone linked him with the deaths.

Of course no one had any idea. And they never would. Gilles knew that the truth defied belief—no one would guess and if they did they would dismiss it as impossible. They were safe, all of them.

No, he didn't need to buy a paper to see if anything new had come from the latest murder. What he needed, quite desperately, was a weather prediction. What he needed, quite desperately, was more rain.

* * *

Claire sat alone in the kitchen of the huge old apartment, delicate hands cradling the mug of coffee. Marc was gone, promising to call every few nights. She hated answering the telephone. Most of the time it was someone babbling at her in French, talking too fast and too loud, never giving her a chance for her halting explanations.

As often as she could she had Nicole answer the phone. But arrangements had been made for Nicole to spend each day with her grandmother, being transported by the old woman's chauffeur. There was no need for Claire to present herself to Harriette Langlois—that much had been made clear. And indeed, Claire had no wish to subject herself to the humiliation of trying to converse with someone Marc stigmatized as an old harridan, with a reluctant Nicole as translator.

No, she was happy to have her days free, and if part of that freedom meant she was lonely, she would learn to deal with it. She would have Nicole write something in French to leave by the phone, something she could read to whomever was trying to communicate without listening.

She shoved the coffee away. The day stretched ahead of her, bright and clear and shining, with no duties, no responsibilities. She could even leave the dishes sitting in the sink without fear of reprisals.

All she had to do was relax and enjoy herself. She had every intention of doing so when the telephone rang, its shrill bell racing across her nerve endings.

She sat at the table letting brief fantasies play across her mind. It was the man from the park—he'd somehow found out who she was. It was Marc—he couldn't bear to be away from her. It was Nicole—no, it was her grandmother, and Nicole was hurt.

She couldn't ignore the telephone. Slowly she rose from the table, crossing the room with dragging feet. Without Marc around she went barefoot, not minding the chill in exchange for the blessed feeling of freedom. The ring was angry, insistent, and Claire held her breath for a long moment before snatching it from its cradle.

Hello was a universal word. The voice on the other end spoke English, and she wished it hadn't.

"Ms. MacIntyre?" The voice had flat American vowels. "This is James Donner at the United States embassy. We'd like you to come in and answer a few questions for us."

And Claire dropped the phone from nerveless fingers, watching it clatter to the floor.

⚜ CHAPTER 6

Paris was blessed with six sunny days in a row, a miraculous phenomenon after the ceaseless rain. Someone, Nicole perhaps, had told Claire that the old women had only been murdered on rainy days. That knowledge, coupled with the relief from various different sources, was enough to send her into a mood of almost lightheaded happiness, one Nicole tolerated with cynical patience.

Claire hadn't asked the man from the embassy a thing when she'd retrieved the telephone from the floor, except, "What time would be convenient for you?" Her voice had been wooden, lifeless, a martyr heading for the stake, but James Donner had noticed nothing.

"At your convenience, Ms. MacIntyre," he'd replied, and Claire had almost laughed into the telephone. There was no convenient time for the conversation she'd been dreading for the last six months, but part of her had been relieved it was over with. They'd send her back to the States, of course. She'd probably be charged as an accessory, or something. She'd have to see Brian again, something she dreaded. But the worst part of all would be to leave Nicole, sullen, prickly Nicole.

And Marc, she amended swiftly. Of course leaving Marc would be the worst. Would he forgive her for not telling him?

Three hours later Claire stepped outside the U.S. embassy, relief, irritation, and confusion all warring for control. It had been nothing, a minor bureaucratic hassle that took only a moment to clear up. She hadn't applied for her residence permit, something all foreigners were required to do after they'd been in Paris for three months. For some reason Marc hadn't mentioned it to her, but the workings of the French government were extremely efficient, tracking her down and ready to extend a sharp reprimand.

James Donner, a Southern aristocrat of indeterminate age and sexual preference, took care of it all with bland charm, dismissing her into the Paris streets and the prospect of another harrowing taxi ride, and Claire, dizzy with relief, couldn't stop herself from asking one question.

"Is there anything else?" Marc had told her the American police were looking for her, that they'd been in touch with the embassy. The police would have no interest in a French residence permit; it had to be something else. Unless Marc lied, and he'd have no reason to do so.

"Nothing for now," Donner had said with practiced political charm. "If we need you we know where to find you."

For a moment the words rang ominously in her head. And then she dismissed them as she headed out into the bright, chilly sunshine. Marc must have misunderstood, though that was unlike him. He was such a perfectionist that he seldom made mistakes, and his command of English was almost that of a native.

It must have been some inept employee of the embassy, getting the messages garbled, and Claire's understandable paranoia had done the rest. She'd suffered three days of panic, all for nothing. Deliberately she shut off the little voice in her head, the one that told her she deserved all the panic and guilt she got. She would celebrate.

During the taxi ride to the embassy she had recognized an area of wonderful shops only a brisk walk northward, shops where obsequious employees spoke a dozen languages, English among them. She would go and buy herself something—perhaps a new silk dress or a clinging nightgown for when Marc returned. Or maybe, just maybe, she'd find a shop specializing in comfortable jeans and running suits and wear only what she wanted until Marc returned. Maybe she'd even find a pair of jeans for Nicole.

The sky was very blue—the brisk winds of Sunday had blown the pollution over to England where the Parisians no doubt felt it belonged. Puffy white clouds were scudding through the heavens, and Claire could smell the wet damp smell of newly awakening earth, even in the midst of the city. For the first time in longer than she could remember, she was happy. Surely nothing terrible could happen in such a beautiful world as this.

Chief Inspector Malgreave sat at his desk, pushing papers around. The weather report called for days of sunshine—no rain in sight. There would be no more murders, for a few days at least, and that would give them time. Time to find where Rocco Guillère was the night Marcelle Boisrond was murdered, time to follow up on other leads. There were too damned many of them. Too many leads, and Malgreave's intellect told him there couldn't be so many murderers.

His instincts told him there could be.

Thirty-nine files spread out over his desk, some fat, some thin. All elderly women who'd been neatly stabbed in the heart and then laid out like medieval corpses. There were photographs in each file, photographs Malgreave knew by heart. They were all starting to blur in his mind, all the old ones, and he was beginning to forget important details. Were the fingerprints found at the nun's body or with the twins in La Défense? Had the Comtesse de Tourney been the one who'd been sexually molested after her death, or was it Marthe Hubert?

He pushed away from the desk, running a weary hand through his thinning hair. Somewhere there was an answer, something he was overlooking. He would start again, read through the reports one by one, stare at the gory photos with a jaundiced eye, memorize each insignificant detail until it all began to coalesce and make sense.

Josef came in several times during the long afternoon,

bothering him with questions, distracting him with his reverent silence. Someone brought in fresh coffee, stale brioches; someone, probably not the disapproving Josef, replaced his empty pack of cigarettes with a fresh box. The dank room was blue with smoke, a layer of oil had formed on Malgreave's half-drunk cup of black coffee, and at six forty-seven he sat back, dropped his half-smoked cigarette into the cold coffee, and sighed.

Josef was still there, sitting patiently by the door. "I called your wife," he said. "I told her you were delayed."

Malgreave reached for another cigarette. "What did she say?"

Josef flushed. Mme. Malgreave had said a great many things, none of them encouraging or even kind. "She said she understood."

Malgreave laughed, a short, cynical bark of a sound. "I imagine she did. What about your wife? Did you call her?"

"Helga knows we can't keep regular hours when something like this is going on." Josef gestured to the littered desk. "Once we catch the murderer I'll make it up to her."

"The difference between your wife and mine," Malgreave sighed. "Your wife has only been neglected for the seven years you've been in the department. Marie has had to suffer for more than twenty."

Josef swallowed. "And Helga is ambitious."

Malgreave grinned suddenly, appreciating Josef's frankness. "True enough. Helga has more ambition for you than Marie ever even dreamed of. Do you mind?"

"Helga's ambition? No. I am not a driven man—I need Helga to give me a push now and then, or I would be content to do nothing."

"And does she ever push too much?" Malgreave inquired, tapping a pencil against his long, thin fingers.

"Not yet."

"Bon," said Malgreave. "And there are four."

"Pardon?"

"You said you'd make it up to Helga once we caught the murderer. There are four of them." He gestured to the piles of manila files littering his desk. "In the left corner I have the files of those I'm sure are the work of Rocco. Next to that pile is a smaller one, with those I only suspect are his. The rest of them fall into three categories, each with its own subtle differences. Then we have the two files where we found a fingerprint, and another couple of folders where I'm not sure where they fit. In other words, Josef, my desk is such a mess that I'm giving up and going home to my wife." He rose, and glared at the littered desk.

"Er . . ." said Josef. "Madame Malgreave said she wouldn't be back until late."

Malgreave had looked tired before; now the last ounce of life drained from him. "In that case," he said, sitting back down again, "there's no need for me to go anywhere." And picking up the top folder, he stared once more at an old lady's corpse.

Yvon Alpert worked late that night. He usually worked late. He was an ambitious man, eager to please his employers, eager to get ahead in the world and make a name for himself. With his wedding coming up he wanted to make all the extra money he could, so that he could treat Jeanne to the kind of honeymoon she deserved.

When the days were bright and sunny, when the nights were calm and clear, he could forget his burden. Forget the past, think only of the bright, wonderful future that lay ahead of him. The orphanage in Marie-le-Croix was a distant memory, something that happened to someone else, and he would always hope that the next time it rained, he wouldn't even notice.

It hadn't worked that way. Each time the rain fell it called to him, louder and louder, called to him so he couldn't ignore it, couldn't escape. But still he hoped.

He headed out of the square, ugly building that held the ministry. Jeanne would be waiting at his apartment, dinner ready, that pouty little look on her piquant face, ready to play the game once more. Tonight he had energy, tonight he would throw himself into the charade, woo and cajole her into bed where she'd turn into a tigress. For a moment he wondered how she'd respond when there was no longer any game to play, when her legal and moral place was in his bed. Would she be complaisant, would she lose interest?

Yvon noticed the evening paper as he headed down the street, the dark headlines a screaming blur. He ignored it, knowing there couldn't have been another murder, not with the sky so clear and calm. There was no need to buy the paper, no need to turn around, fish in his pocket for a few coins, and toss them to the news dealer. It would be a mistake—what he didn't know couldn't possibly hurt him. Still, he couldn't resist.

He stood in the middle of the almost empty sidewalk, staring down at the headlines, and his tense shoulders relaxed. More bombings, he read. More terrorists infiltrating the city. Animals, he thought contemptuously, folding the paper. And then he grew very still, as his reluctant eyes caught the weather forecast up by the masthead. Clear and cold tonight, it read. Chance of rain by Friday.

And once more the darkness closed in.

He liked watching the children. Even more, he liked having them watch him. He'd been doing it more often recently, putting on whiteface and his baggy clothes, leaving the tiny hotel room and showing up in some of the small parks that dotted Paris, the parks where the children played. He liked them much better than the parks where old people congregated. The old ones never paid him proper attention.

The children were different. They would flock around him like pigeons around a bag of peanuts, and he would string them along, play them, tease and entice them. Like the Pied Piper of Hamelin, he could lead them down a narrow path to the sea, and they would go willingly, happily.

But not yet. He had other things to do first, a covenant to keep. Later he would turn to the children.

Claire wasn't sure why she'd come back to the old people's park. She'd picked a lousy day for it—after six days of sunshine the sky was dark and overcast, threatening rain. She should have come back several days ago, after she'd gone to the U.S. embassy. But then, several days ago she hadn't been so lonely, she'd been riding a high of complete relief. Several days ago she hadn't had such a frustrating, confusing conversation with Marc on the telephone with the best long-distance connection she'd heard since she moved to France.

She almost wished there'd been more static on the line. He'd been brief, almost monosyllabic, and for the first time she realized how little he usually spoke. He communicated more with his mobile face and expressive body than with words, and over the telephone it left something to be desired. His long silences left Claire feeling uneasy, oddly guilty, and inane attempts to fill that silence with breathless chatter only increased her disquiet.

He'd had nothing to say about the current tour, ignoring her when she'd asked where he was. He had no desire to speak with Nicole, who clearly had no desire to speak to him, and he had nothing to say to her. It was an odd, meaningless conversation, made even worse by his final words.

"Don't worry, darling," he murmured with some of his usual sweetness. "When you least expect it I'll be back."

She'd had nightmares that night, with Marc looming over her, a dark, silent shadow, tracking her every movement, never saying a word. Nicole was there, equally silent, making no noise but to scream whenever Marc grew too close. They were running, running through a dark forest, with fire all around them, and the fire turned into a score of funeral pyres, and at the center of each conflagration was an old woman, her mouth open in a silent scream.

Someone was standing at the edge of the forest. As Claire ran she dragged Nicole behind her, all the time knowing that Marc's shadow was following her, looming over her like a bird of prey. The man ahead of her was Marc, the other Marc, gentle, loving, protecting her from the hideous mistakes of her past. She reached him, and it was the American she'd met in the park, smiling at her, a coffee ice cream cone in one hand. In the other, he held a gleaming knife to plunge into her heart, and once more he was Marc, and he was going to kill her.

Claire sat bolt upright in bed. The room was dark, the curtained windows letting in only a sliver of moonlight. Her body was covered with sweat, her hands were trembling, and panic still beat against her eyelids. She reached for the phone, then drew her hand back. Whom could she call?

It had been almost dawn before she slept again, and when she finally awakened, Nicole was dressed and gone. Another layer of guilt, Claire thought as she made herself a pot of coffee. Nine years old was too young to arrange your own life. She'd make it up to her. She'd go to the confectioner's shop and buy some of the apricot creams Nicole loved so much, even if she had to use sign language to get her meaning across.

She pulled on blue jeans and a heavy cotton sweater and slipped her narrow feet into the pair of Reeboks she'd found in a little store on the Champs Élysée, of all places.

She'd done better than expected. There was a new girl working at the confectioner's shop, one who spoke English, and Claire was able to get Nicole everything from a packet of Gummi Bears to a chocolate Easter bunny. Trying to buy the love of a sour, unloving child, she chided herself. There was no better bet than chocolates for someone of Nicole's insatiable sweet tooth. She'd tucked the package in her purse and headed on, feeling absurdly confident and optimistic.

The park benches were nearly empty when Claire reached the entrance. White posters were affixed to several trees, and she remembered Marc had told her they were going to post warnings. It certainly had an insalubrious effect on the elderly inhabitants of the park. Even on a warm, slightly overcast day the park was sparsely inhabited. The ice cream vendor stood by his cart, staring disconsolately at the pigeons.

Claire's happy mood began to flag, and it took all her

determination to pull it back. She was going to get herself an ice cream cone and enjoy the day, she told herself, come hell or high water.

Maybe the ice cream vendor would respond to charades, Claire thought, walking down the winding pathway, her sneakered feet crunching agreeably on the gravel. He'd been friendly enough to the American—maybe he'd be patient enough with her, too. She'd been good at games as a child. Maybe, when Marc returned, she could have him teach her how to be a mime. She could go around Paris in whiteface and no one would ever know she couldn't speak or understand a word of French.

She laughed aloud at the absurd idea. There was someone sitting on the park bench, engrossed in a newspaper, but the sound of her voice must have startled him, for he dropped the paper and looked up, directly into her eyes.

And then Claire knew why she'd walked blocks out of her way to get to a park that held no interest for her. She looked down into Thomas Jefferson Parkhurt's eyes, smiling in pleasure and relief. "I've been looking for you," she said, suddenly knowing it was true.

A range of emotions crossed his face. For a moment Claire thought she saw anger, disappointment, and regret. And then he grinned back, and the skin around his blue eyes crinkled, and he got to his feet, all shambling grace. "And I've been waiting for you," he said, his voice that slow, pleasant drawl that she found so attractive. "For a while there I wasn't sure if you were ever coming back."

She shrugged. "I'm here," she said simply.

"I know why, too."

Claire ignored the shaft of guilt that spiked through her. "Why?"

"Coffee ice cream."

She felt her shoulders relax. "There's that," she agreed.

"I'll do the honors," Tom said. "And then we can sit down over there on that bench and you can tell me what you've been doing since Sunday."

She eyed him warily. "All right. Anything for coffee ice cream."

"And you can tell me who that man was. Your husband?" Beneath the banter there was a thread of emotion, and Claire knew she hadn't imagined the anger.

"Not my husband," she said. "And if you want the story of my life you'll have to get me two scoops."

He looked down at her for a long, silent moment. He was very tall, Claire thought. She wasn't usually attracted to tall men. No, cancel that thought, she ordered herself on a note of panic. She wasn't attracted to Tom, either. He was just a compatriot, a stranger she could talk to, nothing more. She had no room for anyone but Marc. Marc made sure of that.

"Two scoops," he agreed, and she knew suddenly that he wanted to kiss her. She should run. He didn't want to offer her friendship. He wanted to give her something more, something she couldn't accept. She watched him go, watched his broad shoulders, long back, the way his scruffy brown hair brushed the collar of his rough fisherman's sweater. With a sigh she moved over to the park bench, sat down, and waited.

At four o'clock Yvon Alpert looked out the sixth-floor window of the ministry. The sky was a roiling, blackish gray, the sun had disappeared entirely, and wind was whipping through the bare trees. He looked down at his hands, square, strong hands that were now curved into fists.

Looking up again, he saw that the first fat drops had splattered against the windows, and the black hole in his heart expanded and grew until it devoured everything inside him.

He reached forward and picked up the phone, dialing from memory. "Jeanne," he said, his voice uncharacteristically husky. "I have to cancel tonight. Something's come up." He listened mindlessly to her whining chatter for a moment. "No, it's something I have to do," he said. "I have to go see my grandmother." He replaced the receiver very quietly, pushed back from his desk, and headed for the door.

No one said a word, no one tried to stop him. Yvon Alpert had worked there for seven years; he was a good, conscientious, unimaginative man. The perfect bureaucrat. If he was walking out of the office in the middle of the day he must certainly have the best of all reasons.

Jeanne stared at the phone for a long, uneasy moment. Yvon hadn't sounded like himself. He'd had moments like this recently, moments that unnerved her and made her wonder if she was right to plan a life with a man who'd seemed so dependable but was now becoming prey to moods. There was something wrong. He'd sounded different, as if he were lying to her, and Yvon never lied.

Then she realized what was wrong. Yvon had no grandmother. He'd grown up in an orphanage, and then with foster parents who'd been more businesslike than affectionate. His mother's mother had died not long after placing Yvon in the Marie-le-Croix orphanage.

She called him back immediately, but Yvon had already left, though no one knew where he'd gone or how long he'd be away. Slamming down the phone, she did her best to squash down the sense of foreboding that washed over her. Jeanne's grandmother had been a Gypsy, and she had the sight, or so she told people. And all her senses were warning her of very grave trouble.

She too walked out of her office without excuses. She reached the street and ran through the heavy rain to her car, holding her breath as her heart hammered inside her. She would drive straight to Yvon's apartment and wait for him. Sooner or later he'd come back and explain to her what was going on.

But she knew, deep in her heart of hearts, that it was going to be later. Too late. Driving through the rain, she thought of the little house in the suburbs, the wedding dress her mother was making for her. She knew she would never wear it, that no one would ever wear it. It would turn yellow in a trunk in her mother's attic, and when Jeanne did marry she'd wear a white suit, ignoring the existence of the lace-trimmed dress. And as she drove through the downpour, she cried.

❧ CHAPTER 7

It was getting darker. Claire scarcely noticed the deepening shadows as she sat with Tom on the narrow park bench. The ice cream vendor had packed up and left long ago; the few old people who had lingered despite the warnings had long since disappeared. They were alone in a cozy little world, the two of them caught up in discoveries and shared memories of separate lives, only dimly aware of the growing storm. Claire looked up, suddenly uneasy. The cloudy sky had darkened to an ominous black, the bare tree limbs trembled and shook like angry spiders' legs, and last winter's dead leaves scuttled up the pebbled pathways. A first, fat drop of rain splatted down on Claire's upturned face, and she shivered.

Tom shifted, his long legs stretched out in front of him. "Just my luck," he muttered gloomily. "You finally show up and it starts to rain. We've had almost six days of perfect weather and I've spent those six days on a park bench hoping you'd show up. Now when you do, it rains."

"You've been here every day?" Claire didn't know whether to be flattered or worried.

Tom shrugged, smiling ruefully. "What can I say? It's Paris in the spring, and I'm an incurable romantic."

"And I'm engaged." The rain was coming down in

earnest now. Claire pulled her sweater up around her ears and stood up. "I should be getting back."

He rose, towering over her, and his large hand caught her arm. "Don't go yet. Let me buy you a cup of coffee, a glass of wine, anything. Take pity on a poor lonely fellow American."

She looked up at him. She knew she shouldn't. If she wanted to keep safe in her own little cocoon, shut away from pain and hurting, she would turn right around and head back to the apartment, shut and lock the doors, and count the days until Marc returned.

Even two days ago she would have done exactly that. But the sun had been out too long, Marc had been gone too long, and Claire was finally sick of cowering. "Okay," she said softly, inevitably. And putting her chilled hand in his large, capable one, she raced through the steady downpour, out of the small, sad park.

His hands were sweating. His palms were damp, and as he tried to dry them on his trousers they left wet streaks. It didn't matter, though—he was already soaked with rain. The marks of nervous sweat would scarcely be noticeable.

Yvon wondered what time it was. He didn't bother to check the elegant gold watch Jeanne had given him, even though its presence on his wrist was like a second skin. He stood there in the doorway, huddled out of the rain, waiting.

He'd known exactly where he was going when he'd left work. As the rain started to fall a compulsion had come over him, a blind, mindless need that had sent him out into the rain-drenched streets, walking aimlessly until he'd ended up in this small, residential neighborhood in Beaubourg, not far from the Pompidou Centre.

On good days he would walk to work, and his path would take him by this old town house. He'd seen the woman before, watched her slow, stately grace as she walked her tiny little dog around the corner. On the sunny days it would amuse him to watch her patrician calm as she monitored her dog's basic biological functions.

But now it was raining, night was falling, and there was

no amusement in Yvon Alpert's wintry heart. He stood in the rain outside the old lady's home, hidden in the doorway, and wondered whether she'd fight him, whether she'd scream and struggle. And he wondered if the black hole in his heart would take over and consume him, or if his damp hands would continue to shake.

"Where were you today?" Nicole's sallow face was accusing as she sat at one end of the formal table, buttering an overlarge piece of bread. When Marc had left, Claire had suggested she move closer, to the seat beside her, but Nicole had declined with unconcealed contempt, and they'd continued their stilted dinners from across a wide expanse of polished walnut.

Claire dropped her fork with a clatter, then looked anxiously at the dinner plate, terrified that she might have chipped the scalloped gold edge of the Limoges. It was still intact, and she breathed a sigh of relief, followed by a wave of anger as intense as it was unexpected. She was damned if she was going to live in fear of Marc and his possessions. Tomorrow she would go out and find a store that had cheap dishes. Failing that, she'd buy paper plates and plop them down on Marc's priceless walnut table, and to hell with everyone.

"I asked you where you went today," Nicole repeated with the faint sense of hauteur that sat so well on her nine-year-old shoulders. "You weren't here when the taxi brought me home. We had to drive around the block for hours and hours, waiting for you."

Claire stifled the guilt that had been plaguing her. "Nicole, I got back here at five-thirty. You leave Madame Langlois's apartment at five every day. You couldn't have been waiting for more than fifteen minutes."

"What if I told you *Grand-mère* was ill today? That she sent me home early?"

More guilt, Claire thought wearily, squashing it down. Nicole wore the expression she'd long ago perfected, the testing, manipulative smirk that lingered in the back of her flat brown eyes, and for not the first time Claire wondered why she cared. Why such a prickly, unlovable child mattered to her. She wasn't simply a surrogate for another nine-year-old still recovering from a hit-and-run accident—Nicole was too strong a personality for that.

"Did she send you home early?" Claire asked calmly enough.

Nicole shook her head. "No. We waited only five minutes," she admitted, a rare, mischievous grin lighting her dark face.

Claire smiled back. "You're a beast, Nicole."

"I know," the child said calmly, stuffing another piece of bread into her small mouth. "Did you know, Claire," she continued, mumbling through the food, "that you're a lot happier when Marc isn't around?"

Claire dropped her fork again, her smile vanishing. Damn the child. "Don't be absurd," she snapped. "I miss him terribly."

"Oh, I imagine you do. Marc is very good in bed. All his women say so."

"Nicole!"

"But he's not very comfortable to be around," Nicole continued, unfazed, her precocious, old-woman's face serene. "Don't you find that you like it better when he's not creeping around, watching you?"

"Don't be disrespectful," she murmured, echoing Marc's words absently. She could think of a great many things more important to Nicole's well-being than proper filial respect, but she owed it to Marc to make an effort.

As usual, Claire's reprimand didn't faze Nicole. "But it's true," she insisted calmly. "He does lurk around, watching one. He says it's for research, but I know better. *Grand-mère* says he gives her . . ." For a moment the child looked blank, struggling for the right word, then triumphant as she found it. "He gives her the creeps. Isn't that how you say it?"

"That is not how I say it." Claire hated the prim, repressive sound of her own voice, but she couldn't let Nicole sit there and tear her father apart. It would break Marc's heart if he knew. Wouldn't it? Or did he already know—had his own coldness and distance been part of the cause? "Your father loves you, Nicole. He's just not a demonstrative man."

"What is 'demonstrative'?"

Claire pushed her plate away, no longer hungry. Nicole was so absurdly precocious she'd forgotten that she was talking to a nine-year-old. One with an amazing command of English, but even most American nine-year-olds wouldn't know what *demonstrative* meant.

"When someone is demonstrative they show, they express their emotions and thoughts, rather than talk about them." She was sounding like a schoolteacher again, and Claire felt a sudden, searing loss. She missed it, the work, the children, the sense of being needed, making a difference.

"Then don't you think it strange," Nicole said quietly, "that a mime, someone who never uses words, is not . . . demonstrative at home?"

Claire had no answer, but then, Nicole wasn't expecting one. They finished their meal in strained silence, listening to the steady beat of the rain outside their windows.

Yvon looked down at his hands. They'd clenched into fists, and it took all his strength to open them, flex them. The fingers were cramped, useless, and he held them out into the pouring rain, watching as the water splatted against them. They were still shaking.

It was after eleven. Lights were blazing in the old woman's apartment, but he'd seen no shadows against the heavy curtains for a long time. The old bitch was probably too rich to worry about electricity bills. She probably left all her lights on, afraid of the dark. Tonight, he told himself, it would be a waste of time. The lights wouldn't keep her destiny at bay.

He started to move, out into the heavy rain, oblivious to the passersby, the cars sluicing through the deep puddles, oblivious to everything as he crossed the street. He had no plan, no thought at all beyond the certainty of what he must do. The black hole in his heart grew larger, devouring him as he stood in front of the heavy wooden door that fronted the residential side street. When he reached out to press the bell, his hand no longer shook.

Thomas Jefferson Parkhurst was whistling as he raced up the endless flights of stairs to his artist's garret. Even the final flight failed to wind him, though the whistle became more strained. Nothing could quench his buoyant spirit, not flights of stairs, not the empty apartment, not even the memory of Claire's eyes when he'd asked her about the man.

Because the rest of the time Claire's eyes had been on him, and they'd been warm, happy, and full of promise.

It was after eleven when he got home. Claire had left him at five, but he'd been too restless to go home and work when he knew damned well he ought to. He'd gone out to see friends, spent the entire evening talking about Claire, and then finally ended up back at the apartment, still too dreamy and lightheaded to tackle the novel.

Claire was part of the problem. She'd made her appearance in chapter seven as Elizabeth, the madonna. Then he'd revised her into Violette, the whore. But now he knew her too well, he couldn't turn her into a stereotype and make her do what he wanted.

Ignoring the typewriter, he flopped down on the bed, letting his big body absorb the vibrations from the ancient springs. Who the hell was he fooling? He wasn't a novelist. He wasn't a dancer, a clarinetist, a playwright, or a painter. He couldn't even run a vineyard. He had seven more weeks left, but he already suspected he knew the answer to his quest. He was a damned, dull, boring stockbroker. His creative gifts lay in making money, whether he liked it or not.

He knew something else, too. Irrational, unbelievable as it was, at the age of thirty-two, with a decent amount of experience behind him, he'd fallen hopelessly in love with a stranger. And while common sense told him it was absurd, common sense didn't make a dent in his conviction. For almost two years he'd been convinced he'd come to Paris to find himself. Right now he wasn't so sure. He might very well have come to Paris to find Claire.

The old lady had opened the door, and Yvon knew why. Even soaking wet he looked the model of a French bureaucrat, sane, unimaginative, unthreatening. France had more people in civil service than the rest of Europe combined, and the French were used to interference in their lives.

The old lady was already dressed for bed. Her soft wool bathrobe would have cost him a week's salary, and her faded blue eyes were chilly with hauteur. She believed him when he said they were checking gas meters, though her snobbery and impatience were clear. She didn't look like *Grand-mère* Estelle, but the cool contempt in her eyes brought back his childhood with dizzying force. That, and the smell of her apartment, of papery old skin, of wool and cough drops and strong tea. Of sweet pink roses.

She let him go into the kitchen alone. It didn't take him long to find the knives, and his conviction strengthened. It was right, it was his destiny. Everything was falling into place so easily. The old woman had let him in, the knives were at hand, the rain was falling, beating against the old house.

His hand was still damp with rain, with sweat, as he clutched the knife. He'd chosen a sharp one, not too big, not too small. He would take it with him when he finished, and at last he would be free.

She was just replacing the telephone in its cradle when he walked back into the coolly elegant living room.

"Your meter is in order," he said. "Who were you calling?"

She couldn't see the knife. He'd done nothing to alarm her, he knew that. So why was she backing toward the door? There was no fear in her disdainful old face, only contempt, and he felt the black hole in his heart reach out to engulf him.

"The police," she said in her cool, upper-class voice. "I

75

was very stupid to let you in without proper identification, particularly at this hour. They will be here in less than five minutes. I would suggest you leave."

"Five minutes," said Yvon. He smiled, and he could feel the grin devour his face. "That should be time enough." He started toward her, the knife no longer hidden.

The police car raced through the wet streets, klaxon blaring to warn away the nonexistent traffic. They'd come to fetch Malgreave, Josef and his nemesis, Vidal, driving. Malgreave barely had time to give his excuses to Marie.

Not that excuses would do any good anymore, he thought. It was a lucky thing he hadn't yet gone to bed. He'd pulled on his heavy raincoat and battered old hat and followed his assistants out into the rain. He'd known all along something would happen that night. His instincts were well honed after all his years on the force, and he knew the killer, the killers, would be half mad with bloodlust after their forced inactivity during the last sunny spell. He'd even considered staying late, staying all night if he had to, waiting for the call to come in, but then had decided against it. If he'd been waiting, the call would never come. And he knew, ghoulish as it was, he would have been disappointed.

"This may be a wild-goose chase," Josef said as they careened around a corner. "The call came in and they passed the message on to me while they sent someone to investigate it. Just an old woman near the Pompidou Centre with a late-night intruder. Probably harmless—the man said he was with the Department of Public Works and she said he looked respectable."

"Then why did she call? Why the hell did she let him in in the first place?" Malgreave fumed. "Doesn't she read the papers, doesn't she know old women are being murdered? Why the hell can't these people show some sense?"

"They're probably all senile," Vidal offered from the driver's seat. He was younger than Josef, not nearly as thorough, but he made up for his lack of attention to detail with flashes of intuitive brilliance that couldn't be learned.

Malgreave shook his head. "I wish it were that easy. You heard the report, Josef. Was this woman confused, disturbed?"

"Madame Bonheur? Not according to the dispatcher. She sounded very sensible." Josef glared at his subordinate. There was no love lost between the two men. Josef disapproved of Vidal's cowboy ways and brightly colored jeans. Vidal couldn't be bothered to disapprove of Josef's stodginess in return, a fact which made Josef even more hostile. In easier times Malgreave used to enjoy setting them against each other. He learned a great deal about both of them when they were quarreling.

There was no time for that now. "Not sensible enough to keep strange men out of her apartment on rainy nights." Malgreave leaned forward and tapped Vidal on the shoulder. "Drive fast, Vidal. She'll be chopped into little pieces at the rate you're going."

Vidal nodded, grinning, and the car skidded around a corner. Malgreave leaned back with a sigh. "We'll be too late, I know it."

"The police station was only three blocks away," Josef soothed him. "They should have made it in time."

Malgreave shook his head. "We'll be too late." And leaning back against the uncomfortable seat, he shut his eyes wearily, preparing himself for blood and death.

It shouldn't have been like that, Yvon thought as he stumbled through the back alley. There shouldn't have been so much blood. He was covered with it, swimming in it, and still the old lady had fought. He was so much younger, so much stronger, and yet the frail, aristocratic old woman had had the strength of tigers.

And then there was the dog. The damned stupid yapping dog, attacking his ankles, barking and yelping and raging at him. No sooner had he finally finished with the old lady than he'd had to contend with the furious assault of the tiny poodle.

He chased him all over the apartment, trailing bloody

77

footprints. He'd caught the wretched brute by the back door, finished with him, and flung the little carcass across the room. And then he'd heard them, pounding at the front entrance, and he knew he'd taken too long.

He didn't dare go back to the living room. He'd left the old lady where she'd fallen; he hadn't been able to arrange her properly, to do all the small, ritual things he'd promised he would do. This wouldn't count, he'd bungled it, he'd have to do it again, properly next time, or he wouldn't be free.

He was sobbing as he fumbled with the back door, muttering over and over to himself as he staggered out into the rain. The back alley was dark, deserted, only the rank smell of garbage mixing with the heavy, metallic odor of blood and sour sweat. He slammed the door behind him, seeing his bloody fingerprints with blind eyes, and stumbled into the darkness.

There was no escape. There were dark figures at the end of the alley, milling around. He would have to hide, back among the garbage, and wait for daylight. Wait for them to give up, to go back to their cars and their police station and realize it was hopeless. They were too clever for the police; even hopeless, bumbling Yvon was too clever for them.

He tucked himself back among the battered garbage cans, ducking his head beneath the heavy onslaught of rain. He should have realized, should have planned it better. When they were young he had always screwed things up. The others had teased him unmercifully. Gilles had hit him, hurt him, his brutish bullying somehow less devastating than the quiet contempt of his idol. From him he had suffered pinches, slaps, and soft, jeering laughter.

He would laugh again, if he wasn't too angry. He would read in the paper how Yvon had once more screwed up, and unless it endangered him he would simply shake his beautiful head, sigh, and say, "Poor Yvon. He never could do anything right."

Gilles was another matter. If he made it past the police, made it home safely to his apartment just three blocks over,

Gilles would find him. Gilles wouldn't be able to tell what endangered him and what didn't, and he'd always hated Yvon. No, when it came right down to it he was in as much danger from Gilles as he was from the police milling around.

He must have dozed off. The rain had lessened somewhat, the sky was growing lighter. It must be near dawn. Yvon stirred his cramped muscles, peering out into the darkened alleyway. The police were gone. Standing alone, silhouetted against the street light, was a figure, a man.

It was him. His idol, his hero, the god of his childhood, the one he'd worshiped with blind obedience. He was standing there, waiting, and Yvon could see the gun in his hand. He was there to punish him, punish him for failing in their pact. Yvon hung his head, and the rain sluiced down around his face. His hands were clean of blood now—the steady downpour had washed it away, but his clothes were black with it. He would show him, he would throw himself on his mercy.

But his idol had no mercy. He was waiting there for him, waiting, and Yvon knew he could be a coward no longer. Slowly he rose, knocking over the piled garbage, and stepped into the alley.

Suddenly the place was flooded with light, blinding him. Someone was shouting at him, but he couldn't hear the words. He lifted his arms, and his hand still clutched the knife. And then there was a rushing, roaring sound, a thousand fists struck his chest, and he was hurled backward by an invisible force, thrown against the building. He looked down at his body, and there was still blood everywhere. He would have thought the old lady would have stopped bleeding by now, but there was fresh blood pouring all over his body. He watched with dazed surprise, tumbling forward onto the puddled streets. And before he died he said one word. "Marc."

"Stupid, stupid, stupid!" Malgreave fumed, watching as they carried the corpse away. The black plastic body bag

79

wrapped up the bullet-riddled remains of a minor bureau-crat named Yvon Alpert. It wrapped up Malgreave's only chance at finally getting a few answers.

"I'm sorry, sir," Josef murmured miserably.

"What did the men think? He had a knife, a small knife. He couldn't have thrown it far enough to hit anyone, even if he'd been a circus performer and not a pencil pusher. Damn their trigger-happy stupidity!"

"They saw what was left of the old lady," Vidal offered. "Most of them have grandmothers. This has spooked them all."

"I suppose they think they've solved the problem." Malgreave's voice was bitter. "That they've killed the murderer, that justice is served."

"Yes, sir."

"Well, it isn't. They haven't. Alpert didn't kill the nun in La Défense, or the twins, or the old lady last week. Unless I'm mistaken, Alpert never killed anyone before."

"He won't kill anyone again," Josef offered.

"No, there's that. But he won't help us find the others."

"Are you so sure there are others? Perhaps just Guillère . . . ?"

"More than that, Josef," Malgreave said wearily. "More than that." He looked around at the barely discernible dawn. The rain was continuing in a steady downpour, and he felt as old as the women who were being murdered. "I need some coffee," he said finally, hunching his shoulders and heading back toward the car.

"Is there anything I can do, sir?" Josef scampered after him, miserable and guilt-ridden, and Vidal was already in the driver's seat. They all knew Josef could have kept a tighter rein on the men who'd surrounded the alleyway. They all knew Josef could have stopped it.

Malgreave paused by the door of the car, the rain sliding off the battered brim of his hat. "Pray for sunshine, Josef. Pray for time."

* * *

He backed away, into the fast-disappearing shadows of the night, away from the milling police, the curious early risers. His feet were noiseless in the soft-soled slippers, his face under the slouched hat was unnaturally pale, a pure, unearthly white. He faded into the dawn as silently as a wisp of fog, unseen, unheard. Gone.

❧ CHAPTER 8

The day dawned cloudy and overcast, but at least it wasn't raining. Claire lay motionless in the too-soft bed she'd shared with Marc, thinking of the old ladies who died in the rain. Never again would she enjoy the cozy sound of rain beating against the windows while she sat curled up in front of a warm fire.

Anyway, fires didn't do much to warm this old barn of an apartment. While no one could deny its ancient elegance, *cozy it ain't,* she thought, shifting around in the crumpled sheets. And today wouldn't help matters. She could see the bare branches whipping about outside the multipaned windows. When the wind blew, there was no way they could warm the old place—they'd have to wear heavy wool socks and layers upon layers of sweaters. She could only hope Nicole's grandmother lived in warmer lodgings.

Marc had been gone for almost two weeks. For two weeks she'd slept alone in this bed, left her clothes lying on the now-dusty parquet floor, left the dishes sitting in the sink, eaten junk food and starches and dressed in jeans. Each small act of defiance had given her pleasure, a childish, stupid sort of pleasure, she realized now. Marc had been gone two weeks, and instead of missing him, she was dreading his return.

Rolling over, she buried her face in the goose-down

pillow. The soft percale smothered her, as Marc smothered her. She flipped back, staring at the ceiling. There were cobwebs lurking there, new cobwebs. God knows, she'd spent more than enough of her time lying on her back to have memorized the ceiling. If Marc saw those cobwebs he'd have a fit.

And there was no if about it. If she hadn't gotten rid of them by the time he returned he would walk into the room and his dark eyes would immediately go to whatever imperfection marred the bedroom. She could always distract him, leave her clothes lying on the Aubusson carpet, but the very thought turned her slightly ill with apprehension.

She scooted up in bed, pushing the pillows behind her and staring at the dawn-lit room in dismay. The longer Marc was gone the worse it was getting. Not the missing him. Just the opposite.

She pulled her knees up and wrapped her arms around them. Without his commanding presence, without his formidable sexual technique, she was suddenly beginning to think for herself once more. For six months she'd been in shock, content to follow where Marc led her, content to live an almost cloistered existence, doing penance for Brian's crime and her complicity.

But with no one to tell her what to do, with Nicole depending on her, she'd begun to face life once more. And as the days passed she was coming to the unsettling conclusion that she didn't want to face life with Marc Bonnard.

She was a slob, he demanded compulsive neatness. She was casual, he was formal. She liked to laugh and cry, he disdained emotions. She liked to lie in bed and read and eat chocolate and croissants and dribble crumbs all over the place; for Marc the bed was for sex and for sleep.

He wanted her passive, and for far too long that was exactly what she had been. Suddenly, without Marc around to keep her subdued, she was waking up. And she didn't like what she saw.

The frightening thing, she realized as she leaned forward and stared out into the streets of Paris, is that the alternatives were so unpromising. If she left Marc, where would she go? She couldn't go back to the U.S. and pretend nothing had ever happened. If she went back she would have to go to the authorities and tell them about that night six months ago. She'd have to implicate Brian, implicate herself. She'd probably face criminal charges. Even if she didn't, the publicity would be ghastly, and there'd be no way she'd be able to find work with that kind of past haunting her. She'd be friendless, jobless.

She could always go down to Florida to stay with her mother. But her mother's retirement life of bridge and gossip and cocktail parties drove her crazy—even Marc was preferable to that.

Claire shivered in the drafty old apartment. Even Marc, she echoed, dismayed. When had it turned from passion to repression, when had it turned from idyllic love to resentment and the desperate need to escape? Even prison, an honest, American prison, would be preferable to the straightjacket kind of life Marc had forced on her.

But what about Nicole? Nicole, with no one to love her but her grandmother, a grandmother who was gone far too much of the time. In the early-morning light Claire could no longer come up with excuses for Marc. If he loved his daughter it was a useless kind of love. His behavior toward Nicole was as controlling and repressive as it was toward Claire. Never had she seen him kiss the child, cuddle her, praise her, even greet her warmly. And while Nicole still didn't trust Claire, didn't accept her, at least Claire was able to distract Marc when he grew terrifying.

No, she couldn't leave Nicole. Not unless she made some arrangement with Madame Langlois, made certain the old woman wouldn't desert her again. And in order to do that, she'd have to go see the old lady.

Claire shoved the covers back and climbed out of bed, padding across the floor in the oversized T-shirt that Marc would have disdained. He preferred her in ruffly silk and laces, like a Victorian whore, Claire thought bitterly, yanking the shirt over her head and dropping it on the floor. She picked up the jeans from the Louis XIV slipper chair and headed for the bathroom. The more she thought about it, the more determined she grew. She'd see Madame Langlois, assure herself that Nicole was in good hands, and then she'd make her plans to leave.

Rocco heard the pounding at the door. He'd been in bed less than an hour and he was in no mood for visitors. Giselle was still out, which was fine with him, and normally he wouldn't get out of bed until late afternoon.

The pounding continued, and Rocco squinted at the thin gold watch he'd taken off the Spaniard. Seven-fifteen. Any man who woke another up at seven-fifteen deserved to die. Rocco pulled the huge Magnum from under the grimy pillow, aimed it at the door, and fired twice.

"God damn it!" A furious voice came through the holes in the flimsy pine door. "What the hell do you think you're doing, Guillère?" The door slammed open, bouncing against the peeling wall, revealing a tiny figure vibrating with rage.

"Hubert," Rocco acknowledged, sitting up and pulling his boots on. The man in his doorway was no more than five feet tall, almost as round, and dressed quite nattily in a gray linen suit that emphasized his bulk. His egg-shaped head was completely bald, and there was a long scratch on top of that shiny pate, oozing blood.

Hubert was dabbing at it gingerly with a white handkerchief. "Damn your eyes, Rocco," he said with his unmistakable voice. Upper-class Parisian combined with a lisp, Hubert's voice was his trademark. "You could have killed me."

If anyone could have chastened Rocco, Hubert was the one. No one could. "It's lucky you're so short, Hubert," he said lazily. "Anybody else would have gotten it in the throat."

"Is that what you were hoping?"

"It's effective. That way they die quickly and they can't scream."

"It makes a hell of a mess." Hubert peered at his bloody handkerchief in disgust, then tucked it away in his vest pocket.

"I'm not fastidious."

Hubert wrinkled his nose. "In our long association I have discovered that about you. I have a job, my friend."

"A job that brings you here in the middle of the night?"

"You'd prefer the middle of the night. I don't sleep more than an hour at a time, Rocco. If you wish to work for me you'll have to accommodate yourself to my schedule."

Rocco stared at him stonily, the warm gun clasped loosely in his hand. For a moment he considered shooting one more time. He didn't like to take orders from anyone, even someone as deceptively impressive as Hubert. But the old man was legendary, with connections that reached all the way to the top of the government, and those kinds of connections couldn't be thrown away in a fit of pique. Besides, Hubert's jobs were never boring.

"I wish to work for you." Rocco kept his voice lazy, insolent. "What is it this time?"

Hubert seated himself gingerly on the green plastic American recliner that was Rocco's pride and joy. "It's a tricky one, my boy, but well suited for your talents and reputation." He sighed, dabbing at his eyes with the bloody handkerchief and then grimacing. "It's a favor for an old, dear friend."

"I didn't know you had any."

"Don't be absurd, my boy. It's my friends that serve us so well, that have saved your butt time after time. Though this is somewhat different, and I'm counting on your delicacy to handle it properly."

Rocco looked down at his black-rimmed fingernails and smirked. "Who do you want me to kill?"

"So blunt, my boy." Hubert sighed. "This is not just any friend. This is the woman I almost married. I would do anything for her, no matter how distasteful. For her sake I come to you."

"She has a husband? Is that what you want?"

"She's a widow."

"It's too early for guessing games, Hubert," Rocco snapped. "What is it you want from me?"

"I want you to assist my friend in her plan. I do not know the particulars, nor do I care to. I leave it up to you."

"Who's your friend, Hubert? What does she want from me?"

Hubert sighed again. "Her name is Madame Harriette Langlois. I'll give you her address. You are to go to her apartment this afternoon at five-thirty and there she will tell you what she requires of you."

"And you have no idea what that is?" Rocco persisted.

Hubert's eyes were very small, very flat, very black. "She wishes you to kill her. You should be able to do that, shouldn't you, Rocco? Kill an old lady?"

He knows, Rocco thought. Why should he be surprised? There was very little that Hubert didn't know. But that changed matters. When he took care of Madame Harriette Langlois he would have to take care of Hubert. The old man might know, but he didn't understand. No one could know, and live. It was part of their pact, and Rocco's honor, nonexistent in every other matter, was ironclad in this one.

"I should be able to manage, Hubert," Rocco said gently. And he watched Hubert shiver in the overwarm apartment.

The day was cool and overcast as Claire moved down the sidewalk. She had to force herself to move at a leisurely pace, when all her instincts told her to hurry, hurry. Nerves, she told herself. She still couldn't rid herself of the feeling of being watched. It was bad enough in the apartment—she constantly found herself looking over her shoulder, peering into the dimly lit corners of the rambling old place.

But outside it was even worse. She couldn't walk down a street, go to the market, even buy a newspaper without having the awful sense of being spied upon.

It was all in her imagination, it had to be. No one would care what an American expatriate was doing wandering the streets of Paris. She wasn't pretty enough to attract the attention of the roaming males, she wasn't being furtive enough to interest the police. No, it had to be her paranoia, coupled with a guilty conscience.

Guilt was becoming second nature to her. Guilt over Brian, guilt at the thought of abandoning Nicole, guilt over leaving Marc without a word.

That was exactly what she intended. While she could summon up enough courage to leave, that bravery vanished when she contemplated a confrontation with Marc. Not that she expected unpleasantness. He wouldn't try to force her, he wouldn't beg or plead.

No, he would do far worse. He would mesmerize her, as he always had, he would put his hands on her and swiftly, efficiently drive all rational thought out of her brain. She'd always hated it when she'd read that in books—where normally intelligent women turned into mindless idiots when the swaggering heroes took them to bed. Now she knew it could happen. She just couldn't rid herself of the suspicion that in this case Marc wasn't the hero.

Claire wasn't quite sure where she was, but it didn't matter. All she wanted was some fresh air, some way to pass the time until she confronted Harriette Langlois in her den. She had a little-used French phrasebook in her back pocket. It had never done much good before, it would probably be useless today, but she had to use every weapon available to her. If she had to she could have Nicole translate for her, but that might get a little touchy. It would be better if Nicole didn't know she was leaving until the last possible moment.

She bought a newspaper and a cup of coffee at a sidewalk café, then wished she hadn't. The chair was too hard, the day too cool to sit outside, the waiter too inclined to hover. And the newspaper was too horrific.

She should have known better than to have bought it. She favored one of the splashier rags, one with screaming headlines and lots of pictures. Their choice had been particularly gory, but for once Claire had no difficulty deciphering the lead story. There was a nasty photograph of an old lady, butchered in her apartment near the Pompidou Centre. Another photograph showed a man lying in a littered street, and she didn't need to look at the blood-stained torso to know that he was dead. The somber police behind the corpse suggested they had been responsible for the man's demise, and Claire breathed a small, cautious sigh of relief. Maybe they'd finally caught the man, then, the one who'd been slaughtering the old women.

The waiter appeared at her elbow, looking over her shoulder at the grisly newspaper account. He started talking, so quickly she doubted she would have understood him even in English, and Claire looked around in sudden desperation, that panicked, closed-in feeling washing over her once more. Why did she stop, why did she even attempt something as normal as a midmorning cup of coffee?

"I'm sorry, I don't speak French," she said haltingly.

The waiter looked at her with expected contempt, then jabbed a grimy figure at the grainy photographs in front of her, continuing to jabber at her.

"He's trying to tell you his theory about the murders." The slow, wonderful voice to her left caught her attention, and she turned and flashed a smile of relief and sheer pleasure at Thomas Jefferson Parkhurst. Now she knew why she was in this part of town, why she had chosen this café. She knew nothing of Paris save her own small neighborhood and certain landmarks. She knew Tom lived near this small, tidy café, and she'd headed there, mindlessly, unerringly, hoping to find him.

Find him she had. When she smiled up at him he looked startled, taken aback. And then he'd smiled back, that slow, sexy crinkling around his eyes and mouth, and taken the chair beside her, dismissing the waiter with a few fluent French phrases.

"What was his theory?" Claire tried to wipe what she knew was an idiotic grin off her face. Was it relief that made her overjoyed to see him? Was it coincidence that so soon after meeting him she'd decided to leave Marc? Or was she making another foolish mistake?

Tom reached out and put a hand on hers. The warmth of his flesh was soothing, comforting, and she wanted to turn her palm over and grasp his. She didn't.

Tom shrugged, but he didn't remove his hand. "He thinks

the man the police shot was just a scapegoat. That the police are useless fools and can't find the criminal, so they killed an innocent passerby to make themselves look better."

"What do you think? Did you read the paper?" She didn't want to talk about murders that had nothing to do with her, but the alternative was even more threatening.

"It seems unlikely that the man would have killed all those women. He was just a lower-level bureaucrat. He had no motive and even less opportunity. However, it seems pretty clear that he did kill the woman in the photograph. Why are you here?"

The question came so quickly that she didn't expect it, wasn't prepared to counter it. She looked up into his warm blue eyes and told him the truth. "I don't know. I think I was looking for you."

The hand tightened on hers for a moment, and his wonderful grin lit his face once more. "Good. It saved me the trouble of looking for you. You never told me where you lived."

"I don't think it's a good idea . . ."

"It's a terrific idea," he interrupted. "If you don't tell me I'll follow you home."

Claire shivered in the bright sunlight. "Have you been following me already?" She could still feel the memory of the eyes burning into her back.

"No. Why?"

She gave herself an imperceptible shake. "Guilty conscience, I guess," she said with a self-deprecating grin that didn't reach her eyes. "I shouldn't be here with you."

"Why not? We're just a couple of expatriates sharing news of home and a cup of coffee. There's nothing wrong in that. Unless there's more to it." His voice was calm, implacable, just the tiniest bit goading.

Claire knew she should ignore it, should agree that their meeting was harmless. His hand was still on hers, the heat of his flesh sinking into her chilled bones, and slowly she turned her palm over, her fingers grasping his. She smiled ruefully. "Unless there's more to it," she echoed, her eyes meeting his for a long, breathless moment.

His fingers tightened around hers. "Claire . . ."

"Claire! What on earth are you doing here!"

She hadn't seen them coming. If she had, she would have released Tom's hand, she would have dived under the table to avoid them. As it was, all she could do was look up into two almost identical pairs of dark French eyes and curse the day she was born.

"Robert and I were wondering where you and Marc had gotten to," Solange Capet said, keeping a possessive arm around her husband. "We've seen nothing of you recently. And who is this charming young man?"

Claire suppressed the urge to scream. Solange and Robert Capet were the only people Marc had ever socialized with. Robert was a fellow mime of splendid physical attributes and not much brain power; Solange was much older, much richer, a major patron of the Théâtre du Mime. Claire had always suspected that she and Marc had once been lovers, and the malicious glint in Solange's eyes did nothing to discourage that supposition.

"I'm Claire's brother," Tom said helpfully. "Jeff MacIntyre, from Boston."

Claire swallowed her groan of dismay as Solange's grin widened. "Claire is an only child," she said sweetly. "How very naughty of you, Claire darling. Tell me, does Marc know what you do when you go out? He never was terribly modern about these things."

"Tom is a friend." There was no way she could keep the defensiveness from her voice, but it no longer mattered. She had never liked Solange or her witless husband, and right now she detested them.

"Tom? I thought his name was Jeff?" Solange cooed. Her mauve-tinted eyelids drooped for a moment as she surveyed Claire's companion. "You know, I don't blame you. He's very attractive in a roughhewn sort of way. Marc won't take kindly to being a cuckold, and believe me, he'll find out."

"I'm not cheating on Marc!" Claire said desperately. Tom's fingers clenched warningly around her own, and she realized belatedly that she hadn't let go of his hand. She wasn't about to do it now—the damage had been done, and she needed the reassuring touch of his flesh too badly in the face of Solange's sophisticated malice.

"No?" said Solange. "Well, if I were you I'd be sorely tempted. However, let me give you a piece of advice. I'd wait until Marc is out of town before I'd take a lover. Marc has a nasty temper and a streak of unpleasantness in him that it would be wise to avoid."

Claire opened her mouth to protest once more when Solange's words sunk in. "Marc is out of town," she said slowly.

"Is he?"

"You should know that as well as I do," Claire said. "He's on tour with the Théâtre du Mime."

Was that pity on Solange's face, mixed the amusement? It was too hard to tell. "No, he's not."

"He's been gone two weeks," Claire said desperately.

"He may very well be. But he's not on tour. If he were, Robert would be with him. And I, as a major fund-raiser, would know about it. If Marc told you he was going on tour he lied to you." Reaching over, she patted Claire's shoulder. "Don't worry. Perhaps he's found a lover of his own and just hasn't wanted to break the news to you. When he comes back and finds Jeff/Tom here he might be relieved. Or then again, he might not." She moved away, taking the oblivious Robert with her. "Keep in touch, *chérie*. This is almost as good as 'Dynasty.'"

Slowly Claire removed her hand from Tom's. Slowly she rose from the table. "Would you pay for my coffee? I never know how much they want."

"Claire, don't leave!"

"I have to."

Tom was on his feet, searching his pockets for change, frustration and impatience on his face. "Can't you see that woman was a lying troublemaker? Of course Marc is out of town, and even if he isn't, what does it matter? You haven't done anything wrong. Are you afraid of him? Has he threatened you, hurt you in any way?"

"No. No, he hasn't hurt me," she said slowly. "I'd better

get back." And before he could stop her she was racing down the streets, her Reeboks silent on the sidewalks.

She could feel his eyes watching her hasty departure, but she knew those weren't the eyes that had watched her, followed her. She knew now whose eyes they were. No, Marc hadn't threatened, abused her. But he frightened her. Very much indeed.

And tucking the grisly newspaper under her arm, she turned the corner and raced homeward, a thousand demons riding at her back.

≋ CHAPTER 9

The apartment was empty. Claire made very sure of that fact, starting with the hall closet and working her way back through the huge, stately rooms to the cavernous kitchen. No sign of Marc, no sign that he'd been there in the past two weeks. All that remained was her defiant clutter.

Pushing up the sleeves of her baggy cotton sweater, Claire began to clean. She started in the kitchen, working with single-minded purpose, scrubbing and dusting and straightening, making sure every piece of china was back in place, every piece of silver polished and sparkling, the counters and table scrubbed, the floor spotless, the ceilings free of cobwebs.

Without stopping any longer than she needed to consume too much black coffee, she moved through the bedrooms, the bathrooms, the dining room and formal salon, working with a frenzy only intensified by the silent reproach of the apartment and the caffeine in her system. She kept her mind a perfect blank, refusing to think about why she was doing this, refusing to acknowledge the very real panic that had swamped her when she imagined Marc's reaction when he saw how she had trashed his beloved apartment.

She stopped outside of Nicole's room, exhausted, sweating, almost too weary to continue. But she knew Nicole was just as intrinsically messy as she herself was, knew that as long as her father was out of reach she'd let her own room turn into a shambles.

She opened the door and then stopped, leaning against the door frame and staring at what she hadn't quite comprehended during her previous reconnaissance.

Nicole's room was spotless.

Messy Nicole, who'd left her dishes in the sink just as Claire had, who'd dropped coats in the hallway and crumbs on the silk-covered sofas, had kept her own room scrupulously neat.

Claire shut the door silently, moving back through the empty apartment that didn't feel empty. It hadn't been deeply ingrained instincts that had kept Nicole's room neat. She must have known, deep in her nine-year-old heart, that Marc was still around. Watching.

No one saw him as he made his way back to the shabby hotel room. But then, no one ever saw him. He knew how to blend with those around him, how to disappear into crowds, become invisible. If by any chance someone happened to notice him, they would simply shrug and think no more about it, accepting him as part of the Paris street scene.

He was late coming back. He'd stayed too long at the park, but he couldn't help himself. He liked the little boys the best. The girls, even the five- and six-year-olds, were already too flirtatious, too sure of their own seductive power. Whores at heart, all of them.

The boys were still innocent. Still a challenge. When he was ready he would start with the little boys.

The pain was manageable. Harriette had learned that long ago, learned to control it with her mind, with drugs, with sheer grit and determination. It wouldn't be much longer. Just time to pay off a few debts, and then a blissful nothingness. She simply had to use the formidable strength of mind and will that had supported her for so long. And never weaken.

She watched her granddaughter leave with mixed emotions. She didn't like entrusting her care to some mindless

American besotted with Marc Bonnard's sexuality. But she had Nicole's word that Claire MacIntyre was essentially a decent person, and she trusted her granddaughter's instincts. Nicole had seen through Marc even before Harriette had, looking up at her stepfather with dark, disapproving eyes.

It was no wonder Marc hated her, almost as much as he hated Harriette, as he had hated Isabelle, her daughter. He was such a consummate artist, a trickster, that it was simply unbearable for him to be seen as he was, the shoddy upstart with no origins. He'd taken on Isabelle's apartment, her life-style, her daughter, as if he were born to them all, but Harriette could see through his jumped-up manners. She didn't need to know he'd been brought up by peasants in Rouen to realize he had less breeding than her garbage man.

She wasn't going to die peacefully and let Marc end up with everything—Isabelle's money, Isabelle's apartment, Isabelle's daughter. He wasn't going to profit from murdering her daughter. The damnable thing was that Harriette had no proof. It had been a stormy night when Isabelle had taken off over the steep, winding roads in the south of France, and Isabelle had never been a good driver.

The police had seemed to think it all reasonable, and Marc had been sufficiently broken-hearted to convince some of the most cynical observers.

But not Harriette. She had watched, dry-eyed with a grief too terrible to bear, as her son-in-law moved with dignified grief through the funeral, and she had known. In the years since it had happened she had been consumed with such bitter hatred that it was no wonder her aging body was now eaten up with cancer.

But it wasn't cancer that was going to get her, she was about to make grimly sure of that. And Marc wasn't going to reap the benefit of her money, the money she had no choice but to leave to Nicole, which would, in turn, place it in Marc's greedy hands. No, she was going to take care of Marc, give him just what he deserved.

She heard the rude buzz at the back door, and nodded with satisfaction. She'd told Hubert to make sure his employee—her employee—wasn't seen. She wanted nothing to tie him to her untimely demise.

She moved slowly through the apartment, running a graceful, regretful hand along the elegant old furniture. The door buzzed again as she reached the kitchen, and Harriette frowned. Such a rude, impatient man. But what could you expect from someone in his line of work?

She opened the door and looked up into Rocco Guillère's cruel, pockmarked face. She blocked the doorway, all one hundred frail pounds of her, and looked him over with a withering glance. "You are Hubert's friend?" she inquired coolly.

The man didn't like her attitude, she could tell. Good. It would make him that much more eager to get the job done.

"I'm Hubert's friend," he growled in a gutter-Parisian accent. He hesitated a moment longer, then pushed past her into the kitchen. "I believe you have a job for me." He looked around her small, spotless kitchen in contempt, looked at her with equal disdain.

Harriette felt a final shiver of regret. And then she stiffened her backbone, shut the door, and led her new employee toward her elegant chintz salon.

The woman was crazy, Rocco thought, wishing he could find it funnier than he did. Not only was the woman out of her mind, but life itself was playing tricks, tricks he wasn't sure if he appreciated.

He hated the looks of her, from her snooty, beaked nose to her swollen ankles to her tiny little feet. Even more, he hated the smell of her and her apartment, the wisp of lavender and mothballs, the trace of a perfume so aristocratic it made his lip curl.

He liked the others better, the poor ones. The ones who were just holding on to their dignity, with their overcrowded apartments and their fading memories, the ones who smelled of old sweat and urine, not flowers. He would have taken special pleasure in this one, not because she reminded him of *Grand-mère* Estelle, but because she was so far removed from the old woman. Two centuries ago his

97

ancestors would have watched her ancestors being guillotined. Now it was up to him to continue in that tradition.

But it wasn't going to be up to him. Not when he heard her plan. "I want you to kill me," she'd said in her poker-up-the-ass voice, looking at him as if he were a cockroach.

"My pleasure," he'd rumbled, setting his dirty jeans on her fancy sofa and propping his shiny boots on the rickety table, knocking the artfully arranged magazines askew. "When and how?"

"I would like it to appear to be a murder like the other ones," she'd said, giving him his first taste of uneasiness. "I want you to stab me and lay me out as the other old women, but I want it done at such a time and in such a way as to implicate my son-in-law."

He'd laughed out loud at that, a rough guffaw that rattled the china in that overbred apartment. "With a mother-in-law like you I'd think he'd be more than willing to do it himself," Rocco offered maliciously.

Harriette Langlois had smiled, a chilly little smile, and for the first time he saw the connection between her and *Grand-mère* Estelle. "My son-in-law is too clever for that." She was unruffled by his rudeness, and he hated her all the more. "If he were to kill me he would make absolutely certain he wasn't caught. He murdered my daughter and no one ever suspected. He may very well be planning to kill me, I don't know. It doesn't matter. All that matters is that he pay for his crime, that justice be served."

Rocco reached in his black leather jacket and pulled out the solid gold toothpick he'd stolen off a dead pimp. "I don't give a rat's ass about justice," he said, poking at an old piece of steak that had lodged in a broken molar.

"No, I imagine you don't. But you care about money, don't you? And Hubert thinks very highly of you—he thinks you're the man to carry this off, make it appear like it's simply one more in the string of murders."

Rocco grinned. "I think I can manage that."

He'd finally gotten through to her. She was looking at him

warily, out of filmy blue eyes, as if he were one of those big jungle cats in the Paris zoo. "You haven't . . . you didn't . . ." She stopped on a shuddering sigh. "No. I don't wish to know."

Rocco's grin broadened. "You still haven't answered my question, lady. Where and when?"

"My son-in-law is on tour at the moment. He should be returning to Paris in another two weeks. We'll do it when he comes back. You'll have to plant the knife in his apartment, and I expect Hubert will take care of the anonymous phone call to the police. It should be fairly simple."

It should be, Rocco thought, his uneasiness increasing. "Who's your son-in-law?" he asked suddenly. "What's he doing on tour? I don't want to get involved with anybody famous—it draws too much attention and the police are much more diligent when they've got the newspapers on their back."

"He's nothing. He's a third-class mime with a second-class theater," Harriette said waspishly. "His name is Marc Bonnard." And she watched him stonily as once more Rocco began to laugh.

He hadn't bothered to explain it to her. After all, what could he have said? The irony of it all was so delicious he was bursting, and yet there was no one he could tell. No one, except a man he hadn't seen in over twenty years. Marc Bonnard.

Rocco doubted he was really out of town. Unless he'd changed drastically he was probably holed up somewhere, watching the old lady, waiting for his chance. Maybe he hadn't wanted to do it himself, afraid it might call attention to him. Part of the success of their pact had been the random nature of their victims.

Hubert would be able to find him, Hubert could set up a meeting. Together they could lament the demise of that stupid fool Yvon, together they could share a bottle for the sake of old times. Together they could decide who would get the supreme pleasure of wasting the old lady, and who would take the fall for it.

But Rocco still couldn't rid himself of a trace of nerves. While he could appreciate the irony, he didn't like the coincidence. And he wondered if his childhood buddy would feel the same.

The phone calls began that night. Claire was lying alone in the big bed, the fresh sheets scratchy beneath her silk nightgown, when the ringing broke through her efforts to will herself to sleep. She leaped for the phone, knocking it onto the floor, and scrambled after it, speaking into it breathlessly.

There was no sound on the other end. No French or English obscenities, no heavy breathing, nothing. Just an eerie silence that caused a rash of goose bumps to travel down Claire's bare arms.

She slammed the phone down, restored it to its proper place beside the bed, and crawled back beneath the covers. She should be able to sleep—her body was so achingly weary that it was amazing she could keep her eyes open.

But her brain was still clipping along at twice the normal rate. She'd tried to keep it quiet by bustling around, doing all that she would normally do if Marc were there, telling herself that if he happened to return unexpectedly she wouldn't need to worry. The rumpled sheets had been taken to the laundry, the T-shirt thrown away, every crumb and speck of dust in the house had been banished. Everything was done; she had some breathing space while she decided exactly what she was going to do, how she was going to get out of a mess that was of her own making.

Nicole had watched her panicked industry with maddening calm. She always kept her room neat, she'd said. It was second nature by now. But Claire knew she lied. What was second nature to the nine-year-old was not trusting Marc. If only his thirty-year-old mistress had as much sense.

She shut off the light, snuggling down lower in the sheets. How in the world had she gotten herself into such a fix? Had she no brains at all when it came to men? For two years she'd listened to Brian's lies and believed them, only

100

coming to her senses when he'd run down an innocent child and then driven away from it.

But she'd turned to Marc, a man who'd mesmerized her sexually and terrorized her spiritually. So that here she was, stuck in Paris with nowhere to go and no one to turn to.

That wasn't strictly true. There was someone she could turn to, someone she wanted to run to, but that was the last thing she would do. She'd gone from one mistake to another, and she wasn't about to go tearing into another relationship without thinking first. Her instincts told her Tom Parkhurst was safe, charming, cuddly, and protective, but so far her instincts had done nothing but get her into trouble. Besides, she shouldn't trade sex for protection.

God, what a fool she was. The first thing she should do was take a vow of celibacy, so that her body wouldn't blind her brain. For one year she wouldn't go to bed with anything more active than a hot-water bottle, for one year she'd wait, she'd think, she'd give herself time to know herself and what she wanted in life. When that time was over she'd consider getting involved again. There were plenty of good men like Tom Parkhurst around. She just hadn't been looking for them.

Still and all, there was something about him . . . The telephone shrilled in her ear, breaking through the dangerous reverie. This time when she reached for the phone she didn't knock it on the floor. This time when her greeting met with dead silence she didn't panic. She merely said something extremely Anglo-Saxon and replaced the telephone, breaking the connection. And then she took the receiver off once more, tucked the phone under the extra pillow, and curled up to sleep.

Malgreave didn't leave the office till after eleven. Vidal had left ages ago, Josef had finally gone half an hour before him, and the hallways were dark and deserted as the chief inspector made his way down to the street. He was not in a good mood.

One couldn't be cheerful if one spent hours staring at

photographs of corpses, he reasoned, climbing into his car and heading homeward through the brightly lit streets. Brightly colored pictures, with vivid hues. He should retire, move with Marie to her parents' deserted farm in Normandy and raise chickens.

That's exactly what he would do, once he solved the murders. The newspapers might think it was all over, but he knew otherwise. He knew Yvon Alpert had been an incompetent bungler, messing up his one sloppy murder. The other killings had been handled with more finesse, more expertise, God help him, more loving care.

The other murderers were still free to try again. Rocco Guillère and at least two others, perhaps three. Until he caught them, Normandy would have to wait. Josef's wife's ambition would have to wait, Marie would have to wait. He only hoped she would.

"I'm going with you," Claire announced, draining her third cup of coffee and trying to sound efficient. It was a losing battle. She hadn't been able to sleep. As if she hadn't been spooked enough, those two silent phone calls had put an end to any hope of rest for her. When she finally drifted off, her stubborn brain had tormented her with erotic fantasies of Tom Parkhurst, something her conscious mind had studiously avoided. She doubted she'd ever be able to see those large, long-fingered hands again without remembering the dream-induced feel of them on her bare skin.

Not that she had any intention of seeing him again. Not with the uneasy possibility of Marc lurking around, hiding, watching.

"Going with me?" Nicole echoed, pushing her plate away. "Why?"

"I wish to talk with your grandmother. And don't tell me she doesn't speak English—I know that. We'll have to make do. If worse comes to worst you can translate. Or we can use sign language, or charades." Claire moved to the sink and began washing the paper-thin porcelain tea cup, missing Nicole's look of surprise.

"*Grand-mère* doesn't like unexpected guests," she said. "I

think it would be better if you waited until you were invited."

"Will I be invited?" Claire didn't bother to turn around. The soapy cup slipped from her fingers and dove into the iron sink, smashing into a dozen pieces. Claire stood there, looking at it, her blood running cold.

The running water drowned out the sound of Nicole's footsteps as she crossed the room. She stood beside Claire, looking down at the cup in the sink, then reached over and turned off the water. "Don't worry, Claire," she said in her most practical voice. "Those belonged to Mother, and she's dead. She wouldn't care what happened to them."

"They belong to Marc . . ." Claire began, but Nicole shook her head.

"No, they don't. This apartment and everything in it belongs to me. Marc has the use of it during his lifetime, but my mother's will left everything to me. That's why Marc hates me." Her tone was cheerful, matter-of-fact.

"He doesn't hate you, darling," Claire protested, moving away from the sink, leaving the shattered pieces where they lay. "Fathers don't hate their daughters."

"Perhaps not. But Marc hates me," she said flatly. "I don't know if *Grand-mère* will agree to see you."

Claire dried her shaking hands on the linen towel. "She'll have no choice in the matter. I need some answers to some very important questions."

"Such as?"

Claire hesitated for only a moment. "Such as why your mother would leave everything to you and nothing to her husband," she said finally.

Nicole shrugged. "Suit yourself," she said, her French accent and unnatural gravity making the American idiom amusing. "But I can answer that for you. She didn't trust him." And on that note she left the room, leaving Claire staring after her.

It was depressing to think a nine-year-old had more sense about people than an adult, Claire thought, three hours later. It was unnerving to have her worst fears justified, her paranoia validated, her neuroses exposed for what they were. Only a neurotic fool would have fallen for Marc Bonnard. And Claire was tired of being a fool.

Madame Langlois had been sitting in her pale pink and blue living room, thumbing through a magazine, when the silent maid had ushered the two of them into her presence. Claire had just enough time to notice that the magazine Harriette was reading was an English one when Nicole vaulted herself toward the old lady with the first show of open affection Claire had ever seen from the child. She had begun to think Nicole incapable of it, but now she knew she was wrong. Nicole was capable of great affection, she just hadn't been around anyone who'd earned it.

And then Madame Langlois's steely eyes had spotted her by the door. They had run down Claire's narrow, neatly dressed body with sharp precision, assessing her merits and demerits with ruthless efficiency. And then she'd risen, crossing the room with ancient grace, and stood before her, greeting her in liquid, musical French.

Claire turned to Nicole for translation. "She says welcome. She says you aren't what she expected."

"I'm not?" Claire said warily. "What does that mean?"

Nicole grinned, suddenly looking her age. "I imagine she thought you would look like a bimbo. That's the word, isn't it?"

"Nicole," the old woman said in a reproving voice.

"Tell your grandmother I'm grateful she agreed to see me . . ." Claire began.

"I didn't agree to see you." The old woman spoke in sudden, astonishing English. "You simply appeared in my salon. Now that you're here we might as well talk."

"You speak English?"

"Of course I speak English," Madame Langlois snapped. "Any educated person speaks at least two languages. Whatever gave you the impression that I didn't?"

"Marc." Claire hadn't missed the snub, but she dismissed it in favor of more important things.

"Ah, Marc." The old woman nodded. "That explains a great many things. Nicole, my precious, run out to the

104

kitchen and ask Geneviève to make us some strong coffee. And stay there awhile, would you, my dear? Your stepfather's friend and I have a great deal to talk about."

Claire flinched. "Stepfather? Marc isn't Nicole's real father?"

Harriette smiled, a sour, satisfied pursing of wrinkled lips as she led Claire to the sofa. "Marc lied about that, too? Surely you had enough sense to ask Nicole herself about these things? You can't be that much of an idiot!"

Claire stifled the flash of anger that swept through her, simply because she knew that she had, indeed, been that much of an idiot. "There was no reason to doubt Marc," she said slowly. "Besides, when I referred to Marc as her father, Nicole never corrected me."

"You must have done so in English. Nicole is an intelligent child, but her grasp of that language is understandably limited. Sit, sit!" she ordered. "We have a great deal to talk about. But first you will tell me why you are here."

"And then?" She sank down onto a silk striped chair, gripping the arms of it with cold, sweating fingers.

"And then, my dear Mademoiselle MacIntyre, I will do my best to save your life."

❧ CHAPTER 10

When Claire left Harriette Langlois's apartment it was raining, cold fat drops that splatted down on her head, ran down her collar, and soaked her skin. She usually kept her head down when she walked through the Paris streets, scurrying along determined to avoid meeting anyone's eyes and thereby precipitating a conversation.

But this time she looked up for a moment, around her, at the Parisians huddled against the cold and rain, rushing to their destinations, a gray, desolate lot, each in his own solitary world. They looked as cold and miserable as Claire felt. Somehow she didn't find the thought comforting.

She wrapped her arms around her waist, hugging herself for warmth and comfort as she hurried through the streets. It had been so long since anyone hugged her, anyone offered her comfort, that her heart cried out for it. Right then she would have given anything for a sheltering pair of arms and a place to weep for her own foolishness.

There was such a place. If she had any sense at all it was the last place she should go to. But the last six months, no, the last two and half years had been singularly lacking in sense on her part. Why mar a perfect record? she thought bitterly. And with no hesitation she turned and headed toward Thomas Parkhurst's neighborhood.

It wasn't that she believed Harriette. Nor, for that matter, did she disbelieve her. The woman was bitter, full of anger and hatred, and she directed all that negative energy toward Marc. Whether or not Marc really deserved it was another matter.

Freed from the mesmerizing effect of his presence, Claire could contemplate it calmly. Was the man she'd been living with, the man she'd considered marrying, capable of murdering his wife?

He'd lied to her. The more Claire thought about it the longer the list of lies grew. He'd lied about Harriette's speaking French, he'd lied about Nicole being his own daughter rather than his stepdaughter, he'd lied about the apartment and its expensive furnishings. God, even his precious Limoges had belonged to Nicole's mother; it hadn't been in Marc's family for generations. He'd grown on his aunt and uncle's run-down farm outside of Rouen, dirt poor and distinctly working class.

It should have made Claire's heart ache for the poor, orphaned little boy. He would have been a very handsome child, and doubtless he'd honed his winning ways early. If she had any charity, any understanding at all, she would understand why he had taken Isabelle's ancestry, her apartment, even her daughter for his own identity.

But for some reason her charity and understanding couldn't reach out and enfold him as they had Nicole. No, she didn't believe he was capable of murdering his wealthy wife. But there was an essential coldness, a talent for manipulation that she could see quite clearly, now that the sexual blinders were off. And she wanted nothing more than to get away, as fast and as far as she could.

Through the gray, soaking downpour she began to recognize the neighborhood. Tom had told her where he lived, but she hadn't been paying attention. She'd thought it too dangerous, too tempting. Now she could have kicked herself for not listening.

Did he live to the right or to the left of the café? Was he five or six flights up? That didn't matter—he was definitely on the top floor. It was late enough—a little after eleven. At least she wouldn't be waking a stranger if she made the wrong decision.

She should turn around and go home, back to that apartment where she couldn't escape the sense of being watched. She needed to clean up the broken tea cup she'd left in the sink, she needed to make plans. What she didn't need was another man when her taste had been so execrable in the past.

But needing and wanting were two different things. And without hesitation she entered the building to the left of the café and began to climb the stairs.

Gilles Sahut looked out into the pouring rain as it puddled in the streets, making little pools of filth and garbage along the walkway. Slowly, with deliberate care, he untied his bloody apron and set it on the knife-scarred counter.

"You take over," he said to his assistant, a sturdy young boy from the streets. "Close the shop at six and don't touch a penny or I'll cut your throat myself."

The boy nodded, unperturbed, and Gilles allowed himself a brief moment to watch the play of muscles in Edgar's naked arms. It had been a long time since he'd had a boy. Maybe tonight, after he finished, he'd pay a visit to that small, dank room Edgar rented in a filthy alley in the midst of Belleville. With luck the boy would put up more of a fight than the whores Gilles paid so well.

Gilles pulled on his jacket, not bothering to wash the blood, the smell of death, from his hands. The rain looked as if it would continue all day and well into the night. With a smile that sat oddly on his harsh, beefy features, he headed out the door in search of a grandmother.

By the fifth flight of stairs Claire wished she was dead. Her breath was rasping, burning in her chest, her legs trembling, her heart threatening to burst from her chest. If Tom Parkhurst weren't at the end of this torture then her decision would be made. There was no way she was capable of trying the other building and climbing another five or six flights of stairs.

There was a window at the top of the final flight of stairs, looking out over the rain-drenched Paris skyline. Claire paused, gasping for breath, to peer out over the rooftops. This was more like the Paris of her imaginings, the artist's garret, the metal roofs, the old buildings, and the trees about to bloom. Up here she could imagine that Paris was hers. Down on the streets she knew she was separated from all she longed to enjoy by an impenetrable wall of silence, of incomprehension and confusion. Leaning against the streaked, ancient glass, she closed her eyes and listened to her labored breathing, feeling completely, unutterably alone.

She'd been a fool to come. The only thing she could do to retrieve the situation was to turn around and leave, not bother to find out whether she'd chosen the right building or not, whether that was Tom's garret apartment behind the flimsy, scarred door or if it belonged to some impoverished student.

She turned and started back down the stairs, moving quietly this time, trying to stifle her still-labored breathing. She was only halfway down one flight when she heard the door open at the top of the stairs, heard the clatter of heavy feet start down after her.

He moved so quickly she didn't have time to duck. Tom barreled into her, knocking her against the wall, and the two of them collapsed on the stairs in a tangle of arms and legs. It took him only a second to recognize her.

"Are you all right?" he demanded breathlessly, his hands, his large, clever hands, running over her, checking for damage.

"I'm fine." She tried to move away, but he was lying on top of her, pinning her there, seemingly oblivious to the blatant impropriety, not to mention sexuality, of the situation. "Please, let me up."

He stopped his seemingly careless inventory of her body, holding himself very still as he looked down at her. The window at the top of the stairs let in only a murky amount of light on such a rainy day, and the shadows surrounded them.

"You were leaving," he said quietly.

Unable to deny it, she said nothing, lying quiescent beneath him. She was soaked to the skin—the relentless downpour had penetrated the thin wool dress and silk raincoat she'd worn in deference to Nicole's grandmother. A shiver swept over her, one, and then another, and then she was trembling beneath Tom, shivering, and her eyes filled with sudden, useless tears.

He felt and saw everything. Before she had time to realize what he was doing he'd pulled himself upright and her with him, lifting her into his arms and starting back up the stairs, kicking open his door and angling her into the garret apartment.

Through her tears she saw the huge skylight with the rivulets of rain racing down it. She saw the hot plate and the dirty dishes, the table with the old typewriter and stacks of paper beside it, the bare floor and dusty corners. And the bed, sagging mattress, leaking pillows, tattered blankets and all, as he laid her down carefully upon it.

"What is this?" she gulped through her tears, "the road company for *La Boheme?*"

He sat down beside her, grinning. "It looked even more authentic in my painting stage. If you try you can still smell the turpentine."

"I can't smell anything," she wailed. "I'm crying."

"I noticed."

God, the man was dear. Without another word he leaned over and pulled her into his lap, leaning back against the iron bedstead and cradling her as she drenched him in tears. Somehow or other the raincoat got dumped on the floor, his own jacket followed, and their shoes joined them. Somehow or other she ended up curled up against him, her hand clenching his shirt, her body weary, her tears spent. Somehow or other she slid down in the bed, wrapped around him, sighing with the release of tension and something else. Somehow or other she fell sound asleep.

It was still raining when she woke up, and for a moment

she lay there in the gloomy darkness, trying to orient herself. Her body was cramped, uncomfortable from lying on a sagging mattress, but there was a curious feeling in her chest, half relieved buoyancy, half gloomy apprehension. She moved a fraction of an inch and recognized the cause of the happier part of her emotions. Tom Parkhurst was lying beside her, sound asleep, his thick brown hair tumbled over his high forehead, his eyes closed, his expressive mouth slack and emitting faint, regular snores.

Her gloomy apprehension belonged with the man she usually woke with, she thought, not moving. A man with a great deal more sophistication, charm, and good looks than the shaggy giant next to her. A man any fool could see through, she thought. But then, Claire MacIntyre wasn't just any fool. She was the queen of fools, and deserved everything she got.

She realized suddenly that the snoring had stopped and his startlingly blue eyes were open, watching her. She tried to summon a calm smile, but the attempt failed miserably, and to her annoyance she could feel tears stinging at the back of her eyes. She would have thought she'd cried enough by now. It had never been her habit to turn into a watering pot.

"You want to tell me what precipitated all this?" he inquired, scooting back and sitting up against the pillows. He made no move to touch her this time, but his long leg rested against her thigh, sending warmth and a dangerous sort of comfort through her. "Why were you going to leave without seeing me?"

"I shouldn't have come here," she said with sudden decisiveness, sitting up and scrambling off the bed.

This time he did touch her, reaching out and stopping her, hauling her back onto the bed with a bare minimum of effort. "If you're here you came for a reason." He was very calm, sensible, and that pragmatic quality soothed her. "And I have my stubborn moments. I'm not about to let you go until you tell me what's wrong."

She believed him. She sank back with a sigh, next to him on the sagging bed. It was all she could do to keep from

111

falling into the middle, but she dug her fingers into the mattress and kept to her tenuous perch, unwilling to give in to temptation.

"The man I've been living with lied to me," she said, not looking at her companion, keeping her eyes trained on the sloping window and the steady raindrops. She fell silent for a moment, uncertain how to continue.

"He's been seeing someone else?" Tom prodded gently.

"Oh, God, if only that were true. It would make things so simple," Claire said, her voice weary. "But I don't think so. As far as I can tell, he only wants me."

"I can understand that." The comment was casual, almost thrown away, and Claire wished she dare look at him, to see whether he meant it or not. She kept staring at the rain.

"He lied about the apartment. He said it was his, had been in his family for generations. But it wasn't, it belonged to his dead wife.

"That doesn't seem that terrible a lie. A lot of people make up things to feel more important."

"He told me Nicole was his daughter, but she wasn't. She's only his stepdaughter, and they hate each other. I never could understand how someone could hate their own child, but that explains it. He told me Nicole's grandmother couldn't speak English, and she probably speaks it better than I do."

"Still relatively harmless," Tom said. "How did you find out these were lies?"

"I went with Nicole to see her grandmother anyway. I thought she could translate for us, but there was no need."

"Let me guess. The grandmother hates Marc. And she told you all these things about him. Have you ever stopped to think she might possibly be biased?"

She did turn to look at him then. "Harriette Langlois told me a great many things, most of which I took with a grain of salt. She thinks Marc murdered her daughter. I know that's impossible. Marc simply isn't the type to kill. He can charm, manipulate, twist things around to suit him, but he hasn't got the brutality to kill. He hasn't got the honesty."

Tom shifted on the sagging bed, moving marginally closer. "That's a strange way to put it."

"It is, isn't it? But I think killing requires a certain amount of honesty. You have to admit you hate, you have to confront the evil that lives inside you in order to kill another human being. I don't think Marc has done that."

"So what are you worried about?" Tom prodded gently.

"You heard Solange yesterday in the café. Marc told me he was going on tour. Solange said he couldn't be. She would have no reason to lie."

"And Marc would?"

"I don't know. He doesn't seem to trust me. He's always watching me, waiting for God knows what." She shivered in the chilly air. Her silk dress was still damp, clinging to her, and Tom's garret had little if any heat.

"Is that it?"

She hesitated. She could stop then—the list of lies was long enough. The room was filled with shadows; there was something comfortingly anonymous about sitting on the bed, talking. If she just kept watching the raindrops run relay races with each other down the sloping skylight she could say anything.

"He lied about the police. He said they were looking for me."

"Were they?"

"No," said Claire flatly.

Silence. "Did they have any reason to?"

Claire pulled her knees up, dropping her chin onto them. "Yes," she said finally. "They did."

"And Marc knew that."

"Somehow," she said, talking to her knees. "I never told him."

"So why don't you tell me?" he coaxed gently. "How bad can it be? What did you do, rob a bank?"

She shifted on the bed, turning to look at him in the murky light. "No," she said, steeling herself to say the words she'd never spoken to a living soul. "I was involved in a hit-and-run accident." It sounded terribly mundane when she finally said it. Almost prosaic.

113

"And?" Tom prompted.

"A nine-year-old girl was the victim. She was in a coma for weeks."

"Did she recover?"

"Yes."

"Were you the driver?"

"No."

"Did you try to force the driver to stop, to help her?"

"Of course," Claire said, outraged.

"Then," said Tom with a shrug, "I fail to see why you're going around acting like Lady Macbeth or something. It wasn't your fault and you didn't do it. Lighten up."

She stared at him, uncertain whether to hit him or to laugh. "I broke the law by not going to the police."

"So get a good lawyer and you'll get a slap on the wrist. Don't spend the rest of your life doing penance with an egocentric Frenchman."

"How do you suggest I spend the rest of my life?" she demanded in her stiffest tone of voice, one that would do justice to Madame Langlois at her starchiest.

Tom shrugged, grinning that engaging grin. "It's not for me to say. But while you're thinking about it you might consider that egocentric Americans have their advantages."

The apartment was empty. He moved silently down the hallways, listening, watching. No sign of either of them, but they'd be back, sooner or later.

He'd be back, too. When they least expected it he'd be there. Watching, listening, waiting. He was silence, waiting to engulf them. He laughed soundlessly as he moved over to a window, looking down into the busy street below. He was silence, and they were ceaseless noise. And he would triumph.

Tom wondered whether he'd pushed her too far. That was as close as he could come to a declaration, and once more he felt as if he were on a precipice. Most of his encounters with Claire MacIntyre had felt that way. The two of them seemed to go lurching and staggering from crisis to crisis, and each time he told himself this would make or break them.

Just moments ago he convinced himself if she told him what the police wanted her for, then he'd have a sign to go ahead. If she trusted him more than that elegant lover of hers he'd be halfway there. Now he was simply waiting to see whether she'd jump off the bed and stalk from the room, that lovely little nose of hers in the air.

Tom waited, not even aware that he was holding his breath, while she looked at him, her shadowed, tragic eyes unreadable. And then suddenly, blessedly, she smiled. "You're a swine, Parkhurst," she said. "I think if I'm going to do penance I'd better do it on my own."

"Suit yourself. I'll come visit you in the convent."

"Do that." She did climb off the bed, and he let her go, relieved that the tension was gone. She was accepting him, smiling at him, as if, damn it, he were an old English sheep dog. It wasn't her fault. He'd done his best to foster her opinion of his harmlessness. She didn't need another man coming on to her, not while she was still enmeshed in a situation that sounded sticky indeed.

But he was beginning to get tired of feeling like a eunuch. She'd slept in his arms for close to half an hour before he drifted off himself, lulled by the sound of the incessant rain on the metal roof directly overhead, and during that half hour it had been all he could do to keep from unbuttoning that rumpled silk dress that clung so damply and so enticingly to her curves. Her forehead had rested against his chin, and it wouldn't have taken much to tilt her back a bit, to put his mouth on hers. She was so overwrought she probably wouldn't have objected, more than willing to accept an hour or so of oblivion, even with an old English sheep dog.

He was glad he hadn't succumbed to the temptation. If he had he knew what would happen. Right now she'd be buttoning her clothes, refusing to meet his eyes, emitting brittle, sophisticated conversation. And once she left his rooms he'd never see her again.

115

No, better to wait. Better to ignore the tension in his shoulders, the blood pulsing in his crotch, the itching in his fingers. Hell, Claire probably didn't even think he had a crotch.

"I'll walk you back." He swung his long legs over the side of the bed and started to pull on his sneakers.

"There's no need . . ."

"I'll walk you back."

"What if Marc is watching?"

He handed her the rumpled silk raincoat, then pulled on his own leather bomber jacket. "Then I expect he'll be in touch. You're not afraid of him, are you? You said you didn't think he was capable of murder."

A shadow crossed her face, and he would have given anything to have prodded further, to find out what she was thinking. But he'd pushed enough for one day. "No, I'm not afraid of him," she said, her voice lacking conviction. "Let's go."

It was midafternoon, and the rain was still coming down steadily. The gutters were awash, the passersby an army of bobbing black umbrellas. Tom took Claire's arm when they crossed the first street and didn't let go until they were in front of her building.

She stopped, clearly torn, and he couldn't resist teasing her. "No thanks, I won't come up."

"I'm sorry, of course you should," she murmured, distracted.

"I should, but you're nervous as a cat." She looked pinched and cold and miserable, huddled against the rain, and he wished he could put his arms around her, take her back to his rooms and build a fire in the smoky fireplace and warm her to the bones. He knew he couldn't. Not yet.

"Sorry," she said again, pushing a pale, nervous hand through her red gold hair. "Thank you for everything, Tom. For letting me cry all over you, among other things."

He didn't say anything. She wanted reassurance, she wanted charm, she wanted his easy, nonthreatening smile. Right now he no longer felt like giving them to her. "You're welcome," he said. "Before you go in it's only fair if I mention one thing."

The worry creased her high forehead again. "What's that?"

He moved too quickly for her to duck, to realize his intent. He caught her narrow shoulders in his big hands, pulled her wet, startled face up to his, and kissed her, a brief, thorough kiss that didn't help the uproar his hormones were in.

By the stunned expression on her face he could tell it didn't help calm her hormones much either. Good, he thought with a certain savage satisfaction. "Just that," he said huskily. "Go on in."

She went, quickly, without a backward glance. He stood there in the rain, watching her go, and then looked up at the elegant old building. Someone had been watching them from the first floor, probably some curious old biddy. A curtain moved, falling back into place over a window, and Tom felt little shivers of disquiet along his backbone. At least he knew Bonnard's apartment was on the second floor of the old building. It must simply be a curious neighbor.

But as he walked back through the rain, he couldn't rid himself of the memory of that curtain falling into place. And he wondered if he were being ridiculously paranoid, or far too trusting.

⚜ CHAPTER 11

Claire ran up the steps to the second-floor apartment, her mouth burning. She'd asked for it, hadn't she? She'd been waiting for it, wondering what had taken him so long. If he'd made his move earlier, when they were lying curled up in bed, she wouldn't have stopped him from doing anything he wanted.

Thank God he hadn't. She suspected it had crossed his mind, but he'd deliberately waited until they were on safe, neutral territory. And the kiss had been just right. No overwrought pawing, no chaste salute, it was a simple, effective, surprisingly arousing statement of intent.

Having made that statement, would he continue to allow her to hide from the electricity that was generating between the two of them, hide in her worry and panic? Somehow she didn't think so.

She rummaged in her purse for the heavy set of keys, then began unlocking the three complex locks Marc had insisted upon, her mind still abstracted. She'd actually told him about the accident. Not in detail—that could, and she had no doubt would, come later. But she'd actually spoken the words and he hadn't drawn away from her in disgust. That was probably half the reason for her current, irrational feeling of mild euphoria.

The apartment smelled slightly musty, and the scent of long-dead roses lingered in the air. She shut the door behind her, wishing it were warm enough to open the windows. She hated the smell of this apartment in the rain.

Dumping her wet raincoat in the hall, she slipped off her high heels and headed back toward the kitchen and a much needed cup of coffee. She should be feeling depressed, she thought, filling the kettle and reaching in the freezer for the coffee beans. She should be making feverish plans to escape. Instead she was humming under her breath, dreaming of a shaggy giant of a man with an endearingly clumsy body and deft hands. She was a hundred times a fool.

Madame Langlois, for all her dire warnings, hadn't been very helpful about Nicole's future. She'd made it quite clear she couldn't take her granddaughter in, and that she expected Claire to be responsible for her. But what possible good could Claire be against the superior legal and moral rights of a stepfather?

But Harriette Langlois had been curiously adamant on that issue. And until Claire figured out what to do with the child, she couldn't leave Paris.

Well, to be perfectly honest, right now she didn't want to leave Paris. She didn't want to leave Thomas Jefferson Parkhurst. Fool that she was, she was doing exactly what she had sworn she wouldn't, falling in love with a new man before the old one was gone. When would she ever learn from her mistakes?

But it was hard to believe that trusting Tom was a mistake, that any kind of involvement with him should be avoided. He was worth ten of Marc, worth twenty of Brian. Maybe she'd finally developed some taste in her old age. Even if the timing was all wrong, the smartest thing she could do was accept it, rather than jeopardize the best chance she'd had.

It was quarter past four. Nicole would be back in less than an hour, and Claire had better pull herself together, not sit around mooning like a love-struck teenager. She'd change into something more comfortable, rummage in the freezer

119

for something to eat, and put up with an evening of incomprehensible French television.

She headed for the sink, setting her empty mug down. And then she stopped, a cold, bitter bile settling in her stomach. Six hours ago, when she and Nicole had left the rambling apartment for Madame Langlois's house, the shattered remains of a Limoges tea cup sat in the sink. Now every trace was gone.

Once more she searched the apartment, every room, every closet, searching for a sign, a trace, for Marc himself. Nothing. The now spotless confines of the old apartment yielded not even the faintest clue. For all anyone could tell, Marc hadn't been near the place in more than two weeks.

But who else could it be? Claire thought, shivering in the dimming afternoon light. She pulled off her rumpled silk dress and threw it on the floor of her closet, instinctively reaching for another formal dress. And then she stopped herself, grabbing her jeans and heavy sweater, frowning in disgust. She wasn't going to play these games anymore. If it was Marc he could show himself. For all Madame Langlois's dire warnings, she knew he wasn't dangerous. If he didn't trust her, didn't like the way she kept the apartment or herself, he could come back and tell her.

But even the heavy cotton sweater couldn't keep the chill away from her body. She moved over to the window, staring down into the street below, and for a moment she thought she could smell the faint trace of cologne Marc favored, the bitter almond scent that seemed part of his skin. Leaning forward, she saw the place where Tom had held and kissed her. And she began to shiver.

Rocco stopped long enough to have his big black boots shined. His large, dirty hands were trembling slightly as he lit a Gitane, and he stared at them in surprise. He simply couldn't remember ever being nervous in his life. Not since he was thirteen years old and living in the Marie-le-Croix orphanage.

It had been so long since he'd seen him, since he'd seen any of them. It had been part of their pact, that they'd never be in touch. That they would read in the papers, and know, and that would suffice.

Of course, he'd seen his photograph in magazines. He'd stared at the grainy images for long minutes, looking for traces of the boy he once knew beneath the full-grown man and the passage of twenty years, stared until that nosy Giselle had questioned him. It was hard to see anything beneath the whiteface.

And then there was that idiot, Yvon. The picture of his corpse, spread-eagled against the garbage cans, hadn't given anything away. Even in childhood he'd never been able to do anything right—it was no wonder he bungled it with the old woman. Messy, Rocco thought, tossing the cigarette out and reaching for his gold toothpick. Very, very messy.

He headed down the street, his black leather jacket shedding some but not all of the rain. It had probably been a waste of time having his boots shined when they had to wade through this slop, but he didn't regret it. As long as he had a shine on his shoes he could face Marc Bonnard with his bravado intact.

It hadn't taken Hubert long at all to arrange a meeting, but then, Hubert knew everything there was to know in Paris, or knew someone else who had the information wanted. In an hour it had been set. Rocco had to admire the choice of meeting places. The small park where the old people congregated was a wonderfully ironic spot for the two of them.

He wanted to be late, but he couldn't bring himself to do it. He found he was hurrying through the streets, shoving people out of his way in his haste to make it to the park on time. He only hoped they wouldn't be too noticeable on a stormy day like this one.

But Marc must have taken that into account. Marc always took every possibility into account, and just as he had twenty years ago, Rocco would follow blindly.

The notices were still up at the entrance of the park, warning the old people to be on their guard. Against him, Rocco thought cheerfully. The rain had slowed to a steady mist, and while a few damp pedestrians were taking a

SEEN AND NOT HEARD

shortcut through the park, the benches were deserted. All
except one.

Rocco recognized the set of his head, the line of his jaw,
the elegant nose. He always was a handsome fucker, he
thought, even as a child. It had helped him get what he
wanted back then, when the others had been hard pressed to
protect themselves. He would always remember that summer morning, with Marc sitting on *Grand-mère* Estelle's
desk, his high, well-bred little voice calmly outlining his
plan.

Not that he'd been any better born than the rest of them,
Rocco thought, sneering and staring at him. He'd just been
an excellent mimic, picking up the accent and manners of
his betters, using them to charm and infuriate *Grand-mère*
Estelle and Georges, the gardener, using them to charm and
intimidate the others.

He must have felt Rocco's inimical gaze on him. He
turned his head, his dark, fathomless eyes meeting Rocco's
across the rain-swept park, and his beautiful mouth curved
up in a smile. And Rocco, fearless Rocco, a man who could
cut the throat of a nun without flinching, shivered in the
cold spring rain.

Nicole was asleep on the damask sofa, her dark eyes
closed, purple shadows lurking underneath, staining her
sallow skin. Claire sat there, watching her, ignoring the
babbling of the television set with its dubbed sit-com.
Nicole would usually disappear into her room at nine
o'clock and reappear the next morning at seven. During
those long hours the lights were off and no sounds issued
forth, but it was clear by the shadows beneath her solemn
brown eyes that she wasn't sleeping soundly.

Who could blame her? Madame Langlois probably fed
her fears, turning the tension between stepfather and stepdaughter into something more sinister. Damn the woman
with her paranoia! Claire could no more entrust Nicole to
her than she could to Jack the Ripper, even if Harriette had
been willing to take her.

The television blared at her, the light and darkness shifting over the room. Marc would never have approved of its arrival, but Claire had ignored that during her defiant stage. Now she wished she hadn't. The constant noise drove her crazy, as American television never had, but Nicole was entranced by it, preferring to keep it on all evening rather than suffer the silent apartment and Claire's nervous chatter.

Claire sighed, leaning back and stretching her feet out in front of her. At least the dubbed French drowned out the sound of the rain outside. If only the apartment would warm up. But she knew from icy experience that there was no way to warm up the old barn of a place. She and Marc would usually just retire to bed, filling the long hours with pleasuring each other.

No, that wasn't true. He would pleasure her, torment her, excite and arouse her. She was given very little chance to participate. He usually kept her so busy, so overwrought, that she had little to do but lie there and react.

Brian had been the other way around, expecting to be serviced when the mood struck him. Claire sat there, an expression of distaste marring her face. Surely there was something in between the two extremes? Surely sex should be give-and-take, a sharing of pleasure.

Her thoughts started to drift toward what it would be like to share, who would be likely to do so, and she pulled them back. The last thing she should do was sit there having erotic fantasies with Marc's stepdaughter asleep at her feet. She had to make plans, for her and for Nicole, for the self-possessed child who wouldn't let her in, but for the life of her she couldn't think what.

Claire heard the phone ring, but she didn't move. It wouldn't be anyone she wanted to talk to. She would let it ring, try to make sense out of the sit-com on TV, try to make sense out of her life.

Nicole stirred, opening her eyes and blinking up at Claire. "Aren't you going to answer the phone?" she inquired sleepily.

Claire sighed. It was easier getting up than explaining her reservations. With a weary sigh she pulled herself from the sofa, hoping the ringing would stop before she reached it.

The large, old-fashioned black phone in the hallway kept up its shrill, incessant tone. She picked it up, steeling herself for the spate of French that would greet her cautious "Hello."

Silence. The same, absolute silence that had greeted her the night before. She'd almost forgotten about those calls, but now the memory came flooding back. No heavy breathing, no muttered obscenities, no background noise. Just complete, utter silence.

The vision came unbidden, eerie, sudden, unavoidable. Marc was on the other end of the line, in whiteface, miming desperately, communicating with her in breathless silence.

She slammed the phone down, her hands trembling. She stood there for a long moment, trying to compose herself before facing Nicole's too-observant eyes, when the phone began to ring once more.

Without thinking she yanked the phone from the wall, the long black cord snaking free. In the distance she could hear the extensions still ringing, in the kitchen, in the bedroom. And in the doorway stood Nicole, watching her.

"Was it Marc?" she questioned calmly.

"Of course not." Claire marveled at her own self-possession. "A wrong number."

"Then why did you rip the phone out of the wall?"

Damn the child. "All right, it wasn't a wrong number. It was a crank call."

Nicole's face whitened in the dim light. Suddenly she was no longer a distant, precocious stranger, she was a frightened child. "Did someone talk to you, Claire? Or was it silent?"

Claire could feel her own blood drain away from her skin. "Silent. How did you know? Have you had the same thing happen?"

Nicole shook her head slowly, painfully. "No," she said. "Just before my mother died she began receiving phone calls like that. When Marc said he was out of town."

Claire just stared at her, fighting the nausea that was rising from the pit of her stomach. And for the first time she wondered if Madame Langlois was a bitter, paranoid old woman, or wise even beyond her years.

For a large, graceless man Gilles Sahut could move silently enough. He walked down the street, his heavy boots quiet on the pavement, heading toward Belleville. The rain was coming down heavily now, pouring over his bare head and running down his face. His hair was cut so short one could see the skull beneath it, and the short stubbly growth did nothing to slow the descent of the rain. He shook his head to clear the water from his eyes, like a large, evil dog, and continued on, single-minded in his purpose.

He'd had a few bad moments tonight. He'd been inside the apartment of the old one, moving through the clutter of furniture, when he realized the rain had stopped. He'd halted, motionless, not even daring to breathe, as he listened for the sound of rain against the window of the apartment. Nothing.

She'd been asleep. She was a plump one, her black stockings rolled down below her knees, crumbs and food dribbled on her massive bosom, an impressive mustache above her pursed and wrinkled mouth. She wore a wig, an elaborate, blue white affair, and it had slipped to one side, revealing the thin strands of yellow gray beneath it.

She was snoring, her head drooping, her plump hands resting in her capacious lap. The rooms smelled of cabbage and roses, and he remembered the roses in the garden at the orphanage, Georges's pride. He remembered the thorns, and how they'd been embedded in his young boy's flesh.

He could turn and go. He couldn't touch her when the sky was clear—he'd sooner kill himself. But he could wait. It wouldn't stay clear for long. Sooner or later the rain would return, and he'd be ready for it.

Without a sound he moved closer, dropping his massive bulk into the chair opposite the old lady. She stirred for a moment, then began snoring more loudly, as Gilles had settled down to wait.

In the end it had happened fast, too fast. A loud rumble of thunder, a renewed downpour, and the old one had woken up, her rheumy eyes opening to view her killer just as he plunged the knife into her chest.

It was always too fast. He felt cheated, frustrated, and he knew what he was going to do about it. Edgar lived alone on the top floor of one of the mean little houses on this narrow, dirty little alleyway. The only other occupant was a drug dealer who minded his own business. He wouldn't interfere if there was a struggle. It was time Edgar learned his place.

The door was a flimsy one, and the lock didn't hold against a man of Gilles's bulk. The stairway was narrow and dank, and Gilles remembered the one other time he was here. Edgar had been sick, and Gilles had come to drag him into work. He accepted no excuses—if Edgar wished to work for him he would come to work with the runs, with a streaming nose, with typhus if need be. And Edgar had come.

He remembered the mattress on the floor, the dirty gray sheets that had once been white, with Edgar's pale face and strong boy's body lying there. He grew hard as he remembered, as he thought about just what he would do to the boy on that mattress. Something would be salvaged out of this miserable night. And then maybe he'd move the boy in with him, for as long as it amused him.

The room was very dark when he opened the door. No moonlight filtered through on such a rainy night, and the light from the hallway barely reached the mattress. He could see Edgar lying there, the smoothly muscled shoulder and tousle of dark hair. Gilles reached down and unfastened his pants, moving across the room on his silent cat's feet.

Edgar moved, and a dim light speared across the room. The boy looked at him, at his erect flesh and the determination, and he moved back against the mattress. He was naked, and Gilles felt himself grow even harder.

"No," said Edgar, the first time he had ever said such a thing to his employer.

Gilles grinned. He would have enjoyed this if Edgar had been passive, but a fight would add spice to the whole thing.

He outweighed the boy by more than a hundred pounds, and his muscles, honed by years of slinging dead animals around, were impressive. He carried his knife loosely, the knife that had served him well once this evening, secure in the knowledge that he wouldn't need it to overpower the boy.

"Yes," he said, mocking, advancing. "But yes."

He could smell the boy's fear, and the sour, sweaty smell was an aphrodisiac. He remembered his own fear, when he was much younger than Edgar and Georges had come after him, and his excitement increased. Suddenly impatient, he went down on his knees on the mattress, dropped his knife, and lunged for the terrified boy.

It happened so quickly. One moment he was ready to draw the boy underneath him, in the next he felt the sharp thrust up against his throat. It was wet, hot and wet all around him, pouring over him, and he knew blood too well not to recognize the feel of it, the warmth of it, the ironlike smell of it.

It amazed him to realize it was his own. Somehow Edgar had managed to get hold of his own knife and stick it in his throat. He was dying, Gilles thought in surprise. His blood was soaking them both, and he was dying.

He tried to laugh, but the sound was a gurgling noise. Years ago he had killed a man for buggering him, and now he had met the very same fate. You had to laugh at the tricks life would play on you, he thought, falling onto the mattress. It was Edgar's mistake, though. If he could talk he would have told him. He should have waited, put up with him until he was old enough to inherit the boucherie. That was what Gilles had done, and it had served him well.

No, Edgar had botched it. He was standing there, naked, watching his employer bleed to death on his mattress, and he didn't make a sound. And just before he died Gilles noticed, with grim satisfaction, that Edgar had an erection too.

Tom couldn't stop thinking about that curtain falling into place. He lay stretched out on his narrow, sagging bed, breathing in the lingering traces of Claire's elusive scent, and thought about the watcher in the window.

Stupid, stupid, stupid, he chided himself. He hadn't been able to resist the romantic gesture of kissing her good-bye, the two of them standing outside in the pouring rain. There would have been no problem with it if she didn't already have a live-in lover with a possibly murderous streak. He'd been alone too long. He shouldn't be in a garret trying to write the great American novel, he should be writing romances.

He wished he could share Claire's faith that Marc Bonnard was harmless. He knew that he should—after all, he'd never met the man and Claire had lived with him for the past four or more months.

But Claire, for all her denials, had a hunted look in her eyes, one that wasn't caused solely by her guilt over the hit-and-run accident. And she'd never told Bonnard about that, yet she'd confided in him within days of meeting him. That ought to count for something.

No, her common sense might tell her Bonnard was safe, but her instincts were disagreeing. He wished he knew which he could believe.

He stretched out in the bed, his feet touching the bottom railing, his head brushing the top. He'd planned to leave her alone for a couple of days, to think about that kiss, but right now he didn't think he could do it. For one thing he didn't want to go for days without seeing her; for another, that curtain still bothered him. He'd find out who lived on the first floor, in the apartment below her, and set his mind at ease.

He was almost asleep when a sudden, disquieting thought slid into his mind, disrupting what little chance he had of a decent night's rest. The watcher had been on the first floor of the old building, just above the ground floor. Did Claire know the difference when she told him she lived on the second story? Did she know that in Europe the first floor was the ground floor, the second was the first, etc.? Did she actually live in the apartment that held the silent watcher?

He reached for the phone, then pulled his hand back. He

would only make things worse. If it hadn't been Marc he would worry her needlessly. If it was, she was already dealing with it, and she didn't need his interference. He looked at his watch. Quarter past one in the morning. The earliest he could show up on her doorstep was eight A.M. Not until then would he be certain she was all right.

He sighed, sitting up. It was going to be a long night.

⚜ CHAPTER 12

"Isn't modern science wonderful, Josef?" Malgreave lit another cigarette as he stared down at the medical examiner's report. "A butcher gets his throat cut and his body gets dumped in an alley in Belleville. There's so much blood on his corpse you can't even tell what color his clothes were originally, and yet the coroner was able to determine some of that blood came from someone else. Someone with very rare AB negative blood."

"Ah," said Josef, putting his fingertips together and waiting.

"Now you and I both know that it's always possible that Sahut's attacker had that rare blood, and Sahut was able to inflict some damage before he died. That would make sense, wouldn't it? So why am I searching further, Josef? Let me hear what you've deduced from all this." Malgreave stabbed the air with his cigarette. "Don't just sit there nodding portentously."

"I don't think the blood came from his attacker," Josef said after careful consideration. "For one thing, the butcher was a huge, powerful man. The only way anyone could have gotten him is by surprise. If he'd had time to fight back, there would have been more than that trace of AB blood, there probably would have been a second body."

"A good point," Malgreave conceded. "But what have we

got to tie a butcher from Belleville with the murder in the Latin Quarter? What do you think, Vidal? You must be here for some reason other than to look pretty. Give me your thoughts. What have we got to tie him to Rocco Guillère, to Yvon Alpert?"

"Nothing," Vidal said, unruffled. His pants were lavender today, and far too tight. Josef had taken one look at Vidal's apparel and started fuming.

"Nothing indeed." Malgreave took one last, greedy suck of the cigarette and stubbed it out in an already overflowing ashtray. The room was thick with blue smoke. "Nothing but an old cop's instinct. There may be no connection with Guillère, or Alpert for that matter. They may have been acting on their own, random, copycat killers."

"You don't believe that," said Josef.

Malgreave sighed. "I never have. It would be so much easier if I did. Such a nice, neat answer to a nasty problem. But I stake my career, my reputation, on my instincts. The victims may be random, the acts aren't. The blood on Gilles Sahut's clothes, that which didn't belong to him or the animals he'd slaughtered, that blood came from Marcelle du Paine."

Josef leaned back in his chair and crossed his legs, an almost unheard-of act of relaxation in his precise lieutenant, while Vidal pulled himself upright from his lounging position in the doorway. Always at opposites, Malgreave thought with a sigh.

"How do you intend to find the connection, sir?" Josef said.

"Ah, Josef, that's where the trouble comes in. Two years ago Rocco's file disappeared from central records. It's no wonder—the man has informers and friends everywhere. But it contained the only information we had about his early years. What we have now covers the criminal highlights of the last ten years of his life as we were able to reconstruct them, and there is no possible connection between him and the butcher and the bureaucrat."

"What about the other two?"

"We're still working on that. Alpert's life is an open book.

131

He grew up outside of Paris in the Marie-le-Croix orphanage, worked his way through college, got a job with the government, and was a model, industrious Frenchman. He was all set to get married next month. There is no clue, no hint as to why he would suddenly show up at a stranger's apartment and murder her."

"Do we know they were strangers?"

"It's a logical assumption. The woman had very nosy neighbors, and no one had ever seen him before."

"Besides, she said so in her phone call to the police," Vidal offered.

"So she did." Malgreave nodded his approval.

"Why don't I check and see what records I can find concerning the orphanage?" Josef suggested, glaring at Vidal's lavender jeans. "There might be something that would explain Alpert's sudden derangement. Maybe he was a difficult child, maybe he came from an abusive home."

Malgreave shook his head. "Another dead end. The place burned down years ago."

"Before or after Alpert left?"

Malgreave grew very still. "Josef," he said gruffly, "you cheer me enormously. I will be leaving this department in good hands when I retire." He stood up, shuffling the papers briskly. "First things first. You start with the orphanage. Find out when the fire took place, see if any records survived the blaze, or if records were kept elsewhere. In the meantime, Vidal can scout out Sahut's boucherie and see what he can find."

"Yes, sir."

"Maybe, my friends, just maybe, fate has decided to be kind. We may solve this case after all."

"With you in charge, sir, I never had any doubts," Josef said with complete sincerity.

He was going to kill her. He had always known he would, deep inside, but he'd hoped that this time his trust wouldn't be misplaced. This time a woman would prove worthy of his love.

But deep inside he'd known. She'd lied to him, from the very beginning. She'd kept a tiny part of her hidden from him, no matter how he tried to charm it out, into the light and into his possession. She'd always held back.

A part of him had been glad when she'd kissed the American. He was sick of wondering, sick of giving her the benefit of the doubt. Now all questions were answered. Now it was up to him, to pick the time, the place. And how much he was going to make it hurt.

The predawn light was a faint pearly glow in the east. The rain had, for the moment, stopped, and streaks of pale blue were edging across the Paris sky. Claire lay there, curled in on herself, trying to fight her way back to oblivion, when she realized she wasn't alone.

She could hear the steady, deep breathing. She could feel the weight on the bed behind her. Terror sliced through her, complete, mindless panic, as she lay there, not daring to move. Had Marc returned?

But no, Marc wouldn't simply have crawled in bed with her, would he? Marc had very definite ideas about what the bed and Claire's presence in it signified. And besides, why should she be frightened of Marc? He had never hurt her, and she had only Madame Langlois's word for it that he'd hurt her daughter. No, her growing distrust of Marc had no logical basis in physical fear.

Still, she was frightened. In the predawn light and her sleep-disrupted panic she had to consider whether the stranger in her bed was the murderer who'd been haunting Paris the last few months. But no, they only murdered old women, didn't they? Not thirty-year-old Americans.

Slowly, carefully, she turned her head, terrified of what she might find, of the monster that had invaded her bed during the night, waiting to rip her limb from limb.

Lying next to her, on top of the covers, was the small, defenseless form of Nicole.

Relief and wonder washed over Claire. She shifted carefully, so as not to wake her visitor, and stared down at the

child's face. Nicole looked younger in her sleep, less terrify-
ingly precocious. Her eyes were puffy and swollen, with the
dried trace of tears beneath them, and she was curled in a
fetal ball, as if even in sleep she knew she had to protect
herself.

Yet she'd come to Claire, a fact that amazed her. Despite
the uneasy truce that characterized their relationship, she'd
sought out Claire for a comforting presence.

The room was damp and chilly in the early-morning light.
Claire had made the bed the way Marc liked it, with a top
sheet and a duvet, no blankets. Carefully Claire lifted the
duvet away and wrapped it around the child's body. Nicole
shifted once, sighing, and sank back into a deep, dreamless
sleep.

Claire lay there, shivering under the light sheet, watching
the child, fighting the wave of maternal tenderness that had
swept over her. It was too much for a little girl, first to lose a
mother, then to be caught between a stepfather's coldness
and a grandmother's paranoia. It should come as no surprise when Nicole turned to the only person who demanded
no allegiance and only wished to offer comfort.

Usually Nicole wouldn't accept that comfort. Last night's
dreams must have been particularly bad to send her into
Claire's bedroom, a bedroom Nicole always assiduously
avoided. Looking down at her, Claire's indecision vanished,
the last of her doubts fled. She wouldn't, couldn't leave
Nicole behind to the tender mercies of Marc and Madame
Langlois.

Didn't Nicole have a great-aunt somewhere outside of
L.A.? Hadn't that been where Madame Langlois spent the
last year or so? If Claire moved swiftly, before Marc decided
to return from his so-called tour, she could take Nicole out
of the country, leave her with her great-aunt, and then
disappear.

It would doubtless be against the law. Could France
extradite her for kidnapping? And was it kidnapping if she
was taking the child to a close blood relative?

All that was academic. She had already committed a
criminal act and hurt a child in doing so. Perhaps another

criminal act to help a child might even the score a bit. Not in the eyes of the law, but in her own, troubled soul.

She wouldn't hesitate. This morning, after Nicole went off to Madame Langlois, she would go to the American Express office where, thank God, everyone spoke English. She would get two tickets for Los Angeles on the next possible flight, and then they would simply leave.

She imagined Marc's anger when he returned from his nonexistent tour and found them gone. Not that he cared for Nicole, but he wasn't likely to willingly give up ownership of anything, even an unwelcome nine-year-old. And to lose his control over Claire would make him livid.

Claire shivered in the dawn light, telling herself it was the chilly room. She allowed herself a brief, longing thought of Tom, then forcibly dismissed it from her mind. The right man, but the wrong time and place. It wasn't meant to be.

She'd have more than enough to keep her mind occupied, away from regrets for what might have been. She'd have to find Nicole's passport and put it with her own, she'd have to find the great-aunt's name and address. She'd have to pack for both of them, surreptitiously, and think of something reasonable to get Nicole on the plane. While she'd be more than happy to leave her stepfather and the coldly elegant apartment that had once belonged to her mother, she wouldn't willingly part with her grandmother.

Of course, Harriette Langlois might very well assist Claire in her plan. If she truly believed Marc was so dangerous, she should be glad to have her granddaughter sent out of harm's way.

But could Claire trust her? Would Madame assist her, help cover for her if Marc should return unexpectedly, support her in case the French courts were more active than Claire hoped? Or would she demand that Nicole stay with her, a constant audience to her persecution complex, until Marc took her away again?

No, she didn't dare risk it. She'd leave Madame a note, explaining what she had done, and it would be up to the old lady to help or hinder the aftermath. At least she wouldn't be able to interfere with their escape.

Nicole stirred in her sleep, murmuring something low. The word was universal; even in its French form Claire understood it. She was calling for her mother.

Claire blinked back the hot tears that had suddenly formed in her eyes. Come hell or high water she'd get Nicole safely away. Then, and not until then, she'd begin to deal with her own problems.

Harriette Langlois lay alone in the bed, watching the sunrise as she had every morning for the last thirty years. Except for her hideous, self-imposed exile in America, she corrected herself, watching the sky slowly lighten. The bed beneath her frail body had long ago conformed to her contours, so that she lay, cradled in the softness in a place that clearly belonged to no one but her.

The Americans bought new mattresses every ten years or so, her sister had said. They turned their mattresses every few months to keep the surfaces hard. Just another example of new-world stupidity, Harriette thought, sniffing contemptuously. With their constant need to spend money they would never have the luxury of owning a mattress that really knew them.

It was a shame she couldn't die in this comfortable bed, but she'd already mourned that fact. She had never shirked her duty in her life, and she wasn't about to do so now. She wasn't going to die without taking Marc Bonnard down with her, and since fate and medicine had decreed her death was growing imminent, her need to act was also imminent.

She thought back to the man dear Hubert had sent her. She didn't even know his name, nor did she want to. She'd originally planned to ask whoever appeared to do it as painlessly as possible. One look into the man's flat, dark eyes and she knew it would be a waste of her breath.

She'd faced terrible things in her life. She'd stayed during the long, terrible years when the Boches invaded Paris, she'd watched her beloved husband die slowly, painfully, she'd survived the cruellest blow of all, the death of her only child. She would face this, and do it without flinching.

But Lord, the bed was so comfortable, the scent of her lilac toilet water hung lightly in the air, and all around her were the dear, familiar things she'd had for so long. If only fate had decided, for once, to be kind.

In the early-morning hours, Harriette Langlois allowed herself a brief, uncharacteristic moment of self-pity. No one would see, no one would know. In another few hours she would face the day, stalwart, unmoved, waiting for the moment when the dark, evil-looking creature would reappear.

It might be today, it might be a week from now. Harriette hoped it wouldn't be too long. The pain was getting very bad indeed, and Nicole had such sharp eyes.

At least Marc's American mistress was a blessed surprise. The woman had more brains than Harriette would have imagined, coupled with an honest concern for the child. She would see to Nicole.

And the man in the leather coat and dirty fingernails would see to her, Harriette thought. Soon, she hoped. Please God, make it soon.

The passports were gone. Claire sat back on her heels, staring at the scattered contents of her traveling bag in horrified disbelief. There was no sign of the slim blue folder with its unflattering photograph anywhere in the jumbled bag where she usually kept it. That bag usually sat at the back of the bedroom closet, where no one knew of its existence; no one could get to it except Claire. And Marc, of course.

Nicole's passport had been missing from its cubbyhole in the kitchen desk, but Claire had forced herself to be calm. To be sure, she thought she'd seen it just a couple of days ago. But she hadn't been looking, its presence or absence hadn't mattered then, and her perception of time might be unreliable.

But she knew where her passport should be. And it was most definitely gone.

Maybe, just maybe, in a moment of mindless distraction,

she'd taken both of them and put them in her purse. Lord knows she'd had enough on her mind in the last few days to compromise the concentration of an automaton. Perhaps she'd been sleepwalking.

She raced through the empty apartment, grabbed her leather purse, and upended it on the pale rose Aubusson carpet that graced the formal salon. Lint and shreds of cigarette tobacco littered the floor, and a pen landed, making a small black spot. Claire stared at it in horror. No one else would notice the spot, no one but Marc. It would be the first thing he saw when he walked in, and her panic grew.

No passports in her purse, nothing. She flipped through her large wallet, hoping it might be tucked in there, but there was nothing, the little leather pockets yielding only more lint. She started to put it away when she realized something else. Her American Express card, her one link with financial freedom, was gone.

She heard the sound of the muffled moan, and knew it came from her. She'd seen the card yesterday—she had no doubt at all of that. Someone had been in the apartment, in her purse, removing the broken Limoges cup, the passports, her one way of escape. That someone had to be Marc.

"Stop it," she ordered herself sharply, her voice unnaturally loud in the still apartment. "He's just trying to frighten you. The American embassy will get you a new passport, American Express will get you a new card. You aren't trapped."

Brave words. But how was she going to get another passport for Nicole? Even if she spoke French, how would she be able to convince the suspicious French bureaucrats that she had the right to replace a French child's passport, had the right to take her out of the country?

Could she leave her behind? Claire thought back to the small form curled up on her bed, her shy, ultimately defiant awakening, the surprisingly peaceful breakfast they'd shared. Their relationship had passed to a new level last night, one of reluctantly admitted trust. No, Claire couldn't leave Nicole behind.

"First things first," she said out loud, her voice deliberate. Was Marc hiding somewhere in the apartment, someplace she couldn't find? She wasn't about to go searching again. Twice she'd searched this apartment in the last two days. She didn't want three to be the charm. She didn't want to open a closet door and see Marc's face there, watching her.

She dumped the contents of her purse back inside, shoveling everything in, stabbing herself on the pen. It was cold and damp and raw looking outside, but Claire was afraid to open the hall closet to fetch her raincoat. She ran back to the bedroom, to the closet she already knew was empty, and grabbed what she could find, a heavy wool sweater that would repel the rain. It didn't matter that it would go oddly with the thin challis dress and leather pumps. All that mattered was that she get the hell out of the apartment and get her passport and American Express card replaced. And then she'd worry about Nicole.

Rocco sat in the dark corner of the café, drinking his coffee. This was his home territory, everyone knew that the table was his, that the café was under his protection, and everyone stayed out of his way. He sat there, smoking, thinking, left in peace because everyone was too afraid of him to bother him. Even Bobo behind the bar moved very carefully when he came over to refill Rocco's cup.

It had been a strange meeting yesterday afternoon. Odd indeed to see him after so long, to still feel the same pull, the same excitement. Marc Bonnard had always had it, that magic something that drew people to him. It was no wonder he'd been able to lead a motley band of downtrodden orphans into a revolt against their tormentors.

What had been surprising was the violence that had erupted from Marc's lily-white fingers. In Gilles and himself it was to be expected—they were rough boys from the slums of Paris. Gilles had been sent away by a weary grandmother for torturing and killing animals, cats and dogs and the like. Rocco had, at age thirteen, been the oldest and already a hardened criminal. He was an adept pickpocket, and he'd killed a man just before his own rattled *grand-mère* had sent him down. The man had caught him with his wallet and started yelling for the police. Rocco had had no choice. What had surprised him was how easy it was. And what a feeling of power it had given him.

His father's mother had soon deprived him of that power. Whether she'd suspected his criminal activities or not, she'd had enough of an unwanted boy watching her every move. She still plied her trade every now and then, when she could find someone unfastidious enough to want a fat, fifty-year-old whore, and a grandson got in the way. So she'd sent him away from his beloved streets of Paris, to the Marie-le-Croix orphanage and the tender mercies of *Grand-mère* Estelle and Georges.

He'd paid her back for it, the moment he'd returned to Paris. The memory still had the ability to make him smile.

But Marc's preorphanage upbringing had been different. Middle-class, respectable, his childhood was all that Rocco's wasn't. He didn't know how Marc's parents had died—Marc would never talk about them. But his grandmother, a well-dressed bitch with a mink coat, had dropped Marc off not long after Rocco had arrived. And she'd never come back.

Still and all, it had been Marc who'd talked them into resisting. Marc who'd planned the fire. Marc who'd honed the kitchen knives for them, passing them out that night so long ago. And it was Marc who'd struck the first blow, a savage grin on his angelic boy's face. Marc who'd taken the first bite.

That was a memory Rocco wasn't comfortable with, and he lit another cigarette, shuddering slightly. He'd always considered himself a tough kid, a hard, remorseless man, but there were certain things that had the ability to shake even him.

Marc hadn't changed. He was still almost unnaturally handsome, with mesmerizing dark eyes and a charming, ready smile. He seemed perfectly at ease, doing his best to make Rocco feel as comfortable, but it had all been in vain. Too many years, too many strange and terrible things, lay between them. Rocco sat far away from him on the park bench and wished he'd never come.

"So my *belle-mère* wants you to murder her?" Marc had said gently, his upper-class accent making Rocco want to puke. "And frame me? Bless her heart, I didn't know the old bitch had it in her."

"She's sick. Probably dying anyway," Rocco said, looking at his rain-soaked boots rather than the man next to him. "She had too many pills by her kitchen sink, and her eyes were yellow."

"I expect she would like to take me with her." Bonnard's voice was dreamy, musing. "I'm afraid we'll have to thwart that final wish of hers, much as it grieves me."

Rocco only nodded, staring at his boots.

"I must say, I appreciate this, old friend," Marc continued softly. "While part of me deplores the necessity of our meeting, another part welcomes it. I've wanted to compliment you on your artistry. It's always been easy to tell which has been you and which has been poor Gilles."

"You heard about him?"

"And Yvon. So our ranks are diminished, Rocco. We must be careful."

Rocco nodded, not raising his head. "Shall I take care of your mother-in-law?"

"I think not. I will reserve that pleasure for myself."

"Is that wise?"

"Probably not. But we all have to take risks sometimes, and this is one I can't resist. We can put this one to good use, though. The police have had their suspicions of you, am I right?"

Rocco nodded. For some reason he felt thirteen again, listening to his leader with mingled resentment and respect. He sat very still, waiting for Marc to make his plans, to give him his orders.

"Well, we must make sure that Madame Langlois meets her fate at a time when you are very well, and publicly accounted for. It should make the police livid." Bonnard laughed softly, and the sound ran like a razor across Rocco's backbone.

"The man in charge of the investigation is Louis Malgreave," Rocco mumbled, despising himself. "He's a fool, of course, but not as big a fool as most."

"He hasn't caught us yet," Marc pointed out gently. He looked upward, at the gray, drizzling sky. "We're due for more rain, are we not?"

"Something more than this stupid gray piss?" Rocco said. "So I hear. Tomorrow and the day after."

"All right. The first rainy day. At five-thirty in the afternoon, I think. By that time my darling little stepdaughter will be home, and Harriette will be all alone. I'll take care of the old lady, making enough noise when I leave so that she'll be found immediately. In the meantime, you might choose that time to make a little visit to Malgreave. Take your lawyer with you, and demand he stop harassing you. It should be very effective." Bonnard's beautiful face shone with delicious anticipation.

"How can you be sure the old bitch won't leave something incriminating? She thinks she'll be able to frame you."

"She never was a match for me, and she never will be. It was stupid of her to even think she could attempt it. Never fear, old friend. By the end of the next rainy day Harriette Langlois will be dead and we will both have perfect alibis."

And without hesitation Rocco had believed him.

He sat in the café, staring into the coffee cup. The rain was supposed to start later that morning. Today would be the day—Bonnard had never been one for procrastinating. It would serve them both well, Rocco had to admit it, and it would drive Malgreave utterly crazy.

Still and all, old habits died hard. The moment he came within his sphere he was an underling once more, a skinny pickpocket from the streets of Paris in awe of the upper classes. And he didn't like that feeling, not one tiny bit.

With any luck at all he'd never have to meet with him again. Once more he had to admit that Marc had been right, and the rules he had laid down twenty years ago had been wise ones. They should never meet. Better to go their own ways, without having any contact with each other, any the police could trace.

For Rocco's sense of well-being, he was more than happy to keep that covenant from now on. As far as he was concerned he would be happy never to see Marc again. He hadn't deferred to anyone for years, and now he was feeling like an adolescent again, awed by a boy younger and weaker than he was. Not anymore. He didn't like the feeling, and he had no intention of letting Marc gain power over him again. He'd kill him first, and break the chain of dependence.

The more he thought about it the calmer he felt. That was exactly what he would do. As long as Bonnard kept away from him things would be fine. Otherwise Bonnard would simply join Achilles and the Spaniard in the limitless repository of the Seine.

Twenty-four hours for a new American Express card. Three to five days for a new passport. Claire was back out on the damp streets in less than an hour, her pleas and anguished demands going for nothing. Finally she gave up, accepting defeat at the hands of the State Department and James Donner for the time being. At least the wheels had started turning. Maybe there was some way it could be expedited, some way she hadn't yet discovered. There was no way on earth she could sit in that apartment for three days, waiting for Marc to come back.

It was raining again. According to Donner's secretary it was going to rain for the rest of the week. And Claire knew if she didn't get out soon she'd go absolutely mad.

At least she'd arranged for Nicole to stay longer with her grandmother today. While the old lady might have paranoid delusions, anything was better than the haunted apartment. She would go pick Nicole up herself after six today, and they'd eat dinner at a bistro instead of cooking. She might even drag Nicole to an English-language movie on the pretext of improving her vocabulary. That is, if she could find one suitable for a nine-year-old.

One more night in the apartment. Tomorrow she'd have the new American Express card, and they'd start making the rounds of hotels, moving every couple of days so Marc wouldn't be able to find them.

Tomorrow, when Claire felt more able to face it, she would tell Madame Langlois what she had planned. The old woman might even have Nicole's passport. If she didn't, she would know how to get a new one. With the number of bureaucrats working in Paris they would doubtless be able to get it faster than Claire's.

One more night. Surely they could all survive that long?

❧ CHAPTER 13

Typewriter keyboards were made for smaller fingers, Tom thought, staring down at the X'ed-out mess in front of him. How in the hell did Hemingway, not to mention Thomas Wolfe, manage to control one of these tiny keyboards without his fingers getting stuck?

Maybe he didn't. Tom pushed back from the table in disgust. The room was dark and gloomy on such a rainy day, and he couldn't concentrate. It was no wonder. Bonnard's apartment had been deserted—no ghostly images at either the second- or third-floor windows, no answer to his insistent pounding on the doors on both floors, no answers to his telephone calls when he gave up and went back to his apartment. For a moment he allowed himself the macabre fantasy of Claire lying bruised and bleeding behind one of those heavy doors, and then he dismissed the notion. Claire was right—Bonnard wasn't the violent type. Was he?

Tom shook his head, trying to wipe the grisly image from his mind. The sooner he faced life and his own limitations, the sooner he returned to New York and reality, the better. He'd take with him the memory of two years spent chasing rainbows, a time when he'd indulged every creative whim that had passed his way. That memory should help him through a life devoted to more prosaic matters.

Of course he could take something else back from Paris besides memories and uncomfortable self-knowledge. He could take Claire MacIntyre. And he had every intention of doing his damnedest to ensure that happened.

He got up and crossed the room, restless, edgy, uncertain, ending up by the rain-streaked skylight. It was no wonder he was going nuts. This constant rain was enough to drive anyone crazy.

Where the hell was Claire? Why didn't she answer the goddamned telephone, why didn't she show up at his doorstep and sleep in his bed again? Damn it, had he scared her off so badly with that simple kiss?

He didn't think so. Despite her confusion, despite her anxiety and uncertainty, he had the suspicion that she didn't scare easily. If she didn't want him to kiss her again she'd simply tell him.

Most likely she didn't know whether she wanted him to or not. Or even better, she knew, but didn't like the answer. Tom stood staring over the gloomy, rain-swept rooftops of Paris, wishing there was something he could do to help her make up her mind. He knew, with a depressing certainty, that the best thing he could do was give her time.

In the meantime, he had friends in Paris, friends who either knew things or could find them out. Claude was a journalist for one of the leftist newspapers. While the Théâtre du Mime didn't normally fall under their jurisdiction, Tom had great faith in Claude's contacts. If Claude couldn't find out something about Marc Bonnard, then no one could.

He looked out into the rain once more. The last thing he wanted was to spend more time on the cold, wet streets of Paris. With a resigned sigh he reached for his navy jacket and pulled the collar up around his neck. Some things were worth the trouble, some things weren't. There was no question at all in his mind where Claire MacIntyre fit in the scheme of things. And he headed out into the icy rain.

He wasn't home, damn it. Claire leaned against the flimsy, locked door, panting from the six-flight climb. She could feel tears of exhaustion and frustration burn her eyes, and angrily she rubbed them away, smearing her flawless makeup. She couldn't afford to spend her time moping around weeping. Too much depended on her, Nicole depended on her.

She moved to the landing window. Why in the world had Tom gone out on such a miserable day? She'd never even considered he might not be home. It had taken every ounce of her courage, every ounce of self-justification, to make the climb, to steel herself to face him, to tell him what she'd planned.

All that courage screwed up for nothing. Damn and double damn. She looked down at the thin, feminine watch on her slender wrist. Marc had given it to her, disliking the flat, masculine diver's watch she'd always worn. When she got back to the apartment she'd take off the watch and dump it, she promised herself.

In the meantime it was only two in the afternoon, hours before she was due to pick up Nicole, and nothing to fill her time. She wasn't going back to that apartment alone, she couldn't walk the chilly, damp streets of Paris or she'd be courting double pneumonia, and she couldn't just sit here and wait.

Or could she? Tom lived alone on the top floor—no one would come along and bother her. She sank down on the top step, ignoring the dust and mud, and leaned her head against the stained, peeling wall. It had been so long since she'd slept through the night. One more night, and there'd be the safety of an anonymous hotel room, with clean white sheets and no one knowing where to find them. Closing her eyes, she smiled faintly at the delicious picture and fell sound asleep.

"Nothing," said Josef, looking disgusted and quite human for a change. "Absolutely nothing."

Malgreave roused himself from his contemplation of his pencil. Things had gotten worse, so much worse. He and Marie had exchanged no more than ten words in the last two days. Of course, he had never been a loquacious man.

147

And his hours had been longer than usual, as the case heated up. Two suspects dead within forty-eight hours, three new victims in the last week. They'd picked up the butcher's assistant on suspicion of murder, but they were going to have to let him go. There wasn't enough to pin Sahut's death on the boy, and Malgreave didn't give a damn. If anything, young Edgar had done the world a favor.

Malgreave ran a weary hand through his thinning hair. Things were escalating, usually a good sign. He'd dealt with enough homicides over the years to know—when the killing frenzy became overwhelming the victims began to pile up. And mistakes were made.

He looked over at Josef. "Nothing?" he echoed, hoping he sounded knowledgeable. He spent far too much time mooning over Marie. He had to learn to let go, to accept whatever she decided. He had to keep his mind on business.

"The orphanage," Josef said patiently. "There were no records left."

"That's absurd. There must have been something. We're a nation of bureaucrats, Josef. Somewhere in the Ministry of Records there must be folders and folders of information on the Marie-le-Croix orphanage." Josef had gotten his interest by now, his domestic problems forgotten.

Josef shook his head. "As far as I can tell the place was started for war orphans. It was in existence less than twenty years, and there is nothing, absolutely nothing, on file since the late nineteen-forties."

Malgreave stared at his assistant, at the uncharacteristic smugness around Josef's prim mouth. "What is it? There's something you're just waiting to spring on me, I know you too well."

Josef's smile broadened to an outright grin. "I was fortunate enough to talk with the deputy assistant to the under–associate secretary. You may remember him, a man by the name of Balfour?"

Malgreave shook his head impatiently, waiting.

But Josef was not to be hurried. "Well, he remembered you. He remembered the fuss you made when Rocco Guillère's file disappeared two years ago, and your demand that a thorough investigation be made, to see what else was missing. He doesn't like you very much, sir."

Malgreave waved away such inconsequential information. "Get on with it, Josef. Though I hope and pray I know where you're going."

"Of course you do, sir. The only other files taken at the time of the Guillère file were the Marie-le-Croix orphanage files. Including records of inmates and the complete investigation of its destruction."

Malgreave leaned back, sighing, a broad smile wreathing his lined face. "Josef," he said, "we're going to get them."

"Yes, sir," said Josef, beaming. "I believe we are."

Tom trudged upward. He had to admit, he was getting tired of a sixth-floor walk-up. It wasn't that he minded the exercise. He just didn't like it forced upon him, particularly on a cold, gray day following a sleepless night. As he paused on the fourth-floor landing he thought longingly of clean, soulless condos and self-service elevators.

The smells of the ancient hallways surrounded him, that familiar smell of cabbage and dead fish and fresh bread and cats. It wasn't as unpleasant as it sounded, and he had no doubt he'd miss it when he was back in the manufactured air of his New York apartment.

Today the smell was subtly different, and he paused, sniffing, trying to place it. The dampness brought out the worst of the old building, adding mildew to the aromatic pot, but there was something new. The faint, lingering trace of flowers in the air. Someone must have a new lover, he thought as he climbed higher. Or a new perfume. If the scent was bottled, he'd have to find out what it was. There was something indefinably arousing about it. It reminded him of warm summer afternoons, and soft breezes, and spring flowers, and . . . Claire, it reminded him of Claire.

He took the next flight three steps at a time, racing around the corner landing and stopping short, staring up at her. She was still asleep, her red gold head against the wall, her hands resting lightly in her lap. She was wearing those ridiculous high-heeled shoes, and from his vantage point he could see her slender, silk-covered ankles were splashed with mud. The heavy sweater was beaded with moisture, and it looked far too big for her slender body.

There were purple circles under her eyes, and she looked pale. Even in sleep her soft mouth looked determined, and he knew he was right. She might be confused, but she didn't frighten easily.

As he started up the final flight of stairs, she opened her eyes and looked down at him. He stopped, not moving, standing a few feet below her.

"You're all right." His voice, when it came out, sounded like a boy in the throes of adolescence. It cracked, betraying his fear, betraying his caring.

"I'm all right," she said.

"I was out looking for you."

"I was here."

"Bonnard didn't come home last night?"

He couldn't miss the faint tremor of fright that danced across her pale face. "No. Why would you think so?"

Now that his immediate hormonal rush was under control he continued on up the stairs, slowly, so as not to panic her into instant flight. He answered her question with his own. "What floor do you live on?"

"I thought I told you. The second floor."

"What do you consider the second floor? How many flights of stairs do you take?"

"I take the elevator." The small attempt at a joke came out rather forlorn, and she accompanied it with a self-deprecating smile.

He'd reached her side by then, and it was all he could do not to pull her into his arms. "If the elevator was broken?"

"One flight of stairs. I'm lazy."

"You're on the first floor, then," he said wearily, his worst fears confirmed. "In Europe the first floor is the ground floor, the second the first, etc. I don't suppose there's another apartment on that floor?"

"No, there isn't," she said. "Do I want to know why you're asking me these things?"

"Probably not. Someone was upstairs watching us yesterday afternoon."

She flinched. "You mean, when you kissed me?"

"Yes." He waited, half hoping she'd dissolve in tears again as she had yesterday, hoping he'd have an excuse to touch her. She didn't and while he regretted the lost opportunity he felt his longing and admiration increase.

She stood up, slowly, straightening her shoulders as if preparing to face an invisible enemy. "It must have been Marc."

"Why do you say that?"

"I don't think he is gone. I think he's been hiding, somewhere, sneaking into the apartment and watching me. How's that for paranoia?" Her voice was cool, brittle.

"I'd say you might have reason to be paranoid."

"I might indeed."

"Come inside," he said. "I'll make you a cup of tea, or we'll open a bottle of wine and we'll figure out what you're going to do."

She shook her head, the damp, red gold hair swirling, and he could smell that wonderful, elusive scent again. "Could we go to a café, please?"

"Out into the rain again? My apartment's drier and quieter, and we're here already."

"No," she said.

"Why not?" He knew the answer, but he wanted to hear her say it, admit it.

"Because if we go in there we'll end up in bed. And I'm not ready to do that." She looked up into his eyes, her gaze fearless and unflinching. "I can't keep hopping from bed to bed, looking for someone to take care of my problems. I got myself into this mess and I need to get myself out of it."

"Before you get yourself into another one with me." He finished it for her, his light tone took the sting out of the words. "I bow to your superior wisdom. There's a café close by—we should only get slightly drowned. And once we get there you can tell me what you've decided to do, and how you're going to let me help you."

"You can buy the coffee," she said. "And you can lend me your American Express card." And without waiting for his response she started down the stairs.

He was chilled and wet to the bone. He was going to get pneumonia, he knew it. She was absolutely right—if they'd gone into his apartment they would have ended up in bed. And what a divine place to be, warm and dry and then hot and damp. Instead it was back out into the streets again, and he didn't even have the wistful fantasy that he was suffering for his art.

He was suffering for Claire MacIntyre, and she was more important than a dozen muddy paintings, an execrable play, three chapters of the worst novel in history, and cases and cases of bad wine. Without any hesitation Tom started after her. And if he was becoming obsessed with how soon he could get her back up all those interminable flights of stairs, he wasn't about to let her see it.

"For once I should get home on time," Malgreave announced, shuffling the folders on his desk and stacking them in a neat pile. Normally he hadn't such a precise nature—he left fussy behavior to his assistant. But the Grandmother Murders were of interest to too many people, and if he left his desk cluttered with his work in progress he would return hours later to find things shifted about.

Josef looked at his watch. "Five-thirty," he said. "Madame Malgreave will be pleased."

"You see too much," Malgreave grumbled. "And I'm no longer sure there's any way to please my wife." He rose, stretching wearily. "If only the damned rain would stop, maybe we'd have a night or two without interruptions."

Josef shook his head. "The forecast is for rain through Thursday."

"Damn," said Malgreave, reaching for the rumpled, still-damp raincoat that hung on a hook by his office door. He stopped, his arm outstretched, at the sight of the men standing in his doorway. In particular, by the look and smell of the first man, from his shiny black boots to his greasy, thinning black hair.

"Rocco," he said flatly, dropping his arm and heading back to his desk. "And who is this with you?"

"My solicitor." Guillère's voice was both raspy and high, and his flat, soulless eyes glittered with a hidden amusement.

"I thought as much," Malgreave said with a sigh, sinking back into his chair. "I suppose you've come to confess to the murders of the old women."

Rocco grinned, exposing an incomplete set of teeth. "No, Louis," he said with deliberate insolence. "We've come to insist you stop harassing me."

Malgreave smiled faintly. "We could compromise. I'll stop harassing you and you confess. It would make things very neat."

Rocco stepped into the room, and the smell was overpowering. "I didn't come here at . . ." he made an elaborate survey of the very expensive gold watch, ". . . at five-thirty-five to make jokes, Louis."

Malgreave admired the watch, and wondered where its owner rested. In the Seine, most likely. Rocco wasn't making much of an effort to be subtle, his contempt all too plain, but Malgreave could play the game.

"All right, Rocco," he said gently. "You and your lawyer sit down and tell me why you chose . . ." and he made a matching, deliberate perusal of his own utilitarian watch, ". . . a time as late as five-thirty-five to come to me."

Grand-mère's apartment was still and silent. Nicole sat at the kitchen table, chewing steadily on a peanut butter sandwich. Peanut butter was one of the few American things of which *Grand-mère* approved, and every day she and Nicole would eat thick sandwiches made with baguettes and plum preserves and imported peanut butter.

It was after five-thirty, and Nicole didn't really want another one. But she'd seen *Grand-mère*'s eyes drooping, as they did so often after she had to take one of her pills, and she knew that the old woman would welcome a few minutes of peace, to doze.

Nicole was usually gone by now, back at the apartment

she now thought of as His. Claire would be making her silly, inconsequential chatter, and they'd eat something awful, like macaroni and cheese or frozen pizza, and then they could watch TV and Nicole would explain everything to a confused Claire.

Sometimes she lied, and made up stories to fit the people on TV, stories that had nothing to do with what was really happening. Sometimes she lied about things in real life, too. Marc knew, and had punished her for it. Claire knew, and just ignored it. Maybe she'd tell Claire a lie tonight, tell her Marc had called, asking for her. It would be interesting to see if Claire would be happy or sad.

But she didn't need to lie to Claire to know the answer to that, she'd already seen it in her eyes. Claire was going to leave. She'd probably go without saying good-bye, Nicole thought, stolidly chewing the sandwich. She was surprised to find the thought pained her. Her mother had gone without saying good-bye. But then, her mother had died.

Claire wasn't going to die, she was simply going back where she belonged. And then she would be alone with Marc again. The thought gave her . . . what was Claire's wonderful American word . . . the creeps. It gave her the creeps.

Nicole dropped the crust back onto the plate. She'd dispose of the garbage and *Grand-mère* wouldn't have to know that she hadn't finished it all. Maybe she could talk Claire into buying some Coca-Cola. Another excellent American invention, though this one *Grand-mère* didn't approve of. But Nicole loved it with a passion. There were times when she wished she lived in the States and could drink all the Coke and eat all the peanut butter she wished. And never have to put up with Marc watching her, ever again.

He particularly liked to come in when she was in her bath. He would stand in the doorway, watching her, giving her clipped orders where to wash. The one time he tried to wash her himself, her mother had caught him. It was just before *Maman* had died, and Nicole would never forget how angry she was. She'd heard the two of them arguing that night,

154

low, bitter words. Actually she had only heard *Maman*—
Marc had retreated into his customary wall of silence, his
only response a mimed expression that made *Maman*
scream with rage.

At least he didn't fight with Claire. Claire behaved herself,
did everything she was told. As did Nicole herself. Life was
more peaceful now in the old apartment, and with *Grand-
mère* around there was always some place she could run to,
if things got too bad.

She didn't want Claire to go. It surprised her to realize it,
but she would miss her, miss her awful food and her silly
chatter and her clumsy efforts to take care of her. How could
Claire take care of her, protect her from Marc, when she
couldn't even take care of herself?

Nicole rose, scratching her scalp beneath the tightly
braided hair. Claire had tried to get her to wear her hair
down, even get it cut, but she had steadfastly refused. She
didn't like her hair. She could remember too vividly the
night Marc had come in, sat on the edge of her bed, and
stroked her hair—long, soft, horrid sort of strokes—while
he said absolutely nothing.

That was just before he'd left for America. He'd come
back with Claire, and he'd kept out of her room since then.
If Claire went, there'd be no one to stop him. And she didn't
know exactly why, but she didn't want him to come into her
room, ever again.

Maybe she could stay with *Grand-mère*. Marc had always
refused, but maybe if *Grand-mère* offered him some money
he might agree. He never had enough money, he would
often say. If it weren't for Nicole he wouldn't have to worry,
he would say. And Nicole would sit there, eyes downcast,
silent.

Maybe Claire wouldn't come fetch her tonight. Maybe
she'd already left. The thought was depressing. *Grand-mère*
was getting too old, the pills were making her forgetful. If
Claire had gone, who would take care of her?

She heard the noise at the front door with anger and
relief. At least Claire hadn't left yet. With her characteristic
silence she rose from the kitchen table, moved to the door,

155

and pushed it open a crack. She had a perfect view of the living room, of *Grand-mère*'s sleeping figure. It would be interesting to hear what the two women had to say to each other when they thought Nicole wasn't around.

She hadn't been able to hear a word yesterday, but *Grand-mère*'s maid Geneviève had been there, watching her to make sure she didn't eavesdrop. Nicole was alone in the apartment now, with no one to stop her from snooping.

She pushed the door open a little more. She couldn't see Claire yet—she was still in the hall. *Grand-mère* was waking up, foggy, befuddled, staring at her visitor in sleepy amazement.

"What in God's name are you doing here?" she demanded in a sleepy croak. In French. The visitor wasn't Claire.

Nicole started to let the door swing shut in silent disappointment. Perhaps she'd left Paris after all.

Then she heard the last voice she would ever have expected. Her stepfather's soft, beguiling tones.

"What do you think I'm doing, Harriette?" he replied gently. "I'm here to fulfill your fantasies." And as he moved into the room, Nicole saw that he held a knife.

⚞ CHAPTER 14

Harriette blinked her eyes rapidly, trying to clear her brain of the mists of sleep and pain-killers that had fogged it. Surely she must be dreaming. It couldn't be her hated son-in-law standing there, a small, charming smile on his too-handsome face, contemplating her with a knife in his hand.

She struggled to sit up, her body protesting. "What fantasies?" she said calmly, as behind her impassive face her brain suddenly began working. How long had she slept? Surely Nicole had left by now, was safely home with Claire. Did she dare say anything to the man standing in front of her? Or would she be signing Nicole's death warrant by doing so?

Marc made no sound at all as he advanced into the room, his every movement a graceful, exaggerated gesture. She half expected him to be in whiteface, but of course he wasn't. That same, exaggerated grief wreathed his face, mocking her, as he sank down on the chintz-covered sofa beside her, the knife clasped loosely in his hand.

Harriette looked down at the knife, trying not to be squeamish. It was long, with a thin blade, and there was no discernible trace of dried blood on it. It looked very sharp, and more than effective, and Marc handled it as if he was quite used to it.

"Harriette, don't fence with me," he said softly, his voice a surprise after the thick silence. "You've been very clumsy. While I admit your plan was ingenious, you weren't aware of a few basic flaws."

He couldn't know. But then, if he didn't, what was he doing here with a knife? "What plan?"

"Don't be childish, it irritates me. You wanted to frame me for the murders that have been plaguing Paris, and you were willing to die in order to do so. Your dedication is admirable, but it won't work."

"Why not?" She sounded icy calm, as, indeed, she was. She wasn't afraid of dying, and there was a certain savage satisfaction at doing so by his hands. He would be caught. He had killed her daughter, now he would kill her, and with any luck at all he would make a mistake, enough of a mistake to get caught. Claire had been warned—she wouldn't just sit by and ignore the possibilities.

"Because they will not catch me."

"You may have been able to cover up Isabelle's murder," she said, "but a second one will prove harder."

"Harriette, my dear, the police will simply consider you to be one more in a string of senseless murders, with nothing whatsoever to tie you to me. I'm in the south of France right now, visiting friends. I will be saddened and distressed to hear about your unfortunate end, and I will rush back to Paris to comfort my grieving, much wealthier stepdaughter."

"Pig."

Marc's smile broadened. "And you're mistaken about something, dear Harriette. You won't be my second murder. You'll be my fourteenth. You get your wish, darling. You will be killed by one of Paris's serial killers, one who's had a great deal of practice getting away with it."

She didn't move. She looked into Marc's flat black eyes and saw calm, implacable madness lurking there. Madness and death. Slowly she nodded, leaning back against the cushions of the sofa. "Very well," she said with calm, icy contempt. "I'll have to hope your luck won't hold out. At least I know that sooner or later you'll be caught. You'll pay for killing Isabelle."

"I doubt it, *Belle-mère*. I expect to . . . what was that?"

Harriette didn't even blink. She'd heard it too, the quiet, almost imperceptible thump from the kitchen, and she realized with dawning horror that Nicole was still there, in the apartment, listening to every word.

"I heard nothing," she said in a flat voice. If only there was some way she could draw him out of the apartment, away from Nicole. It would be impossible. He was only inches away from her—if she tried to run he would catch her before she even left the couch. And she couldn't bear the thought of an undignified struggle. She could scarcely stand the thought of his hands on her at all.

"Of course you heard nothing," Marc said. "You're old."

Distract him, she thought desperately. Make him forget that noise. "Tell me, Marc," she said in a voice suited to infuriate him. "Your slovenly friend who was here yesterday. The one who must have told you about our little arrangement. Does he kill the old ladies too?"

"Very astute, Harriette. Fortunately I have a certain power over him. Otherwise he might have insisted on taking care of you himself. You're a popular woman. If the others were still alive I have no doubt they would have wanted to have a go at you. I would have loved to have left you to Gilles's tender mercies, but alas . . ."

"The others?" Some of her icy calm slipped. "What in God's name have you been doing?"

"I told you, murdering grandmothers," he said. "And we haven't been doing it in God's name at all."

He moved closer to her, so close she could smell the very expensive aftershave he favored. She had bought it for him herself one Christmas, back when Isabelle had first married him and everything had seemed to be fine. She wanted to vomit.

She pulled together the last remnants of calm. She had lived with dignity, she would die with it. She was tempted to ask Marc why, but she controlled her curiosity. In a few more moments it wouldn't matter anyway, and she could tell he longed to brag. She wouldn't ask, she wouldn't fight, she'd keep her contempt intact. "What are you waiting for?" she demanded.

"In a hurry?" he purred. "I don't like to be rushed."

"If I were you I wouldn't linger too long. People come and go around here."

"I won't linger. I have to be gone by six o'clock, and I have only a few minutes left. Long enough to take care of you," he said gently, "and then go out to the kitchen and find who's hiding there."

"There's no one in the kitchen."

"Really? I'm afraid I'll have to check for myself." He leaned closer, so that his scent filled her nostrils, and she felt as if she were choking. She shut her eyes, trying to still the uncontrollable shudders that were wracking her body. Her ancestors had died on the guillotine, died with grace and dignity in the face of a howling mob. She could die just as well.

She felt the shock of his wet lips on her withered, dry ones. His tongue entered her mouth at the same moment the knife entered her heart, and she sighed. So very easy after all.

He laid her out very carefully on the chintz sofa, folding her hands across the neat wound. How many times had he seen her, sitting on that sofa, staring at him with stony contempt? Her early attempts at graciousness had been even worse, burning an implacable hatred into his soul.

How fitting to lay her out on the chintz, with her blood staining the soft pink upholstery. He'd harbored a small wish that she would fight him, but deep down he'd known better than to hope for that. She knew him too well, knew what he wanted from her and refused to give it. He looked down at her, into the milky, staring blue eyes, and smiled.

Five minutes to six. He didn't have much time. If she wasn't found within ten minutes his careful planning would help no one. He couldn't afford to dawdle.

On silent feet he moved to the kitchen door. Pushing it open, he looked into the empty, brightly lit interior, and whispered, "Nicole."

There was no sign of her, but he knew she was there. The back door was bolted on this side, she couldn't have made her escape, and the only other exit would have brought her past him. Granted, he'd been preoccupied for the last few minutes, but even at the point of orgasm he would have noticed his precious little stepdaughter tiptoeing past.

He tried it again, his voice a soft croon. "Nicole," he cajoled. She wasn't under the table, he could see that much, or hiding behind the door. With seeming unconcern he walked over to the sink and began washing the blood from the knife.

Still no sound. If she could see, she would have betrayed herself. A child of nine doesn't view her grandmother's blood lightly. Perhaps he'd been mistaken.

But no, his hearing was more acute than others', honed by years of working in silence. He'd heard that tiny, scuffling noise, and seen Harriette's reaction. He finished cleaning the knife, washing his hands carefully before turning to survey the blank wall of cupboards in front of him.

"I know you're there, Nicole," he said gently. "Come out."

Still nothing. He crossed the room and began opening cabinets, methodically, peering into the neatly arranged interiors. China, casseroles, copper cookware, but no nine-year-old. He slammed the doors shut in fury. There was no need to make it painless with Nicole. She wasn't part of the covenant—he could do whatever he wanted with her, and he would take great pleasure in doing so. He would cram a lifetime of emotion and sensation into her last few hours on earth. Indeed, it would be a kindness.

She wasn't in the cupboards. Maybe he was wrong, maybe in his heightened state he'd only imagined the sound. Or maybe not. If she'd been in the kitchen she was gone now, how he wasn't quite certain.

She usually left quite promptly at five. Chances were

she'd done so today, was safely back with Claire, never realizing her beloved *grand-mère* was breathing her last in the arms of her stepfather.

He needn't worry. He could make his plans carefully. Tomorrow he would return to the bosom of his makeshift family, and the first chance he got he would take care of Nicole. And he would take his time doing so, savoring every moment.

The kitchen door shut behind him. The sound of footsteps died away, but still Nicole didn't move. He was clever, he was hideous and mean and clever, and he knew how to make the right moves, the right noises to make it appear one thing when it was the other. He could be right outside the door, waiting for her to move. She wouldn't.

When she'd seen the knife she'd hidden in the first place she could find. She crawled under the sink, pulling back against the pipes, wrapping herself up in a tight bundle, and waited, silent tears streaming down her face.

There had been no outcry from the front room, not as there was on TV. No screams, nothing but the quiet murmur of voices and then silence. She'd pulled back out of the way when he'd walked in the door, not even breathing as he called her name. All he had to do was squat down and he would have seen her. But he didn't. His legs were only inches away from her nose as he ran the water in the sink. One of the pipes grew very hot, burning her arm, but she still didn't make a sound.

When he began opening the cupboards she knew she was lost. She knew he was going to find her, going to drag her out from under the sink and kill her with the knife he still held. She'd shut her eyes, bit down hard on her lip, and waited.

And then he was gone. Nicole's tears dried on her face, and she felt her heart grow small and hard within her. She waited, unable and unwilling to move, waited for someone to find her, hoping against hope that Claire hadn't abandoned her after all.

* * *

"Don't look at me like that."

"I'm not looking at you in any particular way," Claire said, striving for calm. She reached out and fiddled with her coffee, refusing to meet his eyes.

"All right, it was a stupid, romantic gesture. I wanted to experience life as it really was, without the cushion of credit cards," Tom said somewhat desperately, running a hand through his thick, curly hair. "Listen, I didn't turn them in, I just left them back in the States. I could get a replacement for my American Express card in less than twenty-four hours."

"So can I. Don't worry about it, Tom. We'll be fine. One more night in that apartment won't kill us."

"But what about Bonnard?"

"I'm sure Marc is touring somewhere in the south and that Solange was wrong."

"Then what happened to your passport and credit cards?"

"A sneak thief."

"A sneak thief who specializes in passports and credit cards? Surely there was something of value in that place besides the contents of your wallet?"

"Maybe the thief was part of a band of terrorists, looking for new identification papers to get people out of the country. Under normal circumstances it would have been weeks, months before I looked for my passport. It may have already been missing that long."

"You've been reading too much Ludlum." Tom was clearly disapproving. "Even if a female terrorist wanted to get out of France posing as you, why would she want a passport for a nine-year-old?"

"Maybe terrorists have children too."

"Don't be flippant."

"What else can I do?" She could hear the note of desperation in her voice, and quickly she tamped it down. She wasn't going to lose it, not at this stage of the game. Tomorrow she would get her credit card—after that she had all of France to hide in until she figured out how to get Nicole's passport.

"You can let me help you. For starters you and Nicole could spend the night in my apartment."

She raised her eyes from her rapt contemplation of her coffee cup and looked up into his face, seeing what she was afraid to see. "No, we can't do that. Don't worry about us. I'm sure we'll be fine."

"I'm not."

Claire turned her head to stare out into the streets. The café window was streaked with rain, the tables and chairs outside in the downpour looking oddly forlorn. Quite suddenly she hated Paris, hated the incessant rains of winter and spring, hated the beautiful streets where it was so easy to lose her way, hated the people and their liquid, incomprehensible language.

"God," she whispered, "I want to go home." And it was a cry of desperation.

"Are you certain you can't leave Nicole with her grandmother?"

She shook her head. "As a matter of fact, she's been there too long already. What time is it?"

"Five-thirty."

"I'd better go."

He rose, towering over her, his rangy height protective, not threatening, Claire thought wearily, still fighting. "I'm coming with you."

"Why?"

"Why not? You're so guilty, Claire, and unfortunately there's nothing to be guilty about. I'm simply a fellow expatriate you ran into, who's helping you deal with the vagaries of Paris. Why shouldn't you take me to meet the old lady?"

She shook her head. "I shouldn't." She rose also, pulling her heavy sweater over her head once more. "But I will. Do you think there's any chance of finding a taxi?"

"Where does the old lady live?"

Claire stared at him in mute frustration. "In a red building. Twelve blocks east, two blocks north past the church with the bronze roof."

"This is from your apartment?"

She nodded, anger and misery at her own inability clouding her already furious mind.

"We'll find it," he said, his voice soothing. "Come on. We don't want to be any later than we already are, do we?"

"No," said Claire. "We don't." And she followed him out the door.

Malgreave was staring at Rocco in mute frustration when the call came in. He picked up the phone, barking into it, and then grew very still as he listened to the report.

He replaced the receiver back in the cradle and looked up, smiling for the first time. "Everything become's clear."

Rocco's weaselly little lawyer looked affronted. "Pardon?"

Malgreave rose, shrugging into his jacket with efficient movements, signaling for Josef to follow him. "I wondered what the hell you were doing, wasting my time here. Now I know."

"What's up, boss?" Josef knew when to respond to a cue, and he did so perfectly.

"Another old woman, this time on the Left Bank. And our friend here with such a convenient alibi. Notice how he grins, Josef? We will wipe that grin off his ugly face, *hein?* He's just proven beyond all doubt that he's involved. How else would he know to show up exactly at this point? You've gone too far, Rocco, and I'm going to nail your balls to the wall for it."

"I must protest," the lawyer began, but Rocco shrugged.

"Don't worry about it, Lefèvre. Malgreave's got to think he's a big man. He's pigshit."

Malgreave only smiled faintly. "Shut the door when you leave, Rocco." And he headed out toward Harriette Langlois's apartment.

They could see the flashing lights from the parked police cars from several blocks away. The street itself was cordoned off, and Claire could do nothing but follow Tom, listening to his fluent explanations to the obstructive police as a growing sense of horror filled her. The official vehicles cluttering up the street were centered at Harriette's building, and she didn't need Tom's shuttered expression to tell her something was terribly wrong.

He pulled her to one side, huddled against the building, and his face was grim. "It's Harriette," he said. "She's been murdered."

Claire shut her eyes for a moment, letting the cold, icy rain stream over her eyelids. "Where's Nicole?"

"They haven't found her yet."

Claire's eyes shot open. "Oh, my God." Pulling away, she headed for Harriette's apartment, ignoring the protests of the policemen around her, ignoring Tom's restraining hand.

Claire's first thought was that Harriette wouldn't like all these wet, large men tramping through her apartment, putting muddy footprints on her beautiful carpets, dripping on her furniture. And then she saw her, stretched out on the chintz sofa, withered hands crossed over her chest like a medieval martyr, and she knew Harriette wouldn't mind anything at all.

She felt suddenly faint. Tom was beside her, his hand on her elbow, and she swayed against him for a moment. She had never seen death before, and the polite formality of this one was somehow worse than bloody carnage.

A man detached himself from the group standing over the body, one who looked vaguely familiar, though Claire couldn't place him. He spoke to her, and she looked up, blinking rapidly, as Tom intervened.

"I speak English, Mademoiselle MacIntyre," he said. "I am Chief Inspector Louis Malgreave, in charge of the investigation. You knew Madame Langlois?"

"She was my . . . fiancé's mother-in-law." God, it sounded like one of those French exercises that had always defeated her.

But Malgreave had apparently mastered the English equivalent. "I see. Who is your fiancé, and where is he now?"

"His name is Marc Bonnard. He's on tour in the south of France with the Théâtre du Mime. His daughter . . ."

"Do you know where he can be reached?"

"No. He usually calls in. Nicole . . ."

"Do you know why anyone would want to kill Madame Langlois? Had anyone threatened her, did anyone wish her harm?"

For a moment Harriette's fears came back to her. Claire looked over at the still, shrunken body, shivering. The doors were open, letting in the damp, chilly air, and it seemed as if she'd never get warm again.

"No one," she said.

Tom's hand tightened on her elbow for a moment, and she waited for him to say something, to contradict her. He didn't know Marc, he still thought it was a possibility that Marc could have done such a thing. Looking at the eerie stillness of Mme. Langlois's body, Claire knew it was impossible. She couldn't have lived with a man capable of murder. Her instincts couldn't be that awry. As if by magic her doubts had vanished. A small part of her brain had shut down in protest against what was unacceptable. It couldn't be Marc.

Malgreave nodded. "We're assuming it is part of the string of murders plaguing Paris."

"Where is her granddaughter? We were coming to fetch her . . ."

"There was no one else in the apartment."

"But she would have waited for me."

"No one else was here, and there was no sign of a struggle. My men are searching most diligently, and of course we shall want to talk with her when she's found. But I suspect she left long before anything happened. Fortunate for her sake, unfortunate for ours."

"But . . ."

"Go back home, mademoiselle. We will be in touch as soon as we find out anything. And you will call us if the child is waiting for you at home, yes?"

"But . . ."

"I will send you in a squad car. We will need to talk to you, but tomorrow will be soon enough."

"But . . ."

"Bon soir, mademoiselle, monsieur."

They were being dismissed, like obnoxious children. For one moment Claire considered behaving like one, throwing herself on the floor and refusing to move, and then thought better of it. The French equivalent of a coroner was examining Harriette's body, moving the stiffening hands to expose a red, gaping wound, and Claire felt her stomach turn.

"Let's get out of here," Tom said quietly. "He is right—if we're lucky Nicole is already at home, waiting for us. She probably doesn't have any idea what happened."

"But I told her to stay until I came!"

"Does she always do what you tell her?"

"What nine-year-old would?" Claire countered miserably. "You're right. Let's go home."

If she'd hoped the apartment would be a blaze of lights she was disappointed. Everything was dark and empty when she let herself in the front door. Tom followed, looking about him with a curious air, and his hands were gentle and impersonal as they stripped her of her sodden sweater and took her purse out of numb hands.

"I suppose I'd better call the police and tell them she's not here," Claire said woodenly.

"I'll do it. Why don't you go and make us both drinks? Something very strong."

She nodded, not moving. She wanted to sink back against Tom, lean against his strong, comforting body, but she wouldn't allow herself that luxury. "If he's hurt her I'll kill him," she said, her voice low and fierce.

"Who? Marc?"

"No. It couldn't have been Marc. If there was even the faintest possibility I would have said something to the police."

"Do you think," Tom said gently, "that you have the right to make that determination? Don't you think you should have told Malgreave about the old lady's fears?"

She shook her head fiercely, fighting the doubts. "Impossible," she said. "It was a coincidence, a random murder."

"I don't believe in coincidence," Tom said.

She looked up at him. "Neither do I," she said finally. "You make the drinks. I'm going to check Nicole's room."

The faint glow of the street lights cast a tiny pool of light into the spotless confines of the room. Claire reached for the light, then stopped. She could see the small figure lying in bed and, as her eyes grew accustomed to the dark, make out the sodden shape of a raincoat lying on the floor.

She moved into the room and sat down carefully on the bed. "Nicole?"

The small, familiar shape shifted. "I don't feel well, Claire," she said in a tiny voice. "I just wish to sleep."

"When did you leave your grandmother's?"

There was such a slight hesitation Claire thought she might have imagined it. "Early. I'm sorry, I know you told me to wait, but I had a stomachache. So she sent me home in a taxi quite early. I don't remember when."

For a long moment Claire said nothing. Nicole had an unfortunate habit of making up tales, and this sounded like one of them, but there was no earthly reason for her to lie. "How are you now?"

"I threw up and I'm feeling much better," her muffled little voice replied. "I just want to sleep now."

Claire knew a dismissal when she heard it. She also thought she knew a lie when she heard one, but she had no proof. "All right. You sleep, and I'll check on you during the night and make certain you're okay."

"That would be nice," she said in a woebegone little voice. "I thought I heard voices. Is . . . is Marc back?"

"Not for a few more days. It's just a friend of mine. He'll be leaving soon."

"If he spends the night I won't tell anyone."

Claire stared down at her, astounded. "Well, he's not going to spend the night. I can't imagine . . ."

"If he doesn't, can I come in and sleep with you again?"

"Certainly. If you want I'll send him home now."

"No. He should stay. I just want to sleep. Good night, Claire."

Claire shut the door behind her, her face creased in worry. Now was not the time to tell her about her grandmother—tomorrow would be soon enough. But she couldn't rid herself of the notion that Nicole already knew.

❧ CHAPTER 15

Nicole burrowed deeper into her bed, scarcely daring to breathe. Beneath the crisp white sheets she was still fully dressed, and her clothes were damp from her walk home through the pouring rain.

She'd run more than walked, looking over her shoulder, terrified Marc would reappear. But she'd made it back safely, back to the dark, empty apartment, moments before Claire returned.

She'd had enough time to think it through, to realize how hopeless the truth was. Claire wouldn't believe her. Women always believed Marc—the same thing had happened with her mother. When she'd tried to tell *Maman* about Marc her mother would get very angry and accuse her of lying.

So why should Claire believe her? If she was able to convince everyone she had seen nothing, maybe she'd be safe. Marc hadn't found her—he couldn't be sure she'd been there. Maybe if she lied and said she came home early people would believe her, Marc would go away and leave her alone, and no one would hurt her.

She hunched down deeper in the bed, her teeth chattering. When she'd first heard the man's voice she'd been terrified that Marc had come. But she knew even before she asked Claire that it was someone else, someone with a slow, deep, American voice.

As long as the person with that voice was here, she'd be safe. And if he left, she would go and sleep in Claire's big bed. Either way, no one could harm her for now. She could close her eyes and sleep.

Tomorrow she would think about *Grand-mère.* Tomorrow she would mourn properly, would decide how much to tell Claire. For now all she wanted to do was sleep. And blot out the memory of Marc walking into the kitchen, a bloody knife in his hand.

Claire walked slowly back to the living room, trying to rationalize her fears. It was no wonder she was troubled, she told herself. She'd seen violent death, murder. It should come as no surprise that she was filled with a nameless, overwhelming dread.

At least Nicole was safe. That, for the moment, was the most important thing.

"She's here?" Tom was standing by the door. Ready to leave, Claire realized with numb panic.

"She says she came back early. She doesn't know what happened to her grandmother."

"Thank God for that."

"Yes."

"Don't you believe her? Why would she lie?" He still hadn't moved away from the door, and Claire resigned herself to the fact that he was leaving, knowing it was best for both of them.

"Nicole lies sometimes. She makes up fantastic stories with no connection to reality."

"Surely this time she'd tell the truth? If she'd seen her grandmother murdered, seen the murderer, she'd say something."

Claire gave herself a tiny mental shake. "Of course she would. I'm just being neurotic." She moved over to the doorway, to him. "You're leaving?"

He hesitated. "It seems wisest. I imagine the police will be keeping an eye on you. You'll be safe here."

"I imagine," she echoed.

"Unless you want me to stay?"

Yes, she thought. "No," she said. "Would you call Inspector Malgreave for me and tell him Nicole is here and safe? I don't want to have to hassle with trying to get through to him."

"Of course." He still didn't move. The apartment was brightly lit, the rain had stopped, and Claire could smell the faint scent of the cognac he'd poured for her. "I'll call you later."

"I don't think I'll be answering the phone. I don't really like to, and I've had some crank calls recently."

Tom's hand had been on the brass doorknob, but he let it fall. "What kind of crank phone calls?"

"Just silence. No heavy breathing, no obscenities. Just absolute silence. I suppose it could be someone who simply doesn't understand English and doesn't know what to say. I could be jumping to conclusions."

"I'll ring twice, hang up, and then call again."

"All right."

"If you don't answer I'll come back."

"I'll answer."

"I don't want to go," he said flatly.

"I know," she said.

He stood there, indecisive, frustrated, angry. "Be careful," he said finally. And without touching her he left, slamming the heavy door behind him.

She moved to the window, staring out into the wet streets, waiting for him to emerge from the building. He appeared moments later, pausing in the lamplight, staring up at her. And then his gaze drifted sideways, across the length of the building, then back to hers, and he nodded, satisfied.

Suddenly she was desperate to call him back. She tugged at the window, but it had been painted shut years ago. She rapped at it sharply, but he'd already turned away, heading down the busy Paris streets.

For a moment she was tempted to slam her fist through the pane of thick glass. But common sense prevailed. She was safe, locked in the apartment. And spending the night with Tom Parkhurst was probably more dangerous than any imaginary threat from the serial killer or Marc Bonnard.

She moved away from the window, reaching for the glass of cognac Tom had poured before he left. Sinking down on the sofa, she curled her bare feet up under her and leaned back, sighing. At least Nicole was safe.

The small house in the Paris suburbs was dark and silent when Malgreave let himself in that night. He called Marie's name, but there was no answer.

He shouldn't be surprised. He was home earlier than usual. The killers usually struck late at night, rousing Malgreave from a troubled sleep. Tonight he or they had been thoughtful enough to do it while Malgreave was still on duty. He'd had time to take care of the formalities, view the initial evidence, and make it home before nine.

He needn't have hurried. Not with Marie gone. He could have stayed late, called Rocco Guillère back in, and pounded at him until he made the little weasel confess to prior knowledge. Malgreave wasn't a man who believed in coincidence. Rocco never came near the police if he could help it. For him to have chosen to appear at a time the killer struck was just a bit too fortuitous. A few minutes alone with him, after hours, with no one to interfere, and Malgreave could work off some of his anger . . .

Who the hell was he kidding? Rocco was twenty years younger, a great deal taller, and perhaps a bit more ruthless. He hurt people for a living. No matter how much rage and frustration were building up inside of Malgreave, he was no match for Guillère's brute strength. But God, he needed to hit someone. On nights like these, he needed to hit someone very badly.

He'd seen one corpse too many. Harriette Langlois, with her silks and her spotless apartment, with her silver-framed photographs and her hothouse roses. She should have been allowed to die in peace.

That was one curious aspect of this latest case, Malgreave thought, some of his anger leaving him as his brain started traveling down the familiar twisted pathways. He sat down on the new sofa he and Marie had bought last year, not bothering to turn on the lights, and thought back to the old woman's face.

Usually the old women were peaceful, laid out in state, their arms folded across their wounds. But Harriette Langlois hadn't died peacefully. Her wrinkled face was still twisted in rage, settled forever into an expression of absolute fury, her blue eyes still and staring.

She hadn't been frightened. Of that Malgreave was fairly certain. A cursory examination of her medicine chest had given him a reason for that. She'd already come to terms with impending death. No, she'd been angry, very angry, at the form it had taken, but not afraid.

He shook his head, sinking down into the sofa. Something was eluding him, something hadn't quite clicked into place. He thought back to the photographs, the serene, rather beautiful young woman, the handsome, oddly familiar young man, the plain little girl.

At least the child had been found. Word had come through just as he was leaving work. Apparently she'd left early, missing the murderer. He didn't know whether to be relieved or disappointed. While he didn't want another murder, particularly not one of a child, the girl might have seen something.

She still might have noticed something. The killer might have been waiting for her to leave, for the apartment to empty. She may have passed him, unknowing. Skillful questioning could bring out all sorts of information, and Vidal was nothing less than inspired when it came to questioning children. He put them at ease with his ridiculous clothes and his hot-dog ways. First thing tomorrow he would send him over to get a statement. The *Américaine* had looked protective, but Vidal could get around that too. Who knows, tomorrow they might be a little bit ahead of the game. While each murder was an outrage, a victory of darkness over light, each murder also brought new chances for the killer or killers to make mistakes. To start the chain of events that would lead to their being caught. To justice.

His stomach growled, but Malgreave ignored it. He

should partake of something besides strong coffee and cigarettes, but right now he hadn't the energy. Something was holding back, there was something he noticed tonight that hadn't moved into his consciousness. No matter how he tried to force it, it stayed buried.

He reached for his crumpled pack of cigarettes. Marie didn't like him to smoke in the living room. But then, Marie wasn't there. If he got up, went to the kitchen, he'd probably find a note and instructions on where to find a frozen dinner. She'd probably gone out with one of her friends, to the ballet, to the movies, to one of a thousand innocent places she'd taken to frequenting. Or so she said.

Or maybe, just maybe, there'd be no note at all on the kitchen counter. Maybe it would be in the bedroom, and all her clothes would be gone. Each day brought that possibility closer and closer.

Merde, he was being a maudlin, neurotic old fool! One of Marie's American frozen dinners, a good night's sleep, and he'd feel better. And maybe, just maybe, he'd remember what he'd never really known.

His arms slid around her in the darkness, scooping her up from the couch. Claire stirred, putting her arms around his neck and turning her face against his shoulder. She didn't want to wake up. All that mattered to her sleep-dazed brain was that Tom had changed his mind, had come back to her. If she woke up completely they'd have to talk, to work things out, to face issues that she wasn't ready to face. All she wanted right now was comfort, comfort and faceless sex. Tomorrow they could sort things out.

He didn't bother to switch on the light when they reached the bedroom. He kicked the door shut behind him, carrying her over to the bed and dropping her down on the cool cotton sheets. There was a moon that night, but the clouds covered it, and no light penetrated the cavernous room.

His hands were deft, careful as they unfastened the row of tiny pearl buttons on her silk blouse, pushing it off her shoulders and down her arms. His mouth followed, hot, wet, covering her skin, tasting, biting. He tugged at the skirt,

176

pulling it down over her legs and yanking her slip and panties with it. She wanted to say something, to protest, but she didn't. Tom was shy—she didn't want to inhibit him by any hint of criticism. Perhaps he was used to women who liked a rough approach.

She considered waking up long enough to take his hand and slow his assault. But waking up would require more of a commitment, one she wasn't ready to make. He knew what he was doing with his hands; he was arousing her in a crude, efficient fashion.

She tried to will her mind back into a dreamlike state. To imagine the gentle, protective Tom in this businesslike lover. But his hands were hurting her even as they were arousing her, and his mouth on her breasts was painful, and when he climbed on top of her, suddenly naked, he gave her no time to prepare for him, simply shoved his hard penis into her.

. She couldn't pretend anymore. Tears of pain stung her eyes, and her mouth opened in a tiny cry. He put his mouth on hers, shoved his tongue in deep, in rhythm with his invasive body, thrusting, pushing, his body hunching beneath her vainly protesting hands, slick with sweat and coiled strength.

She wanted to say something, wanted to slow him, stop him, but his mouth was raping hers, his fingers dug into her breasts, and she lay there, desperate, praying for it to be over.

It ended quickly enough, his body jerking, then collapsing against hers. His mouth left hers, his head lolling against her shoulder, and she could feel his hot breath panting against her tear-streaked face.

Misery and confusion washed over her as she lay imprisoned beneath his sweat-slick body. How could she have been so mistaken? How could she have let herself in for such a nightmare? As the calm, quiet night air flowed around her trembling body, common sense and understanding began to filter through, and the answer was almost worse than what she'd imagined.

The man raised his head, and in the heavy darkness she

could see his eyes glittering down at her. "Miss me, *chérie?*" Marc said.

And Claire, numb with guilt and distaste and a sudden, unreasoning fear, said, "Yes."

Malgreave was up early the next morning. Marie slept soundlessly in the narrow bed beside his, her mouth open, soft, sweet snores fluttering the tranquility of the morning. He'd heard her come in last night, had lain there, pretending to sleep, all the time knowing that it was almost two in the morning and that instead of being furtive, she was being almost defiantly noisy. He could tell from her jerky movements that she wanted a confrontation. He wasn't about to give it to her, not then. A confrontation could result in steps being taken, steps which could never be reversed.

No, as long as he avoided it, avoided meeting her angry, reproachful gaze, she wouldn't leave him. Marie was too honest to sneak out, no matter what he sometimes feared. So he lay very still, ignoring the thump of her shoes on the floor, the thud of the drawer pushed shut, the rush of water from behind a bathroom door left deliberately ajar.

No matter what time he got to work, Josef was there before him. It must be hell to be so ambitious, Malgreave thought with a trace of wry humor as he drove through the empty morning streets of Paris. You always had to be one step ahead of the game, one step ahead of the boss, and even then it wasn't enough. He could remember his own ambitious years as if they were yesterday. And where had they gotten him? Old before his time, his marriage on the skids, children he'd never had time to know. It wasn't worth it.

He'd tried to tell Josef that, and if it weren't for Madame Summer it would probably have sunk in. But Josef didn't have a soul to call his own, and Malgreave knew with grim certainty that Josef would continue to appear at work before he did, even at six in the morning.

Vidal was another matter, always late, always rushing in at the last moment with coffee and excuses overflowing. He shouldn't complain about Josef, Malgreave thought, moving through the empty offices to his own cluttered desk and dropping down. At least he had coffee in the morning, and someone to bounce ideas off. He wouldn't be nearly as efficient without Josef.

He was nowhere in sight, but Malgreave wasn't fooled. The spotless desk just outside his private office had a folder sitting atop it. Josef's gray polyester jacket rested on the wooden hanger he'd brought from home. He was somewhere about, bound to appear when needed.

The file on Harriette Langlois was waiting. Malgreave lit a cigarette, picked up the coroner's preliminary report, and stood there in the outer office, waiting for Josef to appear with the coffee and brioches Malgreave was old-fashioned enough to still love.

"You're in early, sir." Josef came up behind him, discreet as ever, and only a man of Malgreave's trained senses would have heard him coming. "I thought you might be."

"You are phenomenal, Josef." He took the cup of coffee and drank it down in one gulp, ignoring the searing heat of it, ignoring the delicate taste. "What's the latest?"

"You have the report." Josef followed him into his office, shutting the door behind him. "She was dying of cancer. Riddled with it, as a matter of fact. She must have been in great pain."

"Do you think that has anything to do with her killer?" Malgreave blew a stream of smoke above Josef's head.

It was his assistant's turn to be startled. "How could it?"

Malgreave leaned back, a satisfied smile on his face. "I noticed two things about Madame Langlois, my friend. One, that she wasn't afraid of death, of her killer. Only very, very angry."

"The cancer would explain that. She already knew she was going to die. I expect she'd prepared herself for the inevitable, and having a stranger break into her apartment with a butcher knife was not what she'd accepted."

"That was the other thing. I couldn't pinpoint it last night—it wasn't until just after dawn that I realized what it

179

was. I don't think it was a stranger, Josef. I think Madame Langlois knew her murderer."

Josef shook his head in disbelief. "So you don't think it's part of the chain of murders? You think this was someone with a personal grudge, copying the others? I would think you'd be disappointed."

"I'm not the slightest bit disappointed. I think this was someone with a personal grudge, someone the victim knew. But I think Madame Langlois's murderer has killed many times over. This was his first mistake, to choose someone he knew."

"His second mistake." Josef slid a piece of paper across Malgreave's cluttered desk. "I just got this from the lab. There were fingerprints in the old one's apartment, lots and lots of them. We have a match with the one found at the convent and in the twelfth arrondissement."

Malgreave felt positively buoyant with excitement. He stubbed out his cigarette. "Why didn't you tell me this at once?"

"It may mean absolutely nothing. The matching fingerprint was quite old, half-covered over by new ones."

"Even better. Don't you see, if Madame Langlois knew her killer, he would have been in her apartment before. He would have no reason to wear gloves as he did last night. We're getting somewhere, Josef. I can feel it in my bones." The troubles with Marie vanished in his excitement, and he rubbed his chilly hands together.

"But what if it is a copycat killer?" Josef protested stubbornly.

"You've forgotten the feet."

"The feet?"

"Madame Langlois's feet were bare, just as all the victims had bare feet. That's the one piece of information we've kept from the papers. No, last night's killer was one of the men we were looking for."

"As you say."

"We have our work cut out for us today, Josef. I need you to go down to Marie-le-Croix and see what you can discover about the orphanage and any of its inhabitants. I'm going back to the apartment and have a look around again. I particularly want to look at her photographs. Something, someone looked vaguely familiar, and it's been teasing my brain." Malgreave positively beamed at his assistant. "It won't be long, Josef."

"No, sir. It won't be long."

❦ CHAPTER 16

It was cold in the apartment, bitterly cold. Claire sat at the well-scrubbed table, drinking inky black coffee, trying to warm her hands on the thin Limoges cup. Her mugs had disappeared, and she had to hold very tightly to the delicate china to still the trembling in her hands. The coffee still sloshed against the eggshell-thin sides of the cup.

It was late. After eight o'clock in the morning, and Claire hadn't done all the myriad things required of her on a normal morning. She hadn't gone to get Marc's paper and croissants, she hadn't picked up the laundry, she hadn't dressed in a silk dress and applied the expensive makeup Marc had insisted she buy. She had crawled out of the bed like a wounded puppy, pulled on jeans and a sweatshirt, and gone to make herself coffee. Waiting, dreading the moment when Marc would wake up and join her.

Did he know about Harriette's murder? He must, why else would he have returned from his so-called tour of the Corte d'Azur? Did he have her and Nicole's passports? Who else would have them? Did she have a chance in hell of escaping, of taking Nicole with her? She didn't know. All she knew was that she had to try.

Her American Express card would be ready, and probably her passport. Tom would help her, Tom would hide both of them until she could figure out what to do about Nicole. Her suspicions, her fears, were confused, hazy, but unavoidable. All she knew was she had to get away, and had to take Nicole with her.

She couldn't afford to wait much longer. Marc usually slept late, waking between ten and eleven in the morning. If they left right now, raced through the maze of blocks to Tom's flat, they would be out of reach before Marc awakened. Nicole was exhausted—Claire's glance in on her showed a pale, huddled figure curled up in a deep sleep. It would take long, frustrating minutes awakening her, making her pull on clothes and keep completely silent.

Would Nicole fight her? Claire doubted it. Nicole had always distrusted Marc, had always held herself aloof from the man Claire had assumed was her father. Perhaps Claire was crazy, full of paranoid fantasies with no basis in reality. It didn't matter. All that mattered was escape, safety, breathing space so she could figure out what they could do, should do. Tom would help them find it.

Nicole's bedroom was dark and chilly when Claire tiptoed back in, her sneakered feet silent on the parquet floor. She touched Nicole's shoulder, that thin, bony shoulder that was hunched against some imagined terror. Nicole didn't move.

Claire squatted down beside the bed, keeping her voice low, and shook Nicole harder. "Nicole, wake up."

Nicole still didn't move. Her breathing was loud and shallow, her color a sickly white. Claire shook her again, quite hard, rattling the bed in her sudden panic. Nicole rolled over on her back, still dressed in yesterday's clothes, still caught in a deep, unbreakable sleep.

Calm, Claire ordered herself. Be very, very calm. She sat on the bed, pulling Nicole's limp body into a sitting position, and slapped her. Her sunken eyes didn't open, her head lolled to one side, and her mouth hung open slackly. Pressing her head against Nicole's thin chest, Claire listened for a heartbeat. It was there, slow and strong, and her lungs sounded clear. Nicole wasn't sick. She was drugged.

Claire let her drop back onto the bed. While Nicole's frail body was birdlike in its delicacy, there was no way Claire could cart her limp form through the streets of Paris. The one time she'd gotten a taxi it had been a nightmare of misunderstanding. No, her only chance was to go for help, and go quickly, before Marc awakened.

If luck were on her side they could be back in time. If Marc were to wake up and find her gone he would assume Nicole was gone also. The child wasn't going to awaken in the near future—Marc might even forget her existence.

Don't be an idiot, she stopped herself. Marc wouldn't forget Nicole's existence, not if he drugged her in the first place. And if he hadn't, who could have?

Of course, he might have made a habit of drugging Nicole. Looking back over the past few months, there were any number of times that Nicole had slept unnaturally long hours and awoken pale and sluggish. Maybe Nicole's current state wasn't as singular an occurrence as Claire imagined.

It didn't matter. What mattered was to get help, to get both of them out of there. If she couldn't drag Nicole's drugged body out of the apartment, she could at least hide her. Sliding her arms under Nicole's, she half-tugged, half-dragged the little girl out of the bed.

She hit the floor with a muffled thud, falling on Claire, and the two of them sat there, the woman breathless with fright, the child still unconscious. The apartment was well-soundproofed, protected by thick walls and heavy carpets, but Claire had no idea how deeply Marc slept. He awoke when he wanted to, usually at times she least expected.

For a long moment she didn't move, waiting for some telltale sound. But the air, the silence, was thick and still, surrounding them like a cocoon. With a whispered murmur of apology, Claire rolled Nicole's body under the bed, yanking a pillow and a blanket off and making swift, futile attempts at wrapping the drugged child. Then she rose, tugging the bedspread down almost to the floor, so that it covered any sign of Nicole's hiding place.

She left the scribbled note on the kitchen table beside the pot of coffee that was much stronger than what Marc usually preferred. "Nicole and I have gone to visit Harriette. Meet us over there. C."

Even if he knew Harriette was dead, he couldn't be certain they did. If they were due any sort of luck he would go after them without bothering to search the apartment, and once he arrived at the building the police would detain him, ask him all sorts of curious questions. Maybe even that sad-looking Inspector Malgreave would take him in for a statement. At the very least it would give Tom and Claire time to spirit Nicole away.

She let herself out the back door, closing it with a silent click. She sped down the back stairs and out into the sunny streets without a backward glance, her sneakered feet flying over the pavement as she raced down the broad sidewalks toward Tom Parkhurst's romantic garret. And as she ran she prayed.

"The mime." Malgreave was alone in his office. It was late morning, he'd smoked half a pack of cigarettes, eaten two brioches, and was in the midst of his fifth cup of very strong coffee. All morning he had sat there, staring at the walls in his windowless office as his brain chased around that one elusive memory. Josef had gone to Marie-le-Croix; Vidal and the others had come and gone in respectful silence, knowing Malgreave's expression of old. It had taken a long time, longer than usual, but in the end he had come up with the missing piece. He stubbed out his cigarette, sat back in his chair, and grinned, a savage, hunter's look that Marie had never seen.

"The goddamned mime," he said again. "His picture on the old lady's dresser. Him and his American girlfriend in the park just after the other murder. I do not believe in coincidence."

"Did you say something, sir?" Vidal poked his head inside the door.

"See if you can track down Josef," he ordered, leaning forward again and shuffling papers that were beginning to make sense. "If you have to, send someone down after him."

185

"I'll go myself."

Malgreave had expected that response, and was pleased with it. "Do that. Have him ask particularly about a boy who might have lived in the orphanage just before it burned back in the fifties. A boy named Marc Bonnard."

"The mime?"

"You've heard of him?"

"He's well-known if you like that sort of thing. My girlfriend does." He made a disparaging gesture with his shoulders.

"Do yourself a favor, Vidal. Don't marry her."

Vidal grinned. "No, sir. I'll call in as soon as I find Summer."

"Bon." Malgreave watched him leave. It was a visceral thing, this excitement when things finally began to fall together. The Grandmother Murders had gone on longer than most, and been more baffling, more frustrating. In the end, it would be his greatest triumph. And the perfect swan song. Let Summer deal with Vidal and all the other hounds at his heels. It would soon be time to rest.

Rocco wasn't a man to believe in premonitions. He believed in facts, in flesh and blood and pain and death. He'd heard the preliminary reports of the old lady's murder and emptied a bottle of red wine to celebrate. But his sleep had been troubled, and even reading the newspaper accounts the next morning, the typical vagueness of the police reports, hadn't soothed his worries. It was almost noon now, he was well into a cheaper bottle of Beaujolais, and the bright sunny day was casting shadows into his soul.

He was sitting outside at his favorite café, his shiny black boots propped up on a chair, the newspaper open on the table in front of him. He had nothing to do, no jobs to complete. Nothing until next week, when he promised Hubert he'd oversee a transfer of boxes trucked in from Spain. He had a fairly good idea what was inside those boxes, but he didn't care. The one person he would never dare mess with was Hubert. His reach was long, endless, and Rocco always knew which side to favor.

Marc must be celebrating. Would he have gone back into seclusion, or would he be with that tight-assed *Américaine?* He wouldn't have minded having a piece of her himself. He liked the *Américaines,* with their love of excitement and their lack of Catholic scruples. They were particularly fascinated with him, with his air of danger and amorality. Part of the perfect college vacation—see the Notre Dame, the Louvre, and the bed of a French criminal. He liked to hurt them first, just a little bit. Not enough to scare them away, just enough so that they'd know they were in for something different.

But maybe Marc shouldn't be celebrating. Rocco hadn't liked the expression on Malgreave's face when he'd stormed out yesterday afternoon. And it was getting dangerous, when you picked someone you knew. It wasn't wise to underestimate Malgreave. He would have made a great criminal, Hubert had always said so. He knew how to think along gutter lines, he knew the inside of madness when he dared to look. No, Malgreave was a definite threat, and more than once Rocco had considered wasting him.

He'd always changed his mind. The murder of little old ladies could be overlooked. None of them had much family to bother about them, and they would have died soon enough anyway. And no one cared about drug dealers found floating in the Seine, apart from those damned environmentalists who didn't care for pollution messing up their beloved river.

But a chief inspector was a different matter. Cop-killers were hunted down with a determination bordering on fanaticism, and Rocco had no desire to be the object of such a manhunt. Malgreave was respected and even more unusual, well liked. There wasn't a *flic* in all of Paris, perhaps all of France, who would rest before Malgreave's killer was found.

Marc was the smartest man Rocco had ever known. He would have covered his tracks. There was no way Malgreave could figure out anything, no matter how good he was. If Rocco could get away with it for so long, no one could take Marc Bonnard.

187

But he still couldn't get rid of that uneasy feeling lurking at the back of his neck. Maybe if he talked with Marc he'd feel better. He couldn't go to the apartment on the Left Bank—he'd be walking into the police's hands if they'd happened to find anything. No, he'd check with Hubert. Hubert would know if everything was well. Hubert would be able to make the contact with Marc if need be, or at least set his mind at rest. Hubert would take care of things.

He leaned forward and folded the paper. A shadow covered the sunny table, a hand reached over and took the paper from him. He looked up into Chief Inspector Louis Malgreave's world-weary gray eyes and an unlikely shiver of foreboding swept along his backbone.

"Mind if I join you, Rocco?" Malgreave inquired amiably, pulling up a chair. "I wanted to talk to you about your childhood."

Nicole felt absolutely horrible. She couldn't open her eyes, the air was close and smothering, the bed hard as a board beneath her, and she wanted to throw up. She was cold, and frightened, and something was terribly, terribly wrong.

She would go back to sleep. That would improve matters. If things were too miserable to face, then sleep was the answer. Maybe then her stomach would stop jumping about. She hated to throw up. She hated kneeling on the hard marble floor in the bathroom, staring down into the dark cracks in the toilet bowl. She hated the burning along her throat, the horrid, childhood fear that she would throw up all her insides and then die.

No, if she just lay very still on the hard surface and tried not to breathe, maybe the sickness would pass. Maybe she would wake up and *Grand-mère* would still be alive. Maybe it had all been a nasty dream, Marc with the knife, *Grand-mère* dying.

But there'd been another dream, hadn't there? Someone in the night, making her swallow something nasty. It hadn't been the first time. And she knew that Marc was back.

At that her stomach finally gave up the fight. She crawled

out from under the bed, gagging, and scrambled toward the bathroom. She didn't make it in time, ending on her hands and knees, vomiting on the carpet. Marc had beaten her once when she'd tracked mud on it. What would he do when he found she'd thrown up on it?

It didn't matter. Her stomach wasn't worried about Marc—all it wanted to do was empty itself quickly and efficiently. When she'd finally thrown up everything, when the dry heaves finally shuddered into silence, Nicole sat back, wiping the mess from her mouth, shivering. She looked up, to the right, to the open door to her bedroom.

Marc was standing there. No knife in his hand, no blood on his clothes. He looked distant, almost affable, as he stared down at her.

"Sick, *chérie?*" he inquired softly, too softly. "We'll have to clean it up, won't we? And then I have a little game in mind." And slowly, silently, he began to move toward her.

Claire couldn't speak by the time she reached the sixth floor of Tom's apartment. She'd passed any number of police along the way, and racing through her panicked brain had been the thought that maybe one of them might speak English, might help her.

But even the most sweeping command of the English language didn't mean they'd believe her. Didn't mean they'd let an American woman remove a French child from the custody of her French stepfather. And Marc could be so persuasive, so charming. What did it matter that his mother-in-law had been murdered last night? He would only use it as an excuse for Claire's paranoia.

No, she didn't dare stop, not until she reached Tom. But by the time she'd collapsed against his door, banging loudly, by the time she fell into his arms, she was sobbing and gasping for breath, unable to choke out more than a few struggling phrases, none of which made sense.

"Calm down," Tom said, his hands steady on her arms. He gave her a slight, rattling shake. "You're not making any sense. What about Marc? And Nicole? And you? Claire, are you all right?" His hand came up and caught her chin, forcing her face up to meet his, and his blue eyes were searching.

She still couldn't manage more than a few disjointed sentences. "Marc's . . . back.   Nicole . . . drugged. . . . Afraid . . ."

The hand on her arm tightened almost painfully. "When did he come back?"

"Last night. I . . . thought . . . you . . ." She gave up the struggle for a moment, leaning against him and shuddering in remembered distaste.

Tom began to swear, a low string of obscenities that was curiously comforting. "I should never have left you."

"It . . . would have . . . made things worse."

"I should have brought you home with me, then."

She lifted her head. "We've got to get Nicole. I couldn't . . . move her. She was too heavy. He's given her something, and I don't think it's the first time. I didn't dare stay, but I was afraid if he woke up and found her . . ."

"We'll get her." He'd already put her aside and was pulling on a jacket. He was dressed as she was, in jeans and sweater and running shoes, and even with his superior height Claire had to wonder whether he'd be a match for Marc. She couldn't imagine it would come to that, but so much had happened already that was beyond her wildest nightmares. Something was very, very wrong in that apartment, with her lover of the last four months, and that wrongness was so evil, so permeating, that it defeated even her overblown fantasies.

"Should we call the police?" She didn't even flinch as she headed toward the door, prepared to retrace her mad dash of only minutes before.

"After we get Nicole out of there. The French do everything at their own speed, and I don't think they're going to like taking the word of a couple of Americans against that of a fellow Parisian. Bonnard is a fairly well-known figure in certain circles—it will only make it more difficult."

There was no reply she could make to that, only swallow the groan of despair that threatened to overwhelm her. She was halfway out the door, ahead of him, when the phone rang. She stopped dead still at the top of the stairs, and Tom careened into her, almost knocking her down the steep flight.

"Answer it," she said.

"Don't be ridiculous. We have to get back as quickly as . . ."

"Answer it," she said again, her voice dull and resigned.

He didn't argue, simply turned and went back into the apartment, picking up the serviceable black phone and barking a French greeting into it.

She could tell by the sudden whiteness of his face that her instincts had been right. He held out the receiver to her. "It's Bonnard."

She didn't ask how he knew where to find her. Tom wouldn't know any more than she did. All that mattered was that Marc knew.

She took the receiver from him, holding it gingerly, as if it were a cobra about to bite her. She held it to her ear. "Marc?" she said, and her voice was surprisingly calm.

There was no answer. Just the same thick, impenetrable silence she'd heard on those other occasions. She could see him at the other end, the exaggerated expressions, the perfect command of his trained body, but God only knew what he was telling her in his silence.

And then she heard Nicole scream.

❦ CHAPTER 17

The call came in just before three in the afternoon. Malgreave had assigned one of the newer detectives to manning the phone. Over the last two years there'd been so many false leads and crazies calling in with messages from God that Malgreave no longer bothered to deal with them directly. He left it up to Pierre Gauge, a not very bright transfer from the police department in Rouen. What he lacked in brains he more than made up for in doggedness, and Malgreave knew he could count on having a complete transcript of every call concerning the old women that came in, be they from concerned citizens or Saint Joan herself.

Gauge even taped them all, keeping the tapes for a week at a time, long enough for Malgreave or Josef to review them to see whether Gauge might have missed something. He seldom did. Even with his limited command of languages other than French, he managed to do a creditable job, and his nighttime replacement, a weary old veteran on the edge of retirement, did the same.

Gauge knew enough to recognize Vidal's voice when he heard it, patching the call directly through to the Chief Inspector. "Summer's still talking with the mayor," Vidal said. "But he thought this couldn't wait any longer. You were right—Yvon Alpert, Rocco Guillère, and Gilles Sahut were all inmates at the Marie-le-Croix orphanage at the

time it burned down. Two people were killed in the blaze—
an elderly gardener and the matron of the house, an old
woman named Estelle Marti. There was a question of arson
at the time, but nothing could be proven. Besides, the boys
were only about ten or twelve years old. Not old enough to
be criminals."

"You'd be surprised," Malgreave said, tapping his pencil
thoughtfully. "Anybody remember the old people? Were
they locals?"

"People old enough to remember have been pretty close-
mouthed about the whole thing. As far as we can tell, the
victims weren't well liked, either of them. It sounds as if the
investigation into the fire was dropped for lack of interest,
not evidence."

"Interesting. What about Bonnard?"

"No one by the name of Marc Bonnard was in residence
here at the time of the fire."

"I don't believe it."

Vidal laughed on the other end. "I should mention that a
young boy named Marc de Salles arrived about a year
before the fire. A very handsome boy, younger than the
others, with a talent for theatrics and a particularly winning
way with the locals."

"It should be easy enough to check. The boys would have
been sent to other institutions, farmed out to foster homes.
Probably our young friend de Salles was taken in by a family
named Bonnard."

"Chief Inspector, the boy was ten years old when the
place burned. Surely you don't think he could have been
involved?"

"I'm convinced they all were involved, and they may have
had a damned good motive. When you finish up there see
what you can find about the gardener and Estelle Marti.
Whether they had any criminal record, any history of child
abuse, of sexual deviations. It would explain a great deal."

"Yes, sir."

Malgreave replaced the phone, a faint expression of
amusement momentarily lightening his features. Josef
would have to watch himself with that one. Vidal was an

eager beaver if ever there was one. It must have killed Josef to let him make that call, but Josef was ever conscientious, putting a case ahead of his wife's ambitions. Malgreave would have to make sure Josef felt appreciated.

He heard the phone ring in the outer office. He reached for the receiver again, but Gauge was ahead of him, his broad face creased in concentration as he took studious notes, and Malgreave pulled his hand back, reaching for a cigarette instead. He could hear the voice on the other end through a lull in the office noise, some hysterical woman babbling in what sounded like English. Another crazy, Malgreave thought, lighting the cigarette and taking a deep, appreciative pull on it. Thank God he could count on Gauge to deal with it.

It all came together in an instant of pure, disbelieving horror. She knew, the moment she heard Nicole scream, she knew. She didn't need Marc's voice, the sudden, rasping, giggly sound of Marc's voice breaking in, speaking to her at last, to confirm what she'd never wanted to face.

"I am going to kill her, *chérie*," he said, his voice high, breathless. "I only like to kill old women, grandmothers like Harriette, but in Nicole's case I'll make an exception. She saw me last night with her grandmother, and she's always suspected about her mother. If it weren't for Nicole you would have loved me."

"Marc . . ."

"She's trying to hide from me, Claire. She's running, but she's so drugged that she won't be able to get far. I won't kill her right away once I catch her. I like little girls. I like to touch them. I'll make it last, *chérie*. I'll make it last a long, long time."

There was no background noise beyond Marc's eerie voice. Maybe she had gotten away, maybe if she could just keep him on the phone long enough Nicole could run for help. Claire took a deep, struggling breath, only dimly aware of Tom's arm around her hunched shoulders. "Marc," she said, and stopped, momentarily astonished at how calm her voice was. "Marc," she said again. "You don't want to hurt anyone . . ."

"*Au contraire, chérie,* I do. I want to hurt Nicole, I want to hurt you, I want to hurt the old women that watch me, that tease and torture me, I want to hurt them all. I want . . ." His ranting changed swiftly from English to French, his voice rising to an almost incomprehensible shriek. Tom jerked the phone away from her, listening with growing horror, and Claire thanked God she couldn't understand French.

And then the line went dead. Silence once more, but not the listening, waiting silence. A few seconds later an impartial buzz informed them that Marc had hung up the phone. That now he could search for Nicole.

Nicole sat huddled against the wall in the hallway, the scream of terror still caught in her throat as she stared at Marc. Nothing seemed to be working, not her legs, not her arms, not her voice, certainly not her brain. She'd felt like this before, the time she'd fallen into a swimming pool, going down, down, deep under the water, fighting through the heaviness that pulled and tugged at her, drowning her. Her mother had saved her, jumped in and pulled her to the surface, where she could struggle and breathe again, scream and cry in terror and life.

But her mother was dead, killed by the monster in front of her, and there was no one to save her. No way she could struggle out of the heavy folds of death that were wrapping around her. Claire had deserted her. Claire who had promised to take care of her, Claire had left her to Marc.

He'd forgotten her for the moment. He was laughing into the telephone, and his eyes were bright with joy and malice. He was telling Claire what he would do to her, what he could do to both of them. Summoning her last ounce of strength, Nicole began to scuttle backward like a crab, along the side of the wall.

Marc stood between her and the front door. She could make it to the back door, but he might catch her, and there were knives in the kitchen, too many long, sharp knives. There was a chance, one chance that he might not know about. Claire would come. Claire had abandoned her, but Claire would come. If she could just find a place to hide, long enough for Claire to get there, she'd be safe.

She must have banged against the wall. Marc turned, looking at her, and his mouth curved in cheerful anticipation before turning his attention back to the phone. He knew she was too weak to walk. She wouldn't have the strength to go far enough to get away from him.

But pray God he didn't know about the old heating duct in her closet. She'd pulled the grate off years ago, and sometimes she used to crawl in there and hide, curled up in her own misery, missing her father, hating the interloper who smiled too much and watched her in her bath. She was bigger now, and it might be a tight squeeze, but she could pull the grate after her, hide back there, and he might not find her.

She could hear his voice, getting higher, louder, saying things she couldn't understand and didn't want to. Her legs were getting stronger, finally beginning to respond to her brain's orders, and she scrambled into her bedroom, across the rug, and into the closet.

For a moment the grate stuck, and she panicked. Someone must have found it was loose, must have put new screws in. But then it moved, and she yanked it open, crawling into the narrow chute.

Her numb fingers could barely lift the heavy grate. It made a loud, clanging noise as she pulled it into place, and the silence from the hallway told her Marc had finished with Claire. Had he seen where she went? Had he heard the sound and recognized it? Was he just behind her, watching her, about to reach for her with those long, cruel fingers?

She let go of the grate and tried to scramble backward into the narrow tunnel, but the heavy iron began to fall forward, and she caught it just in time. She had no choice. She would have to sit at the end of the tunnel, holding the grate in place, hoping Marc wouldn't be able to see her pale fingers through the hatches, wouldn't yank the grate open and grab her before she could edge away into the narrow ductwork.

And if she was able to get away, into the maze of tunnels, what would happen? What if she got stuck, and no one ever found her? She'd starve to death, stuck in the heating vent, trapped, unable to break free.

She heard a whimper of terror, and knew it was her own. And then, in her room, close, too close, came the almost imperceptible sound of footsteps. The footsteps of a man used to silence.

She stopped breathing. He made no sound, the madly cheerful voice stilled. She heard the rustle of bedclothes, the creak of an old floorboard. He was looking beneath her bed, in the corner, behind the curtains. She could sense him moving closer, toward the closet, and she knew if he opened the door he would see her pale white fingers against the gray iron of the grate. She had no choice, she would have to release the grate and scuttle back into the tunnel.

Light flooded the end of the duct just as she released her death grip. She held still, waiting for the heavy iron to fall, exposing her hiding place. She held still, waiting for death.

The hangers rattled overhead. The neatly polished shoes in front of the grate were kicked by a slippered foot. And the grate, held by an uncertain gravity and her terrified prayers, stayed in place.

The closet door remained open, but the footsteps edged away. She leaned forward, watching his shadowed figure as it moved toward the hallway, and as she did so her forehead brushed the iron grate, sending it tumbling toward the wooden floor.

She caught it, inches from the floor, clenching the heavy piece of iron in impossibly weak hands, half in, half out of the vent, not daring to move, waiting, waiting for Marc to come back and find her.

But he'd already gone, moving into the hallway, intent on his own hunt, dismissing her room as a possible haven.

Slowly, silently, she sat back, pulling the heavy grate with her. Her fingers were clutched so tightly around the iron that she found she couldn't release them. She no longer cared. She leaned back against the cold metal sides of the vent and shut her eyes. She would wait until someone found her. If it was Marc, so be it.

Claire didn't wait to see if Tom was following her. She raced down the flights of stairs, holding on to the railing to keep herself from falling in her unthinking panic. The late-morning streets were crowded on the first sunny day in ages, and she careened into passersby, bouncing off them without so much as a mumbled apology.

She didn't bother to look for a taxi—with the traffic it would take less time to run. And run she did, numbly aware of Tom's long-legged figure keeping pace with her, numbly aware of the burning pain in her heart as she gasped for breath. And all the time she prayed, a silent litany begging a heretofore unfriendly God to keep Nicole safe. She promised everything in a tumbling flurry of rash thoughts. She'd become a nun, she'd die herself, she'd go back to the States and face charges, she'd never go near another man again. But please, dear God, let Nicole escape from that madman.

She half expected the street outside Marc's apartment to be jammed with police cars and ambulances. As she stormed into the ancient brick building she had a split second to marvel at the ordinary charm of the day, the tourists crowding the streets, the elegant Parisians taking the infrequent sunshine to heart.

Tom caught her halfway up the broad marble stairs, jerking her to a halt, and for a moment all she could do was lean against the walls and stare at him as she struggled for breath.

If Tom wasn't equally winded it was probably due to his six flights of stairs. Even so, it took him a moment to be able to speak.

"We can't just . . . storm in there," he said. "It might push him over the edge."

"He *is* over the edge, damn it! Didn't you hear what he said? He's going to kill Nicole."

"I heard him. I heard what he said in French, too, and it was far worse than what he was threatening in English. He

198

told us exactly what he was planning to do to Nicole, and then what he'd do to you when he caught you." Tom's face was pale beneath the sweat, and Claire shivered.

"I don't care. We can't wait . . ."

"We have one advantage," Tom said ruthlessly, holding her still when she tried to break free. "He only uses a knife. That's what he was talking about, that's what the papers have said. So he'll have to get fairly close to either of us to hurt us."

"The papers," she said numbly. "Do you really think he's the one who's been killing these old women?"

"Do you really think there's a chance he isn't?"

"God," Claire moaned. "What sort of monster have I been living with?"

"I don't know. But I think we're about to find out. Carefully now. Stay behind me. It's you he wants to hurt. He seems to want to prey on women. Maybe he'll think twice about hurting me."

"Bullshit." She pushed herself away from the wall. "You heard him. I don't think he's capable of thinking about it one way or the other. He'll go through you to get to me. And I don't give a damn. Anything to get him away from Nicole." She yanked herself out of his grip and started back up the stairs, moving swiftly, dreading what she knew she'd find in the apartment.

Tom gave up arguing and came with her. The heavy green door stood open into the deserted hallway. There was no sign, no sound, of a living human being anywhere near the apartment.

Claire started forward, and once more Tom caught her arm. "He might be lying in wait for you," he warned.

She shook her head impatiently. "He's gone," she said with great certainty, moving into the apartment with Tom beside her, slowly, carefully, listening for any unexpected sounds, watching for movement out of the corner of her eyes.

She half expected, half dreaded to see blood stains on the floor. There were none. No sign of a struggle. No sign of Marc. No sign of Nicole. The apartment was deserted.

"I'm calling the police."

Claire barely heard him. "She's still here."

"No one's here, Claire," Tom said impatiently. "Marc's taken her somewhere, and the sooner we get help the better."

"Go ahead and call them. I'm going to keep looking." She headed back toward the bedrooms, and with a sigh Tom replaced the telephone and followed her. "I thought you were going to call the police."

"In a minute. If Nicole is here I don't want you to have to find her alone."

Claire shivered. "She's not dead."

"If you say so."

"God damn it, Tom, I'd know . . ."

The sound was very faint. If every nerve in Claire's body hadn't been tuned in, waiting for it, she might never have heard it. Just a whisper of noise, calling her name.

"Nicole?" She kept her voice calm, as hope and panic threatened to swamp her. "Nicole, honey, where are you?"

The call came again, so softly she could scarcely hear it. She knew the voice, but the words were distant, incomprehensible.

"Nicole, where are you?"

The voice was louder as they ran toward the bedroom, and clearly in muffled French. Tom shook his head. "I don't understand what she's saying. She says she's in something, but I don't know the word."

As they reached her bedroom they were greeted by a loud clang that shook the bedroom floor. Moments later Nicole crawled out of a hole in the bedroom closet, her sallow face pale, her dark hair hanging limply, her eyes still dilated and glassy. She looked up at Claire, murmured something in French, and collapsed on the floor, crying.

Within seconds Claire was on the floor beside her, pulling her into her lap, cradling her, murmuring ridiculous, comforting phrases as she pushed her damp hair out of her face. She rocked her, back and forth, for long, soothing moments, until Nicole's tears shuddered to a halt, turning into occasional whimpers of fear as she clung to Claire, until she'd drifted back into an exhausted, semi-drugged sleep.

Claire turned and looked up at Tom. "Lock the doors," she said. "We have to make sure he can't get in." And her arms tightened protectively around Nicole's shivering figure as she jerked in fear.

Tom nodded, heading for the door, when her voice called him back.

"What did Nicole say when she saw me?"

A semblance of a smile lit Tom's face. "She said she knew you'd come. She knew you'd save her."

Claire managed the ghost of a smile in response. "I hope she's right."

"You're the last person I expected to see." Hubert's voice was chilly with high-pitched disdain as he looked up into Rocco's face. The old man was wearing mourning—a beautifully cut black suit with a single white rose in the lapel. Mourning the old bitch, Rocco thought with a sneer he didn't let show.

"I'm in trouble, Hubert."

"And? You expect something from me?"

Rocco shrugged. "Information, perhaps. I've been useful to you in the past. It might be in your best interests to keep me around in case I could prove useful in the future."

"It could be that you've outlived your usefulness. Things become dangerous when you start enjoying your job, Rocco. You were always such a professional. When you start killing for pleasure you run into trouble. Things are bound to catch up with you."

Rocco veiled the hatred in his opaque black eyes. "We all have to have some sort of hobby, Hubert."

"When you're in a dangerous line of work you ought to find a discreet hobby, not one that will call more attention to yourself. Malgreave is after you, isn't he?"

Rocco wasn't surprised at Hubert's knowledge. Little escaped the old man. "Malgreave has always been after me."

"But he's beginning to put things together. Your friend Bonnard is in deep trouble, and he's going to drag you down with him."

"Where is he?"

"Is that what this is about?" Hubert sniffed. "I haven't the faintest idea."

"Don't give me that shit. You know everything. Where the hell is Bonnard?"

"Out looking for his girlfriend, I expect. Not to mention her lover and Bonnard's stepchild. You find them, you'll find Bonnard." Hubert took a black silk handkerchief from his breast pocket and dabbed at his pursed mouth. "Come to think of it, you might be able to assist me after all. And in the end, you'll assist both Bonnard and yourself."

"Name it."

Hubert smiled. "You really have gotten the wind up, haven't you, my boy? I never thought to see the day you'd be so thoroughly spooked. It's very simple. Find the *Américaine* and her lover and kill them. Bring the child to me. I'll be grateful, and you know I'm capable of astonishing things in my gratitude. Malgreave could be forced to take an early retirement. Or given a promotion to a police department in Lyon or somewhere equally distant."

"Why do you want the child?"

"I'm a sentimental old man. She's the last living relative of a woman I loved dearly. For Harriette's sake I want to protect her."

"And Bonnard?"

"Once the woman and the man who cuckolded him are dead he will regain reason. He's had times like this before, word has it. But if you wish to survive you'll have to stop your nasty little hobby. Even if I can manage to get rid of Malgreave, someone else will be after you and if you're almost caught once, someone else can put the same facts together. And next time it won't take them so long."

Rocco wished he had a silk handkerchief of his own to wipe the sweat from his forehead. "I'll stop. I don't know if it will be possible for Bonnard."

Hubert smiled sweetly. "Then you'll simply have to stop him."

Rocco shut his eyes for a moment, feeling the sweat roll down his back and under his arms, pooling in his groin. If he was frightened of anyone in this world he was frightened of Marc Bonnard. He met Hubert's grave expression and nodded.

"And take good care of the child for me. I would be very distressed if Bonnard got to her first."

"I'll find her. And the Americans."

"And Bonnard," Hubert said gently.

"And Bonnard," agreed Rocco.

⚜ CHAPTER 18

Claire slammed down the telephone, crashing it into the receiver. Nicole slept onward, curled in a fetal position on the uncomfortable sofa in the salon, and Tom stood by the window, looking out into the afternoon streets. "They won't listen," she said, her voice raw with frustration and unshed tears. "Damn their souls to hell."

"What did the police say?"

"Just the same garbage they told you. They would record my complaints and pass the information on to the next available officer. That they appreciated my assistance in this matter. Damn them!"

"You couldn't remember who's in charge of the investigation?"

"I know who's in charge of the investigation." Claire wrapped her arms around her shivering body. "He's a tall man, in his late fifties, with gray eyes and a deeply lined face."

"I hate to be nitpicking, Claire, but what was the man's name?"

"For God's sake, don't you think I'm trying to remember?" she cried. "It was something French. And don't tell me that isn't any help. I know most people who work for the Paris police have French names. It was something like . . . Mal . . . Malgreave."

He still hadn't moved from his spot by the window, and she wanted nothing more than to cross the elegant, haunted room and lean against him, huddle in the shelter of his warmth and strength. She couldn't do it. She couldn't give in to the weakness and terror she was fighting so hard. Tom couldn't take responsibility for the three of them, much as she wished she could simply hide her head in the sand and let him. She had gotten herself, and to some extent, the two of them, into this mess, and she had to get them out.

"Did you leave your number with the police?" Tom asked. "Are they going to call you back?"

"Yes. Not that I'm holding my breath. It was clear they thought I was a crazy American lady."

"They wouldn't listen to me either."

"You're a crazy American man. They're not going to take our word against that of a man with Marc's reputation, not unless we can prove it. At this point it's our word against his."

"And you don't think there's enough proof? What about when Nicole wakes up? Won't they believe her?"

"She's a child, a child who's recently lost her mother and her grandmother in violent, unexpected ways. They'll think she's fantasizing."

"I think you're being needlessly pessimistic. Let's wake her up, go outside, and get a taxi to police headquarters. We can just camp there until someone listens to us. At least Bonnard couldn't get to you there." She could tell Tom was making an effort at being reasonable, but she couldn't listen.

"No!" she said, fighting panic at the very idea. "I know how charming Marc can be, and when it comes right down to it, I have no right keeping Nicole with me. He could even tell the police that I drugged her, I kidnapped her. They'd take her from me and give her back to him, and there'd be nothing I could do about it."

"I don't know if Bonnard is capable of such rational behavior anymore," Tom said slowly. "He sounded like he'd slipped over the edge."

"Maybe. I can't count on it." She moved over and sank down on the couch, inches from Nicole's bare feet. Tom had been surprisingly patient all afternoon, calling the police and trying to get through in his adequate French, making tea that neither of them drank, his very presence a comfort, a defense against the forces of evil. She wouldn't be surprised if he'd had enough. After all, he had no ties to her. They were merely chance-met strangers in Paris, and she'd managed to draw him into a web of murder and madness from which there seemed to be no escape. It would be little wonder if he wanted to wash his hands of the whole sordid affair.

"Damn it, Claire, we can't just sit here . . ." he began, rumpling his already tousled hair in frustration.

"No, we can't," she said, pulling a hard-gained serenity back around her. "And I've decided what I have to do."

"Have you?" His tone of voice wasn't promising, but Claire ignored it. The sooner Tom was out of this mess, the better.

"Nicole and I are going into hiding. My new American Express card should be ready. With that I'll rent a car, take Nicole, and go off someplace where Marc can't find us. Just long enough for the police to realize we've been handing them their murderer on a silver platter. Once I read in the paper that Marc's been arrested I'll bring Nicole back."

He'd listened to this all with an enigmatic expression on his face. "And what am I supposed to be doing during all this?"

"Working on your novel. While we're gone you could keep after the police, tell them how crazy Marc is. With you to badger them, they should eventually see reason."

"Sounds very efficient. Where were you planning on going?" His voice was mild, and Claire found herself struggling between relief and disappointment. She had thought, had hoped, he'd put up more of a fight.

"I wasn't quite sure. South, I suppose, maybe near the Riviera. We'd call in, check to see if anything's happened. We'll be fine."

"You'll be dead," he said flatly.

"Tom . . ."

"For one thing, you can't rent a car without proper identification, and that includes a passport. For another, Bonnard knows the Riviera, you don't. You'd be much safer in a less-inhabited part of the country. God knows that's easy enough to find—most of the population is crowded around Paris and the southeast coast. And in case it's slipped your mind, you can't speak French. Not a god-damned word of it. So how do you expect to fade into the woodwork for God knows how long without Marc finding you?"

"I can't involve you in this."

"I'm already involved. He knows me, he knows where I live. He called you at my apartment, remember? I'm just as likely to wind up with a knife in my throat while you're off sunning yourself at Cap Ferrat."

"Don't." Claire shuddered.

"Sorry, lady. I'm in this all the way. You'll find I have my uses. I'm a jack of all trades—I'll be your chauffeur, your translator, and your bodyguard. And I work cheap. Just an occasional pat on the head, a crumb of affection, and I'll be your slave."

"I can't let you do it."

"You have no choice," he said flatly, and Claire wondered how she had ever thought he was easygoing. "It's very simple. First, I don't have a car, but I have a friend who has an old Peugeot that simply sits around getting rusty. Second, I don't think we should bother with your American Express card. Bonnard will expect you to get a new one—it would be his best chance of tracing you. We'll manage without. I can get plenty of cash, and where we're headed we won't need much money."

"Where are we headed?"

He grinned at her, and suddenly she found herself grinning back, feeling reckless and oddly carefree. Whether she liked it or not, she did have someone to turn to. "We're going toward one of the darkest, emptiest corners in the back of beyond. A place where the goats outnumber the dogs, and the dogs outnumber the people. The only place in

France where grapes don't grow. In other words, we're going to my vineyard."

"You have a vineyard?"

"For want of a better word. It's a bleak and barren outcropping of earth where the sun never shines and it only rains when you don't want it to. What grapes survived three different kinds of blight are at this moment fermenting into one of the world's worst wines. We closed down last year and as far as I know no one's been back since. It'll be the perfect place to hide out. No one speaks English, but they'll remember the crazy American who tried to grow grapes where grapes won't grow. And Bonnard will never find us."

Claire shook her head in disbelief. "And where is this Garden of Eden?"

"About four hours away if we drive directly. I propose we take a roundabout way in case anyone follows us. We don't have a telephone at the vineyard, but there's a public phone in town. Once I get you settled into the farmhouse I can go down and call the police again. Maybe by then they'll be more receptive."

"Or maybe by then Marc will have convinced them that he's innocent."

"Maybe. We'll cross that bridge when we come to it. In the meantime, I want you to pack some clothes for you and Nicole. Just the bare essentials—we want to travel as light as possible. Then we'll head out across town to my friend's house."

"Couldn't you just get the car yourself and come back here?" she suggested, bowing to the blessed inevitable. "I could pack while you're gone, and I promise we'd keep the doors locked."

He shook his head. "I haven't wanted to point this out to you, darling," he said gently, "but this is Bonnard's apartment. A locked door isn't keeping him out. He has keys."

Claire could feel her face turn pale, her small measure of security ripped away from her. "How could I be so stupid?"

"It's all right, Claire. As far as I can tell he hasn't come near all day."

"I'll get our clothes," she said numbly. "You call your friend. I'll be ready to leave in five minutes. If Nicole's still asleep you can carry her."

"We don't need to rush . . ."

"I need to get out of here," she said, her voice deep and grim. "Call your friend."

Josef dropped the neatly folded paper on Malgreave's desk. "As ordered, sir," he said, dropping wearily into the chair across from his superior. He wiped his domed forehead with a linen handkerchief. "A nasty business."

Malgreave smiled benevolently at his assistant. "A nasty business indeed. Your wallowing in the sewers has brought it closer to completion, my friend."

"Sewers, indeed." He gestured toward the paper. "Is that what you wanted leaked?"

Malgreave picked up the evening paper. The ancient photograph of the Marie-le-Croix orphanage reproduced poorly—it looked shadowy and gothic, full of brooding evil. The headlines were suitably macabre—"Orphans' Sex Ring Tied to Killings" got the message across quite nicely, if without subtlety.

"You did well, Josef. You and Vidal." He kept his face bland at Summer's involuntary wince. "And there's no mention of Bonnard?"

"None at all. Just the dead butcher, Sahut, the bureaucrat, Alpert, and Rocco Guillère described in such intimate detail that you don't need his name to know who they're talking about."

"Very good. And de Salles?"

"Also profiled. I'm afraid Vidal got a bit creative in that part when he talked to the reporter. He said the boy had a marked talent for miming."

Malgreave shrugged. "No harm done. At this point I don't care what we have to do to smoke him out, just so long as we can make it stick in the end."

"Just so."

"You look tired, my friend," Malgreave said. "You've

209

been at work even longer than I have. Go home and spend some time with your wife." Before it's too late, he added silently.

"You've been here almost as long," Josef pointed out politely.

Malgreave shook his head. "You go home. I have to check the telephone calls and then I'll leave."

"I checked with Gauge when I came in," Josef said. "Just the usual crank calls. I'll check the transcripts to make absolutely certain, but it seems ordinary enough. Some hysterical woman insisting the killer was after her stepdaughter, a man with an incomprehensible tale of drugs and such. Gauge was in the midst of typing them up. I'll go over them and then go home."

Malgreave's forehead creased. "Maybe I should take a look . . ."

"Sir!" Josef managed a look of affront. "Surely you can trust me on a matter such as this. I've been checking the phone calls for months now."

"Of course." Malgreave backed down. It had been a long day, and the tension was beginning to tell on both of them. "I'll go home for a bit. But call me if anything turns up."

"Of course, Chief Inspector."

Josef watched the old man leave. It was funny how he'd aged in the last few years. The chief inspector couldn't be more than fifty, yet he looked at least ten years older. Would the job do the same thing to him?

He had every intention of finding out. And the way Malgreave was going, it would be soon. When they cracked this case, Josef had every intention of seeing that he was in line for his share of the glory. Malgreave was always generous in sharing the credit. If he could just keep Vidal down where he belonged, and if Malgreave did as he threatened and retired once they put a stop to the recent killings, then his future looked rosy indeed.

He settled down into Malgreave's chair, his broad bottom fitting nicely into the worn leather seat. He wrinkled his nose at the smell of dead cigarettes. A filthy habit, and as far as he could see it, Malgreave's only weakness. That, and the bitch he was married to.

Lucky for him that Helga was so understanding. Her ambition rivaled his, and she had no objections to late nights, early mornings, and an absentee husband if his salary and prestige continued to rise. And if sometimes he felt a little lonely, if he missed his son and daughter as they grew up without him, then that was the price he had to pay for the good life.

But things would be much better once he took over Malgreave's job, Malgreave's private office with the window overlooking the street. He could set his own hours, not have to put in twelve- and fourteen-hour days to impress his superior. He'd leave that to brownnoses like Vidal.

Pierre Gauge's shaved head ducked inside the door. If he was surprised to see Josef relaxing in his superior's chair his bland face didn't show it. "I'm going off duty, sir," he said, and Josef took pleasure in the respectful title. "Do you want the transcripts in here?"

"Leave them on my desk," he said airily. "I'll check them tomorrow morning."

"Very good, sir." And Pierre Gauge departed, leaving Josef to his dreams of glory.

It had taken them longer than five minutes. Claire had thrown clothes together into a large suitcase, paying little attention to her choices, but Nicole had proven almost impossible to wake. Her clothes were filthy, and she managed to swim to consciousness only long enough to struggle into clean clothes and submit to having her face and hands washed by a maternal Claire before drifting back into a semi-stupor.

Without a word Tom scooped her up, wrapping a blanket around the thin, frail body. "Are you sure she's all right?" Claire worried. "Maybe we should take her to a doctor."

"She's fine, Claire. She's just drugged. All she needs to do is sleep it off."

"You're certain?"

"Reasonably so. If she seems to be falling deeper into sleep we'll stop at the first hospital we can find. Does that satisfy you?"

"It'll have to. A hospital will want to know where her father is, and I'd rather not have to answer those sorts of questions."

"We could tell them I'm her father."

"Which would work fine until she woke up enough to start speaking in French," Claire said. "God knows, I wish you were her father."

"At least Bonnard isn't either. Come on, Claire. Hélène said she'd meet us out front."

"Hélène?" Claire echoed. "Your friend is a woman?"

He managed the ghost of a grin. "I told you I tried being a vintner, a writer, a dancer, and an artist. I never told you I tried being a monk."

"No," she said. "You never did."

The Peugeot had definitely acquired more than its share of rust. Claire wished she could say the same thing for its driver. As she and Nicole bundled into the back seat she caught a whiff of Opium, a mane of black hair, and a decidedly hostile smile from the driver, who then proceeded to involve Tom in a raucous conversation held entirely in French. Claire tried to summon up enough energy to seethe, but the heavily drugged child in her arms took all the emotions she had to spare, so she merely leaned back in the cramped seat and tried not to concentrate on the back of Tom's head as he flirted with the French woman.

His hair was too long. There was a badly mended hole in the thick black sweater, and Claire wondered who'd darned it. Certainly not the exotic creature with the mundane car who couldn't seem to control her high-pitched laughter. Claire told herself if the woman giggled one more time she'd scream. She'd wanted to scream for hours now, and had controlled herself. It wouldn't take much to break that control.

Traffic in Paris was always ghastly; in rush hour it was bordering on criminal. It took forty-five minutes and several close brushes with death for the aging French car to travel

less than a city mile, with Hélène laughing all the way.
When they finally pulled up outside a block of modern,
soulless apartments, the dark-haired woman slipped from
the car, once more casting the subdued Claire a calculating
look, and then proceeded to kiss Tom full on the mouth.

It was a very long, fishy kiss, and while Claire could see
Tom's participation was more polite than enthusiastic, it
didn't keep from arousing at least a trace of fury in her
apathetic body. She glared at the woman's departing wave,
glared at Tom's amused expression, and hugged Nicole's
sleeping body tighter.

"Are you going to sit in the back seat and glower?" he
inquired coolly. "Or are you going to keep me company up
here?"

"I think I should watch Nicole."

"And I think I'll have a hard time driving with you
fuming behind my back. It's not my fault Hélène's an
affectionate girl."

"Hélène's a . . ." Nicole's sleepy moan stopped Claire
before she said something she knew she'd regret. "I'll stay
back here," she said again.

"Suit yourself. It's going to be a long drive."

Her whole body ached with weariness and pain. She
couldn't remember if Marc had ever been as rough as he'd
been last night. He probably had and she'd been too
besotted to notice. But she noticed now. At least she'd
managed a long shower, but even twenty minutes under a
steaming spray hadn't managed to make her feel clean.

"The longer, the farther away from Paris and Marc, the
better," she said, turning her face into the cracked leather
seats.

And without another word Tom pulled into the rush hour
traffic with all the reckless self-concern of a kamikaze pilot
intent on his mission.

The battered white Fiat looked like a thousand other cars
caught in the maelstrom of Paris rush hour. The interior of
the car was shadowed in the early-evening light, and the
driver wore a broad-brimmed hat pulled low over his face.

213

It would have taken a discerning eye indeed to realize that face was covered with thick white makeup, the mouth painted in a grin of maniacal glee at odds with the stylized tears dotting the clown-white cheeks.

The Fiat pulled away from the curb, following the Peugeot through the crowded streets of Paris, heading toward the northeast. And in the car there was absolute silence.

⚜ CHAPTER 19

Claire slept. How and why she couldn't quite figure out, but when she awoke in the back seat of the borrowed Peugeot she was stiff and sore and it was dark outside. She could hear the muffled noise of the car radio above the raucous engine, see Tom's profile in the reflected light of the oncoming cars. He looked distant, preoccupied, and once more she was swamped with guilt for having dragged him into this sordid mess.

And then she looked down at the child curled up next to her. Nicole was still asleep, though her breathing was more regular and even in the dimness Claire could see her color had improved. Her skin felt normal, not too hot, not the clammy coldness of earlier. Any lingering guilt vanished. For Nicole she would have endangered anyone. For the pale, helpless, not particularly endearing child still wrapped in a drugged sleep she would have done anything, and to hell with the consequences.

"Feel any better?" Tom pitched his voice low, flicking off the staticky radio.

"I guess so. Nicole seems to be doing okay."

"Good. If you hadn't woken in the next half hour I was going to pull over and check on you both, and I'd rather not do that. I've already lost one tail, and I don't want to chance picking up another one."

"Someone was following us?"

He shrugged. "Maybe I was being paranoid. It was probably just some French suburbanite on his way home for the weekend. He never got too close, but every time I looked in the mirror there he was. You missed my fancy driving—it was pretty impressive. Maybe I should have tried being a race-car driver instead of heading for the arts."

Claire managed a weak smile. He was trying to amuse her, to lighten the oppressive atmosphere of the car, and the least she could do was show some appreciation. "What kind of car?"

"An old Fiat. White, I think. The driver was wearing a hat."

Relief washed over her. "It must have been your paranoia. Marc has a Mercedes, and he hates hats."

"Okay, that rules out Marc."

"Maybe."

"How are you doing?" Tom asked.

Claire laughed shakily. "Not too good." She leaned forward over the front seat, close enough to touch him. "I find the man I've been living with, the man I was going to marry, is a crazed murderer. He said he's been killing those old women, and I don't know whether to believe him or not." She pressed her head against the cracked leather seat. "How could I have lived with him and not noticed? I can't believe he could be that crazy. I keep thinking he must have been lying to me. He always liked fantasy. He could be making this up, just to terrorize me."

"Do you really think so?" Tom said, his voice noncommittal.

"I don't know what to think," she said desperately. "He could be so strange. There were days when he'd be completely silent, moving around the apartment like Marcel Marceau, refusing to talk to me."

"How did you react to that?"

"It drove me crazy. I tried screaming at him, but it didn't work. He'd just stretch it out even longer. Do you realize how hard it is to argue with someone who won't talk, just

216

stares at you and shrugs?" She shivered. "Those were the worst times. I should have realized."

"When would he start talking again?"

"Usually the next morning. After . . ."

"After?" he prompted.

"Those nights were very bad," she said simply, shocked at the belated realization. At the time she'd accepted it, passive, as she'd been passive for so long.

"Why didn't you leave him?"

"It wasn't that simple. He didn't hurt me. It's just . . . there was a nightmarish quality about it all. An eerie feel to it, with Marc in control and me simply reacting to him. It was weird—sort of a pleasure-pain. And the next morning I'd feel sick to my stomach, and Marc would be talkative and charming and I'd forget."

Tom didn't say anything for a long moment, but Claire could see his long fingers tighten around the steering wheel. "You don't think Marc really murdered the old women?"

"I can't believe I wouldn't have known."

"That's not an answer. Do you think he murdered the old women? Do you think he's capable of it?"

"I think he's capable of it," she said. "I just can't think why he'd do it."

"There've been some interesting reports on the radio. Apparently the police believe there are several killers with one thing in common. They all went to the same orphanage in a small town outside of Paris."

"Are they sure?"

"Pretty certain. Two of the suspects are dead, a butcher and someone who worked for the government. A third, a minor-league gangster, is still on the loose, and they're not saying much about the fourth."

"But he must have been in this orphanage? Thank God," she said, her voice faint with relief. "Marc grew up in Rouen with his aunt and uncle. His parents died in a car crash when he was eight. He never spent time in an orphanage."

"You're sure?"

"He would have had no reason to lie to me."

"Unless lying had become second nature."

"I've seen pictures of him with his aunt and uncle. They look like a very happy family. They took care of him, nursed him . . ."

"Nursed him?"

"He burnt himself quite badly when he was ten years old. He still has scars on his hands. He'd been playing with matches in the Bonnards' barn and the hay caught on fire, and he'd tried to put it out with his hands."

"Interesting," Tom remarked in a neutral voice.

"Why do you use that tone of voice?" she demanded.

"Still trying to find an excuse for him? What year would he have been ten?"

"Nineteen sixty-three. Why?"

"Because in nineteen sixty-three the Marie-le-Croix orphanage burned to the ground, with an old woman inside. Several of the orphans were suspected of being involved. The same orphans that grew up to murder grandmothers."

"No!"

"Yes. Whether you like it or not, Claire, you've spent the last four months making love with a mass murderer."

And Claire retreated into the darkness of the back seat without a word, hugging her horror to herself.

Tom waited until she fell back asleep before he flicked the radio on again. He couldn't rid himself of the certain knowledge that he was the world's worst shit, and half a dozen times he opened his mouth to apologize, to lie to her and give her hope that Marc Bonnard was simply playing some sort of sadistic mind game with her.

But half a dozen times he closed his mouth again. Comforting lies wouldn't help her, much as he wanted to comfort her. As long as she clung to the ridiculous, infuriating hope that Marc was innocent, she was vulnerable. Bonnard could trace them, show up all charm and sweetness, and she'd probably go to him like the besotted fool she was.

No, that was his own jealousy talking. She was no longer besotted with Bonnard; she was sick and frightened and

218

trying to make some sort of sense of what had happened. If she was looking for excuses, rationalizations, she didn't need him blowing them all to pieces. She knew, deep down inside, just how dangerous Bonnard was. She was just having trouble admitting it.

And it was his own crazy jealousy that was making him act like such a bastard. He wanted to drive Bonnard from her heart and soul, leaving no room for anyone but himself. And the more he pushed, the more Claire held on.

He had to get himself back under control. No more cheap shots; he had to be strong and supportive while she dealt with all this. In a few more hours they'd be at Jassy. There they'd be safe. The head vintner's cottage was in reasonably decent shape—he'd stayed there last fall when he went down for a final visit. It would provide a haven, a place to hide while they dealt with the unbelievable events of the last thirty-six hours, while they dealt with Claire's denial and his own anger. Sooner or later the police had to listen.

And sooner or later Claire had to listen. When Nicole finally awoke from her drugged sleep and told her what she'd seen, then Claire wouldn't be able to lie to herself anymore. And then he could give her the comfort she needed, instead of giving in to his own frustration and rage.

He glanced in the rearview mirror. No white Fiat—either he'd lost him or he'd been ridiculously paranoid. The green Citroën had been shadowing him for quite a while now, but Tom had learned his lesson. He couldn't let his imagination get the better of him. This was the only major road heading toward the northeast—probably he'd been traveling in the company of the same half dozen cars for hours now, and they all couldn't hold Marc Bonnard.

He peered behind him just as a car passed, and the headlights illuminated the driver, putting Tom's lingering fears to rest. The dark, heavy-featured face of the driver was far removed from Bonnard's almost celestial beauty. The man behind him looked like a hoodlum, with his black leather jacket and cigarette drooping from his surly lips. No, it was a coincidence that he was following so closely.

Putting the Citroën and its unprepossessing driver out of

his mind, Tom stepped on the gas and moved a little closer toward their destination.

Malgreave surveyed the practically deserted offices with a feeling of triumph. At six-thirty the following morning he'd finally managed to beat the ever-determined Josef in to work. He nodded as he passed various yawning members of the night shift, moving in to his darkened office and flicking on the light.

Someone had emptied his overflowing ashtray, someone had shifted his chair, and it didn't take the full power of Malgreave's deductive reasoning to guess who. The cleaning staff had orders not to touch his office—it could only have been Josef auditioning for the future. Some of Malgreave's good-humored anticipation abated. Usually Summer's ambition amused him. Today, this early morning, it crowded him.

He sat down heavily in his chair, lighting his sixth cigarette of the morning and pulling the files toward him. Vidal had managed to unearth an old photograph of some of the boys from Marie-le-Croix participating in a Christmas pantomime. The delicate, almost angelically beautiful child in the center of the grainy photo certainly could have grown up to be Marc Bonnard, but then, that might have been an illusion of the whiteface makeup. He simply didn't have enough to issue an arrest warrant. Not yet.

But it was coming. He could feel it in the back of his neck, the tips of his fingers. Soon, soon now, he'd have what he needed to bring in both Rocco and Bonnard, to nail them to the wall and send them, an unlikely couple, to the guillotine. And then Josef could empty his ashtrays and sit in his chair, decorate the offices with no-smoking signs, and Malgreave would no longer give a damn.

Anything he did right now would be killing time. The stage was set—they had to wait for their actors to make a move, a final, incriminating move. Pray God another old woman wouldn't have to die in order to catch the bastards.

He smelled the coffee first, and looked up, expecting to

see Josef's doglike devotion. Instead Vidal was there, holding a steaming mug in his hand. No brioches, Malgreave noticed. And he was wearing peacock blue trousers. Nobody was perfect.

Vidal set the mug down beside the concentric circles of coffee stain on Malgreave's desk, and Malgreave accepted the pale brown liquid with a resigned sigh. He liked his coffee black, but it did play hell with his stomach.

"Morning, sir." Vidal slung his lanky body into the chair opposite him. "Where's Josef?"

"Not in yet." Malgreave took a careful sip of the coffee. It was surprisingly good, and easier to take. And he didn't need the brioches—he'd been putting on a little weight recently as Marie had been slimming down. One had to keep up appearances.

Vidal nodded, but Malgreave could see the surprise and faint trace of malicious pleasure in the young man's face. Perfectly understandable, he thought. Josef was the front-runner, but Vidal was coming up fast.

"Guillère's left town," Vidal announced abruptly.

"Damn." Malgreave spilled hot coffee on his conservative blue shirt. "When did you hear that?"

"Robert called in a few minutes ago. He lost him somewhere outside of Epernay. He was driving an old green Citroën and he hadn't packed. Maybe he's just off on a job."

"And maybe he had enough sense to get out while he still could. Damn," he said again, furious. "Have you notified the local gendarmes?"

"They're keeping an eye out for him. I presumed you didn't want him picked up if they could help, just watched."

"You presumed correctly. Any word on Bonnard?"

"No one seems to know where he is. His apartment's deserted—the Americans and the little girl drove off yesterday and haven't returned."

"I don't suppose anyone had the sense to follow them?"

Vidal shook his head. "The man assigned to watch Bonnard's apartment took his instructions very literally. He was waiting for Bonnard and only Bonnard."

"God preserve me from dogmatic fools," Malgreave said, lighting a fresh cigarette from the tail of his dying one. Without asking, Vidal fished in his pocket for his own pack and lit one, and Malgreave's approval rose another notch. In this world of militant nonsmokers it was good to find another warrior in the battle.

He looked up. Josef had finally appeared, his face flushed, his thinning hair awry as he practically sprinted through the office toward Malgreave's inner sanctum. He stopped in the doorway, and the expression on his face was ludicrous in his outrage at finding Malgreave keeping company with his greatest rival.

He started mumbling excuses as he darted warning glances at an unrepentant Vidal, but Malgreave cut him off, uninterested in car problems and recalcitrant alarm clocks. "Guillère's flown the coop," he said. "So has Bonnard's mistress and stepdaughter. I want them located."

"What's been done so far?" Josef drew himself upright, and Malgreave caught him wrinkling his nose at the heavy smell of cigarettes surrounding the two men like a cloud. If Josef was truly ambitious he'd start smoking, Malgreave thought with the last trace of amusement he would feel for days.

"Vidal's informed the gendarmes in the northeast. Guillère was headed toward Epernay when his tail lost him, and God only knows where the American's gone. Probably to meet with her lover, though she went in company with another American."

"Maybe she's leaving Bonnard. Maybe she knows something?" Vidal suggested.

"Maybe." Josef's tone was dismissive. "What would you have me do, sir?"

Malgreave rose, stubbing out his cigarette. "One thing's for sure—this won't be a day spent sitting on our tails. We'll check out Bonnard's apartment, see if there's anything inside to tell us where he might be, where the *Américaine* would have gone to. And then we'll head over to Guillère's pigsty and see what we can come up with."

"We?" Josef echoed.

"The three of us, Josef," Malgreave said gently. "Unless you'd rather stay behind and deal with paperwork?"

"I'm coming," he said fiercely. And the telephone transcripts remained unnoticed on his desk as he followed Malgreave out into the early-morning streets.

The sky was just beginning to lighten when Tom pulled the car to a stop. Claire moved, stretching her cramped body, and to her relief Nicole did the same. The child yawned, opening her puffy eyes, and then a sudden tremor of panic shook the slight body. Until she focused on Claire, and the tension drained from her narrow little shoulders.

She said something in French, in a low, sleepy voice, and Claire bent her head down to listen. "In English, darling," she said.

"Where are we?"

Claire looked up, meeting Tom's gaze. "I haven't the faintest idea. Somewhere far away, where Marc can't find us."

"Bon," said Nicole, shutting her eyes again.

By then Tom had opened the back door and lifted the drowsy child into his arms. Nicole stiffened again, then relaxed. She looked very small and slight indeed against Tom's broad frame, and Claire scrambled after her, her face still creased with worry.

Tom hadn't exaggerated when he said he was taking them to a bleak and barren spot. Even in the predawn light she could see the dryness, the rocky soil where grapes couldn't grow.

The building looked oddly like an American ranch house —long and low with a porch running along the front of it. It was built from stone, however, as were the various outbuildings looming through the gray shadows, and the interior, though spotless, was hardly welcoming. The night chill lingered, clinging to the thick stone, and Claire shivered, wrapping her arms around her narrow body as she followed Tom into one of the small bedrooms.

He lay Nicole gently on the bare mattress, covering her with the rough blanket that had been folded at the foot of the bed. Claire headed for the straight chair beside the bed, determined to continue her vigil, but Tom's hand caught her, yanking her back.

"She's fine," he said. "She just needs to finish sleeping it off, and you're not going to do her any good sitting there."

"I'm not leaving her."

"The hell you're not." Without another word he scooped her up, slinging her over his shoulder and carting her out the door. She considered screaming, but she didn't want to wake Nicole, to frighten her any more than she'd already been frightened. She contented herself with pounding her fists against Tom's strong back. He took the punishment without a sound, heading into the adjoining bedroom and tossing her down on the bed.

She immediately tried to jump up, but he simply pushed her back down again. "Stay put," he ordered. "You can hear if Nicole makes any noise. In the meantime you need to get some sleep."

"I can sleep later," she said mutinously.

"I hate to bring this up, but what if Bonnard finds us? I certainly took a circuitous route getting here, but anything's possible. Don't you want to be rested, ready to face him if he does?"

"I don't want to leave Nicole alone and unprotected."

"You aren't. I sleep very lightly—if anyone makes a sound I'll know it. I want you to promise me you'll stay there."

"Where are you going?" Her voice sounded damnably plaintive, but she was too cold and too frightened to worry about it.

"First I'm going to hide the car in one of the sheds. Then I'm going to see if I can find the gun that used to be here. The vintner liked taking potshots at rabbits. And then I'm coming back in here and getting in bed with you, for the sole purpose of getting a little sleep myself."

"Why don't I just sit with Nicole while you're hiding the car . . . ?"

"I can lock you in," he said flatly.

"You wouldn't."

"I would. Lie down." He tossed a worn quilt around her shivering body as she reluctantly complied. Leaning over her, he tucked the cover around her shoulders, and his face was very close. "You're only a few feet away from Nicole, and she's just fine. Stay put. Okay?"

The soft, concave bed was deceptively comfortable. Warmth was beginning to penetrate from the threadbare quilt, and there was no denying Tom was right. "Okay," she said in a small voice.

Her reward was his smile. "Good woman," he said, brushing his mouth against hers. "I'll be right back."

She watched him go, half her brain listening for Nicole's slightest sound. "Good woman," he'd said. Marc, Brian, most men she knew would have said, good girl. She rolled over, curling up, listening to Nicole's steady breathing, as she considered the last few moments. The timing was all off, the situation hellish in the extreme, but there was no denying it. She'd found the man of her dreams. And for just a few hours she would put her trust in him and do what he told her.

She didn't wake when he joined her on the sagging bed. She moved into his arms, curling into his warmth, breathing a sigh of comfort and pleasure as she huddled against him.

They slept for hours, as the sun tried to fight its way through the clouds to shine on another damp, rainy day. She wasn't sure what woke her, ravenous hunger or something just as elemental. When she awoke fitful daylight filtered through the shuttered windows, Tom's hands were on her breasts, and her mouth was pressed against his chest.

He'd dispensed with his sweater, and his rough cotton shirt was unbuttoned and pulled from his jeans. She didn't know whether she'd unfastened it or he had, and she didn't care. His flesh was hot and smooth beneath her mouth, tasting, smelling of safety and delight. She wanted him, with a desperation and suddenness that shocked her. She wanted him inside her, replacing Marc, filling her and overwhelming her and ridding her of the repulsion that had threatened to crush her. He was awake, a willing partner to her mouth's exploration, and she slid her hands down to the waistband

225

of his jeans, her fingers trembling with fear and determination. Hurry, hurry, she thought, wishing he'd take over, wishing he'd take care of it all, leaving her a passive partner in delight, when she heard the noise.

A creak. A rustle of bedclothes from the room beside theirs. And a piercing shriek of complete, agonized terror split the thick dampness of the morning air, tearing Claire from the bed and her short-lived, erotic daze.

☙ CHAPTER 20

Nicole was alone in the stark room, sitting upright in the middle of the narrow bed, her eyes wide and dilated with terror, her mouth still open in an unending scream. The windows were shuttered, the house still seemingly deserted.

Without hesitation Claire climbed onto the bed and pulled the terrified child into her arms, muffling the screams in the folds of her cotton sweater as Tom ran to the front room. He was back moments later, just as Nicole's panic was subsiding into shivering gasps for air, and Claire met his gaze above the child's head.

"No one's here."

"You're certain?" Claire stroked the lank hair that clung to Nicole's fragile skull.

"Positive. The door was still locked and barred from the inside. It must have been a nightmare."

"And who could blame her?" Claire murmured. "It's all right, sweetheart. There's no one here to hurt you."

The child stirred, pulling herself out of Claire's arms and looking up into her eyes with a touching combination of wariness and trust. "Where's Marc?"

"He can't find us. We've gone so far away that Marc will never be able to catch us," Claire promised rashly.

Nicole sighed, a shuddery little sound that pulled at

Claire's heart. "I hope not." She looked up at Tom without curiosity. "Who's that?"

"A friend. His name is Tom Parkhurst, and he's going to make certain that Marc can't get anywhere near us."

Nicole surveyed him for a long, silent moment, from the top of Tom's tousled head to his bare feet, taking note of the small handgun he held somewhat gingerly, and Claire followed that enigmatic gaze. As a knight errant he looked somewhat less than formidable, but Claire wasn't fooled. She would trust him with her life, and with Nicole's. In fact, she'd done just that.

"Okay," Nicole said finally, accepting him.

Tom moved into the room, tucking the gun self-consciously into the waistband of his jeans. "Tell Claire what happened yesterday, Nicole," he said gently. "What did Marc do to you?"

"There's no need." Claire's voice was sharp, protective. "I don't have any more illusions."

"It doesn't matter," Nicole said, her voice absurdly adult. "I've always known Marc is a bad man. I just knew no one would believe me."

"You didn't come home early from your grandmother's, did you?" Tom prodded gently.

Claire opened her mouth to protest once more, then shut it as Tom glared at her.

"No," said Nicole in a very small voice.

"Did you see him kill your grandmother?"

A shudder passed through Nicole's body. "I didn't watch. I heard him come in and I hid in the kitchen. At first he didn't know I was there, but when he came in to wash off the knife I must have made a noise."

Claire shut her eyes in horror. "Why didn't you tell me?"

"You wouldn't have believed me," Nicole said simply. "My mother didn't believe me when I told her things about him. She said I was lying to get attention."

"What things?" Claire didn't want to ask, couldn't keep herself from asking.

"The way he used to touch me. The way he used to watch me in the bathtub, the way he used to hurt me when he thought *Maman* wasn't looking. And then, when *Maman* finally did believe me, it was too late. She was dead." As always, Nicole was practical, prosaic. *"Grand-mère* insisted I go away to school, and Marc went on tour to America, so things were all right for a while. And then you came, and you believed everything he told you." Nicole's contempt was more than plain. "I knew it wouldn't do any good to tell you, but at least he was too busy with you to bother me."

Claire was beyond guilt. "What happened yesterday?"

Nicole shook her head. "I don't remember much. He was laughing, talking about how he was going to hurt me. I couldn't walk, but I was able to crawl away and hide in the heating duct. I thought he was going to find me but he didn't. Something must have scared him away. The next thing I remember, you were there."

"Thank God," Claire murmured. At least things hadn't gone as far as she'd expected. Marc had been driven away before he'd had a chance to molest her. She wanted to grab Nicole once more and hold her, to keep away the evil and fear that had haunted her for so long, but she knew better. Nicole was rapidly recovering her prickly self-possession, and she wouldn't accept Claire's babying her for much longer. Indeed, the best thing for all of them was practicality, not an excess of emotion.

So Claire climbed down from the bed, shoving up the sleeves of her sweater and addressing Tom in her best no-nonsense voice. "First things first. I imagine Nicole would like to use the bathroom." At that Nicole nodded enthusiastically. "And then I need something to eat before I fall down and faint from hunger."

"The first part's easy. The second part will take a little longer." Both females groaned loudly. "I have to go into town to find something to eat and a telephone. In the meantime you'll have to make do with wine and candy bars."

Claire moaned. "Is that all we have?"

Nicole grinned. "Perfect," she said with a blissful expression on her pale face. "And bring back some Coca-Cola."

*   *   *

229

Rocco settled in to wait. He was hungry, he was thirsty, but he made it a practice never to eat before a job. He still hadn't decided whether today's task was business or pleasure. Maybe a little bit of both.

He'd parked the Citroën in a small scraggly patch of bushes. It gave him an unobstructed view of the stone cottage and the sheds. From the dubious comfort of the small car he could watch and wait until one of those American idiots made a move.

It was a dark, rainy day, with a spring chill in the air that made Rocco huddle deeper into his leather jacket. He hated the countryside, hated being cold, hated being cramped into this too-small car. The sooner this was over the sooner he could get back to Paris. He would have given a great deal to be able to chuck it all, to let Bonnard's mess sort itself out. But he knew he couldn't afford to do that. Not if he wanted Hubert's protection.

In a way it was his own fault, for listening to Marc in the first place. It was his own fault all those years ago. He'd been older than the others, he'd had plans of his own. They'd been doing all right, too, protecting each other, until Marc de Salles had shown up, with his angel's face and his devil's soul. He'd been the one to first suggest killing *Grand-mère* Estelle and Georges. He'd been the one to use the knife, and to take pleasure in doing so. And he'd been the one to suggest the pact, using his mesmerizing personality to convince the others.

Rocco had never thought he'd actually carry through with it. The government had rounded up the orphans and sent them to foster homes. Rocco had ended up with a schoolteacher and his family in Lyon. He'd stuck it out for two years and then taken off, back to his beloved Paris, where he killed for a living, not for pleasure.

It had been a simple enough pact, written in their own blood, signed by the fire. When they grew up they would kill the grandmothers of the world, the evil ones who'd sent them away to the orphanage, the evil ones who kept them there and hurt them and abused them. They would never meet, never talk, never in any way acknowledge each other, but each of them must kill twenty old women before they could stop.

There had been all sorts of rules. Boys on the edge of puberty loved ceremony and mystery. They could only kill in the rain, they must remove the shoes of the old ladies and lay them out as they had *Grand-mère* Estelle, they must use a knife and one thrust into the heart. Rocco had added that part, being partial to knives, while Yvon had suggested the bit about the shoes and Gilles had just listened and nodded. It was Marc who had wanted them to rape the old women's corpses.

The other boys had rebelled at that, and he'd given in. They would kiss the dead women, and leave it at that. Rocco always wondered whether Marc had.

In the years that followed Rocco had forgotten the pact, forgotten the orphanage and the other boys. If he couldn't quite forget Marc, the burning eyes and angelic face, then everyone had their own demons. It had been an accident. A rainy night, and he'd been robbing an apartment in Montmartre, when the owner returned. It was a frail, blue-haired lady, with silver-framed pictures of chubby grandchildren adorning her walls. He'd stabbed her quickly, instinctively, one thrust to the heart, and as the rain beat against the windows he found himself removing her shoes and laying her out on the narrow bed, arms folded across the wound. He'd stared down at her for a long, enigmatic moment, surprised at the joy and power he felt coursing through his veins. Killing had become an instinct by then, but this was different.

Vaguely he had remembered the night in the orphanage, the pact written in blood. And he'd bent down and kissed the dead woman on her slack mouth.

Twenty women, he thought back to the original pact. The problem was, he didn't know if he could stop. He was already at eighteen—two more and he'd be finished.

Poor Yvon had bungled things quite badly, managing only one. And between Gilles and Marc there were only about twenty-four. The others were dead, and if Marc was helped to retire then none of them had fulfilled their promise. Twenty each, that made eighty old women, and only forty-three of them gone so far. Maybe Rocco would finish things up for the others.

There was movement at the farmhouse, and Rocco pulled himself out of his reverie, wiping the dreamy smile from his face. The American was leaving. In the darkness of the opened doorway he could make out the slender, fair figure of Marc's mistress. He would have liked a taste of that, but it probably wouldn't work out. Better to finish her quickly, grab the girl, and head back to Paris. Once he'd bought Hubert's protection with the price of the old woman's granddaughter, then he could concentrate on more important things.

The door closed behind the man, and Rocco had no doubt it was firmly locked and possibly barred. He watched the man head to the shed where he'd hidden the Peugeot, and considered cutting him off, killing him there and then. He decided not to bother. The man would be out of the way—he could only be going to the town and that was a good seven miles off. He had more than enough time to get into the house and do his work without bothering with a man who was taller than him and possibly as strong. Rocco was a prudent man, not one to take unnecessary chances when he had a job to do.

He sat in his car, watching the Peugeot disappear down the rutted, rain-soaked road. He had at least half an hour to do the job, perhaps more, but it wouldn't do to waste time. Sliding from the cramped car seat, he headed out into the pouring rain, down the rocky hillside to the farmhouse.

Pierre Gauge blinked his eyes in concentration, ran a pink tongue over his thick lips, and broke the point on his freshly sharpened pencil. "One moment, monsieur," he said laboriously, setting the phone down and crossing the room to sharpen the pencil. He moved back across the crowded room with his usual deliberation, sank back down in his chair, pulled the notebook toward him, perused the name and the opening sentence he'd just transcribed, and then picked up the phone again.

"Yes, monsieur," he said patiently. "Speak slowly and clearly. I can't understand you when you yell." These stupid Americans, Gauge thought, pressing hard with the pencil. Either they speak English too quickly for even a clever man to follow, or they speak French so badly one would think they were speaking Hindustani. They didn't even have the sense to use the same alphabet, or at least they didn't call the letters the same things. The Holy Mother only knew if he'd spelled the man's name right.

The man's voice was getting angrier, making his French even more indistinct. Gauge looked around him, curious to see if a more efficiently bilingual policeman were in sight, but there was no one available.

"Perhaps you should call back when Inspector Summer or Chief Inspector Malgreave is in the office," Gauge broke through his tortuous explanations.

He didn't know the words the man used, but from the tone of voice he expected they were something quite obscene. The man was insisting that lives were at stake, but they all said that. Gauge leaned forward, sighing, and began to write once more, when his pencil broke again.

"One moment, monsieur," he said, putting the receiver down and ignoring the angry squawking. He crossed the room again, sharpened the pencil, moistened it with his tongue, sharpened it again, recrossed the room, and sat down at his desk. When he picked up the phone the line was dead.

Gauge shook his head. It was just as well. He worked better making the transcripts, where he could stop and start the tape and not have to worry whether he'd caught everything. And then Malgreave or that puffed-up Summer could track it down at their leisure, and Gauge didn't need to worry.

He stared at the tape machine that sat prominently on his desk. Even if the man hadn't given complete details, all calls concerning the Grandmother Murders were automatically traced. They were in no danger of losing important information.

The question was, should he start transcribing the harried

message now or wait till more came in? The line had been very busy all morning, what with the latest information going out over the news last night, and the angry American was only one in a long line of crazies who thought people were after them. The American was at least a bit original— he thought a mime wanted to do him in.

Gauge chuckled to himself. He'd wait for two or three more calls to come in before he changed tapes and began the laborious task of transcribing once more. After all, Malgreave and Summer were out and weren't expected back till late afternoon. He had plenty of time.

The ground was rocky underfoot. Rocco's shiny black boots were scuffed and splattered with mud, slippery on the wet earth, and he cursed as he slid down the shallow embankment and moved toward the house. The rain was pouring steadily now, drizzling down his neck, sliding down his back beneath the leather jacket that was like a second skin to him.

The shutters were still tightly shut against the miserable outside world, and a plume of wood smoke sweetened the air. Rocco shivered against the side of the building. Maybe if he hurried, finished the *Américaine* quickly, he'd have time to warm up before heading back out into the rain.

If it weren't for the brat, he'd have time to enjoy the fire and the *Américaine* before returning to Paris. For a moment he considered the alternatives. He could tell Hubert that Bonnard killed the kid. While Hubert wouldn't like it, there wouldn't be much he could do about it. And things had gotten so bad maybe even Hubert couldn't help.

Paris might not be the answer. He had friends in Marseilles, even a cousin or two. Opportunities abounded in that city, for an enterprising man who didn't count squeamishness as one of his character flaws. Maybe the wisest thing he could do would be to silence both of them, leaving the bloody scene for the local gendarmes to deal with. They'd be so busy looking for the murderous Bonnard that they wouldn't even think about Rocco Guillère.

Except for Malgreave, of course. He was like a dog with a

234

rat, worrying it, shaking it, never releasing it until its neck was broken. Malgreave wouldn't give up, even if Rocco disappeared into the Marseilles underground. Sooner or later he'd catch up with him.

But for Malgreave, time was running out. He was getting old, too old for this sort of thing. Sooner or later he'd retire, and that fool Summer was no match for him. Once Malgreave was out of the way Rocco could safely return to Paris. If Hubert had suspected something untoward in the death of the little girl, well, Hubert wouldn't live forever either.

Damn, it was cold. He huddled closer to the building, listening to the quiet voices just barely discernible through the thick stone walls. It was no wonder he was freezing. Those walls still held the icy temperatures of the previous winter, and it was radiating directly into his bones. He looked down at his boots, the pointy toes scuffed and muddy. He was standing directly in a pool of water, and his beloved boots weren't made to suffer such an insult. Water had already seeped through, and the leather was ruined.

He'd have to throw them out, buy new ones. The thought made him ferocious—his feet were large, and the fancy leather boots he preferred were hard to find. Someone would pay for this, someone with a soft voice and Marc Bonnard in her bed. The thought of wasting Bonnard's mistress gave him an odd thrill of pleasure and fear. While the anticipation was sweet, the chilly wet air wasn't. The sooner he iced the child, the longer he'd have to enjoy the woman. He wouldn't even worry about the man returning. A civilized American was no match for someone who'd grown up on the streets as Rocco had. If he came back too quickly Rocco could make short work of him before finishing up with the woman.

Damn, he wanted that fire. Reaching into his pocket, he pulled out his custom-made switchblade knife, the one that had served him so well for years. He'd taken it off a Chinese heroin dealer, and the dragons on the ivory handle had always appealed to his imagination. This place must have a back door, a window where the shutters weren't tightly latched. His boots splashed through the water as he skirted the house. He'd just reached the far corner when the icy dampness reached down into his bones, and he let loose with a loud, uncontrollable sneeze.

And inside the house, Claire looked at Nicole, and the two of them froze in complete, utter panic.

Tom sped along the rutted roadway, cursing. He pounded the steering wheel in impotent rage, damning the Paris police department, their governing Department of Interior, the local gendarmes, the army, the French, and the world, not necessarily in that order. He reached for the windshield wipers, but instead the lights flashed on through the dark afternoon light, and once more Tom cursed. Typical of the French to put everything in a different place, he fumed.

He skidded in the mud, and the groceries in the back seat tumbled to the floor. He wrenched the wheel, turning into the spin, and straightened the car, slamming down on the accelerator once more. At this rate Bonnard would find them and finish them before the Paris police even noticed something was going on.

It was no wonder it had taken them almost three years to come up with anything near approaching a solution to the Grandmother Murders. It would probably take another two to bring Bonnard to justice.

And to top everything off, he thought he'd seen the white Fiat in the tiny village of Jassy. He'd noticed it out of the corner of one eye as he was talking on the phone, and when he'd finally slammed down the receiver and tried looking for it there was no trace. Besides, it probably meant nothing. White Fiats were a dime a dozen throughout Europe, and a great many men wore hats pulled low over their faces. Still, he couldn't rid himself of the nagging sense of familiarity.

At least he'd left Claire the gun, explaining the rudiments of how to aim it and fire it. Not that he was an expert himself—he could only hope he'd shown her the right way to do it. She wouldn't need it—it had simply been a precaution, one to help set his mind at ease when he drove off and left the two of them there. He only wished it had worked.

The car slid again, and Tom cursed Hélène and her bald tires and an engine that tended to choke and splutter in the dampness. Just let it get him back to the farmhouse, quickly, and he'd ask nothing more of it.

And let Claire and Nicole be all right, he added in a silent prayer, giving in to the indismissible fear that was filling him. And he drove on into the afternoon rain.

❧ CHAPTER 21

Nicole was standing motionless, petrified with terror. All her slowly returning sangfroid had vanished with the sound of that furtive sneeze, and she stood in the middle of the room, pale, silent, horrifyingly resigned.

Well, I'm not resigned, Claire thought furiously. "Hide, Nicole," she whispered fiercely. Nicole didn't move, and Claire caught her shoulders in a fierce, desperate grip, propelling her toward the bedroom. The late afternoon was alive with noise, the hiss and pop of the fire, the steady, nerve-wracking beat of the rain against the shuttered windows and the tin roof, the rattling noise of the wind at the door.

But it wasn't the wind. Someone was jiggling the back door, someone was trying to force his way in. "Go away," Claire shouted in a panic that almost equaled Nicole's.

To her astonishment a voice answered, in heavy, guttural French. She stopped propelling Nicole forward, looking down at the child with a questioning expression.

"He says he's a stranger. His car went off the road and he wants to call a garage." Nicole's voice was shaking with terror, her eyes blank.

"We don't have a telephone," Claire shouted. "Go away."

Again the voice came, as the back door rattled noisily. "He says he's wet and cold and wants to come in till the rain passes," Nicole whispered. "Oh, Claire, do you really think it's Marc?"

She shook her head. "I don't know. It doesn't sound like him, but Marc's a trained actor. I'm sure he could disguise his voice if he wanted to."

"But if he had come to get us," Nicole said with eerie common sense, "he wouldn't be making a sound. This man is much too noisy."

Her words were prophetic, if not reassuring. The rattling turned to a loud thudding, and the two of them watched in mute horror as the flimsy back door began to give way beneath the barrage. Seconds later the door splintered open, and a dark figure hurtled through.

"Run, sweetheart," Claire hissed, shoving her into the bedroom and shielding her with her body as she faced the huge, angry intruder. Where the hell had she put the gun Tom had insisted she keep?

The stranger moved into the room, relaxed now, taking his time as he shook the water from his leather jacket. At least it wasn't Marc, Claire told herself, holding her ground. The stranger couldn't have seen Nicole, he would think she was there alone. If he was intent on harming her at least Nicole would be safe.

The man looked up and grinned at her, a terrifying, savage grin that revealed a cruel mouth with several gold teeth. He said something in French, and Claire shook her head.

"I'm sorry, I only speak English," she said with deceptive calm. She'd left the gun on the table somewhere behind her. If she could just back up, casually . . .

"I said, where's the brat?" The man advanced on her, swaggering slightly, and for the first time Claire realized she'd seen that face before. She couldn't remember where or when, but the effect was unnerving.

"Please leave," she said, stumbling backward, away from him, part pretense, part real fear. The table had to be somewhere behind her, the gun in reach.

The man smirked, there was no other word for it. "Not until I get what I came for." He had something in his hand, something slender and cylindrical, something that looked harmless. Until he snapped it, and a thin, wicked-looking blade snicked out. "I'm afraid you've become a problem, *chérie,"* he crooned. "You and the little girl. Not to mention Marc himself. I'm going to clean up a few loose ends. Tell me where the brat is, and when I finish with her we'll have a few minutes to enjoy ourselves. If you're nice to me I promise it won't hurt."

Claire just stared at him in horror. "I don't know what you're talking about," she said, her shaking voice belying her protestations.

"Don't anger me." The man was enjoying this, she could tell. She edged a few inches further, but the table was still maddeningly out of reach. "It's not often I get an audience, someone to talk to. Your man's gone into town, there's just you and the brat, and no one can help you."

She didn't bother to ask how he knew. He'd probably been the one in the white Fiat who'd followed them. "He'll be back any moment . . ."

"And he'll be useless against me." The man began paring his filthy fingernails with the wicked-looking knife. "I kill for a living, *chérie.* I kill for business and for pleasure. Your American won't have a chance against someone like me."

"Who do you kill?"

The man shrugged. "Anyone for a price. Drug dealers, pimps, whores, businessmen, bureaucrats."

"And for pleasure?" Her seeking fingers caught the edge of the small table.

The man smiled his hideous smile. "Why, old ladies, of course."

A last, lingering trace of hope spiked through her. "Then Marc didn't . . ."

"Oh, yes, Marc did. Just as we killed *Grand-mère* Estelle in the orphanage twenty-five years ago. Of course," he added sweetly, "we no longer eat them."

Claire's empty stomach twisted, convulsed, and she doubled over, knocking against the table, the gun skittering into her desperate hands. She collapsed on the rough plank floor, rolled, and came up with the gun in her hands, pointing straight at her murderous intruder.

Except that he was gone. She saw his leather jacket disappearing into Nicole's room, and she didn't even hesitate. She fired, and the damned thing recoiled on her like an angry serpent. She heard Nicole scream, and she raced toward the room, prepared to fire again and again and again.

The man was lying on the floor, clutching his side and cursing furiously, weakly. Claire could see the blood on his hand as he pressed it against his leather jacket, and another wave of nausea and dizziness hit her.

This time she wouldn't give in to it. Nicole was kneeling in the middle of the bed, staring at the bloody tableau in horror. Holding the gun as steady as she could in wildly shaking hands, Claire stepped over the man's writhing form and caught Nicole in her arms. The child clung to her, burying her face in Claire's shoulder, and slowly, carefully, Claire stepped back toward the door.

A steely, bloody hand shot out and wrapped itself around her ankle, the fingers digging in like claws. She fought back the scream that caught in her throat, and still holding Nicole with one protective arm, she leaned over and pointed the gun directly into the man's face.

"I'll count to five," she said, "and then I'll shoot you. Don't think I won't."

His glittering, enraged eyes met hers for a long, thoughtful moment. She knew he was weighing his chances of toppling her over, Nicole and all, weighing that against the possibility of another bullet smashing through his skull.

"One," said Claire, ready to pull the trigger if she felt the slightest tug.

Her ankle was numb, streaks of pain were shooting up her calf and thigh, and Nicole was snuffling into her shoulder, clinging to her for dear life.

"The hell with it," Claire said, and pulled the trigger.

The bullet buried itself in the floor beside the man's head, but she'd still accomplished what she'd set out to do. In his panic he released her ankle and rolled out of the way, slamming up against the foot of the bed and panting in rage and pain. He left a smeared trail of blood on the scrubbed plank floor.

Through a haze of panic and adrenaline-charged determination, she heard the renewed pounding, this time on the front door. Tom's voice came with it, and for the first time the blind rage cleared a little from her head.

"Go around the back," she shouted, not daring to leave the wounded snake untended. His knife lay on the floor, out of his reach, and she kicked it away, into the living room, cradling Nicole as they waited for Tom to arrive.

He took in the bloody scene with admirable efficiency. "You shot him?" he asked calmly.

Her voice no longer worked, so she contented herself with a brief nod. The man's eyes were closed, his breathing labored, but she wasn't fooled. When Tom started toward him she stopped him. "Let him be," she said in a raw voice. "He's too dangerous."

"He could be bleeding to death . . ."

"He deserves it. He kills the old women too."

Tom looked down at him, no surprise showing. "Rocco someone, the radio said. All right. If he bleeds to death he's no great loss. Are you two all right?"

"I'm okay," Claire said, lying. "How about you, baby?"

Nicole lifted her tear-streaked face, nodded, and hid once more in Claire's arms.

"Good," Tom said. "Then let's get the hell out of here."

"The police . . . ?"

He shook his head. "Still no luck. We'll try from our next stop."

"Do you know where we're going?" She found she was still clutching the gun in an iron grip. Carefully Tom pried it from her.

"Not really. We'll just drive till we find a safe place." He reached for Nicole, and surprisingly enough she went, transferring her limpetlike grip to him with an unconscious show of trust. "At least I managed to get some food. We'll have a picnic on the road."

He headed out the door, and for a brief moment Claire remained behind, staring down at the man she'd shot, the man she would have killed in cold blood if her aim had been better. She tried to summon remorse, triumph, at least a sense of justification. She felt nothing, empty inside, as she stared at the pale, sweating face.

Suddenly his eyes shot open, dark, full of pain and malice. He tried to move toward her, but the effort was too much, and he sank back, panting, his eyes shut once more. Claire ran from the room.

Pierre Gauge finished typing the transcript. He was a careful man, working slowly, steadily, so as not to miss or mistake a word. He worked without using his brain, only his ears and his fingers, not bothering to read what he had transcribed until he'd finished. He sat back, his watery brown eyes moving laboriously over the typed words.

And then he whistled to himself, softly, and allowed himself the luxury of a muttered curse. This one sounded different from the usual crackpots that called in, disturbing Pierre's peace and distracting his attention from the day's racing form. He rifled through his copy of yesterday's transcripts and found what he was looking for. The American, Parkhurst, had called two days in a row. And in print he seemed neither deluded nor attention-seeking.

He scanned the page, coming across the call from Claire MacIntyre. He swore again. Well, it wasn't his responsibility, his place, to judge whether a call was important or not. Neither of them had mention Guillère, and up to now that was the only thing Malgreave had been interested in. Pierre had placed those transcripts on Josef Summer's desk. It was up to the bosses to think, not the likes of him. If Summer had screwed himself, well then, that was life.

But Gauge's ass was on the line, too. He couldn't just sit there, waiting for someone to pay attention. Neither Malgreave nor his two assistants were back yet, but they would be, sooner or later. And this time, instead of putting the transcript on Josef's tidy desk, he took the few extra steps and placed it in the center of Malgreave's mess.

And with the righteous sense of a man who'd done his duty, he reapplied himself to the racing form, ignoring the noise around him.

The goddamned bitch, Rocco thought, pulling himself into a sitting position. He knew from experience that the bullet wouldn't kill him, but he'd lost a lot of blood and he was weak, weak. It would take every ounce of strength he had left to crawl out to his car and drive to someplace where he could find help.

Probably back to Paris, much as he hated the thought. Marseilles was too far away. Besides, he knew where to find doctors who were as discreet as they were practiced. He'd get patched up, then disappear. He'd screwed things up but good this time. Hubert wouldn't help him—not since he lost the child. And Marc sounded too crazy to be of much use to anyone.

No, things didn't look good for Rocco. What with Malgreave hot on his trail, no one would be enthusiastic about hiding him. No one he knew would want to let themselves in for police attention.

He levered himself up to the bed, panting slightly. He was slightly disoriented. God only knows how long ago the Americans had left. He must have passed out. There'd be no catching them now, and he no longer gave a damn. He had his own skin to worry about, a more important issue than revenge.

He'd be lucky if he made it as far as Paris, he thought gloomily. He might very well have to stop on the way, but that would only be a last resort. He didn't look like the kind of man who shot himself by accident, and he'd face all sorts of difficult questions if he checked himself into some rural hospital.

No, he'd make it. At least the bitch hadn't taken his knife. She'd kicked it out of the way, but he could see it in the darkened confines of the empty living room. He'd take a minute or two, catch his breath, and then head for his knife.

He blinked. There was no noise but the sound of the rain

beating against the deserted farmhouse, but he thought he saw a shadow. He squinted his eyes, concentrating on the knife, watching in shock as a white-gloved hand reached down and picked it up. He looked up as the figure filled the doorway, and a frisson of horror washed over him.

"Marc," he said, forcing an easy tone of voice. "Old friend, I never expected to see you here."

Marc said nothing. He was dressed in black—tight black leotards and top and mud-soaked black slippers. Only his gloves were white. And his face.

He glided into the room, the knife held loosely in the gloved hand. Rocco tried again, stilling the superstitious terror that threatened to swamp him. "Thank goodness you're here. That damned bitch of yours shot me. I need some help. I'm afraid it's going to have to be a doctor—I'm not sure if I'll make it to Paris before someone patches me up."

Marc said nothing. He kept coming, his feet making no noise, almost as if he were floating a few inches off the ground, Rocco thought dizzily. Every motion was smooth, effortless.

Rocco kept talking. His brain was getting a little muddled, but it no longer seemed to matter. "Remember the orphanage, old friend? Remember *Grand-mère* Estelle and that whip she used? I still have nightmares about her and old Georges. I remember how helpless I used to feel, and how I hated them. Sometimes I wake up at night in a cold sweat, remembering.

"Do you remember the smell? The rain and the charred timbers of the old place? And the roses, Georges's goddamned roses, covering over the stink. I knew a whore once who always wore a cheap rose perfume. I killed her, just for the pleasure of it."

Marc said nothing. He stood only inches away from where Rocco sat, and it took all his effort to lift his head, to look into that white-painted mask of glee and despair. The chocolate brown eyes were quite mad, Rocco decided. But then, they'd always been a little off. Marc was going to kill

245

him. He knew what Rocco had been trying to do, knew that Rocco would kill him if he got a chance. He wasn't going to get that chance.

"Have you ever killed a man before, Marc?" he inquired dreamily. "Of course you have. You were the one who killed Georges, weren't you? And you're going to kill me." It really didn't matter. He was very tired, and he didn't want to go out into that cold, wet rain. Better to stay right here.

And then he remembered what Marc had done to the old gardener, his fitting act of revenge for the endless bouts of sexual torture. A last bit of energy filled him. He didn't want to be mutilated. He reached out a hand, to protest, to stop Marc, but his arms were weak, and Marc was very, very strong. He kept slashing, slashing, and there was nothing Rocco could do but laugh. Marc didn't realize that he was feeling nothing, cheating Marc of the pain. Finally he was cheating Marc of everything, as the blackness closed in, the thick silence settled around him, and he slumped forward on the bloody bed.

Claire was cold, so very cold. It never stopped raining in France; the steady downpour was a constant companion and reflection of the gloom. Rain and death seemed entwined, inescapable. She sat in the front seat of the Peugeot and shivered.

At least Nicole was temporarily distracted. Right now she was probably making herself sick in the back seat, gobbling down chips and candy bars and warm Coca-Cola. Doubtless in the next half hour Claire would have to crawl in back and hold her while she rid her body of everything she was busy stuffing into it. Which certainly wouldn't help Claire's uneasy stomach.

She'd forced herself to nibble on some bread and cheese, to choke down some of Tom's god-awful wine. At least her hands had stopped shaking, even if her stomach still churned and roiled inside her. She kept feeling the cold, hard metal of the gun in her hand, the recoil as she shot, the second time, at the murderous intruder's head.

It had been his quick reflexes and her own rotten aim that had saved her from killing him. Not any sense of morality, or decency, or fairness. She'd always considered herself a pacifist, someone who'd rather turn the other cheek than react with violence when threatened.

But it wasn't her who was being threatened. It was Nicole. And when it came to a helpless child she was no pacifist at all, but the equivalent of a soldier, determined for revenge. No one could hurt or threaten Nicole and get away with it.

She shivered again, looking over her shoulder at the small figure happily gorging herself in the back seat. The amazing thing about children was their resilience. She'd seen it time and again when she was a teacher, hoped and prayed the girl Brian had hit would have that same ability to bounce back. And there was Nicole, who'd gone through a nightmare and a half during the last three days, entirely at ease, on the run with people who bore no relation at all to her.

Claire wished to God she could be that flexible. She wished she could blot unpleasant images out of her mind. But over and over again she saw the man Tom called Rocco, his hand clutching her ankle, his dark, evil eyes glaring up at her, as she shot at him, trying to kill him.

"Cold?" Tom asked gently, his attention still on the rain-swept afternoon, the headlights sweeping down the deserted roads.

"Yes." She huddled deeper against the seat, hugging herself. Sooner or later this nightmare had to end. Sooner or later they'd be safe. "How far are we going?"

"I'm not sure. At least we know we're safe for now. Guillère must have been driving the white Fiat. I thought I saw it in town, and I hurried back rather than waste any more time shopping."

Claire lifted her head, finally giving Tom her full attention. "I don't think so. We heard him outside about ten minutes after you left. You couldn't have seen him in town."

There was silence in the car. "Well," he said finally, "Fiats are a dime a dozen in France, and white's a popular color. It must have been my paranoia."

"It must have been," said Claire, shivering. And neither of them believed it.

"When the hell did this come in?" Malgreave roared through the offices, crumpling the paper in his fist. "God damn it, Gauge, get in here!"

He watched Pierre shuffle forward, cursing the incompetent idiot. Gauge had learned early in his career that you went farther in a bureaucracy if you didn't allow yourself to think. He'd perfected the art of mindlessness, and his somewhat bovine brown eyes blinked at Malgreave innocently.

"Three o'clock this afternoon, Chief Inspector."

"Why wasn't I told?"

"You hadn't given me any particular instructions. And since Inspector Summer had discounted the previous messages . . ."

"Previous messages?" Malgreave's voice shook the windows. "What the hell are you talking about?"

Josef shrank in his chair, bewilderment and panic washing over his face. "I don't know what he's talking about. What previous messages?"

Gauge turned a limpid expression on the inspector. "They came in yesterday, sir. I placed them on your desk as you ordered."

"Good God, I forgot to look at them!" Summer turned even paler.

Malgreave shut his eyes for a moment. It was no wonder so many old women had died. He was surrounded by incompetents; even his most trusted assistant was letting his ambition get in the way of the most rudimentary practices. "Get the other messages," he said, his voice soft and very dangerous.

Summer scrambled from the room, returning moments later with a sheaf of neatly typed pages. "They're on pages three and five . . ." he began, but Malgreave snatched them out of his hand.

"I don't need you to point them out to me, Josef," he

said. "After all, you haven't seen them before either, have you? Have you?"

"No, sir," he mumbled.

At another day, another time, Malgreave would have taken pity on him. But not now. "Do you have any idea where these came from? Was the automatic tracer working?"

"Only on the first ones," Gauge said calmly. "They were made from Paris. The number and address is listed. The one today was a trunk call, and they take longer. The man hung up before we could trace it."

"So what we must do," Malgreave said bitterly, "is wait, and hope that Bonnard or Guillère don't catch up with these poor people. And the French police are left sitting on their hands. Damn you both for your incompetence!"

"Should we call the gendarmes?" Josef suggested timidly. "They have jurisdiction over rural matters . . ." He subsided in the face of Malgreave's fierce glare.

"And tell them what? That we have some people on the run, somewhere in France? I don't think they'll appreciate the information, and I won't appreciate being made a laughingstock by the army. We wait. We already have warrants out for Guillère and Bonnard. If we find them, the Americans are safe."

"And if we don't?"

Malgreave smiled sourly. "Then you can kiss any future advancement good-bye, Josef. And their blood will be on your hands."

And Josef, thinking not of guilt but the anger of his ambitious Helga, groaned softly.

CHAPTER 22

They must have driven for hours. Claire lost track of time, staring into the rain, listening to the incomprehensible crackle and buzz of the car radio. Nicole, once she had finished eating every remaining crumb of junk food, leaned over the back seat and began an amiable conversation with Tom that soon lapsed into French. For once Claire didn't care. It freed her from the necessity of keeping up a front. She could sit there in the front seat with the scent of Hélène's Opium still lingering, mixing with the smell of chocolate and chips and exhaust, and think about the man she would have killed.

There were no headlights following them, spearing through the gradually diminishing rain. They were alone in the growing night, their Peugeot a tiny boat in the vast black sea of rural France, and for a while Claire played with the illusion of safety. It didn't last. For all their sense of isolation, in the end she knew Marc would find them. When they thought they were safely hidden in some rural pension, waiting for the police to finally listen, Marc would appear. She could only hope they would see him first.

"Where are we?" she finally roused herself to ask. "Where are we going?"

She could feel the concern in Tom's eyes as he glanced over at the tightly clenched fists resting in her lap. "I can't say exactly. We're somewhere beyond Jassy, heading into a more rural section. I'm afraid our accommodations aren't going to be up to the old farmhouse. There's an empty barn not too far from here that should do for tonight. Tomorrow we can head back to town and try to get through to those idiots in Paris once more."

"All right." She turned to look back at Nicole. She had chocolate on her face, her lank brown hair was a tangled mess, but she seemed surprisingly at ease amidst the clutter of the back seat. "Are you okay, Nicole?"

She grinned in response. "I like this," she said calmly. "It's an adventure."

Thank God for children, Claire thought. "Yes, it is."

"As long as Marc doesn't catch us," Nicole added soberly. "But he won't. Tom has promised he'll cut his heart out if he tries to touch me again."

Claire controlled the tiny shiver. "Sounds messy."

"It is what he deserves," Nicole said in a complacent tone of voice. "Do you want any chocolate, Claire?"

This time Claire did shudder. "No, thanks. I'm not really hungry."

"Well, I am. Tom promised that when we get to America he'll take me to McDonalds and Burger King and Pizza House . . ."

"Pizza Hut," Tom corrected, carefully keeping his face averted.

"When will this be?" Claire asked calmly.

"When we all go to New York to live. Tom says I may have to spend some time with my great-aunt Jacqueline, but apart from her, you're my only living relative. So I'll stay with you when you and Tom get married and I'll become a real American girl."

Too many things were happening at once. Claire picked the smallest issue she could face. "I thought you hated Americans."

"Oh, I don't hate them. I don't much like them when they're tourists, but once they're home I don't think I'll have any trouble. Besides, your television is much, much better. And you have Burger Kings on every corner."

"Not quite every corner," she said faintly, settling back in her seat.

"Well, close enough," said Nicole with more animation than Claire had ever seen her exhibit. "Tom says we'll have a great time."

"Oh he does, does he?"

Tom took one large, strong hand from the steering wheel and covered her clenched fists. The warmth of his flesh touching hers, the strength in those capable hands, soothed her, chasing away the nightmare they were living through. "He does," Tom murmured.

Claire looked at him, tears stinging her eyes. For a proposal it definitely counted as one of the stranger ones. But then, their entire relationship was peculiar. She wasn't quite sure when it had turned from friendship into courtship, but turn it had. She'd known him only a few weeks; they had kissed, but never made love. How could she consider sharing the rest of her life with a man she hadn't slept with?

She glanced down at the hand covering hers. Honest hands, gentle hands. She didn't have to sleep with him to know he'd never hurt her, would be tender and loving and more than she deserved. She looked up and smiled brilliantly through her unshed tears.

"Yes," she said. "We'll have a great time." And Tom's hand tightened on hers.

The small house in the Paris suburbs was empty when Louis Malgreave let himself in the front door, but then, he hadn't expected Marie to be home. She never was these days, and tonight he was back early. He couldn't stomach one more minute of Josef's hangdog expression, Gauge's bland stupidity, the mute frustration of the telephone that didn't ring. He wanted to hit someone, very hard, and the only thing he could do was leave before he shoved his fist into Gauge's fat face.

So close, so very close. If it weren't for a comedy of errors the Americans would be safe, and Bonnard and Rocco well on their way to being caught. Instead they were still bumbling around like fools in the dark, waiting for still another lucky break that they no longer deserved.

Malgreave snapped on the lights in the living room, illuminating the rain-dark afternoon. For some reason the house felt even emptier than usual. As if part of its soul had been torn away. He held himself very still, not reaching for the cigarette that was second nature to him, not slipping off his soaked raincoat. Fear made him silent, a deep, terrifying fear such as he'd never known. He'd faced death countless times, murderers so savage they surpassed comprehension, and never had he flinched. Right now all he wanted to do was turn around, walk out the door, and run away, run from what awaited him.

But running wouldn't change it. He yanked off the raincoat, dropping it in a puddle on Marie's spotless carpet, and started slowly up the stairs.

The bedroom looked so empty without her. The dresser was stripped of its bottles of scent and makeup, the closet bare of her clothes and shoes. Everything was gone, suitcases full of belongings, and all she'd left in the place of those years of accumulations was a small, lavender piece of paper propped on his pillow.

It was probably dowsed with her own special scent, Malgreave thought, making no move to touch it. The traces of it would linger on his pillow as he tried to sleep, forcing her into his unconsciousness as she would permeate every waking hour.

Turning on his heel, he went back downstairs without reading the note, heading into the kitchen. He had a bottle of American bourbon whiskey, and he poured himself a dark, tall glass of it. The name had always amused him— after the old kings of France. Something so very American, with such a very French name. He opened the refrigerator, hanging on the door and staring at the interior, the neatly labeled leftovers, the packages of meat and cheese and butter. Marie never had strange things growing in the back of her refrigerator. Everything was always accounted for, neatly dated and labeled and used before it grew too old.

He took another sip of the whiskey, then turned away to

the sink to add a bit of water. He reached for the faucet, then dropped his hand. Marie always kept the medicines on the shelf above the old iron sink. His blood pressure medicine was there, along with some old antibiotics and a bottle of aspirin. Usually they jousted with seventeen different bottles of vitamins, minerals, fish oil, rose hips, and the like, all part of Marie's strict beauty regimen since she'd started losing weight and making a life without him. Now his medicine sat alone on the shelf.

As he was alone. He stared at the empty space above the sink for a long, hard moment. And then he began to cry.

"Here we are," Tom announced unnecessarily a few hours later. He'd pulled to a stop in front of a huge, monolithic structure, and Claire peered up at it through the rainy darkness. "Home sweet home," he added, turning off the engine.

"Where are we?" Nicole piped up from the back seat, asking the question Claire had grown tired of repeating.

If Tom was aware of their silent doubts he didn't show it. "It's an old stone barn. It's been abandoned for years—my partner and I considered leasing it to store our wine barrels while we waited for the stuff to age. It would have been perfect, cool and dark and huge."

"Why didn't you?" Claire asked.

"For one thing, we only had twelve barrels—not enough to justify the expense. For another, our wine didn't age. It just turned to vinegar. Come on, you'll love it. It's about five stories tall, with catwalks and haylofts and tiny windows set up high. It's made of solid stone—it could withstand an invading army."

"If we had our own army armed with crossbows at every window," Claire said. "The question is, will it withstand Marc?"

"Bonnard's probably still in Paris, waiting for us to show up back at my apartment. Even if he did have any idea where we were headed, he'd never find us here. This is at the back end of beyond—Jassy's more than twelve miles away over treacherous, twisty roads."

"Only twelve miles away? We've been driving for more than three hours."

Tom managed to look sheepish in the dim light of the car. "I missed my turn a few times. Which is only to our advantage," he hastened to add. "If I couldn't find my way here, how will a stranger manage? I threw some blankets in the trunk; there's probably some old straw left in here. We'll bed down for the night and deal with things in the daylight. We'll try the police one more time, and if they still won't . listen I suggest we head over the border into Switzerland."

"No passports."

Tom grimaced. "I forgot. Well, we'll make the police listen. If worse comes to worst we'll get in touch with the local gendarmes. Even if they're worse than the Paris police, at least they could offer us decent protection."

"What's the difference between the police and the gendarmes? I thought they were the same." Claire pulled the sleeves down on her sweater, shivering in the cool night air.

"Nope. The police are urban, and under the direction of the Department of the Interior. The gendarmes are rural and belong to the army. Needless to say there's a fair amount of rivalry going on. We might be able to use that competitiveness to our advantage."

"I'll take any advantage we can get," Claire said wearily, reaching for the handle. Nicole had already scrambled out the back door and was busy poking about in the lightly falling rain.

"Come on, Claire," she shouted over her shoulder. "This is wonderful."

Wonderful was not the word for the old stone barn, Claire thought an hour later. The place was huge and damp and musty, the catwalks running around the stone walls looked practically suicidal, and it took most of Claire's concentration to keep Nicole off them. The steep walls disappeared up into darkness above them, and it was apparent from the puddles on the cobbled floor and the intermittent splashes on their heads that the roof was in uncertain condition.

There was hay all right, damp and moldy and smelling of rodents. Tom mounded piles of the stuff into makeshift beds, tossing blankets on top of them. Two beds, she noticed, one large, one much too small for Tom to sleep on, even if he were alone. Clearly he wasn't planning on sleeping alone.

They made a meager meal of the leftover bread and cheese. Nicole had already demolished the junk food, but even she pronounced Tom's wine unfit for human consumption. They sat around in the semi-darkness, lit only by a few candles and a quickly fading flashlight, and gradually the wind abated, the rain softened, the night seemed to mellow around them.

"I don't suppose anyone wants to tell ghost stories," Tom suggested lazily. He was stretched out on the larger of the two makeshift beds, seemingly at ease.

"No!" Claire said.

"Yes!" Nicole said with equal enthusiasm.

"I think we have more than enough cause for nightmares right now," Claire added.

"Don't sound like a repressive schoolmarm," Tom said, rolling over onto his back. "I sure as hell would rather dream about werewolves and ghosts than Marc Bonnard."

"I don't want to dream about anything," Nicole said, some of her animation leaving her.

"You don't have to, sweetheart," Claire murmured. "Why don't we go find this stream Tom swears is nearby, wash our hands and face, and then settle down for the night?"

"It's only eight o'clock," Tom protested.

"The sooner we sleep the sooner it will be daylight, and the sooner we can go find another telephone," Claire said. "At least the rain's stopped for now. Which way is the stream?"

"Out the back. There's a path leading down to it. You shouldn't have any trouble—you can hear the sound of rushing water even in here."

Claire nodded, climbing wearily to her feet and holding out a hand to Nicole. She was going to have to get Tom to regroup the sleeping arrangements. Much as she wanted the comfort of his body wrapped around hers, Nicole needed comfort more. Soon, when this was all over, they could sleep together in peace.

Nicole took her hand, making no effort to pull away as they headed for the narrow opening in the back wall of the barn. The fading flashlight provided meager illumination into the rainy darkness, and Claire hesitated.

"Want me to come with you?" Tom asked, pulling himself into a sitting position.

"Nope. We ladies need a little bit of privacy, don't we, Nicole?"

Nicole nodded vigorously, clearly pleased to hear herself described with such an adult word. "We have to use the bathroom," she confided.

Tom nodded solemnly. "Give a holler if you can't find your way back in the dark."

"I think the flashlight will last that long. In the meantime you can rearrange the beds a bit. I don't think you're going to fit too well on that one," Claire said calmly, trying to stifle her amusement as Tom's face fell.

Then he sighed in theatrical resignation. "All right," he said. "Don't be gone too long."

"We won't," Claire promised. She stared at him for a long moment, wanting to say so much to him, not knowing where to begin. In the end she didn't have to say a word. He took her upturned face in his two strong hands and brushed his mouth over hers.

"Be careful," he murmured, his eyes warm and loving.

"We will be." But in the end it took much longer than she expected. Despite the noise of the rushing water, the stream was quite far away. The path twisted and turned through trees and overgrown bushes, the dirt had turned to mud beneath their feet, and while Nicole had no qualms about squatting in the woods, it took Claire a moment to overcome her New England inhibitions. They washed in the icy, rushing stream, and for a moment Claire thought longingly of a deep, hot bath soaking away the aches, the pains, the sticky grime of two days on the road. And then she shook herself, as the rain began to fall once more.

"Let's get back to the barn," she said, pulling herself upright. "This is one day I can't wait for to end."

Nicole murmured something in French, adding in English a succinct "me, too." Going back was rougher—the batteries in the flashlight were ready to give up the ghost, the path was uphill and even more slippery, and the rain grew heavier as they climbed. The barn loomed ahead of them, and the faint glow of candlelight from the open door was welcoming.

Claire hurried in, stumbling slightly on the rotting door sill, with Nicole at her heels. "Tom . . ." she began, but he was nowhere in sight.

She turned back to Nicole. "He must have headed for the little boys' room," she said.

"Comment?"

Claire understood the tone if not the word. "He's probably gone to the bathroom himself," she explained more prosaically. "Why don't we get settled?"

"He's made a third bed." Nicole pointed to a pile of clothing a good distance from the two blanket-covered piles of hay.

"How absurd," Claire said with a sigh, heading over toward the new pile. "He didn't have to move that far . . ." Her voice trailed off. As she drew closer in the shadowy darkness of the old barn she began to recognize the clothes. She hadn't realized Nicole was following her until the child started screaming.

Blood was everywhere, pooling around Tom's body. He lay face down in it, and Claire knew with heart-numbing certainty that no one could lose that much blood and still live. She bit back her own horrified scream, grabbed Nicole's limp arm, and ran, straight out into the pouring rain toward the old Peugeot, hoping and praying they'd make it there before Marc.

The keys were still in it. She shoved Nicole into the seat beside her, locked the doors, and began grinding the starter. For long, desperate moments it just coughed and choked, and Claire bit her lip until it bled, ignoring the tears of panic and despair that rolled down her face, cursing and praying and beating on the steering wheel, certain that Marc's hideously grinning face would appear at the window.

Finally the damned thing caught. There was no sign of anyone, no shadows in the darkness. Claire slammed the car into gear, slid in the mud until she rested up against a tree, and then, yanking the steering wheel with all her strength, she tore off down the narrow, muddy track.

Malgreave sat alone in the darkness of his living room, listening to the rain. He heard the car pull up outside, and only for a brief moment did he allow himself the fantasy that it might be Marie, changing her mind. He knew the sound of a police car when he heard it, he recognized Josef's hurried tread on the front steps. He'd heard them often enough to memorize them. He stared at the overflowing ashtray on the table in front of him, listening to the sound of his doorbell, the frenzied pounding on his front door.

They'd been trying to get him for a while, but he hadn't answered the phone. He'd been afraid it would be Marie, and he didn't know what he could say to her; he was afraid it wasn't Marie, and he'd be speechless with rage and disappointment. In the end he simply hadn't answered. If the rest of his department could be a bunch of self-absorbed incompetents why not him, too? He might as well be as inept as the rest of them.

He leaned forward and stubbed out his cigarette, nudging some of the butts aside, out onto Marie's treasured walnut coffee table. The glass of whiskey sat there, barely touched. For all his determined inattention to duty Malgreave couldn't bring himself to get as drunk as he so desperately wanted. The game with Bonnard and Guillère wasn't finished. Even if he'd screwed up his family life, his professional life was still worth salvaging.

He rose, not hurrying, and headed for the door, flicking on the light in the hall as he went. He noted with a distant interest that Josef hadn't come alone. Vidal, his hated rival, was with him.

"Yes?" He kept his voice low and unpromising.

"They've found Guillère," Vidal announced, and Josef glared at him for stealing his thunder.

"In a small town in the northeast named Jassy," he added importantly.

"Found him?" Malgreave echoed. "Is he dead?"

"Very much so," Vidal said.

"He had a bullet in his shoulder, his throat was cut, and his body had been mutilated," Josef broke in. "And you'll never guess where he was found."

"I don't want to guess," Louis said evenly, retrieving his still-wet raincoat from the hall floor. "I expect you to tell me, and quickly."

"He was found in the farmhouse of an old vineyard that belongs in part to Thomas J. Parkhurst." Josef looked pleased with himself.

"The American friend of Bonnard's mistress. Interesting," Malgreave murmured, following them out into the rain.

"And the farmhouse had been recently occupied. Two beds were slept in, clothes were left behind, according to the local gendarmes. Clothes belonging to a woman, a man, and a girl."

"So it appears Rocco ran afoul of our fugitives. There've been no more phone calls?"

"None." Josef looked abashed. He held the door of the police car for his superior, but Malgreave opened the front door himself and slid in beside Vidal. Josef had no choice but to get in back alone, something that didn't please him. He knew better than to object.

"Surely you don't think they killed Rocco?" Vidal demanded, heading out into the traffic at suicidal speed.

"What do you think?" Malgreave countered.

Vidal thought about it. "I would guess the American shot him, and left him there. The bullet would slow him down enough so they could make their escape. Someone else must have used the knife. Someone who's made a recent habit of using knives. Bonnard?"

"I'd put good money on it," Malgreave replied. "What do you think, Josef?"

Poor Josef was torn, but a fair man in the end. "I hadn't thought of it that way. But I think Vidal is right. The Americans wouldn't be likely to butcher him. It had to have been Bonnard."

"And I expect he's after the Americans right now," Louis said grimly. "How long will it take us to reach Jassy?"

"Four hours if we drive directly and the weather's not too bad," Vidal replied.

"Make it three," Malgreave answered. "And we may find a promotion for you."

And Vidal, whose ambition more than equaled Josef's, stepped on the gas.

⚜ CHAPTER 23

Claire gripped the steering wheel, hunched forward, peering into the rainy night. "We'll be all right, Nicole. We'll find a phone, we'll call the police again. If they won't listen we'll stop and find a farmhouse, a store, anyplace where someone will help us. We'll be all right." Deliberately she kept from mentioning Tom, his body lying in that ever-spreading pool of blood, his long limbs stretched out, limp, useless. Dead.

Nicole said nothing, but Claire needed all her concentration for the road, and she didn't dare glance at her. "We must have just missed Marc," she murmured, more for her own sake than Nicole's. "He probably went looking for us after he . . . hit Tom. We must have passed him in the dark and he didn't even realize it. We've been lucky, Nicole. Really, we've been very lucky."

Still no response. "And maybe Tom's not hurt too badly," she said, knowing she was lying, knowing he was dead. "Maybe Marc just clubbed him on the head. Head wounds bleed terribly, but they're not always that bad. Maybe he just knocked him unconscious. We'll go get help, and get him to the hospital, and I bet he'll be fine. Just fine." Even to her own ears the excuses sounded lame. She ventured a brief, worried glance at the child beside her. Nicole was sitting very still, her hands clasped loosely in her lap, her body swaying with the turns of the old car, her face completely, frighteningly blank.

"Nicole," Claire said, hearing the panic in her voice and no longer caring. "Nicole, sweetheart, talk to me. Are you all right?"

Absolute silence. She didn't turn her head, didn't blink her solemn black eyes, didn't do a thing but sway with the motion of the speeding car.

"God damn his soul to hell," Claire muttered tearfully under her breath. "I'll make him pay for this." And Nicole, lost in some safe, peaceful world of her own, merely stared straight ahead, into the stormy night.

He moved from the shadows on silent feet. He'd enjoyed watching them, watching her panic and tears. She'd be back. He knew it, he knew it with instincts that were so well-honed they were automatic. She would be back, and he would punish her then.

He looked down at the American's body. He would have rather used his knife, but the man was too big and too fast for him. He'd settled for hitting him over the head, and the satisfying crunch of wood against bone and flesh had told him it was enough.

He would have liked to have taken his time. He'd paid Rocco back for his disloyalty, for his coveting Claire and Nicole. This man, who'd stolen his women, deserved worse.

But not now. Later, after Claire came back. He'd make the two of them watch. Then Nicole, and then Claire.

If only he had more time. He didn't dare stretch it out much past dawn. The police would come looking, and he had to be back in Paris, mourning the death of his mother-in-law and the disappearance of his stepdaughter and the deranged woman he'd been living with. It must have been the accident she'd been involved in in the States, he would say, his eyes wide and innocent. Somehow it must have turned her mind, until she confused poor Nicole with the child in Massachusetts. He'd had no idea how her madness had flowered until Nicole said something to him.

And he'd been too late to stop her. She'd killed the American who'd befriended her, murdered the child, and then taken her own life in a fit of remorse. He would have to be very careful in his punishment of her. Any signs, any marks on her slender, pale body, would have to be in keeping with the story he wanted the police to believe. He'd have to forgo the pleasure of teaching her the lesson she deserved. Still, having her watch him with Parkhurst's corpse and Nicole would be consolation enough.

He sank to the cobbled floor, his legs folding gracefully beneath him. He would wait. Wait for Claire to return, as return she must. And he would be ready.

Claire lost track of the time. She took a dozen wrong turns, the narrow, muddy roads ending in front of the skidding tires of the Peugeot. Each time she yanked the car around and tried another way, all the while keeping up an idiotic, cheery, one-sided conversation with the silent Nicole. Nothing seemed to dent the wall of silence that surrounded the child. She'd shut herself off from everything, having seen too much death.

Claire couldn't blame her. If only there was someplace they'd be safe, someplace they could hide. But wherever they went, Marc would find them. The police, those stupid fools, would stand by and wait until they were slaughtered, would wait until Marc wiped out half the old women in Paris before they finally did something. By then it would be much too late for them.

When she first saw the lights in the distance she didn't even notice them. Too many times had she hoped for signs of civilization, only to be passed by a speeding, oblivious driver who had no intention of stopping to give directions or aid to a fellow motorist. Besides, she would have been afraid to signal, terrified that one of them would be a white Fiat with a familiar figure in the driver's seat.

But this time the lights weren't headlights. They were the dim, unmistakable lights of a small village, the warm glow emanating from windows, and shining overhead the small public phone that sat conspicuously by the local market.

"There's a phone, Nicole," she said, her voice raw from its nonstop monologue. "We'll call the police, and they'll send someone to help us. I promise you, darling, I won't let him get us."

Nicole said nothing. Claire pulled up beside the phone, climbed out, and pulled Nicole with her. Like most pay telephones in France, the instructions were in both English and French, and Claire sent up a silent prayer of thanksgiving as she fumbled for the proper coins. This time she had to get through, this time someone would help her.

Goddamnit, didn't anyone speak English in the Paris police? she fumed as she repeated, over and over again, her name, her nationality, as she was passed from barely bilingual subordinate to slightly more bilingual superior. "Someone is trying to kill me," she finally shrieked into the telephone. "He's already murdered countless people, he just killed my friend, and now he's trying to kill me and my little girl. You've got to help me."

The calm, expressionless voice came again. "Please to give your name, visa number, nationality, and address."

"I've given you my name," Claire shouted, in tears. "I can't give you my visa number—I've lost my passport."

"That's a very serious matter, madame," the voice said sternly.

"Not as serious as murder. Listen, I've been living with someone who's been killing old women. His name is Marc Bonnard, and he's absolutely crazy. He's going to kill me and the child with me, and if you don't send help . . ."

"Please hold," the damned voice said again.

And Claire, staring at the telephone in mute fury, slammed down the receiver. "Nicole . . ."

But Nicole was staring straight ahead, oblivious to the thwarted phone conversation, oblivious to the rain pouring down on her head, oblivious to the dark, deadly night.

The streets of the tiny village had been deserted when Claire first placed her call, but now in the distance she could see a door open, a small pool of light flooding the rainy darkness. She gently pushed Nicole back into the car, then raced down the roadway to the door, only to have it slam shut in her face. She threw herself against it, pounding on it, screaming and crying for help.

The only response was an incomprehensible babble of French. Claire didn't need a translation to know she was being told to go away. For a moment her knees buckled, and she sagged against the door, weeping. But only for a moment. She shoved herself back, upright, and turned to the car, to the oblivious, waiting Nicole.

"No help here," she said briskly, ignoring the tears staining her face, climbing in the car, and starting the motor. This time it purred to life, one tiny blessing in a world turned angry and hostile. "We'll have to head for a larger city. At least we've got . . ." Her voice trailed off in sudden horror. "No," she said after a moment, "we don't have money. Tom has it all."

Nicole said nothing. "We don't have any protection either," Claire said aloud, despairing. "Tom had the money, and the gun. We'll have to go back." She turned and looked at Nicole, waiting for a protest, a change of expression. Nothing.

"All right," she muttered under her breath. "We'll go back. Marc should be long gone by now. He'd never think we'd be stupid enough to hang around. We'll go back, get the gun and the money, and then drive straight to . . . God, I don't even know where we are! I don't know where the nearest city is, I don't know where the frontier is." Her voice was rising in desperation, and she forced herself to calmness.

"We'll be all right," she said, refusing to think how she was going to find the money and the gun. She'd have to search Tom's corpse, have to rifle in his dead pockets, and if she hadn't gone mad with grief and fear yet, that could be enough to push her over the edge.

But not with Nicole depending on her. She could hold out long enough to get them to safety, hold out long enough to get Nicole to her great-aunt. And then she could give in to all the misery and guilt that were battering at her. Then she could give in to anguish and despair.

It took her just as long to retrace her path to the old barn.

Every wrong turn, every dead end she'd hit on the way out, she hit on the way in. She'd lost all consciousness of time, dreading the moment when she found the old barn again, content to spend the night driving through the deserted, muddy roads, the silent child by her side.

And then she thought to check the gas gauge. It took her a while to find it, and then she wished she hadn't. The car was smack dead on empty, and there was no telling how long it had been there. If she got to the barn, found the money and the gun, they might not be able to escape. Marc could be hiding somewhere there, watching, waiting for them.

She had to take the chance. If she didn't get the money she wouldn't be able to fill the tank, and sooner or later they'd run out, and be left like sitting ducks for Marc to finish with them. It was her only choice, and she had to take it. But God, she wished there was someone else who could do it for her.

The rain had stopped when she finally found the old barn. There was no sign of another car, but the night was dark, and a white Fiat could be hiding anywhere nearby, and Claire wouldn't be able to see. Nicole was still sitting upright in the front seat, eyes blank and staring, and for a moment Claire considered leaving her in the car, rather than subject her to the sight of Tom's body once more.

She didn't dare. She had no idea if they were alone there in the woods, but she couldn't take the chance. The only way she could protect Nicole was to keep her with her. It was unlikely the child could be any more traumatized than she was already. One more view of a dead man she had barely known wouldn't be the end.

But Nicole had liked him. She'd opened up to Tom more than she'd opened up to anyone before—she'd laughed with him, the first time Claire had ever heard her laugh. He would have been a marvelous father, full of fun and life, willing to take chances, willing to try anything. And Marc had finished all that, wiped it out, just as he'd wiped out a child's innocence.

The candles were still burning, just as they had been when Claire had grabbed Nicole and run, but the flames were burning down low, casting eerie shadows in the huge old building. Claire had Nicole's cold, limp hand grasped tightly in her own as she edged inside the doorway, looking around her, every sense, every instinct, tuned in to the night air around them.

"Stay here," she whispered, releasing Nicole's hand and pushing her gently against the thick stone wall. Nicole stayed, her face blank, as Claire turned to the bloody spot where Tom's body lay.

The blood was still there, a thick, congealed pool of it. The body was gone.

"She's called in, sir." The voice came crackling over the police car phone. "She hung up while I was getting Chief Inspector Clery to talk with her. She said Bonnard's killed the American, and he's after her and the little girl."

"Shit." Malgreave leaned back. "We've got to get that murdering bastard before he kills anyone else. Did she say where she was?"

"The dispatcher didn't speak English very well . . ."

Malgreave almost put his fist through the windshield. "Why the hell didn't they have someone who could speak English answer the goddamned phone?"

"They were trying to get someone . . ."

"So we don't know where she was?" Malgreave cut him off ruthlessly.

"We were able to trace her, sir. She was calling from a public phone in the village of Jassy. The call came in about thirty-five minutes ago . . ."

"And it took you that long to call me?"

"She said the dead man was in an abandoned barn somewhere outside of Jassy."

"Just great," Malgreave fumed, slamming down the phone. "How many abandoned barns do you think are in that depressed part of the country?"

"We'll find it, sir," Vidal said.

"I'm glad you have confidence, Vidal," Malgreave said wearily. "I hope it's justified."

"We're within ten miles of Jassy, sir. We know they were

driving a beige Peugeot, and there certainly isn't much traffic on the road. The local gendarmes know we're coming —they'll know where to look first," Josef said earnestly.

Malgreave turned and stared into the back seat. "For all our sakes, I hope so, Josef." And turning back, he lit another cigarette.

There was no sound, no noise at all in the huge old barn. Just the distant rushing of the stream, the wind in the trees overhead, the eerie echo of the huge stone building. Yet with sudden, horrifying certainty Claire knew they weren't alone.

She backed up, slowly, lifting her gaze overhead to the rickety catwalks lacing the stone walls. No sign of anyone, but she knew he was up there, waiting. She reached behind her, catching Nicole's limp hand in hers.

"Nicole," she whispered, her voice a breath of sound. "I know you don't want to listen, don't want to wake up, but you have to. You have to help me, or I won't be able to stop him. I want you to run and hide. I want you to go back to the car, get in, and lock all the doors. No matter what happens, no matter what you hear, don't open those doors. He can't get you in there, he can't open locked doors. He's only human. You'll be safe in the car, Nicole. Please, baby, run."

Nicole didn't move. Her hand remained loose in Claire's desperate grip, and her eyes were blank. Claire swallowed the desperation that was beating against her throat. "All right," she said softly. "You don't want to leave. I'll still keep you safe. I won't let him hurt you, Nicole. I swear I won't."

There was the slightest answering twitch in the cold, clammy hand, and Claire gripped it with renewed hope. "If you won't go to the car, I want you to go hide in the corner. Behind the haystacks, in the shadows. He won't be able to see you unless he's looking, and he's more interested in me right now. Can you do that for me, sweetie?"

Still no answer. With a silent, desperate prayer, Claire dropped Nicole's hand. Slowly, with zombielike precision, ole began to edge backward into the shadows, her eyes blank.

aire closed her eyes in relief as she listened to the ing sounds of Nicole seeking shelter. And then, lifting ad, she threw her shoulders back and stepped into the of the huge old barn, staring up into the shadowy darkness.

"Marc?" she called, her voice firm and loud. "I'm here." And she started for the first flight of stairs.

"This is the fourth goddamn barn we've tried in the last hour," Josef fumed. "Can't your men do any better?"

"This is a poor section of France, Inspector Summer," the local prefect said. "We have more than our share of barns standing empty."

"How many more?" Malgreave interrupted.

The local shrugged. "Perhaps a half dozen, perhaps less. There's one not far from here, though I doubt it's what you're looking for. It hasn't been used for much during the last few years—too remote. Americans could never find it."

"These Americans are particularly inventive," Vidal said.

"They must be, to have eluded the illustrious Paris police for so long," the man sneered.

"Damn you . . . ." Josef began, but Malgreave interrupted.

"We'll check this next one," he announced, "and then we'll split up. At this rate it will take all night, and I don't know if Nicole Bonnard or Claire MacIntyre have all night."

The petty bickering abruptly ceased. "Maybe this time we'll be lucky," Vidal said diplomatically. Josef looked at him and snarled.

Claire had never liked heights. She'd grown dizzy at the Grand Canyon, she'd never attempted the Eiffel Tower, and hadn't even been too happy with the outside escalators at one of the museums Marc had taken her to. She'd had a moment of suspecting he'd subjected her to it on purpose, knowing her fear, and then she'd dismissed the idea, thinking she was being absurdly paranoid. In retrospect it was clear that was exactly what he'd done.

The wooden walkways were set into the old stone walls with thick, splintery chunks of wood. Here and there the braces had rotted through, and the narrow balcony swung a bit over the stone floor. She refused to look down once she passed the first flight. Somewhere down there was Tom's body. Somewhere down there was Nicole, hiding, waiting, unable to protect herself.

Somewhere above her was Marc, moving silently along the walkways. She could hear the unmistakable creak of aging wood. Even someone as graceful as Marc couldn't overcome the hazards of ancient, rotting wood, and his noiseless tread could bring forth occasional, telltale sounds.

From the moment she'd looked over her head and known Marc was up there, Claire had had no choice. There was only one way down, and she had to cut off that exit. He would have to go through her to get to Nicole, and she had no intention of letting him do so. She had no weapon, other than her hands and a fury so deep and powerful it frightened her, but she had no hesitation. She would stop Marc, no matter what the cost.

"I know you're up there, Marc," she said again, holding on to the railing and pulling herself upward. "You're not as good as you think you are. I can hear you. I can see your shadow on the walls, I can hear you moving. You're moving away from me. Why? Do I frighten you, Marc? Have you finally found someone who won't cower before you, who won't just sit there and let you kill them?" she taunted. "It's no wonder you kill old women. They're the only ones who are too weak to fight back. You're a bully, Marc. A childish, murdering bully."

Another creak, directly overhead, and she jerked her head up. She could see his slippered feet, the flash of white gloves and something else, something shiny and metallic and very deadly, before he disappeared into the shadows once more, silent as the grave.

"Did you think I didn't know?" she continued, climbing

higher, splinters in her hand from the railing. "Did you think I didn't see through your little games, your twisted idea of lovemaking? I knew. I knew a long time ago. I just hadn't decided what to do, especially about Nicole. I knew you were crazy, I just didn't know how crazy you were."

A sudden, hideous, high-pitched shriek tore the air above her head, and she nearly lost her grip on the railing. Something dove at her head, followed by another, and she ducked, stilling her own terrified scream, wondering what Marc was throwing at her.

Bats, she realized as they flew blindly away. Marc had disturbed a horde of sleeping bats overhead, sending them flying wildly into the night. She only hoped they scared him half as much as they scared her.

She allowed herself one brief glimpse down to the stone floor beneath them. There was no sign of Nicole in the candlelit darkness, no sign of life at all. Maybe Nicole had come to her senses, had gone to hide in the car. Or maybe she was just waiting for death to come and claim her.

Out of the corner of her eye Claire thought she saw a flash of light through one of the narrow slits of windows. She dismissed it as wishful thinking, and climbed higher. "I'm not going to let you get away with this," she announced, her voice calm and dispassionate. "To get to Nicole you'll have to go through me. And I'm not going to let you."

The silence above her was as thick as a velvet shroud. One more flight, one more rickety expanse of walkway, and there'd be nowhere else to go. Maybe he'd found a place to hide, maybe she'd been fooling herself and there was another way down. Sudden panic clamped a fierce hand around her heart.

"Marc?" She cursed the fear that came through her voice, but she couldn't help it. She willed herself to calm. "Cat got your tongue?" she taunted, climbing up the final flight. The walkway swung beneath her weight, pulling from the wall, the flimsy wood rotting beneath her fingertips. "Marc?"

He was there. It was so dark she could scarcely see him, but the white gloves and face stood out with eerie luminescence. He stood absolutely still, not making any move toward her, waiting for her to come to him.

"Two can play at this game," she said, holding still. "If you think I'm going to come any further you're crazier than I thought, and that would be downright impossible, my friend. Why are you wearing face paint?"

His body moved, an expressive pantomime with short, graceful gestures that were a perfect communication. His face was himself, he said, sorrow and laughter hiding from the world. He reached up a white-gloved hand and gestured her closer, that gesture promising her love and redemption and oblivion, and for one brief, horrifying moment she was tempted.

"I'm not taking one step further," she said, her voice deliberately mocking, "so you can stop making like the Ghost of Christmas Future. If you want me, Marc, you're going to have to come and get me."

He twisted in the darkness, and she could see the silvery glitter of the knife in his hand. In a weird, inexplicable way it was reassuring. He was so mesmerizing in his grace and talent that she was half ready to do or believe anything. The knife was a blessedly prosaic instrument of death.

She could make gestures, too. She held up a hand in the murky darkness, beckoning him. Her hand didn't shake. "Come and get me," she cooed again. "Or we can just stand here all night long."

She thought she heard noises far beneath her, but she didn't dare look. Maybe Nicole was fool enough to come out into the open, but it wouldn't matter. As long as she stood between Marc and Nicole, the child would be safe. And Claire was prepared to stand there forever.

He moved again in the darkness, coming infinitesimally closer, shrugging his shoulders, curving his arms in a defenseless gesture only slightly marred by the knife. His head was cocked to one side; his whole body shivered with sorrow and longing and a twisted sort of love.

And then he lunged. She could never be certain where her energy came from. She was standing motionless, awaiting the knife, when she heard the noise from below, jerking her from her dreamy state. "Damn you, no!" she shrieked as he leapt on her, hitting at him, the knife slicing painlessly into her hand.

He was standing there, motionless, staring at her for a timeless moment, shock and sorrow in his mad dark eyes. And she realized he was standing on air, as he fell, slowly, silently, his soundless scream filling her ears as she watched him tumble, gracefully—oh, so gracefully—to his death on the flagstones far below.

There were people below, people surrounding the curiously flattened shape of Marc Bonnard. The catwalk shifted and swayed as Claire climbed down, her bloody hand clinging to the splintery railing. When she reached the ground floor, men rushed up to help her, but she hit them away. In her confusion she saw two men lying on the floor. One was Tom, and people were working feverishly on him. She wanted to rush to his side, to assure herself that he was still alive, but her feet refused to obey her.

Slowly, dazedly, she crossed the stone floor, pushing the huddle of police aside, until she stood over Marc's body. There was no doubt about him—the back of his head was crushed, his neck at a hideous angle, his beautiful, graceful body destroyed. The black, mad eyes were still and staring, and he was very, very dead.

She looked across the corpse into Nicole's eyes. The blankness was gone as she looked down at the man who'd murdered her mother and grandmother, the man who had tried to kill her.

"*Bon,*" she said succinctly, meeting Claire's questioning gaze.

"*Bon,*" said Claire, speaking French for the first and only time in her life. And holding out her arms, she waited for Nicole to run into them.

EPILOGUE

Malgreave lit another cigarette. God, he was getting sick of the taste of these wretched things. He ought to toss them out. After all, he was going to have to accustom himself to a new life. Might as well make a clean sweep.

It was eleven o'clock the next morning. He hadn't been back to his house in the suburbs, and if it were up to him he wouldn't return. The house was empty without Marie, and he didn't know if he could stand it.

Josef was standing in the office he coveted, staring out the window. His thinning hair was standing up on his high, domed forehead, his suit was rumpled, his face set in an expression of gloom and disappointment.

Malgreave grinned sourly. Helga was going to give him hell, and Josef deserved it. "Look at it this way, old friend," Malgreave said gently, "at least the Americans are alive. Both of them, and the child, too."

Josef snorted, and Malgreave felt once more that disquieting feeling. When it came to the human angle Josef was missing something. Malgreave could sympathize—fifteen years of Paris police work could take the humanity out of anybody. You had to fight to keep it. Malgreave had, Vidal had. If Josef had lost it, he'd be a worse cop for it.

Finally Josef whirled around. "Did you see what the

275

papers said? Calling us inept, incompetent, a bunch of Keystone Kops bumbling around while people were being murdered?"

"No, I didn't see it. What good would it do? We did some things well, some things very badly. The problem with this job, Josef, is that when we screw up, people die. And we screwed up."

Josef swore, an obscenity unusual from his chaste lips. "You said you were going to retire when we caught the killers?"

Malgreave nodded. "I am."

Josef's face brightened. "Then . . ."

"Then you can prepare yourself for your next assignment," Malgreave said gently.

"Assignment?"

"Vidal is being named chief inspector in my place. You'll be his assistant."

Josef's face whitened. "You haven't even handed in your resignation yet. How do you know . . . ?"

"I handed it in several hours ago. In it I made my recommendations."

"And I get screwed," Josef said bitterly. "All for one little fuck-up."

"For one little fuck-up that nearly cost three innocent people their lives, Josef. I'm sorry."

"The hell you are!" Josef slammed out of the office, out of the building, without a backward glance.

Malgreave stubbed out his cigarette. God, it was about time he retired. He was getting too old for this. He'd finish his report, give it to Gauge to type, and then take off. He'd spent too much of his life swamped by the Grandmother Murders. It was time to break free.

He stared down at the torn and tattered paper in front of him. They'd found it on Bonnard's body, and it explained a great deal of what Malgreave had begun to suspect. Scrawled in a boyish, almost illegible hand, written in human blood, it was the pact, made by a bunch of abused young boys. It was all spelled out, from the weather to the victims, all very ritualistic and depressing. And twenty-five

years later they'd all tried to live up to it, with varyi
degrees of success.

He leaned closer to the paper, peering at it. He'd left his
glasses at home, and his eyesight wasn't as good as it used to
be. Half the words were illegible; he could make out two of
the signatures, but he had to guess at the other two. Except
that it looked as if there were five signatures on the shredded
paper, and only four murderers accounted for.

Claire sat outside the hospital room, her bandaged hand
resting lightly on Nicole's shoulder. They both looked like
hell, she thought. Exhausted, tear-stained, filthy and hungry, they looked like refugees. But neither of them was going
anyplace until she found out whether Tom was going to
make it.

The police said he would, but the police were very low on
her list of trusted personnel. The gash on his head required
countless stitches, but at least Marc hadn't had a chance to
use his knife. Rest was what he needed, rest and antibiotics
to ward off infection. The hay Marc had stashed him under
was laced with chicken manure. Neither the smell nor the
sanitation of it was to be recommended.

The door to Tom's room opened, and Claire rose, followed by Nicole. "How is he?"

The doctor launched into a spate of French, but Claire,
instead of feeling miserable and inadequate, held up her
hand. "In English, please," she said regally, knowing full
well the doctor could manage if he tried.

The doctor, like his American counterparts, considered
himself to be one step below the Almighty and didn't like
taking orders from a mere mortal. With an irritated sigh he
launched into a halting explanation. "He's resting comfortably. With luck we'll take him off the intravenous tube
tomorrow. We've given him something to help him sleep,
and by tomorrow he'll be feeling much better. Go home."

Claire smiled sweetly. "Thank you, doctor." And pushing
past him, she walked into Tom's room, with Nicole trailing
behind her.

He looked like hell, tubes going into him, tubes coming

277

..., his face pale, his sandy hair in a tangle around his face. or a moment Claire panicked, wondering if the doctor had led to her, when he opened his beautiful blue eyes and smiled at her.

"I forced my way in here," she announced without preamble.

"I'm sure you did," he said, his voice weak, his grin a semblance of his usual charm.

"I had to make sure you were okay."

"Fit as a fiddle," he said, though she could see the effort was costing him.

"I just thought I ought to mention something," Claire said, coming closer and taking the hand that wasn't encumbered with an i.v.

"What?"

"I love you."

His grin broadened. "That's right. We never got around to mentioning that, did we?"

"No, we didn't." Her fingers gently stroked the warm flesh.

"In case you didn't catch on, I love you, too," he said.

She nodded. "I just wanted to make sure. After all, we promised Nicole a Burger King on every corner. Go to sleep. We'll be back tomorrow."

"Tomorrow," he said softly, shutting his eyes again.

"Tomorrow," she said, leaning over and brushing her lips against his.

It was early afternoon when Malgreave let himself in his front door. He hadn't wanted to go home, but he was never a man to shirk his duty. He couldn't run away from the empty house—he would have to deal with it, learn to live without Marie, sooner or later, and the longer he put it off the worse it would be.

For some reason the house didn't feel as desolate when he walked in the door. He looked over at the walnut coffee table. His half-drunk glass of whiskey was gone, the overflowing ashtray had disappeared.

He wrinkled his forehead. Maybe he'd dumped them in

278

the kitchen last night, but he didn't remember doing so. H headed toward the kitchen, moving to the sink to pour himself a glass of water, when he heard her. Marie's voice. "Louis, are you home?" she called from upstairs.

He looked at the sink. There on the shelf, tucked neatly beside his blood pressure medicine and the ancient aspirin, were vitamins and minerals and fish oil and rose hips. And closing his eyes for a moment, his whole body trembled in joy and relief.

It was raining in London. They'd had an unusual streak of sunny weather that spring, but now it was raining again, coming down in buckets.

Jean-Pierre Simon sat at his desk at the Bank of France, staring out into the pouring rain. He'd lived in London for fifteen years; there were times when he felt more English than French. But not when it rained.

When it rained he remembered a dark day twenty-five years ago, the smell of fire and roses and burnt flesh. And he felt urges so dark and evil he wanted to wipe them from his brain. But each year they grew stronger, more unmanageable.

"Nasty day, isn't it, Mr. Simon?" Mrs. Grandy said cheerfully, her wrinkled old face creased in a smile. She was well past retirement age, but she enjoyed her work as a teller in the bank, and his boss kept her on. She always made him nervous, as all old women did, and he tried not to remember why.

But this time Jean-Pierre didn't snub her, and his long fingers toyed with the silver letter opener on his spotless desk. "Nasty indeed, Mrs. Grandy." And he watched her walk away with a dreamy smile on his face. The time had come.